CA

Books should be returned or renewed by the last
date above. Renew by phone **03000 41 31 31** or
online *www.kent.gov.uk/libs*

by the same author

CASTRO'S DREAM

LOST

Lucy Wadham

—

ff

faber and faber

for my children, Felix and Lily

First published in 2000
by Faber and Faber Limited
3 Queen Square London WC1N 3AU

Typeset by Faber and Faber Ltd
Printed and bound in Great Britain by Bookmarque Ltd, Croydon

A CIP record for this book
is available from the British Library

ISBN 0–571–20551–8

2 4 6 8 10 9 7 5 3

Prologue

Mickey da Cruz sits, his great barrelled torso tipped forward, his elbows resting on his knees, his little hands clasped between his legs. Out of his good eye he watches the swing doors of the cafeteria letting people in and out like a valve, while his weak eye keeps sliding towards his temple, his own private stress signal: their plane is late. .

A young woman in an Avis uniform walks up to the bar ahead of him, drops her bag at her feet and slides her arse on to the stool. Behind her, like a reprimand, comes a priest wearing a black soutane buttoned to the floor. Mickey thinks he sees the priest slowing at the space beside the woman, then passing on to settle two places further along.

Mickey leans back and takes his cigarettes from his pocket. He lifts the soft packet to his lips and pulls one out with his teeth: you never know, the Avis woman might have eyes in the back of her head. He can see from the way the priest is counting out the change for his coffee that he is a foreigner; probably Italian, like the two brothers waiting for him in the car park. But there are Italians and Italians, and Mickey knows that the Scatti brothers are the scum.

The plane comes in with a sound like wind in a tunnel and he drops his cigarette, stands up, and turns to look through the plate glass at the runway. People begin to move towards the windows to watch, the men holding their suit jackets over their shoulders. Mickey squeezes the tiny camera in his pocket. It has cost him his savings, but he believes that he will not regret the investment. With it he has the opportunity to show everyone how elaborate his mind can be. When they are still reeling he will be on his way out of here for ever.

Through the plate glass he hears the engines moan as they

slow and stop. He keeps his good eye on the door at the front of the plane. The stairs are long in coming and his anxiety grows as he watches the driver dicking around with his manoeuvre. At last the first passengers step out into the kerosene haze. His eye is aching from watching the stairs and then he spots her, on the ground, moving quickly on the outside of the crowd. Her shape is distorted for a moment by a fault in the plate glass in front of him or the heat rising from the tarmac, he is unsure which. He shifts and she is righted again. She is overtaking the other passengers making their way towards the terminal entrance beneath him. As she draws nearer, he can see the mass at her side is a bag with a coat draped over it. And there are her boys, behind and to either side of her, running to keep up. The elder seems to be wearing a pair of strange spectacles and the younger is clutching a piece of her dress.

Mickey pushes through the swing doors and runs down the stairs. He takes up his position in the blind spot to the left of the arrivals gate where the first passengers are coming through at a shuffle. The woman is tall and holds her chin up as if to drive the point home. Her arms are long and sinewy, not his idea of how a woman's limbs should be. And here is the child, the heir, smaller than he had imagined, his yellow rucksack bouncing on his back with each step. The glasses are swimming goggles. Now the mother is passing him, so close he could reach out and touch her. He follows them to the arrivals hall. The woman's hair sways in one dark block from side to side. She stands still and leans down to hear what her youngest son is saying, holding her hair away from her face. The boy reaches up and locks his hands around her neck, and she straightens, gathering him up, placing him on her hip and moving straight on in one movement so graceful he suddenly feels cold inside, as though a draught were blowing on his entrails.

As she waits for her luggage, the younger child still in her arms, he smokes another cigarette to settle himself. He notices how she watches the other passengers waiting. She is watching the little flutter of aggression as the moment approaches to grab their possessions and haul them on to the trolley they have fought for. Her eldest is circling her in ever wider orbits. Mickey watches her mother's radar blinking on and off. He can now feel the adrenaline running to his finger-ends and his heart is booming in his oversized thorax, his body in revolt as he sets himself against the wisdom of the island. He breathes the smoke in deeply. When at last he treads on his cigarette and follows her out into the hot afternoon, he knows he is ready.

They cross a strip of grass watered by sprinklers. The boys run back and forth through the hanging mist, but she does not wait for them and they tear themselves away and out again with her into the white sunlight that bounces off the road. Mickey turns and walks back to the car, keeping her in sight.

He sits in the driver's seat, the Scattis in the back as if he is their chauffeur. The three of them wait with the windows up, the air-conditioning humming. They watch the mother in silence as she emerges from the Hertz cabin. She throws the two bags and the rucksack into the boot and her handbag in through the driver's door. They can see her irritation as the elder boy fools around. When at last he climbs in she slams the door hard behind him.

She drives fast, hardly braking on the sharp turns that lead up into the mountains. Mickey opens the window to smoke and swears at her in admiration out of the corner of his mouth: '*Putain*,' he says. '*La garce.*'

In the back the brothers sit side by side, each looking out of his own tinted window, in their dour, foreign silence.

Chapter One

As they drove past the playground at the entrance to the village of Santarosa, Sam pulled off his swimming goggles, twisting his head round to get a better look.

'Sit down.'

His mother's arm came up in front of him like a barrier. He glanced at her, then turned round again to look through the dust wake of the car at the deserted playground.

'Sit down, Sam. Please.'

Dan was asleep in the back, his hair glued to his forehead with sweat. Sam picked a crisp off the seat and ate it.

'I said please.'

He faced forward.

'Can we go to the beach?'

She looked at him. Her eyes told him she was not in a good mood.

'Sam. Not now.'

She glanced at Dan in the mirror.

'How fast does a scorpion run? Does it go faster than a snake? Which is faster?'

'I've no idea.'

'Come on.'

'I don't know.'

'Just say what you think.'

'You want me to make up an answer? What's the point?'

'No, but just tell me what you think. The scorpion or the snake?'

'The snake.'

'Why?'

'It's bigger and it has more muscles. Look, we're here.'

Sam raised himself on his hands and looked out at the

main square. There were three old people, a man and two women, sitting on the fountain. His mother always made him kiss the old people in the village, one by one, four times each. That made twelve. As they drove past he slid down in his seat.

His mother was trying to turn into the very narrow street that led up to the big house, but she was not managing. The car was too big to turn. He watched her changing gear, forward and back, forward and back, her silver bracelets clinking on her arm and her forehead worried as she looked in the mirror. He opened his window.

'How much can you drink before you explode?'

'Just be quiet.' She changed gear and the engine made a grinding noise.

Sam turned, took another crisp from the back seat and heard the car scraping along the wall on his mother's side.

'You've scraped the car.'

She jerked the car back and then climbed out. Sam turned and looked at his brother's sleeping face. He was dribbling out of the side of his mouth. Sam reached out and touched his red cheek.

'Leave him!' his mother hissed. She was at his window.

Then he remembered: 'My fish!'

'Oh, Sam. You didn't bring it.'

He opened the door, pushed past her and ran to the boot.

'Quick, Mummy.'

She opened the boot for him and he pulled out his rucksack. It was dripping.

'I told you not to bring him.'

Sam dropped to his knees and unzipped the yellow rucksack. He felt inside and took out the Tupperware box, which had emptied of water, then tipped out the contents on to the road. His goldfish lay unnaturally straight among his plastic men. He picked up the fish and held it on his palm, feeling the softness of it and the coldness, and he looked at its open mouth, and his own throat dried up.

[6]

'It's all right, Sam. He's not dead.'

She took the fish from him and was gone. He watched her disappear into the Hôtel Napoléon on the other side of the square. She was gone too long, and he sat there staring at his plastic men lying stupidly on the ground and tried not to cry. Then she was there, holding out a glass of water, and they looked into it at his fish lying on the rotating surface, dead as dead could be.

Sunday

Chapter Two

The morning heat sprang Antoine Stuart as he opened the wired-glass door to his flat and stepped on to the outside steps. He rented a room on the top floor of this large, clumsy house, built to resemble a chalet. The landlord had painted it peppermint green for the summer – to make it seem cooler, he had said, but it looked like icing sweating in the sun. Stuart locked the door and descended the steps. Behind the sound of a coffee-grinder, he could hear a child crying somewhere in the building. He had noted that parents these days seemed unable to leave their children alone.

The place was full of summer tenants who filled their balconies with brightly coloured inflatable junk and strewed their bathing suits among the vegetation. Stuart said a brief prayer for winter, when he could be alone again and feel the cool, protective silence of the floors below. He had taken the flat for the lock-up garage. He now threw up the metal door and felt for the torch that hung from a nail just inside. A single cicada ground away in the undergrowth. He crouched down and shone the torch beneath his car to check for a bomb. He replaced the torch, then climbed into the car, closed his eyes and turned the key in the ignition.

There were times when his fear of exploding into oblivion at the turn of the key occupied his body so powerfully it could rub out whole areas of him, shutting off parts of his nervous system so that he could not feel his fingers, his hands, his arms or his stomach. As he drove to work, all he could feel was his feet on the pedals, his physical self reduced to a pair of size forty-one shoes. He knew at such times that when his body returned it would be with one of his great white headaches.

Stuart backed out of the garage and down the ramp on to the road. He turned left in front of the parasol pine under which Coco Santini's men had so often stood astride their motorbikes, smoking, watching his comings and goings, for no reason he could see other than to remind him at all times of who his enemy was. Now more and more, as testimony to his own dwindling importance, there was no one there.

He drove over the sleeping policemen in his street, his head kissing the roof each time. His brown Datsun had lost its suspension and was a disgrace, but the car cult on the island had always sickened him and so he kept his own in protest. He wound down the window, heard sprinklers working behind the hedges and caught the strong scent of eucalyptus.

He drove to the beach the back way to avoid town. The road wound through a series of garden suburbs in the low hills behind Massaccio. Dogs barked as he drove by. There had once been a craze for poodles, but now there was a preference for dogs that could rip your throat out. He saw Dobermanns everywhere, jogging along the beach at dawn with their skinhead masters, lying across the threshold to more and more cafés, or walking along the pavements wearing woollen caps with holes for their ears. For most of the kids on the island a pit bull was their first weapon. Stuart had never begrudged the islanders their violence. He understood it; he had been bred for it too. And he could see that it was the only thing they had that fitted in the modern world. But since Santini the violence had become incoherent. It was no longer the simple language of grievance and revenge. It was all around them like airwaves and no one understood it any more.

Stuart glanced at the empty road in the mirror. They were right: he was no longer worth tailing. He tried to remember when this feeling of detachment had begun. The symptoms were predominantly physical – a drying up in his mouth and nostrils, a tightening of his skin, as though he were withering fast, as though some hot wind were blowing and he was shrinking a little every day. Soon Gérard, his deputy, would walk into his office and discover his remains, take him for a peach stone carelessly forgotten on his swivel chair, pick him up and bowl him expertly into the metal waste bin.

Stuart had stopped calling meetings. The secretaries, Annie and Inès, no longer hovered on the threshold of his office to ask when the next one might be. Narcotics no longer came to him to complain about Homicide, and Zanetecci from Central Office rang and rang on his direct line, but no one answered because he usually pulled it out of the wall. He would have liked to hide at work, but he had never dared close his door – he felt it to be somehow mean-spirited – and so Annie and Inès, just outside, were aware of his every move and he of theirs. On some days they chatted and laughed; on other days there were feuds and they worked in silence. Stuart often felt hemmed in by the women, affected by their moods, which flowed through the open door of his office and lapped at his feet like a toxic tide.

He drove into the car park. It was early and there were still spaces under the bamboo awning in the centre. Stuart chose this beach because he was not likely to meet anyone he knew here. It was a family beach with a huge inflatable castle for children to bounce on and there were no bars anywhere near it. Even Gérard did not know he came here and so no one could reach him. He slammed the door of his car and took off his shoes. He walked barefoot over the hot sand to the concrete steps that led down to the beach. He did not search for a spot but laid down his towel midway between the sea and the steps. There was a scattering of family units, arranged at neat intervals along the sand. As the sun climbed they would become less subdued and take out their beach toys, and the cries would mount and Stuart would be driven away.

He took off his jeans and his shirt and began to make a mound for his head, pushing the sand with his feet; then he arranged the towel over it and lay down. The few women he had shared a bed with did not like the way he slept. It didn't suit women, perhaps, if you slept on your stomach. He had sensed that he was expected to include them in his sleeping position, but to feel a head pressing down on his chest had suffocated him even then and would now be out of the question. He remembered what it felt like to be inside a woman. The memory would come to him suddenly and be followed, as now, by a sickening feeling, as though a bridge were giving way beneath him. Sometimes he saw his wife's face below him, her eyes closed, her chin raised as though she were straining towards her own pleasure, biting her lip in concentration. With the memory of Maya always came the smell of almonds. When he had first met her she had called herself a *coiffeuse-shampouineuse*. That he had not jumped at the touch of her fingers, but closed his eyes, had been a sign. He had felt the cold, hard porcelain against his neck, listened to the scratching noise of her white coat while she moved, her fingers working, drawing a tree of pleasure that branched across his scalp, down his neck and down his spine, straight to his genitals. He had kept silent while the childish timbre of her voice ran on and on, and he had felt her desire for him, cold as ambition. It suited him that women seemed no longer to notice him, except for Annie at work – a woman, he could tell, given to pity.

He could feel the skin of his back starting to smart in the heat. He lifted his head and glanced at the group that had settled only a few paces away from him towards the steps. Two teenage couples languished side by side and intertwined. Stuart lay down again and closed his eyes.

'You'll get cancer.' The voice was not familiar. Stuart raised his head and looked at the man's shadow on the sand before him. He saw that the teenagers had gone. He sat up and shielded his eyes with his hand. It was Santini's bodyguard, Georges Rocca. He was standing over him with his hands in the pockets of his black suit.

'Did someone die?' Stuart asked.

Georges squeezed the knot of his red tie.

'Monsieur Santini wants to talk to you. He's waiting in the car.'

Stuart brushed the sand from his hands.

'Okay, but I haven't had my swim yet. I won't be long.' And he stood up and walked past Georges to the water.

He dived in, opened his eyes and saw the milky sea, striped with bars of sunlight, heard the muted sounds of his own body moving through the water and felt the air bubbles run along on his neck as he rotated, turning and turning and smiling, letting the water enter his mouth and stream out again as he turned, smiling at the idea that Santini had sought him out.

When he returned to his towel, Georges had gone. He pulled on his shirt, wrapped his jeans in his towel and walked quickly towards the steps, leaving behind him the little mound he had made for his head.

When he saw Santini's new black Saab in the car park he slowed his pace. Santini was sitting in the back, behind Georges. Before Georges had time to climb out, Stuart opened the back door and leaned in.

'Stuart. Get in.'

Stuart nodded at the beige leather seats.

'I'm wet.'

Santini opened his hand. 'Please.'

When Santini used this word there was never any plea in it. Stuart climbed in next to him. He folded his arms. Santini could speak first. As Stuart waited he felt the salt water dripping pleasantly from his hair down the back of his shirt.

Santini looked away from him out of the window.

'I was here for the zeppelin and I happened to see your car . . .'

'What zeppelin?'

Santini turned his pale eyes on him.

'Casino just launched one of those advertising zeppelins over the beach.'

It had been a while since Stuart had seen Santini and he

had put on a little weight. Stuart looked at his ink-black beard and considered for the first time that it might now be coming from a bottle.

'I'm on the board of directors. So . . .' He opened his hand again. 'I saw your car. You can't miss it. You should get the headlight fixed. It looks . . .' Santini closed one eye and leered like Stuart's Datsun.

Stuart smiled. He could feel Santini's aggression, always there, just below the surface.

'What's this bullshit about Father Pierre, Stuart?' Santini took a good-humoured tone.

'What bullshit's that?'

Santini pinched his nose and glanced at Georges' reflection in the rear-view mirror.

'They've just ruled against my visits. Like that.' He clicked his fingers. 'Out of the blue.' He was still using his pal's voice.

'I see.'

'It's pointless,' Santini said.

Stuart raised his eyebrows. 'Pointless for whom?'

'For you. You won't gain anything by stopping me from going to confession. It just looks petty.'

'Confession?'

'Yes. Confession. You can't get to me through him. You know that. You've already tried. The man's life is ruined. A year is a long time in a shithole like that and I'm all he's got.'

'La Santé isn't bad as prisons go. Fresnes is a lot worse.'

Santini's eyes took him in for a moment then slid over him in the way they did.

'You're getting petty, Stuart.'

'You said.'

'To me it's proof you've lost it. I gather they're sending Mesguish in. I'd say that's pretty much the end, isn't it?' He paused. 'You should go out gracefully.'

'Listen, Santini. You ruined your priest's life. Before you decided to use him, he was just a weak man and a not very good priest. You nudged him over the edge. We've talked. A man who thinks he's dammed hasn't got much to lose.'

Santini spoke to Georges' reflection in the rear-view mirror.

'I'm bored of this.'

Stuart opened his door and climbed out.

'I know how much you like prisons, Santini. The only reason you keep going to see him is to keep him sure.' He leaned into the car. 'And that was Madame Lasserre's view and the reason why she put an end to your visiting rights. Which were an aberration in the first place.'

'Drive, Georges,' Santini said.

And to Georges' credit, the response was so rapid that Stuart only just had time to take his hand from the door before the car ripped away in a sweep of floating sand.

Chapter Three

Coco Santini could see from the way Georges kept glancing at him in the mirror that he was limbering up to talk to him.

'What is it, Georges?'

Georges had lost a cap from one of his front teeth and so he kept his mouth closed, making his smile mawkish. He was ugly. His features slid; his eyes, nose and mouth looked as if they had been planted roughly and hazardously in greyish dough and there was a growth the size and colour of a muscat grape on the side of his nose. Georges was eternally grateful for Santini's decision to employ him at a time when the fashion was for good-looking bodyguards. Coco had guessed, rightly as it turned out, that monsters would catch on.

'I feel bad about last night,' Georges said.

Coco looked at Georges' hands on the steering wheel. He wore a square jet ring on his little finger with a tiny diamond in it. His appearance was often cause for concern. Because of it, there were a number of places – one restaurant where they served tiny, crescent-shaped vol-au-vents with the vegetables – that Coco couldn't take him. But what did it matter? Georges Rocca was a human shield and there weren't many bodyguards about whom you could say that.

'Evelyne was great,' Georges went on, encouraged by Coco's silence. 'She really was.'

'Just as well there was someone there who can keep their head.'

'You're right, Coco. She can certainly do that. She certainly can do that.' Georges glanced at him, unsure. 'The Movement can be . . . impressive.'

'No, Georges. The Movement is not impressive. Not ever.' He held up his index finger to stress the point. 'The Movement, as you so wrongly call it – because a movement implies mass support, Georges – the FNL, you should say, is a band of second-rate criminals posing as freedom-fighters. They are an insult to the very idea of the independence movement. There is not a scrap of ideology left between them.' There it was again, a shooting pain in the back of his neck. He closed his eyes. 'The FNL is not a political movement, Georges. It's a gang.'

'You're right,' Georges said solemnly. 'They're not really a political movement at all.'

'They're extortionists,' Coco said, rubbing his neck.

Coco consoled himself with the fact that Georges was too stupid to recognise the paradox: that he himself had helped to build up the FNL to the point where they could now hold a knife to his throat. Coco knew he had made a bad mistake today; probably the first mistake of his life. In exchange for the FLN votes at the election of the last Island Assembly, he had let them use his villa for an arms cache.

Coco had slept badly in anticipation of Georges' call. He had known it was Georges because he could hear his breath whistling through his permanently obstructed nasal passages.

'What happened?'

'There were two Sam-7s in the delivery.'

Coco had then felt the pinching at the base of his neck.

'I said no heavy arms.'

'They think you're Saddam Hussein.' Georges gave a snort. 'Just kidding.' He kept talking: 'It was not good,' he said. 'But Evelyne was . . . Evelyne was great.'

'Shut up.' Coco put his hand to the back of his neck. 'What happened?'

'I lost it when I saw the missiles and I hit a kid.'

'Who?'

'No one, just a kid. A new one.'

'And?'

'Evelyne drove him to the hospital. His nose was broken. She calmed everyone down. She was terrific. Then we carried on filling the hole. It was fine after that.'

[19]

'Is she refilling the pool?'

'I think so.'

'Did she start filling it last night? Did you see that she started filling the pool?'

'She's filling it. Coco, I said you'd have something to say about the Sam-7s.'

'You're an arsehole, Georges.'

He had pictured Georges rooting obscenely in his ear with his index finger, his posture of compliance.

Coco looked out of the window at the swamps around the airport. This land had always been useless. It was a disappointing blot right in the heart of his territory. There was no more malaria, but the land was still worthless. Only foreigners poured their money into it and watched it disappear into the sand. As he looked out over the marshes, he fondled his beard, pinching the coarse, blue-black hair and rolling it between his fingers. His wife, Liliane, had clipped it that morning before he left for the launch of the zeppelin. She had held his face with her small, cold hands, letting his head rest against her bosom. It was good to be tended by his wife. Without Liliane, he knew, he could lose sight of what it meant to be an islander.

'Georges? What time was it when the kid was admitted to hospital?'

'About two-thirty in the morning.' He smiled solicitously at his boss. 'Don't worry, Coco. They admitted him as "X".'

'You didn't know the kid?'

'No. He was a new one. A skinhead.'

They were all skinheads these days. Coco reflected on the days when the FNL could have been considered worthy of the great independence movements such as the IRA or even ETA. They were the days when Titi, the founder, had still been alive. It was rumoured that Titi had planned a summit with ETA. A Basque emissary had come to the island to talk to him. With the thought of Titi came another bout of pain in his neck.

He looked out at the vegetation, dense as rainforest, hanging over the road that led up to Santarosa. Evelyne had told him recently that his stress load was too great. She had said she could feel it in his trapeziums as she massaged him. First the cache, then the disagreeable encounter with Antoine Stuart and the business with Father Pierre, Evelyne would agree, made the stress load unacceptably heavy. Still, he had noted with satisfaction how Stuart had aged. There was not a patch of skin without a line running through it.

'Georges?'

'Monsieur?'

'Do you know what the definition of real power is?'

'No, monsieur.'

'It's not doing what you want, but never ever doing what you don't want.'

Georges beamed, showing his ruined tooth.

Coco looked away. For the first time in his adult life he had done something he didn't want to do. Against his better judgement he had given in to the arms cache and they had proved his mistake by adding the missiles. They had voted for Russo, the only man out there who did not threaten his interests, but they clearly believed they had come out on top. Now that Russo was safely in power he wouldn't help. Russo never cared how Coco got him there: 'I'm your benefactor, Santini,' he would say. 'Not your confidant.'

Coco now cursed himself for not having tried to make an alliance with the pompous old clansmen from the MPR, or even the socialists.

He rested his head against the seat back and practised the breathing exercises Evelyne had taught him: 'In, out; in, out . . . Count your breaths and let them go,' she had said. But it didn't work. The pain in his neck persisted. He decided to break his summer rule and go down to have his siesta with Evelyne at the villa. He wanted to be sure the pool was filling up. He didn't particularly want to screw Evelyne, just smell her. What he liked most about her was her smell: something tangy like orange peel and something else, warm and soft, like vanilla.

'Come and pick me up after lunch, will you?'

'After your sleep?'

'No. Before. I'm going to the villa.'

Georges glanced at his boss.

'What time?'

'Two.'

Now Coco was irritated. There were countless little signs of his disharmony. Changing his routine and going to the villa for his siesta was one of them. 'Don't refer to the FNL as the Movement any more, please, Georges.'

'Okay, Coco.'

They were passing the petrol station at the entrance to the village. Really, it was time to leave Evelyne. Her body was losing its contours and had begun to depress him. In September he would look for someone else. Evelyne could stay in the villa until the cache had been emptied, then she'd have to move out. He reflected that she hadn't done badly from her twelve years with him: her own driving school and a forty-nine per cent share in one of the most successful night clubs on the island. She wanted him to turn La Bomba into a revue bar. There was no reason why they shouldn't stay in business together. She was good.

'Has the Aron woman arrived yet?' he asked. This new thought lifted him a little.

'Last night.' Georges looked at him, reining in a grin. 'She didn't go up to the house, though. They stayed at the Napoléon.'

'Why?'

'Don't know.'

'What's her first name, Georges? I've forgotten.'

'Alice. But she's English, so you pronounce it "Alès". Like the town.'

Alice Aron. Since the cocktail party for the opening of the modern art gallery in Massaccio the summer before, Coco had started hoarding images of her. He would see her heavy hair falling forward as she leaned down to listen to someone beside her. He saw her holding it back, gathering it with her fingers; her long neck; the quality of her skin. And with the image came the same intense excitement he had experienced as a child when he had hit his first rabbit, watched it struggle then fall.

'She won't be selling her house.' Georges winked. 'You don't have to worry about that.'

'Just drop me here. I'll walk home.'

He got out in the main square. There was a youth with long, matted hair sitting on the dried-up fountain playing the guitar. Coco tapped on Georges' window as he was about to reverse. Georges wound down the window.

'Have the German hippie removed before you go.'

Georges looked in his wing mirror at the youth and nodded. Coco turned and walked towards the alley that led up to his house. A large blue Mercedes was obstructing the alley. Coco looked through the open window of the car. Beneath the pedals lay the Hertz hire contract in its envelope. The back seat was scattered with the debris of their journey: toys, sweet-wrappers, crisps. On the passenger seat was an incorrectly folded map of the island, an orange headscarf, and on her seat was a squashed packet of biscuits. There was a deep scratch on the paintwork the full length of the car. She might be young and classy, but she was a slob.

Yes, a woman had to be clean, that was essential. Clean Evelyne was. She was also a safe harbour at a time when things were shifting unpleasantly. Perhaps she had one more good year in her, Coco reflected, as he walked home.

Chapter Four

Alice lay in bed with the sheet over her head. The long morning had been staked out by the buzzing of a single fly taking
off and landing on different parts of her body. She had just
pulled in her exposed foot and the fly had moved swiftly to
her bottom lip, settling there and sending a trill of disgust
through her. She did not know how long she had been pin-
ioned like this on the edge of sleep, when she heard her
younger son's voice.

'Wake up, Alice.'

She answered from beneath the sheet, which the little one
began to tug: 'Call me Mummy.'

'Alice,' Dan's voice whined again. 'Wake up, Mummy.'

'The fish's gone,' Samuel said. She heard the sadness in his
voice and sat up. He was standing by the window, holding
the glass of water in his hand. He had dressed himself.

She climbed out of bed, pulling the sheet around her. As
she rose, the little one tugged hard, uncovering her breasts.

'Bosoms,' he said.

'Let go, Dan,' she said, retrieving the sheet. She crossed the
room and stood behind Samuel, laying her hands on his bony
shoulders.

'Look. He's gone,' he said, peering into the glass. 'Has he
gone to heaven?'

'Yes,' she said. 'He probably has.'

She could see the fine blond hairs forming a perfect spiral
on the back of his neck.

'Look,' he said, holding the glass up to the light coming
through the curtains. 'He's completely gone.'

'Has it got wings?' Dan asked her, tugging on the sheet
again.

'Probably,' Alice said, drawing the curtains.

They had a view over the square. It was empty but for a freckled dog lying directly below, panting on the hot, white pavement. She was disappointed to see that the moss-stained fountain in the centre was dry.

'I don't want to go to heaven,' Dan said.

'Why not, little one?'

She turned round. Dan was lying on the floor with his feet on her bed.

'I don't want wings. I don't want wings; they'll hurt.'

'You can't fly if you don't have wings,' Samuel said. He was leaning out of the window and slowly emptying the glass of water on to the street below. The dog, who was getting spattered, was blinking tolerantly, apparently too hot to move.

'Don't do that, Samuel,' she said, taking the glass from him.

'You can,' Dan said. 'Peter Pan doesn't have wings. Nor does Robin Hood.'

'Robin Hood can't fly,' Samuel said.

'He can.'

'Mummy. Can Robin Hood fly?'

'No.'

'See?' Samuel said.

Alice put the glass down and went to pick up Dan's clothes from the floor. As she straightened up she felt dizzy and sat down again on her bed.

'I don't want to be an angel,' Dan whined.

Alice stood up, stepped over Dan and offered him her hand. He let her pull him up and then went limp.

'Oh Dan, please. Let's get ready and go up to the big house.' She told herself to watch the high note in her voice.

'I don't like it there.'

'You're scared,' Sam said.

Dan looked up to retaliate.

'Sam!' he shrieked. 'Not the goggles. It's my turn.'

'They're mine,' Sam said calmly.

'Make him take them off, Mummy!'

But Sam walked past his brother and made for the door. 'It's my turn!'

'Stay in the square, Sam!' she called.

He slammed the door.

'Push,' she told Dan. 'Please.'

She was trying to feed his limp foot into his sandal. He was blowing bubbles with his spit.

'Shall we go and have breakfast now?' she asked him.

'I haven't played.'

She touched his forehead. He was still hot.

'You can play for five minutes in the square with Sam. I'll call you when it's time.'

They held hands on the way downstairs. On the half-landing a little girl was lolling against the banisters. She stared at Dan as he came towards her. She could not have been more than five but she had dark eyes with heavy lids that gave her a precociously weary look. She wore earrings and a little medallion on a chain around her neck that she passed back and forth across her lips while she stared. A man's voice echoed in the hall: 'Ophélie!'

The little girl suddenly stood straight and ran, like a punctilious ballerina, down the stairs in front of them, across the hall, her little gold earrings catching the light. Alice let go of Dan's hand and watched him pass through the open door of the hotel and disappear into the sunlight. Then she pushed the glass door into the dining room.

Its theme was a Napoleonic encampment: pink, red and gold striped wallpaper hung with sombre prints and an array of military paraphernalia, mostly swords and pistols. The room was empty. A few tables were still strewn with debris from breakfast. She made her way to the only one that was laid and sat down.

She had let Sam into her bed the night before. Dan had stayed asleep on the other side of her and she and Sam had lain awake together, listening to the incongruously urbane percussion of service from the dining room and the shrieks of children in the square. Before he fell asleep he said, 'I know what we'll call him.' He had never been able to think of a name for the fish while it was alive. 'We'll call him Fish Breath.' She had told him it was a lovely name.

Later she had gathered up his sleeping body and carried him across the room to the camp bed near the window. She had laid him down, never taking her eyes off his face, closed and perfect like a lilac mask in the light from the square. She had leaned over him and felt the breath from his nostrils on her lips and then kissed his cheek, and he had moaned and brushed his face as though he had stumps for hands. Then she had taken the glass from the window sill, flushed the dead fish down the lavatory and refilled the glass.

Alice sat in the room and savoured the moment of peace before the boys returned. Someone was whisking eggs in the next-door room. She saw the summer with the boys stretching before her; she should learn to pace herself better. The man from the check-in desk came to take her order. He had a baker's livid complexion and he was wearing a dirty white T-shirt with the island's emblem printed in black across his chest. There was a sound like footsteps on gravel inside her ears and her own voice was muffled to her. He scratched his arm and listened without looking at her, then left.

This refusal of the islanders to behave in any manner approaching servility had always irritated her husband. There were so many things he hated about the island. He even said he had chosen her because she was as far away as he could get from it. Mathieu had spent much of his short life trying to shed all traces the place had left in him. Still, she knew that if she kept returning here with his children, it was because it was here that she felt closest to him.

The little girl with the earrings peeped round the swing door that led to the kitchen. Alice smiled at her, too late: she had vanished. Thinking of Mathieu had become a luxury. She was deeply impressed by this process operating within her by which a source of pain had become a source of pleasure. His death had become intelligible to her; he was a story she told herself and the boys and his absence was as much a part of her life as her children were. Her mother had dug this out in her infallible way: 'You've got to stop carrying your dead husband around with you, my love. You're scaring people off.' She had meant men, of course. Alice had slept with two men since his death, both friends of his. But now sex made her cry. She realised that she would have done better to sleep with a stranger, if only estrangement were an immutable state.

Dan was standing at her side.

'Can't find Sam,' he said.

Alice studied his face.

'I told him to stay in the square.'

She stood up and followed him through the hall and into the sun. On the threshold of the hotel she shielded her eyes with her hand. No sunlight had ever seemed so white. The dog had gone and the square was empty. 'Shit,' she said. At the far end was a cluster of trees planted in thick rows. She strode out into the heat cursing Sam. Dan ran at her side.

'Are you cross with him?'

'Yes. Samuel!' she called.

'Shit,' Dan said.

The trees were huge chestnuts and her voice spiralled upwards into their heavy leaves. She stood and looked about her, waiting for his answer. There was not a breath of wind.

'Call again,' Dan said, tugging at her dress.

'Sam!' Her voice was angry. The tree trunks were perfect for hiding behind, but she knew he was not in earshot. He would not dare push her so far. She turned on Dan. 'Where is he?'

He stared up at her, opened his hands and shrugged his shoulders. Keeping his eyes on her, he shouted his brother's name in two high-pitched syllables. 'Sa-am!'

'Come with me.' She pulled Dan roughly by the arm and walked towards the main road that led up to the church. Two old women dressed in black were walking down the hill towards them.

'Have you seen a little boy? Blond.' She held out her hand to indicate his height. The two women registered Alice's anxiety and began to try to calm her. They had not seen him. But Alice was already looking up the hill, her eyes scanning the narrow street, and she moved on, pulling Dan behind her, leaving the two women staring after her.

'Sam!' Her voice echoed against the parched, shuttered houses. She lifted Dan on to her hip and began to run up the hill, the full heat of the day pressing down on her.

She reached the dusty promenade in front of the church. She could not call because she was out of breath. She sat Dan down on a green metal bench and straightened up, heaving for breath. A few paces away three men were playing boules.

'Stay there,' she said harshly, pointing at Dan. 'Don't move.'

She walked up to the men and stood before them, hooking her hair behind her ears, still out of breath.

'Have you seen a little boy? About this tall? Blond hair?'

The three men stared at her. Only one answered. He had a purple web of broken capillaries across his cheeks and black eyebrows, comically thick and wiry.

'There haven't been any children.' He turned to his companions for confirmation and they both shook their heads. The man with the eyebrows now studied her, ignoring the silent pressure of the other two to resume the game. 'As far as I know, there have been no children in the esplanade since the end of Mass.' He stood still, defying his friends. On his lips she saw the dark tide mark of red wine.

'Would you mind watching him for a moment?' she asked, nodding at Dan, who was now trying to cram little pieces of gravel through the perforations in the metal bench. 'I'm going to look in the church.'

The man closed his eyes and slowly inclined his head in assent.

Alice ran up the three broad steps to the church, lost her

footing and fell forward on to her hands. She stood up, rubbing her stinging palms together, and stepped into the cool, dark interior. This was the kind of place Sam enjoyed. He would be here, staring into the candles beneath the Virgin. He would be offering a prayer for Fish Breath. As she walked up the side aisle, she heard her anxiety in the sound of her heels striking the flagstones. A figure moved behind the spiral stairs that led up to the pulpit.

'Sam?' she whispered.

A priest in a pale robe appeared, his face in shadow. He came forward and she saw his dark beard and, above, a forehead and bald pate, shining white. She stood still and tears filled her eyes.

'I can't find my son.' Her voice was shrill from the effort not to cry. 'Have you seen a little boy?'

The priest stepped forward and put his arm out, not to touch her but to guide her to some other place, more appropriate, for this young woman was sending a ripple of disquiet around his cool, silent church.

'We can talk in the vestry, madame.'

But she was looking past him to the row of candles blinking in their red glass pots at the Virgin's feet. Then she turned, so suddenly the priest thought of a bird flying out of a hedge, and ran back down the side aisle to the door.

When she reached Dan her throat was dry and painful. He had covered the bench in gravel. The men had moved off towards the far end of the esplanade. The man with the eyebrows had his back to her.

'Shit,' Dan said again.

She snatched him off the bench and clasped him to her. She descended the hill towards the square, all the time calling out Sam's name. People were having lunch and the sounds of kitchens and TV voices came through the closed shutters.

In the hotel she set Dan down in the lobby. She pushed open the door to the dining room. The tables were now laid for lunch, but the place was empty. Each time she called his name, the knowledge of his absence seemed to deepen within her. She could now see herself as though from a distance, running up the stairs, along the corridor, opening the door of their room. She saw herself register the room's emptiness without even looking. Panic had settled in her voice and a cold, liquid feeling had crept into her chest.

She passed the concierge on her way back downstairs. 'My son's disappeared. I don't understand.'

The man stood on the landing, looking at his feet in embarrassment.

Dan was in the lobby, walking round and round in increasingly small circles. She grabbed his hand. 'We'll try the big house,' she said, pulling him out into the sun.

She began to run, pulling him after her, past her car and into the narrow alley. This part of Santarosa echoed and seemed always to be empty. She ran between what she thought were blind walls, but the windows were there, high up in the façades. Dan was slowing her down, hanging back. She turned and took him in. His chin was raised and he was panting, his little chest heaving. She picked him up and walked on. Her mouth was dry and her throat was burning.

'Mummy,' Dan said, burying his face in her neck.

She put him on her back and carried on, walking fast and rhythmically, invoking Sam's name with each step, making the walking an incantation.

'It's too far,' Dan murmured.

The street began to broaden and climb in a steep curve. They passed the last house before the property. A dog on a chain bounded towards them and was gagged into silence. Dan clung to her.

'It's all right. We're nearly there.'

When they reached the entrance to the grounds, Alice put Dan down and stopped for a moment to catch her breath. Dan stood there looking at her, plucking nervously at his hands. She picked him up again and passed through the entrance to the property marked by two stone pillars. She began to run along the gravel path that wound through a cluster of pine trees and scrub oaks to a circle of lawn at the front of the house. She put Dan down on the lawn and ran across to the flight of stone steps that led up to the main door. She tugged at the bell but heard no sound. She called out once, but no one came. Gathering Dan into her arms again, she went round to the side and climbed the steps to the broad terrace that ran the full length of the house and overlooked the sea in the distance.

Babette appeared at the far end of the terrace. She was carrying a bunch of orange gladioli with purple stalks that she set down on the stone parapet. She came towards them smiling, her arms open for Dan. Alice handed him to her.

'Is Sam here?'

Babette looked fondly at Dan. He was her favourite.

'He's grown,' she said.

'I've lost Sam,' Alice said, wiping away her tears. Babette looked up and saw her distress for the first time. 'He was in the square. We can't find him anywhere.' Her voice was trembling.

'Have you tried the café? They've got computer games there now. Kids love that.'

Alice stared at Babette.

'No,' she said. 'No I haven't.' She held out her arms for Dan. Babette kissed Dan on the cheek.

'I'll go. You stay here. You're exhausted.'

'No, no. I'd rather go.'

'We'll telephone. Come inside.'

Alice followed Babette along the terrace to the back door filled with glass panes that gave on to a narrow passage leading to the kitchen. The telephone was an old black model that hung on the wall beside the cooker. Babette set Dan down on a chair beside a long wooden table covered with empty jam jars, gleaming in the sunlight. Dan kept his eyes on his mother. Alice felt the cold feeling in her chest spreading, settling in.

'Bettie?' Babette spoke loudly into the phone. Alice could see that Babette was speaking but she could no longer hear her. There was a silence beginning to fill her head. Her mind's eye was now moving like a breeze in the empty village, around the tree trunks and in the leaves, looking down on to the deserted square. And up the hill, past the church and into the graveyard she knew was there but had never seen. She knew where to go and where to look. All of the places seemed to stare back at her. You see, they said. Empty. No tricks. 'Thanks, Bettie. Call us if you see him.'

Alice turned on Dan.

'Where is he, Dan? Dan, did you see him outside in the square?' Dan seemed to pull back. 'Dan. Did you see him at all? Answer me!' She caught sight of his expression and touched her boy's face. 'Please, Dan.' Babette stepped forward. 'Did you see Sam?'

He shook his head. 'He wasn't there.'

'Have something to drink,' Babette said. 'Sit down a moment. He's probably found a friend in the village. I'll go and look for him. I can ask everyone.'

Alice felt a wave of calm like an anaesthetic. She heard Babette's voice fade as though she were being carried rapidly away from her. 'Do you want to come with me, find your brother?' she was saying to Dan.

Then she was out of the room and running back along the terrace. The feeling of calm had gone and her heart was a crazed, unhelpful mechanism banging in her chest. Her eyes and nose streamed as she ran down the steps and along the path towards the gate. At the gate she stopped, gasping for breath.

Samuel. Little boy. Where are you?

She clutched her stomach, her eyes searching the woods around her, the tree trunks poking through the emptiness. She closed her eyes and saw his face, his lips closed, curved upwards at the edges, his round eyes, their perpetual enquiry. She looked about her. The woods were still there, the path, the grassy clearing and the bench made of concrete masquerading as wood, a bench for lovers needful of sea views. In her mind she was calling her husband, begging him to forgive her.

A wave of sickness overcame her and she threw up an acid shower, spattering the ground. She wiped her mouth with her hand and looked past the bench to the thorny precipice. Beyond, between two mauve hills, metallic and scintillating, was the inevitable triangle of sea. She looked up and saw the perfect curve of a vapour trail cutting through the thick blue sky. The tears had dried on her cheeks, leaving a film. The coldness in her chest had grown hard as plaster. She watched the vapour trail swelling and beginning to disintegrate. As though she could see the world reflected in the sky, she knew he had gone. She drew breath and shouted her son's name into the unyielding heat, once and with such force that her voice cracked and broke.

Chapter Five

The telephone stopped ringing while Stuart was unlocking the door to his flat. Only Gérard rang him at home. Poor Gérard, who watched the gradual transfer of authority from Stuart to Mesguish, unable to fight for what was due to him after twenty-five years as an inspector in all the worst postings Central Office could find. When they finally pushed Stuart out and put Mesguish in his place, he would plead for Gérard, but he wouldn't get anywhere. Gérard would be transferred off the island and so would he.

He stepped into the dark room and bolted the door from the inside. He had stayed on the beach until the sand had cooled and the first stars appeared. The large window at the far end of the room was now a rectangle of purple sky. He did not turn on the light, because he had a headache, but went straight to the fridge. Inside was a jar of milky gherkins, a saucepan full of last night's spaghetti in tomato sauce and six small cartons of chocolate milk with straws attached. He took one and drank it without pausing. Then he took off his shoes and, with sand still stuck to his feet, lay face down on his narrow bed.

It was his mother who had made him sleep on his stomach. As a child his hair had been matted at the back and the other children had found in this one of the many things to tease him about. She had tried combing olive oil into it at night and even made him sleep with a rubber bonnet to flatten it. Then she had died, but it had pained her, his hair, and she had tried to help him, but nothing had worked. He remembered the sound his mother had made as she walked: a gentle swishing sound like wind in barley. Now he knew it was her big thighs in nylon tights rubbing together. He remembered her voice calling him in the village when he went missing, patiently and insistently repeating his first name – Antoine – a name no one used any more. He liked listening to her calling him. He would crouch in his hiding place between the church and the graveyard, a narrow passageway full of stones, barred by a blackberry bush with a tunnel through it, and listen to his mother's voice. She was twice the size of his father and several times his worth as a human being. He would have gone on loving his mother if she had not died. As for his father, there was a great hole where his feelings for him should have been. And his sister Beatrice – he was afraid of her and always had been.

His body jolted him out of sleep. He rose from his bed to go and find food. The spaghetti in the fridge would do. He leaned against the sink, eating it cold from the saucepan and listening to himself chewing. In the background, the house was improbably quiet. He spoke aloud, his mouth full. 'We just keep sliding off him, don't we, Titi?' He consoled himself with the thought that Coco had looked rattled when he had talked about his fictional conversation with Father Pierre. And he had got the seats of his Saab wet.

Stuart felt a wave of self-disgust. He put down his spaghetti and inwardly apologised. To his mother, to his sister and to Titi, his brother; almost his brother, for he and Titi had been born the same week and had both been breast-fed by the same woman, Stuart's mother. In spite of this, Titi's life was so to outshine his own that he had become a local god and now, years after his death, not a week went by without someone in the village mentioning his name. Titi's own mother was fifteen when she gave birth to him. She had the body of a sick child and no milk in her, and no love either as far as Stuart could remember. So Titi fed from Stuart's mother, took what he needed and thrived. He grew tall. His eyes were full of light and everybody loved him. He played the best football Santarosa had ever seen and when he ran his dark curls bounced on his shoulders. At night the girls slept with their bedroom windows open and their hair spread out on their pillows, just in case he should climb the drainpipe.

Titi was the only person besides his mother who had looked for Stuart when he went missing. Titi had tried to help him by putting him in goal, but it had not worked; Stuart could not remember why. It was as if the other kids could smell his weakness. Soon Titi was rising too fast to notice him. He had begun to take trips into the mountains on his own that would last longer and longer. At first he had left for a few days, then a month, then the whole summer. Stuart would follow him up the path to the edge of the woods and watch his thin, dusty legs sticking out from beneath his rucksack. Then, without turning round, Titi would disappear into the trees. When he was sixteen he had left for good.

After his mother had died Stuart hid even more. When she could still sit on the fountain with the other women and talk about him, about his appetite and his bowel movements, praise him or complain about him, she was defending his place in the village. When she had died he had become an urchin, without status. His father had gone into the dark recesses of Santarosa's bar and drunk pastis until he was half-blind and half-deaf and could hardly remember he had any children. Titi's mother, who had become fatter but no more loving, had come in every day to cook and wash until his sister Beatrice was ten and old enough to do it herself.

The telephone rang again. Stuart stared at it. On the fourth ring he made his way over to the table beneath the window and picked up the receiver. He listened to Gérard's fat man's tenor.

There was a woman crying in his office.

'I've been calling since six. I sent someone to Enrico's . . . The child disappeared at midday. In your village,' Gérard said.

His village. The idea was amusing. Santarosa, for the whole island, was the place where Coco Santini came from.

'How old?' Stuart asked.

[37]

'Seven.' Gérard paused for Stuart's questions but none came. 'The gendarmerie came in at two,' he went on. 'They ran their checks and came up with nothing. They called the prosecutor at six.'

The thought of Van Ruytens, the prosecutor, wearied Stuart. The man was an indolent bourgeois from the mainland who had chosen the island because he liked to sail. His previous posting had been in Brest and Stuart could not forgive him for his interminable lectures about the Breton character, about its courage, its rigour and its industry. The man had no lessons to give anyone. After five in the afternoon, calls to his office were often rerouted to his portable because he was on his yacht.

Stuart wondered why Van Ruytens had called them in so soon. The judiciary police was rarely called in until the prosecutor had established sufficient grounds for an investigation.

'Why did he take the gendarmes off so fast? They haven't had time to do anything.'

'It was the woman. She insisted.

'Who is she?'

'Her name's Aron. She's English. The wife of Mathieu Aron.'

'Never heard of him.'

'Aron of "Machines Aron". Textiles.' Stuart had never heard of that either. 'He's from the island.'

'The name isn't,' Stuart said.

'He's a Colonna, on his mother's side. Was – he died three years ago.'

'The Colonnas as in Constance Colonna?'

'Yes.'

Stuart remembered how the old woman had frightened him as a child. He remembered her horse's teeth and the translucent skin of her hands.

'The mother managed to convince Van Ruytens over the phone that her child's been lifted,' Gérard said.

'You could convince him of anything. What do you think?'

'I think she's completely hysterical. The kid disappeared in the main square in broad daylight.'

'Midday's quiet in Santarosa. It can be dead at lunchtime.'

'Stuart.' He had lowered his voice. 'She's been here for four hours.'

'Where is she?'

'Next door, in your office. I'm on Annie's phone.'

'What about the search? When is it?'

'Five-thirty at the *mairie* in Santarosa. She's a mess,' Gérard whispered. 'She thinks we're in Colombia. It's Van Ruytens' fault. She got him all excited. Some old friend of her brother-in-law's rang him from the Ministry. So he called us in to cover himself. I told her kidnapping just doesn't happen here.'

'She doesn't want to hear that,' Stuart said. 'All she wants to hear is that it's not a paedophile. What is it, a boy or a girl?'

'Boy.'

'Where's Santini? With his wife, or with Evelyne?'

'No idea.'

'Find out, will you? I'll be there in twenty minutes.'

Stuart drove fast through the centre of town. The first tourists, as always too scantily clad for the island, were wandering inelegantly along the seafront sucking on morsels of fast food. They looked livid and ugly in the new globe lamps that lit the promenade. As he approached the main port, the traffic thickened. Stuart turned on the siren but he had lost his rotating light, so the drivers could not identify the origin of the noise and braked in confusion. Stuart pulled on to the wide stone pavement beside the docks and accelerated. When he was clear of the dock he turned off the siren and drove back on to the road. He wound up the window to shut out the fumes of his own diesel engine. He thought of Santini's Saab, with its purified exhaust, and recalled Santini's first Mercedes and the crowds it had drawn when he had brought it back to the island. Coco had returned triumphant from the mainland with a fortune made in slot machines and found Titi barring his way. By then Titi had been head of the FNL for five years. He had stopped coming down from the *maquis* and people said he had stayed pure as the air up there. He had become a hero even beyond the island, but no journalist had ever managed to interview him. People had started to talk about him as a saint.

Santini had got a kid from Marseilles to kill him. No islander would have dared, they were too superstitious. The kid from Marseilles had stalked Titi for three months, and then shot him with a crossbow in his sleep. Stuart had been in the middle of a law degree at Massaccio in preparation to join the FNL. He had felt he would be of more use as a jurist than as a soldier. When Titi died he took Stuart's vocation with him. He had dropped the law and left for the mainland. He had become a policeman because he couldn't think of anything else to do: he could not be on the same side as Santini. It had taken Coco only one year to gain control of the FNL. Now, only twenty years later, no one even mentioned the word independence any more.

Stuart pressed the remote control and watched the gates to the compound open. If Santini had stooped to kidnapping, the island would not forgive him. As he drove in, Stuart smiled at the thought that Coco might have made his first mistake.

Stuart met Gérard in the hall. He was wearing the mackintosh he always wore, even in summer, a khaki raincoat with epaulettes and a belt he never used. Draped over his bulk, he said the coat made him feel less like a slob and more like a general.

'The beeper didn't respond,' Gérard said.

Stuart had left it at home where it had been for months, lying in the chalky green deposit that grew in his bathroom cabinet.

'Go home,' he said. 'You look tired.'

Gérard took a handkerchief from the pocket of his raincoat and wiped the perspiration from his forehead.

'I'll wait for you. I'm fine. She's in your office.'

This was the difference between them: Gérard liked the

[40]

job. It still made Stuart feel dirty; it was only that he had grown used to the feeling. Stuart was struck by Gérard's capacity to remain so intact, so resolutely good-natured in spite of everything. He thought only children were so stubbornly blind to ugliness.

Gérard inspected his handkerchief and returned it to his pocket. 'Get some Kleenex, I would, before you go in there.'

Stuart was in no hurry.

'What about the search?' he asked. 'What have we got?'

Gérard leaned against the table covered with union pamphlets that Annie conscientiously put on display, like freshly cut flowers, each time Central Office sent new ones.

'A hundred men,' he said. 'With the gendarmerie and the CRS.* The gendarmes have a helicopter and we've got two dogs, one from the CRS and the other from Civil Protection. The prosecutor's coming to the *mairie* first thing. He says he wants you to call him, whatever time it is.'

'She must be a woman of influence.'

'She knows about procedure,' Gérard said.

'How come?'

'Her husband was a lawyer.'

'I thought he was in textiles.'

'That's the family business, run by the elder brother, David Aron. It looks like he's the one with the money.'

'How much is she worth?' Stuart asked.

'She's not clear on that. She says she owns twenty-nine per cent of the business; then she says she's hardly worth anything.'

'How did the husband die?'

'Skiing accident.'

Skiing seemed to Stuart like a particularly humiliating way to go. He noticed that his headache had lifted.

'I'm thirsty,' he said.

He pushed open the swing doors that led into the ground-

* Riot police.

[41]

floor corridor and pressed the time-switch for the light. It clicked like a detonator. 'Did you find Santini?' he asked, holding the door for Gérard.

'He's at Evelyne's,' Gérard said, following him to the kitchen.

'So he broke his summer rule,' Stuart said, turning on the light. The room smelled of Annie's bizarre microwave dishes. He took a glass from the draining board. Water spurted from the tap, hitting the steel sink and spraying his trousers. Stuart gulped back his water, which tasted of bleach.

'This isn't Coco, Stuart. If it's anything, it's foreigners.'

Stuart rinsed the glass and put it back on the draining board. 'Maybe,' he said.

Gérard followed him back into the hall.

'You go home,' Stuart told him. He watched his deputy pat his pockets. 'What is it?'

Gérard contemplated his keys.

'The prosecutor's called in Mesguish,' he said, without looking up. He began working the keys with his tapering fingers.

'Right,' Stuart said. 'When's he coming?'

'Tomorrow morning.'

'What time?'

'I don't know.'

'Is he bringing his men?'

'Six of them.'

Stuart let the anger rise and then fall.

'Right,' he said. 'We'll deal with it when it happens.'

Gérard looked at him with too much compassion, and Stuart turned and walked towards his office.

'Good luck,' Gérard called. 'By the way. She's lost her voice.'

Stuart walked on through the secretaries' room. He paused as Gérard slammed the front door. Then he stepped into his office.

The woman's back was to him. She did not move as he entered. Her hair was parted in the middle and her scalp shone through, too livid against her dark hair, too human.

The sight made Stuart want to retreat.

The room smelled stale. He walked round his desk and sat down opposite the woman. She was looking down at her hands, lying inert in her lap. He scanned the top sheet of her statement: ARON, Alice.

'Madame Aron.' He waited for her to look up, counting her fingers while he waited. They were all there. He would like to have turned off the main light. He preferred the anglepoise on his desk but he knew that this was out of the question. Two bands of straight hair partially veiled her face from him.

'Madame,' he said again.

She looked up. Her eyes were swollen almost shut from crying, her mouth seemed smeared and she looked as if she had been hit. He thought of car-crash victims he had seen, their ghoulish surprise. He decided against holding out his hand.

'My name's Stuart.' He was thirsty again. 'Would you like something to drink?'

She shook her head.

'What is being done to find my son?'

He had to lean forward to hear the rasping whisper. He could not detect an accent.

'You don't believe he's lost. Or run away?'

Her hand leapt from her lap and hit the table. Stuart pulled back. She snatched a biro from the cup on his desk, knocking it over. Stuart restored it, replacing the contents. She was writing on his blotter, pressing hard. He read: 'Do something. Please.'

Stuart looked up. She had turned her face towards the open window. The air was perfectly still behind the closed shutters. The cicadas trilled on. Without turning, the woman hissed, 'It's night. He's afraid.'

She held her hand over her mouth and closed her eyes, but the tears came anyway. Stuart watched her crying, locked in behind his desk, unable to move. He saw himself rising to his feet, walking round the desk and kneeling beside her chair.

He saw himself reaching up and gripping her shoulders, holding on to stop her shaking. Instead he looked down at the papers on his desk. Gérard's writing slanted across the page:

ARON, *Alice*
AGE: 26
NATIONALITY: *British*
CHILDREN: *Daniel (5), Samuel (7)*
MARITAL STATUS: *Widowed*

'What are you going to do?' Her harsh whisper startled him.

He looked up. 'We'll begin the search as soon as it's light,' he said. She was wiping her nose with the back of her hand. He opened the drawer in his desk and pulled out the pocket-sized pack of tissues Annie always put there. 'Here.'

She reached and took them. 'Then?' she urged.

Stuart was so appalled by the woman's tear-stained face that for a moment he did not understand.

'After the search. Then what?'

'If we don't find Sam tomorrow, the prosecutor will nominate an investigative magistrate and we'll take over the investigation. It will be treated as a kidnapping.'

She stared at him. Stuart was aware that this was not the answer to her question. He did not wish to reveal to her how little she could hope from him; not yet.

'You're related to Constance Colonna.'

She blew her nose.

'My husband was her nephew,' she whispered.

Stuart stared. He remembered the two fair-haired boys who had come from the mainland every summer. One of these had been her husband. Once every summer Stuart and his sister Beatrice had gone to the Colonna house for lemon cordial and chocolate biscuits. The fair-haired boys would always disappear. As the twenty or thirty village children ran wild in the huge house, slamming doors and spitting out of the attic windows, Stuart would wander along the corridors, opening doors, checking alcoves, hoping to discover them. He had never found their hiding place.

Stuart detached a small colour photograph of the missing child that had been stapled to the woman's statement. He was blond but otherwise bore no resemblance to either of the boys in his memory. This child was laughing joyously at the camera, the sun in his eyes, a gleeful grin, full of gaps.

'This is Sam?' he said, looking up at her.

She nodded. A single vein, thick and obstinate, the pilot-light of her suffering, stood out on her forehead.

'A circular's being printed up tonight with his photo and description. Every police station on the island will receive copies.'

The woman covered her face with her hands. Stuart leaned closer but could not hear what she was saying. He looked at the long fingers.

'Have you got a car?' he said. 'Did you drive here?'

She took her hands from her face.

'The gendarmerie brought me.'

'I'll take you back to Santarosa. I can't do much at night, but you can show me where your son was.'

She was looking at him. She was no longer sobbing, but tears still seeped from her eyes, which were very dark. They seemed to be taking him in for the first time. He looked down at the papers on his desk.

'I couldn't sleep,' she whispered.

'No.'

'Your boss doesn't believe he's been kidnapped.' She was holding her face up to him and he found it discomforting to look at her. 'I spent four hours answering the same questions. He had such . . . he showed no respect.'

'He's not my boss,' Stuart said, glancing up. 'I'm the commissaire.'

She wiped the tears from her cheeks with the back of her hand like a child.

'I see.'

Stuart could not help looking for the meaning behind her words. He felt an unfamiliar feeling of engagement in the conversation. He stood up as though to shrug it off.

'Will you wait for me next door? I have to make a call. I'll be quick.'

'What call?' she asked, facing him.

'To the prosecutor,' he said.

'He's a fool,' she whispered.

Stuart smiled sadly at her.

'Yes. But he won't be involved any more.'

'Who's the investigating magistrate?' There it was, the trace of an accent. 'Is he experienced?' she asked.

'She. Her name's Christine Lasserre. There's no one here who's experienced in kidnapping. But she's good.' A new alertness had come over the woman. Straight answers seemed to calm her. 'She was in finance. She has a good brain and she's calm. She's lucid, I mean.' He was rambling.

'My husband was a lawyer,' she whispered. 'He disliked investigative magistrates. He said they were cowboys, that they shot from the hip.'

'Your husband was right. In most cases. Lasserre isn't a cowboy. I think that was what I was trying to say.'

The woman stared up at him from her chair. Stuart stood there sustaining her scrutiny with a growing awareness that he was not what she hoped for in a commissaire. He folded his arms across his chest.

'I'll take you up to Santarosa,' he said. 'I'll stay at the house tonight. From now on someone will always be in the house with you in case of a call. If he's been taken, they'll call and we'll try and trace it.'

'Have they called?' she whispered. 'Will they have called?'

Stuart did not wish to look at her. He picked up the biro on his desk and looked at that instead.

'No. Not yet, it's too soon.'

He began to gather the sheets covered with Gérard's meticulous writing. He put the papers with the woman's statement in his drawer. The woman stood up and made for the door. 'Your bag,' he said. He walked round his desk and picked up her handbag from beside her chair. He held it out to her and watched her hook the strap over her shoulder with that movement women made, and he thought of its contents, the bric-à-brac that they carried about with them. He walked her into the secretaries' office and held out his arm towards Annie's chair. She sat, her back to him.

He looked at the back of her head, tilted forward slightly. He felt comfortable watching her from behind. If only his interrogations could be conducted from this perspective. He could tell more from the back of a person's head than from their face, which usually confused him. He closed the door.

He dialled Van Ruytens' number and hoped he was waking him. Stuart imagined him patting the bedside table for his glasses. The man's tone was always sycophantic, no matter how much he disliked you.

'Ah, Stuart. Yes. You were unreachable. I told Gérard it would be prudent at this stage to believe the worst. Let's hope we're wrong. After talking to Madame Aron, though, I think she has good grounds.'

'Grounds for what?'

Van Ruytens hesitated.

'For what?' Stuart said again.

'For believing this is a kidnapping.'

Stuart kept silent. The prosecutor persevered.

'She's very distressed. She feels time has been wasted.'

Stuart waited.

'This is a first, I understand. The Movement hasn't gone in for kidnapping in the past.'

'It's only happened once and it was done by outsiders. It involved an adult, not a child,' Stuart said.

'So the Movement wouldn't be involved in a kidnapping.'

'It's not the FNL.'

'I'm sorry?'

'It's not the Movement, as you call it. They wouldn't survive it.'

'Why, what's your view?'

'I don't have a view.'

Stuart let the silence vibrate a little.

'Of course, this must be kept away from the press,' Van Ruytens added.

Stuart lowered his voice.

'A child is missing. Children are sacred on this island. Tomorrow morning a search involving over a hundred men will set out from a village that has always made it its business to know everything at all times. If the press doesn't know yet, I can guarantee they will by tomorrow.'

'This island . . .' Van Ruytens stopped himself.

'Another thing, Prosecutor. Putting Mesguish on the front of this case is a mistake.'

'No one's said anything about putting Mesguish on the front . . .'

'If they put mainlanders on the front of this case the whole place will close down. We'll get no help and we'll become the enemy. This island doesn't tolerate crimes against children. For once they might help us. Don't confuse them by sending in outsiders.'

There was a pause. Stuart felt elated. His ears were burning. It had been a long time since he had cared enough about anything to get angry.

'I take your point, Stuart. But Mesguish is reinforcement. Nothing more.'

'I hope so.'

When Stuart hung up he held the receiver firmly in its cradle. Then he went and opened the window to let the air in through the shutters and turned on the fan. He stood by the door for a moment watching the fan turning above him. The secretaries had always wanted fans and for years he had fought Central Office on the matter. Only a week before, when he had long given up, they had installed them. That day the women had given him their sweetest smiles. Inès had said, as though he'd done himself a great favour, 'I'll be able to wear my hair down now.' Stuart felt that nothing scared him any more – not his loneliness, or the fact that he was losing his job, or that he could feel himself skidding towards death. Only women, with their expectations, scared him.

He opened the door and found her standing beside the window, her arms folded, her senseless bag hanging from her shoulder.

'We can go now,' he said.

As he led the way past the secretaries' desks to the hall, he felt grateful that she had come in the middle of the night when there was no one to see them, for he worried that the presence of other people made him look worse.

He held open the door of his car and watched her climb in. She was wearing a blue dress with small white buttons down the front. When she had put it on that morning she had still had her son. He pressed the remote control for the compound gates. As they opened, he glanced at her. She was clasping her bag in her lap. He saw her knees glowing in the compound lights.

They drove out into the quiet streets. Stuart started when the woman spoke. Her whisper was too close in the car. He wanted to open the window.

'Everyone keeps telling me kidnapping doesn't happen here.'

'Not usually.'

'Has it ever?'

'No. Yes. There was an attempt. Once. But it was between foreigners. Italians. And it was somebody's wife.'

'No children.'

'Never.'

She did not move but stared straight ahead, her eyes fixed on the disappearing road, as though her lost child might at any moment step out from a side street into the headlights.

'He has been kidnapped,' she whispered. 'I can feel it.'

'I'm not ruling it out.' He wished he could find a more appropriate way of talking to her.

Avoiding the night crowds in the centre of town, he drove through deserted residential streets towards the docks. He wound down the window, letting in the breeze from the bay. They passed the biggest housing estate on the island, where Stuart had lived when he had first returned from the mainland. It was called Les Mimosas, after the three mimosas that had grown defiantly out of stony ground and bloomed every February, in spite of their torture by malevolent children and the knife graffiti of junkies who would shoot up in their shade. The mimosa trees had gone and the junkies had retreated into the dark utility rooms.

'Who knew you were coming?'

'Just the housekeeper.'

'Babette?'

She nodded.

'You didn't plan to stay at the hotel?'

'I couldn't get the car up the alley to the big house. Dan was asleep and Sam was tired and upset . . .'

'Why?'

She shook her head. 'It was nothing. His fish died.'

'Did you telephone Babette to tell her you weren't coming?'

'I've been through this. Yes, I did.' She looked at him. 'Listen, I've thought of everything. I've thought the worst, that some madman's taken him.' She stopped. 'He's not dead.'

They drove along the docks. Liners bound for the Continent stood, tall as department stores, against the quay. Stuart kept his eyes on the road.

'My husband hated this place,' she whispered. 'He really hated it.'

Stuart turned and looked at her. Of course he had.

They drove up into the hills. She was looking out of her window at the view he knew by heart of the hills falling away in tiers to the sea. A lurid moon took away the land's contours, bringing it closer to them, and as they wound further into the island, Stuart felt the discomfort that always accompanied a return to his village.

They drove past the petrol station and the piece of scrubland the mayor tried to call a playground. He had even bought three swings for it, but the brand-new recreational unit had not lasted more than a week. It now stood as a reminder to the village of the sin of overenthusiasm – an empty scaffold, its ropes severed just below the rings. They drove past the gates to the cemetery, cut in neat rows into the hillside directly opposite the village, barring the view to the sea. 'We live with our backs to the sea,' the villagers told outsiders. 'The sea never brought us any good.'.

Chapter Six

Sam kept his eyes wide open in the dark. Through the thin walls he could hear their voices. They spoke in French but their accents made it hard for him to understand. His wrists burned from the man's grip and his finger was numb, but it was still there. He closed his eyes at the memory of the man who had sat beside him in the car, holding his finger in the machine for cutting cigars.

'This is for cutting cigars,' he said. 'If you move I'll close it and you'll lose your finger.'

He had felt a sharp pain just after the blade cut his skin. Because of the glasses they had made him wear, when he looked down he could see only the man's hand covering his own. It was white with black hairs up to his knuckles. They had stuck something on the lenses so that he couldn't see out.

The man had come up to him while he was looking for his swimming goggles. He had asked him where the church was, leaning down to him, his hands resting on his knees. His sunglasses were dark at the top and light at the bottom so Sam could see his eyes. Sam had told him that he didn't know, which was not true. The man had asked him how old he was and when Sam had told him he had said that he had a son the same age. Sam could already smell the man – he smelled of perfume – and he had stepped back. It was then that he had seen the car. It was behind him and close. He had heard the door open. The man's smile had suddenly vanished and Sam's heart had jumped. Then the man had gripped him tightly round the shoulders and driven him backwards and Sam had cried out, and the man had clenched his teeth and said something he didn't understand and pushed him into the car. Inside he had put the glasses on him and then grabbed his finger, pushed it into the cold metal thing and explained what he would do if Sam moved. Then Sam had heard the tyres skidding on the gravel and been thrown against the man, and someone in the car had shouted and he thought they would crash, but they drove on and he felt the smooth road, and knew they were driving downhill along the winding road his mother had taken the day before.

His mother had told him to stay in the square. Perhaps he had left the square without realising. Where had he been playing? His heart beat fast again as he tried to remember.

They had driven straight inside a building. He had seen the darkness through the side of the glasses and heard a heavy metal door slamming behind them. As soon as they opened the car door he could smell garage. They had held his arm so tightly it hurt, and led him to a door that he had to crawl through. Someone had gone before him and grabbed him by the wrists from the other side. It was bright in the room and he could hear the buzzing of a long light bulb like the ones they had in the canteen at school. He had hung back because he was afraid of whoever it was that held his wrists so tightly and he could feel his hands weren't getting any blood. Then they had opened another door and thrown him into this place. When he had taken off the glasses he was in the dark.

He lay curled up and thought of his cousin Jeanne, who had been born with no thumbs. The doctor had sewn on one of her four fingers in place of the missing thumb so that she could pick things up. When he was small, her hands had scared him, but now he liked the feeling of her hand, with its missing finger, so small and soft in his.

He tried to stand up, raising his arms above him in case he bumped his head. He stretched his hand upwards but could feel nothing. He put his arms out to the side and pressed his palms flat against the two walls. Holding his hands in front of him, he stepped forward and after four steps his fingertips touched another wall.

He pressed his hands hard against the walls at his side, and then his feet, and began to climb like he did in the narrow corridor behind the kitchen in his house. It made his mother smile to see him high above her on the ceiling. She would pretend she didn't believe he could jump from right up there. He'd say, I can, and his mother would say, No you can't, and then he'd do it. After five hoists he hit the ceiling and found a square of small holes in the wall. Through the holes he could hear the men's voices more clearly. Here was some light. He lifted his hand to the holes to look at his sore finger. His foot slipped and he fell back, his hands flailing against the sides of his prison, down into the darkness. He hit the floor and the air was knocked out of him, and he lay, unable to breathe or cry out. Pain ran along his spine. 'Mummy,' he gasped, closing his eyes, and the tears came and his whole body shook with them.

'The kid's crying.'

'I can hear.'

Mickey da Cruz stared at the door to the child's prison. They had built it specially for him. They had sound-proofed the room but not the kid's cell. He wished they had, because the noise was distressing. With his fork he speared a piece of ravioli in tomato sauce and put it into his mouth. He chewed hard, glancing repeatedly in the direction of the child's cupboard.

'Oh look,' he said. His fork clattered on the plate. 'I'll feed him. He's probably hungry.' As he stood up, his chair scraped on the cement floor and the two brothers glanced at him.

Mickey poured some ravioli, cold from the tin, on to a plate. Then he put a stocking over his head. When he opened the door he saw the boy shrink back, shielding his eyes from the light. He thrust the plate into the boy's hands and shut the door. The crying had stopped.

'We did well to take him when we did,' he said, peeling the stocking from his head and sitting down.

'It was unprofessional.'

Mickey looked from one brother to the other, unsure of which one had spoken. It was not the first time this had happened and it unnerved him. He believed the timing was a stroke of genius, but he did not say so. He felt inside his jacket pocket for the cold weight of his knife. Opening and shutting the blade with one hand, he watched the brothers smoking their poncy black cigarettes with gold tips.

'They'll waste a lot of time. They won't think it was a kidnapping, will they?' he said, snapping his knife open and shut. He put the knife down on the table. 'The night in the hotel wasn't planned, was it?'

'It was unprofessional.'

It was Paolo, the fatter brother. He was the one who usually spoke for them both. It was he who had negotiated the deal for the kid. Sylvano had stood just behind his shoulder, his hands in his pockets, observing Mickey's every expression, as though that was what he had been told to do and he was going to do it, so conscientiously he wouldn't miss a thing.

'Impromptu,' Mickey said triumphantly. That was the word he had been looking for. The hit had been carefully planned. There had been no denying the brothers' professionalism, but they had no flair. You just had to look at the way they ate. Mickey had fought hard to get them to agree to pick up the child there and then, while he was playing in the square. They had hesitated and nearly missed the moment. The younger child had appeared in the hotel entrance as they were driving off.

'They'll think a pervert got him,' Mickey said, smiling. The brothers rose to their feet. 'You going already?' Mickey asked, watching them take their jackets from the backs of their chairs. 'Get us some fags, will you?' They both buttoned their jackets. 'Winstons.'

Mickey watched Paolo squeeze through the door to the garage and felt a flicker of irritation. Unlike Coco they were completely without style. It was a shame to have to use the Scatti brothers, but they were his only chance for freedom. It was enough for people like Georges Rocca to be Santini's guard dog all their lives but not him. With this deal he'd leave the island and set himself up in Cabo Verde.

He went and stood in front of the kid's cupboard and listened. There was not a sound. He wished there was a mirror. Sadly he had stopped growing upwards in his twelfth year. His shape was dominated by his thorax, artificially large and dense from years of weightlifting. His limbs had proved incapable of following suit. His arms, though muscular, were long and thin and would not lie flat against his sides, and his short, atrophied legs had become bowed beneath the weight of his upper body.

He stood there looking at the room he had chosen for his prison. They had decided not to let it drag on. If after three months they didn't have the money, they would kill the child. These words, formed in his head, caused that unmistakable shrinking of his anus, part pleasure, part fear. The Scatti brothers would bring food and supplies. He would not leave the room until the ransom was paid. There were no windows, just a ventilation shaft high up in the wall that gave on to a small courtyard, invisible from the street. A delicious smell came in waves from the pizzeria on the other side of the courtyard. He had once dined there with Evelyne when Coco had stood her up. As far as he knew it had been their little secret. He liked Evelyne. She had guts. Or maybe she was just stupid. At this idea Mickey began to laugh. His laughter swelled and overcame him until he rocked back and forth on his chair, gripping his stomach. This hit was so . . . what was the word? Audacious. Santini would never believe he was capable of something like this. Mickey laughed until he was so weak he let himself slip from his chair and lay on the cold concrete floor, his knees drawn up to his chest. He remembered the child sitting there in the dark and all the money he was going to make and he stopped laughing and listened, in perfect happiness, to the faint din of the pizza-makers on the other side of the wall.

Chapter Seven

Stuart parked beneath the chestnut trees in the square where Sam had disappeared. Alice climbed out of the car and slammed the door. She heard the breeze moving the leaves and felt the tears rising in her again, so she moved away from the car and began to walk. She walked quickly towards the fountain in the centre of the square.

Too sensitive, his teacher had said of him. The child's too solicitous.

His little hands holding her face: I love you, Mummy.

Me too, my darling. Now go to sleep. You're tired.

Why not just I love you, you're my whole life? Because she didn't know it then.

When she reached the fountain she began pacing before it. Stuart walked round his car, carefully locking the doors. She watched him approach, the man who was supposed to restore Sam to her. He was small, perhaps a little shorter than her, and so slight in his clothes, they might be empty if it weren't for the hands, which seemed to hang from his cuffs, too large and square. She had seen in his office how they shook. His face was hard and seemed to fall at rest into a frown. The brows were a dark ledge that cut across the forehead and overshadowed the eyes. The cheeks were hollow and cut with lines.

He stood beside her with his hands in his pockets, looking stupidly at the square.

'What are you going to do?' she asked. He turned his frown on her. 'What are you planning to do?' Her voice wavered and she put her hand on her throat. 'I haven't seen anyone do anything useful. The gendarme – he just stood around all afternoon like . . . like some local celebrity.' She threw her hand out at the deserted square. 'The whole village was here.' She stepped away from him. 'All the time Sam was getting further away.' She covered her mouth with her hand, gagging her tears.

There was a clatter. She turned and saw a sand-coloured dog rummaging in an upturned dustbin against the wall of the *mairie*.

'We'll set up surveillance,' he said. 'Cover everybody. There are reinforcements coming from the mainland.'

'Then what?'

'Then we watch and wait.'

'Who will you be watching?' she said. 'The people from the Movement?'

'I don't think the FNL would get involved in a kidnapping.'

'Why not?'

'It would be the end of them.'

'Who then?'

The dustbin rolled and the dog sprang back. It looked at the shredded plastic and orange peel on the ground and then, disheartened, turned and came towards them, haunches low, teeth bared. Alice pulled back. Stuart kicked out and shouted 'Getaah!' The dog turned and trotted off as though there were no hard feelings.

'First thing in the morning,' he said. 'We search the country round the village. I don't think we'll find anything.' He looked ashamed.

She turned and walked a few paces to keep herself from hitting this stranger, hitting him hard on the face, because this was the person on whom she now depended.

When she turned again he was squatting, his back to her, looking at something on the ground. He rose and came towards her. He was holding out Sam's green swimming goggles.

'Take them by the strap,' he said.

She took them. They were dusty and scratched.

You never look after anything. I'm always tidying up after you. I'm not your slave.

Oh Mummy, don't be cross; coaxing, a faint smile, full of gentleness and knowing.

'God. How could they have missed them?'

She stood in the square in the empty village, beneath the bright uneven moon, her heart encased, cold and heavy.

She handed back the goggles. Stuart took them from her because it was expected of him. They would go into a transparent plastic bag, with a seal number, an exhibit number, and his pointless initials. He would take prints but with little conviction. This woman would believe in the myth of clues, in the careful scrutiny of detail, conscientiously gathered and reassembled. But there were no such things as clues, only mistakes. Clues suggested some pattern, some internal rules for a game that, with guile and intelligence, he could win. But his job was to sit still as a lizard in the sun and wait for the fallible mechanism to spring and perhaps make a catch, perhaps not. If this woman knew how little he could do.

'I'll take you back.'

He watched her blow her nose. Her eyes were full of tears. The vein stood out on her forehead.

'Your son needs you to be strong,' he said. 'Your grief isn't helpful to you, not now.' He looked down. When he looked up again she was walking away towards the car.

They drove up the narrow road to the Colonna house. He had not seen the place since he was a child. Two stone pillars still marked the entrance to the property, but the iron gates had gone. The drive was still gravel and there was still the tall cedar on the lawn in front of the house, the lower branches now reachable for him. Beside him the woman shivered once.

He stopped in front of the main door. The date 1746 was carved in the granite lintel. All the shutters were closed. He turned off the ignition.

'He was playing,' she said. 'He plays games by himself. He plays the goody and the baddy. Running around doing different voices. I watch him sometimes from a distance. He's so involved; if I interrupt him, he looks ashamed, like he's been caught naked.' Her voice was returning. It was still hoarse, but the robotic whisper had gone. He could hear its contours now, her faint accent and the melody of her class.

He turned and reached into the back for the spare mobile.

'Take this. Keep the phone in the house free for their call.' She took the telephone. He turned on the light above the mirror. He found an old parking ticket in the pocket of his door and wrote down three numbers. 'Here. The top one is my home number, the office, the car.'

He handed her the ticket and she looked at the three numbers. As she climbed out of the car he told himself that he was no more useless to her than the next man.

He followed her round to the side of the house and up the steps to the terrace. He noticed that her arms swung slightly as she walked. She opened the glass door at the back of the house and they stepped into the dark corridor. He recognised the smell instantly: boiled food, flagstone dust and something indeterminable, alluring but sickly, that he still associated with rich old ladies. She patted the wall for the light switch. Two pairs of wall lights came on, mock candles with little pink shades. He considered the fact that Titi had never been in the house. Titi had always refused to go to the parties. Even as a child he had possessed the obscure knowledge that you had to pay for such things. Stuart followed the woman into the kitchen. The fluorescent light buzzed, then flickered on. It was her house now, by inheritance.

'If I could sleep on the ground floor,' he said.

'I'll ask Babette to make a bed up for you in the sitting room.' She stepped back towards the door. 'I'm going to look in on Dan.' Then she turned and was gone.

He tried to recall the expression he had worn. He kept poor track of what his face did. He went to the sink and drank from the tap, closing his eyes and gulping. Once again a woman was asking for his help. Close by, his sister Beatrice lay asleep in their father's house. She would mind when she discovered that he was in the village and had not visited her. But he disliked going there and sitting in silence while she fed him. He straightened up and wiped his mouth with the back of his hand. Food, he thought, had become their only form of exchange.

He looked around the room. An old-fashioned electric clock on the wall above the sink noisily hammered out the seconds. It was the same tin percussion as the clock in his father's kitchen. Stuart had started to believe in the process that had set in over the past year, the growing detachment. He hoped he was freeing himself of the pattern of desire, disappointment and failure. But his memory, that part of his mind which caused him the most discomfort, seemed to be resisting the shrinking process. As his attachment to the present dwindled, the past seemed to take up the deserted ground. He would encounter memories like little pebbles in his shoes and he would have to stop and wearily bend down, retrieve the pebble and throw it away. Like his sister's face as a child, appearing as he fell asleep – a colour slide behind his eyes.

Babette was standing in the doorway in her nightdress, her arms folded under her breasts. She wore a pair of slippers made out of pink teddy-bear skin, horny toes protruding from the ends.

'Madame Aron said to make a bed up for you in the sitting room.' She stepped into the room, careful not to meet his eye. He didn't move. 'She said to wake her if there was anything.' She looked at him, giving in suddenly. 'It's terrible,' she said, appealing to him, looking for a bond in the business of sympathy, but he stared at her unhelpfully.

'When were you informed of Madame Aron's visit?' he asked.

Babette folded her arms more tightly and stared back at him, no doubt remembering how strongly she disliked him.

[61]

'Late May. Why?'

She could not close her mouth completely and her teeth rested on her bottom lip, leaving little dents in the flesh. Her breasts were very large. They sat on her folded arms and stared at him like two heads.

'Did you talk about their arrival in the village?'

'No. I don't know. Maybe. I probably mentioned it. What are you saying?'

'I'm not saying anything. I'm asking questions. How often does Madame Aron come here?'

'More often since her husband's death. She always said how much she liked it. He didn't, though. People don't always like being reminded where they come from, do they?' She dropped her arms, releasing her breasts from their trap.

He noticed that all her fingers had gold rings on them.

'When was the last time she came?'

'Easter and then, before that, last summer. It was last summer she told me she had to sell. But it's been on the market nearly a year.' She shook her head. 'No one's interested. There's too much work to do on it, it's too far from the sea and it's in Santarosa.' She raised her eyebrows encouragingly. 'They wrote on the advert, "an historic village". Historic for what? For the Movement. Anyone from outside thinks that means terrorists, don't they?'

'Do you show people around?'

'Of course I do.'

'No you don't,' he said.

Babette shrugged.

'When was the last time you showed someone round?'

'After her last visit. The end of April.'

'Who?'

'An Italian couple. Young. She was very unfriendly.'

'Does the agency always send the visitors?'

'Yes.'

'Yesterday night when she didn't show up, did you call anyone? What did you do that evening?'

[62]

'I watched telly.' She stopped herself. 'What are you suggesting?' Her voice got on his nerves. It was high-pitched and girlish.

'I'm asking if you told anyone that she hadn't shown up.'

'No. Why should I?' He stared at her, unyielding. 'I might have mentioned it to Liliane. We speak all the time. I don't remember.'

'Liliane.'

'Liliane Santini.'

'I know. Did you?'

'Did I what?' She spat the last word.

'Did you tell Liliane?' he asked calmly.

'Yes.'

'Right. Will you show me where I'm sleeping?' he said. 'And give me keys to the back and front doors.'

Upstairs Alice lay fully clothed on the bed. Next to her on a scant bedside table stood a porcelain dragon with an apricot lampshade. It gave off the only light, a smudged haze that thickened the darkness elsewhere. On the other side of her slept Dan, his mouth open, arms thrown back on the pillow in a posture of triumph. She stared at the brown stain on the ceiling and listened to his gentle breathing.

She pressed her hand hard against the bone between her breasts where the constricted feeling was burning her, affecting her breathing. She tried to breathe deeply. She closed her eyes and searched in her mind for Sam's beginning. He had entered her life before she was ready for him and the expression in his eyes was apologetic, like that of someone who has burst in unannounced.

She saw Mathieu's naked body laid out before her, chest down, the three creases like small commas behind his ears. She saw herself kneeling beside him, hunched over him studiously and carefully, with both hands stroking his back, his bum, his thighs. She could not remember when Sam had been conceived, but it had been at a time when she still

[63]

mistrusted Mathieu. She had sensed his deep, ranging boredom, even then.

The fist around her heart squeezed tighter and she breathed
shallowly, allowing the pain to take over. It was Mathieu who
had convinced her to keep their baby. There had been such an
urgency in his desire for the child that it had frightened her.
Still, the weeks had passed and the hormones had risen in her
like a tide, flooding out her will, and she had held on to his
desire as the only tangible thing in her shifting world.

Before telling Mathieu, she had called her mother in England and told her she was going to keep the baby. She had
thought of this call as an act of rebellion. She had believed
she was cutting loose. Now she saw how she had bypassed
Mathieu. She saw that it was a gesture of which her mother
would have been proud.

Soon she had discovered that for Mathieu her act of faith
made her worthy of a depth of love of which she had never
suspected him capable. He had worshipped the mother in
her. Only since his death had she allowed herself to accept
that this was all she was.

Beside her, Dan slept on. She leaned over to feel his breath
on her face. She touched his hair. This one's existence had
always seemed to her a simple matter, broaching no questions. He had arrived in the world complete, appearing to
lack nothing. The daily minutiae he required from her he
claimed without ceremony. Alice turned off the lamp beside
the bed, lay back and stared into the darkness. She felt unable
to face Dan unless he was asleep like this; he seemed to her
Sam's opposite in so many ways. She saw Dan as invulner-
able and knew she would punish him for it.

She looked at the digital clock beside the bed. Its green digits glowed 4 a.m. She had less than two hours before the
search. In the dark she tried to imagine Sam's fear. But she
could not see him as he was, alone and terrified – only as he
had been. She understood that his little life had brought him
to this night of terror, that it was this terror that had been

waiting for him. All his questions, from the moment he could recognise them, were a manifestation of this fear that had been building up behind him all his life, like a swell growing into a wave that today had broken over him.

'Oh God. What have I done?'

She felt for the lamp and turned it on, then rose and went to the basin in the corner of the room. She turned on the strip light above the mirror. Her face shocked her. The vein running down the centre of her forehead had swelled, altering her expression. Her eyes were opaque, like two holes. She was changed. Nothing, not even the death of her husband, had prepared her for this. She set her teeth hard against each other until her jaw muscles inflated and a pain developed. She stood clutching the basin with both hands, clenching her teeth, letting the desire to cry pass through and leave her. The policeman was right: she should not give in to her grief. She looked at herself again and realised that everything she had idly loved in herself had gone, leaving this behind.

Monday

Chapter Eight

It was just after 5 a.m. and the sky was still navy blue. Stuart walked up the main street towards the *mairie*. Santarosa was at once oppressively familiar and yet so remote; even the houses seemed to shrink from him as he passed. The wind blew dust into his eyes. People had closed their shutters to it because it was the *maestrale*, a wind that brought out the worst in everyone. His mother said it made cats mad and dogs despondent; it made women plague their husbands, men hit their wives and children crueller than ever.

There were some new graffiti in the main square. Huge red letters in support of the FNL bled on the *mairie* wall next to the legend: Raymond's got Aids. A new sum had been daubed on the fountain: Drugs = Capital, and someone had written in elongated black letters: Allah is a faggot.

The wind filled the trees and drove dust in eddies around the empty square, and the weathercock on the church creaked incessantly.

Stuart went and stood in the arched entrance to the *mairie* and listened to the wind. He took a packet of mints from his pocket. They had been left behind in his car by Gérard. On the packet he read, 'Soothing and refreshing. Recommended for smokers and those given to public speaking'. He smiled and put one in his mouth.

He took a small, spiral-bound notebook from his inside pocket. So rare were the occasions that he wrote anything down that he had had it for several years and it was not full. There were pages of notes from meetings with Central Office or with the magistrates. His attention always flagged and the notes were scant and impenetrable. On the last page was a diagram drawn by Monti, the only decent informer he had ever had, the day before he was shot.

Gérard and Paul Fizzi were the first to arrive. Gérard always climbed out of the car in the same way, first one foot, then his hand gripping the roof for leverage to haul out his bulk. Paul Fizzi followed behind. He was in his forties, but his tight jeans and tennis shoes made him walk like a teenager. Stuart pitied his trapped bollocks, which he was always nudging peremptorily. They shook hands, turning their backs to the wind. Paul stood with his feet apart, his hands in the pockets of his leather jacket, bouncing up and down against an imaginary chill. He grinned. 'Ready to go?' he said. Stuart smelled wine on his breath. Through his tan Paul looked pale. Stuart watched him take his cigarettes from the breast pocket of his jacket. His sleeves were rolled up and the veins stood out on his forearms. As he bent his head to light a cigarette, a lock of dark hair fell over his face.

'Did you send the printouts?'

Paul nodded as he drew on his cigarette. Stuart had given up. He considered the fact that smoking had been his only serious occupation. It was a cigarette he wanted, not a mint. He spat it out.

'No good?' Gérard said. Stuart took the bag of mints from his pocket and offered him one.

Gérard looked at the mints.

'No thanks.'

The three of them stood waiting while Paul clicked his gold lighter on and off. He also had a gold wristwatch and a Laguiole knife with which he munificently cut bread for the department at lunchtime. Stuart had heard that these were all presents from women.

The three of them watched the mayor approach. He was wearing a suit instead of his usual blue overalls. He cursed the *maestrale* apologetically as if he were responsible and shook first Stuart's hand, then Gérard's and Paul's, without looking at them. Stuart remembered the mayor's jumpy manner, which someone had once mistaken for the efficiency

that had made his reputation. He stood beside them, surveying the square. He took a handkerchief from his pocket, spat
phlegm into it and put it back, repeating the action several
times while firing questions at Stuart and not waiting for the
answers.

'You've got the old people's clubhouse. That big enough
you think? Who's coming from the gendarmerie? Is it Morin? I
haven't met him. Who's car is that, then? It's the prosecutor's.'

Stuart could feel the mayor's eagerness grow as they
watched Van Ruytens park beneath the chestnut trees and
climb out of his car. The 2CV he drove irritated Stuart – like
the pipe and the tweeds and everything about him. He
walked briskly across the square towards them, carrying his
briefcase, his face to the ground. He shook Stuart's hand vig-
orously and for a long time, his shoulders curved inwards
and his chin jutting forward, faking earnest.

'Well done for getting this thing organised so speedily,
Stuart,' Van Ruytens said.

'I didn't, Prosecutor. It was the gendarmerie.'

Three CRS vans arrived and parked in a line behind the
prosecutor's car, blocking his exit. Van Ruytens watched,
seemed to consider objecting, then decided against it. As the
church clock struck the half-hour the gendarme, Morin,
arrived at the head of four navy-blue buses. The mayor
unlocked the room on the ground floor of the *mairie* with a
large, rusty key.

Stuart stood at the front and watched the men fill the hall.
There was a strong smell of baking bread coming from the
boulangerie on the other side of the wall, filling the room with
the incongruously voluptuous smell of yeast. He spoke
before there was quiet and silence came with an abruptness
that made his voice sound too loud. He kept his speech short,
defining the nature of the search and introducing Morin, the
captain of the gendarmerie, as soon as he could. For he was
aware of Alice Aron standing there at the back of the room
beside two men in CRS uniform, each with a tracker-dog.

As he stood aside for Captain Morin he noticed how his hands were shaking and he hid them in his pockets. The new captain was in his late fifties. He had silver, crew-cut hair and blue eyes that sloped downwards at the corners. He wore the ridiculous new gendarme's sweater with the epaulettes sewn on. His eyes moved conscientiously back and forth from the spreadsheet in his hands to the assembly as he assigned a sector to each group. Stuart could see he had a scout leader's mentality and he did not give him long on the island.

Christine Lasserre, the investigating magistrate, came and stood in the open door as the gendarme was finishing. Stuart nodded at her and she smiled gleefully at him like a mother who has spotted her child. She was a strange woman but he liked her. As the men began to leave, she came over to greet him.

'I came to meet Madame Aron,' she whispered. 'I asked Monsieur Van Ruytens if he minded. If I am called it's simpler for her if she can put a face to my name.'

Stuart nodded. Alice Aron was still at the back of the room, hemmed in by the mayor and the prosecutor.

'You're up early,' Stuart said.

'I'm not a great sleeper anyway,' Lasserre said, touching Stuart's arm.

She stood beside him, fingering the silver pendant she always wore. He was not sure, but he thought it might be a pear. He had always liked Lasserre, even at the beginning when she had just crossed over from civil law, having sat the exams at the age of fifty. The others were irritated by her homeliness. But Stuart saw how quickly she learned. She was not afraid to look stupid.

'Stuart. Are you Scottish?' she asked him.

He shook his head.

'Stuart was the name they gave to the illegitimate children left behind by the English after they occupied the island. It's a generic term for bastard.'

Lasserre smiled.

'You must have English in you then,' she said. She nodded at Alice Aron, who was still trapped. 'Shall we wait for her outside?'

Stuart followed her out through the door. Lasserre leaned back against the wall of the *mairie* and looked earnestly at him. Her very blue eyes were watering from the wind.

'What do you think, Stuart?' A gust of wind swept her grey hair over her face and she held it back with her hand, waiting patiently.

He felt she was on his side, but a policeman's mistrust of investigating magistrates made him hesitate.

'Come on,' she said, smiling. 'You think the child's been kidnapped and you're hoping Santini has something to do with it.'

Stuart spoke his mind, almost in anger at having been encouraged to do so.

'Russo's deputy for the north of the island. So theoretically Santini can hope for a peaceful life . . .'

'Theoretically, yes.'

She held up her hand. The journalist Angel Lopez was coming towards them at a jog, the vents of his suit flapping behind him.

'Your friend.'

Stuart's heart sank.

'Who told him?'

Lasserre smiled. Angel Lopez took her hand and held it, inclining his head slightly.

'*Madame le juge.*'

Lopez had left Spain over twenty years ago but he still spoke with a strong accent. He faced Stuart and clicked his heels then smiled, revealing his little grey teeth. His complexion was sallow and his cheeks were perforated with acne scars.

Lopez slid his hands into the pockets of his suit, and lifted his shoulders.

'Bad wind,' he said. 'When do they set off?'

[73]

'What are you doing here?' Stuart asked.

'I'm doing my job. Like you, Stuart.' He grinned and turned to Lasserre. 'So you've been called, *Madame le juge*,' he said, taking his hands from his pockets and folding his arms.

'Do stop calling me *Madame le juge*, Lopez. No, I have not been called.'

'So . . .' He opened his hands. 'Why are you here?'

'A child's disappeared,' she said. 'I'm here in case they don't find him.'

'A rich child,' Lopez said, nodding sadly. 'Is that the mother I saw? The beautiful dark woman.'

That Lopez should pronounce her beautiful made Stuart suddenly uncomfortable. Lopez knew how to provoke discomfort. His method was always to find out where it hurt and press hard. A former revolutionary from GRAPO, he had come to the island in the seventies after a spell in one of Franco's prisons. He had heard of Titi's movement and had come to join him. When Titi was killed he had come down to the city and started to write for the *Islander*, his past as an anti-Francist giving him an aura that covered his bad writing. Beneath his formal Spanish manners he still had the same uncompromising logic of a revolutionary Marxist.

'Lopez, listen. If you're going to do a story on this, I want to talk to you first.'

'Sure,' Lopez said. 'I can understand that.'

Van Ruytens was coming towards them with Alice Aron at his side.

'I hear she's English,' Lopez said. 'Does she understand everything?'

'She speaks perfectly,' Stuart said.

The prosecutor was wearing new glasses, a ridiculous pair of narrow rectangles without frames that made him look like a glass-blower. He shook hands with everyone with a misplaced enthusiasm. Alice Aron stood on the edge of the group, taller than all the men, her bag on her shoulder.

Van Ruytens introduced her to Lasserre, then to Lopez.

Stuart looked for her reaction to the journalist, but her face was a pale mask.

'And Stuart you know, of course.'

Stuart nodded at Alice and turned quickly to Lopez.

'Meet me in my office at ten.' He nodded at Lasserre, who smiled at him.

'We'll talk after the search,' she said, then turned her attention to Alice. Those in the force who disliked her spread rumours that Christine Lasserre was a lesbian. Stuart knew nothing about her private life but guessed that, like him, she simply did not have one.

He left the two women and crossed the square towards the CRS vans. Gérard was talking to the two CRS with the tracker-dogs. Stuart touched him on the arm as he passed.

'I'll see you at the office.'

Gérard smiled and held up two fat fingers, and Stuart felt a wave of affection for him.

When he reached Santini's house the sky was flecked with the colours of dawn. The wind seemed to have silenced the birds. He stood at the gate, leaning forward and watching a small square of courtyard through a rusty hole in the iron. He pulled on the bell cord and heard it ring in the distance. He remembered the last time he had been at Coco's house, the summer before, for Monti's murder, and watching Coco control his anger while he, Gérard and Paul turned his place upside down and found nothing.

He rang again and then banged on the iron gate with his fist. He glanced up at the passageway that joined the Santinis' house to the Battestis'. Raymond's car, an orange Fiat with a black stripe running along each side, was parked in the tiny square. It was hard to see how he got it in and out. Five cats lay beneath its bonnet, sheltered from the wind. He raised his fist to bang again and the door opened. Liliane Santini stood before him in a yellow nightdress. She held her hands clasped in front of her and looked at him with such distaste that he smiled.

'He's not here,' she said.

'I know.'

Liliane Santini looked up at Stuart, for she was short, shorter these days than most of the village children. She was overweight, had been for as long as she could remember, and had difficulty climbing the stairs, though she was still in her early fifties. Her small, youthful hands were her only adornment and she looked after them. She wore gloves for the vegetable garden and for housework, and she put cream on them regularly. Betty, who was a trained manicurist, often practised on her for free. She looked at her watch.

'You're too early. It's illegal.'

'Not for a friendly visit.'

'I'll tell him you called.' She began to close the gate.

'A child's disappeared,' he said, blocking the gate with his foot.

'I'm sorry?'

'A child. A little boy disappeared without trace yesterday afternoon. He was playing in the square.'

She looked at him benevolently. He showed her the photograph of the blond, smiling child. She looked at it longer than she meant to, took in the big smile and the slightly worried look in the eyes. She thought of her own grandchildren whom she had never seen. What she would have given to have a photo of them like this one. She handed the photograph back and watched him put it into his pocket. If the child's fate depended on Antoine Stuart, she pitied the mother.

'Come on, Liliane. The whole village was out with the gendarmerie yesterday,' he said, putting the photograph back into his wallet. 'You were probably one of the first to know.'

Liliane tried to read the intentions in his face. His eyes, beneath their heavy brows, showed nothing but his habitual anger. His mouth, which had kept its sharp contours, had not changed since he was a boy. She had always felt for Stuart a combination of pity and loathing. He was one of those children who seemed to hang back from life as though half of them were still inside their mothers. She remembered when his mother had died, giving birth to that strange sister of his. He had the look in his eye of a coward, like his father. There was something bloodless about him.

'What do you want? Claude wouldn't have anything to do with the disappearance of a child. You know that.'

'Where is he?'

She stared at him, to steady herself, for she was feeling weak and nauseous.

'You know where he is and you know that he has nothing to do with the child.'

'Get him to call as soon as he gets back, will you? If he comes here.'

'Of course he'll come here.'

'Of course. It's July.'

She held her tongue, watching him turn. When he was a few paces away she called after him. 'I've kept civil. But you can't, can you? You're so bitter.'

He did not turn round but kept on walking.

'Have a good day, Madame Santini!'

She watched him from her doorway as he walked off down the alley. She despised him, but she was not sure that wrong had not been done to him. He had no real family. His sister hardly counted because she was cold as stone. Still, she told herself, that was no reason. All he had was his hatred of her husband, and if he ever caught up with Coco, his life would be over, of that she felt sure.

When Stuart had disappeared, Liliane noted the smell of the *maestrale* in the air. It would be here for three days, or six, or nine, she thought. She was not sure if it was the wind or Stuart's visit that had brought on the nausea. She would boil up some garlic water and drink that. Then she would call Babette. She looked up at the sky and saw the last star. Then she turned and went back into her house.

*

Pushed by the wind, Stuart walked down the main street towards his father's house. He reached the door to his father's cellar and stopped. The door was covered over with washed-out and fraying posters. The village noticeboard was on the wall of the *mairie* further up the hill, but those who could not be bothered to climb that far stopped here. Stuart hesitated. He did not wish to see his sister but he felt a superstitious anxiety about passing beneath her window without doing so.

He climbed the steps to the front door. He did not wait long for her to open. She was wearing a pink bathrobe. A white nightdress showed underneath. She stood aside to let him pass into the dark hall.

'It's early,' he said, leading the way to the kitchen.

She went straight to the stove and lit the gas.

'I was awake,' she said.

'You've repainted it,' he said, looking about him.

She ran the tap and filled a saucepan, which she laid on the hob.

'Manuel did it,' she said, without turning.

Stuart looked at the plait she had made of her hair.

'I can't stay long,' he said.

She turned.

'I heard about the child,' she said. 'I was in the square yesterday. I saw the mother.'

'Yes. I have to make some calls. Can I do it from here?'

He just could not be with her.

'Go ahead. Have you eaten?'

'I'm not hungry. Coffee would be good.'

'I'll make some eggs,' she said as he left the room.

The shutters were closed and the sitting room was dark. Stuart could smell wallpaper glue. He turned on the light and saw the new walls, papered with a motif reminiscent of clouds in fleshy colours, or scar tissue. The room was all Beatrice: her glass animals in the display cabinet, her floral curtains, her paintings-by-numbers of Provence. There was nothing masculine about the room, no trace of Manuel, the father of her child, who now lived at the Hôtel Napoléon because, as the villagers with their cruel euphemisms put it, his sister was 'cold'. On a new set of shelves that spanned the far wall was Beatrice's miniature shoe collection, the sight of which had always chilled him. Stuart made his call standing up, as though to keep physical contact with the place to a minimum.

Annie was already at her desk. Stuart asked her to tell Finance to work on the husband.

'Check all his financial links to the island. Get them to find out who he defended, too.'

Finance always baulked at any extension of their domain, but Annie would not be intimidated.

'Could you check the deviant files, too, both major and minor cases? And prepare a request for phone taps for Madame Lasserre. I'll be in by seven-thirty.'

In the kitchen Beatrice had laid a place for him at the head of the table. Two fried eggs sat on a black plate with a red dice motif.

Heavy-hearted, Stuart made his way to the chair and sat down.

'Really. I've no time.'

'You've time for breakfast.'

Stuart ate fast. His eyes scanned the newly painted walls. They were the colour of egg yolk. Beatrice leaned against the kitchen cupboards, her arms folded, and watched him eat.

'Ophélie chose the colour,' she said.

Stuart nodded his approval, his mouth full of food. Beatrice's daughter, Ophélie, would never belong to her. She bore not a single trace of her mother. Every day she ran off to be with her father at the Napoléon, to be with her own kind. Beatrice fed her, dressed her, put her pigtails in. She did what she had always done, what she was supposed to do, and nothing more.

She sat down beside him at the table and watched him finish his eggs and slurp his coffee.

'I must go,' he said.

She brought her hands from her lap on to the table. He averted his eyes as he always did, though he knew the sight by heart: her left hand, small and slender, like her right, the skin as pale and two fingers missing, severed just above the knuckles of the fist.

'More coffee,' she said.

'I haven't got time,' he said, standing up. He wiped his hands on a cloth she held out to him. She was forty and her lovely face still showed no signs of ageing.

'Have you got any ideas about the child?' she asked suddenly. He looked for some sign of mockery in her expression. Finding none, he looked down at the linoleum. He could make out a bow and arrow in the marble grain.

'I don't know. We'll see.' He smiled at her, a brief, closed smile, which instead of bringing them together, set them further apart. It was a closing signal.

On the way to the door, she said, 'Come and see me soon.'

She did not linger but shut the door behind him the moment he had passed through it. To shut out this terrible wind, he told himself as he hurried down the steps.

Chapter Nine

Alice stood by the window with Dan in her arms and looked out at the pine tree on the lawn before the woods. Its trunk was so curved, its parasol lay almost on its side and its foliage glowed amber, as if it were absorbing all the emerging sunlight and leaving the sky with none. Holding Dan's head against her collarbone, she listened to the suck, suck of his thumb and watched the helicopter battling against the wind. It flew erratically, its tail sweeping dangerously back and forth. She held Dan against her to hide her tears from him. He was requesting nothing of her but to be in her arms, as though he knew this was all she was capable of. She pressed her lips to the top of his head and breathed in the sawdust smell of his hair.

She tried to think of ways out. If Sam didn't come back, she reasoned, she would be no good to Dan anyway. She cursed Mathieu again for being dead. Now if she died, Dan would only have his grandmother. But perhaps her mother could do less damage to a boy whom she could not mould in her image.

Alice turned round to face Babette, walking along the corridor towards them. Her huge breasts moved in circles, one at a time.

'Do you want me to take him for a bit?'

Dan tightened his grip on his mother.

'No. Don't worry. Thank you.'

'I came up for some peace,' Babette said. 'There's another policeman come to take over from the fat one. They're chatting away down there. I'm used to being on my own.' She smiled, then studied Alice for a moment. 'I know they're doing their best,' she said. 'I know things aren't the same on the mainland.' She paused, measuring the effect of her words. 'People here don't like the police. They're unpopular. Stuart in particular. I think you should try' – she hesitated – 'another tack. So as not to leave too much to chance.'

'What do you mean?'

Babette held her hand close to her mouth, partially covering it and forcing Alice to lean closer in order to hear her.

'There's somebody you might want to talk to. He might be able to help. More than Stuart. He can be very kind. If he says he'll help, then he will. He's an important man on this island,' she said. 'Actually he's one of the founders of the independence movement. I mean he was one of the early ones. He's more in politics now. He's no angel but he wouldn't stand for a kidnapping. He knows everybody. If you can get him on your side, he could help you. You wouldn't want to tell Stuart, though. He hates him.'

'Who is this person?'

Babette grinned. 'Claude Santini. People call him Coco.' She put her hand into the pocket of her apron and took out a small piece of folded paper, which she handed to Alice. 'You can call him on this number. He's a bit of a womaniser,' she added, smiling.

Alice put the paper in her pocket. Babette folded her arms.

'If you like I'll get a little girl over so that he'll have someone to play with,' she said, nodding at Dan. 'Her name's Ophélie. She must be about his age. She's Stuart's niece, in actual fact. But she's a nice little girl. It would do him good to play a bit.'

'Yes,' Alice said vaguely. 'He's not very well.'

Babette touched his forehead.

'A little feverish.' She looked at Alice. 'If you do call him, use that portable one you've got. Then they can't listen in.'

Alice nodded.

'Can I get you something to eat, madame?'

'No. Thank you.'

'I'll come up a bit later and see if you don't want anything.'

[82]

Alice went into her bedroom and laid Dan on the bed. She took off his sandals but did not undress him, covering him with a sheet. His eyes blinked open, registered her presence and closed again.

She picked up the mobile Stuart had given her and pressed it against her breastbone. When she had called her brother-in-law she had cried, telling him how much she needed Mathieu with her. Through habit she had talked to David about his brother, but it was not Mathieu she wanted. She wanted to say that, compared to this, Mathieu's death was nothing, nothing at all.

She dialled her mother's number again. The machine answered. She listened to the recorded message, her mother's deep, commanding voice. The tone came, longer this time than all the other times. Once again she left no message.

She lay down close to Dan so that she could feel his little body against her. If she reached her mother she would come immediately and take control. Through habit Alice would shrink back and let her. Even in this environment, so foreign, so inhospitable for women, her mother would be her imperious self. Alice had come far to escape her mother. It occurred to her that it was this flight that had driven her to Mathieu, that had brought her here to this terrible place, to live through this. She thought of her mother's home in the south of England. There was a place near the house where she had gone as a little girl and that still came to her in her dreams. It was a clearing in the pine woods and she would go and stand in the middle and let her stomach fill with fear. The clearing was wide. Clouds floated above it as if it were there only to frame the sky. There were poplar saplings scattered across it and the sound of their leaves moving in the wind was like the whisper of her mother's voice, willing her to go home.

She sat up, unfolded the piece of paper Babette had given her and dialled Santini's number. A woman's voice answered. She hung up.

Chapter Ten

Stuart let Angel Lopez precede him into his office. The man smelled strongly of cigarettes and lavender. Stuart closed the door behind him.

'Sit down,' he said, went to the window and opened the shutters. The harsh light brought by the *maestrale* filled the room. He walked round his desk and faced Lopez, who sat, legs and arms crossed, a small brown bundle in the chair.

'You have a lot of medals,' he said, nodding at the wall behind Stuart.

'They're not medals; they're badges. From other police forces.'

Annie had put them up. She was always decorating his office. He took the Aron file from the drawer.

'You've got the Guardia Civil,' Lopez said, grinning at the wall. '*Todo por la patria.*' He looked at Stuart. 'You have friends there?'

Stuart looked down at the search report.

'I went to Escorial once for a course.'

'Ah, El Escorial. The Francist Mecca. It's a beautiful place. A lot of torturing has gone on in Escorial over the centuries but it's a beautiful place. And nice and near Madrid.' Stuart looked up. 'Nice place to go for the weekend.'

'Do you want a coffee, Lopez?'

Lopez was disarmed only for a moment.

'Sure,' he said, smiling. 'Don't move, I saw the machine. I'll get it.'

Stuart stood up.

'Black?' he asked.

'Please.'

Stuart looked at the file, on his desk, considered putting it away, then decided against it. There was nothing in it Lopez couldn't get from the gendarmerie.

When he returned with the coffee, Lopez was smoking. He held up his cigarette.

'Do you mind? I know you smoke yourself.'

'Not any more.' Stuart put the coffee down on the desk in front of him.

'You've got the Metropolitan Police, too,' Lopez said, nodding at the wall. 'You're well travelled.'

'My deputy is. If there's any travelling to do, I send Gérard.'

'Pinet.' Lopez settled back in his chair. 'He's what I call a new cop. Smooth and sober. I think I prefer the old kind. Like you, Stuart. At least one knows where one stands with policemen like you.'

'You're a nostalgic, Lopez,' Stuart said.

Lopez smiled and picked up the plastic cup; he sipped and blew, sipped and blew.

'I want to ask you something,' Stuart said.

Lopez put down his cup. Stuart slid the heavy glass ashtray across the desk and watched him stub out his cigarette on the Ministry's acronym.

'Please,' Lopez said, rubbing his lips mechanically with his forefinger.

'Don't write anything,' Stuart said. 'Not yet.'

'Why not?'

'Because it would be detrimental to the investigation.'

'Speak normally. You're speaking like a new cop.'

'If you hold back until I tell you, I'll give you sole access to the file.'

'To the file?'

Stuart nodded. Lopez picked up his cup and finished his coffee.

'Why me?' he asked.

'Because you can do the most damage.'

Lopez could not hide his pleasure. Stuart stared at him.

'You've never helped me before,' Lopez said. 'This is

important. Who do you think it is?'

'If you hold back and help me keep it out of the papers, I'll let you in.'

'How do you expect me to do that? Everyone knows he's missing already.'

'Just make sure it stays out of the mainland press. You can do that.'

'Maybe. Who do you think it is?' he asked again.

'Will you give me your word?'

Lopez held up a finger.

'Wait. You want me to take the story and play it down. And what will you give me?'

'Access.'

'Access?'

'Do I have your word, Lopez?'

'If you give me access. To the woman, to the investigators – and then I'll publish when it's over.'

'Not the woman.'

Lopez smiled and threw up his hands.

'But it's no good without the woman.'

'You get the story from me. I'll give you access to all the information. You'll have the file, Lopez, but you leave the woman out. No, it's important.' He hesitated. 'She doesn't need this.' Stuart looked down at the file. 'Not the woman.'

'No interview with the woman,' Lopez repeated, nodding, weighing his options. 'You tell me where you're heading. You keep me informed all the time. And if I lose you, I print.' He held out his hand across the desk. 'It's a deal.' Stuart considered his hand a moment, then shook it once. He wanted him out of his office. 'We were on the same side once,' Lopez said.

'Not for the same reasons.'

'That's not important,' Lopez said, standing up. He took a visiting card from his wallet and held it out to Stuart. Stuart looked at the card.

'We've got your details, Lopez.'

Lopez smiled and returned the card to his wallet.

'I'm happy to work with you,' he said.

'I'm not.'

'That's fine,' he said, holding up his hand and backing to the door. '*Todo por la patria*.' And he shut the door behind him.

Chapter Eleven

Coco looked up at the façade of Santarosa's only bar, at the orange-and-white canopy, torn and flapping in the wind. The bar had not been redecorated since the early seventies and reflected badly on his village. He would offer to redo it. As he stepped down into the bar he listened with distaste to the new electric bell striking midday.

Inside, the TV on a high shelf in the corner gave off most of the light in the room. Coco could make out a football match in what looked like a black snowstorm. The mayor was settling down to a game of cards with Albert, a man who had been in the same year as Coco at school. At the sight of him Coco asked himself if he were the only one not ageing.

'Morning, Mayor. Who's playing?' he asked, nodding up at the television.

'It's a replay of last night,' the mayor said, keeping his back to Coco and surveying his cards.

Albert turned in his chair as though the effort were painful. No Nissan Patrol would bring his youth back, Coco thought. He was already an old man with a dowager's hump. That, Coco believed, was what happened to you if you married a beautiful woman. Coco had understood, even as a young man, that a beautiful wife was ill-advised for anyone interested in power. Nor did he regret his choice: Liliane was ugly and clean and grateful.

'We could have done with you here yesterday, Santini,' the mayor said, still plucking at his cards. Coco was sure the man had throat cancer. 'It was a fiasco,' he rasped. 'The gendarmerie ought to be an outlawed organisation. They're incompetent and they're a threat to public safety.' He shook his head. 'My guess is the kid just went for a walk.'

'The new captain seems . . .' Albert began. 'He seems . . .'

The mayor of Santarosa spat out air.

'He's nothing.' He waved his hand over his cards. 'He's wind.' He pointed at his head. 'In here. Down here. They're all the same.' He looked up and grinned at Coco. 'Eh, Santini?'

Coco jangled the change in his pocket.

'Get the child back to its mother, Coco,' the mayor said, avoiding his eyes. 'The village is already cursed. But this'll pull us over the edge and into the sea. There.' He laid down his hand.

'Get the bell changed, Mayor,' Coco said. 'It's been two years. That electric one's a disgrace.'

The mayor stiffened but did not look up, and Coco moved on. He approached the bar and pointed at Albert's wife Betty who was polishing glasses.

'I'm getting you a new TV.'

Betty smiled. 'What'll you have, Coco?'

'A Ricard, please, Betty,' he said, looking at her so hard she had to turn away.

She put the glass she had been polishing on the shelf and glanced at herself in the mirror that ran the full length of the bar. She licked her finger and wiped away a smudge of mascara from under her eye, checked her teeth for lipstick and smiled again. Her chin was beginning to sag. There was nothing to be done except smile a lot. She let Coco look at her again as she poured water into his pastis, turning the gold syrup cloudy and pale as his eyes. She wouldn't refuse Coco now, she thought. Something she had until recently mistaken for disgust moved inside her when he looked at her. She watched another fly electrocute itself on the new blue neon fly-toaster and join the pile of the dead, and it occurred to her that as a modern woman, able to order American nails by catalogue and get a decent home perm kit for her hair, she had the edge on her mother's generation.

Coco ordered another Ricard, which he downed in one. He

leaned over the bar, pinched Betty's cheek, paid and tipped her, and left.

He crossed the square, the pastis still heating the walls of his mouth. Since he had made his peaceful divorce from the FNL, they had never made a move without consulting him first. The Sam-7s were open defiance. He looked down at the shadows of the chestnut leaves playing on his shoes and he saw for the first time that they were all over him. They were a standing army: it was time to break them up.

He walked down the stone steps that led to the lower part of the village. On either side of him at waist level there were terraced beds planted with vegetables. Children stole the tomatoes and left the rest.

In the alley that led to his house, his soft shoes hardly made a sound. Wasps drank from the open drains. He stayed in the shade of the high wall that ran the length of his vegetable garden, tended every day by his wife. He liked the smell of the alley, of the drains and the honeysuckle fermenting in the heat. His head was turning a little from the pastis, and he stood still a moment and closed his eyes. He could feel his heart beating high up in his chest as if it were in a stranglehold and it was his gut that was doing it. He had lost his peace of mind for twenty-six votes he could have found elsewhere.

Coco crossed the courtyard to the front door. Chickens scattered before him. It was good to be home where nothing changed. Beyond, things had changed so much, people were even lifting kids. He stepped into his dark house and met his daughter in the hall as she was coming out of the kitchen. He took her face in his hands, bent and kissed her forehead. He held her face, his hands squashing her mouth open slightly. She stared back without blinking.

'Where are you going?'

'For a walk.' Her voice sang.

He let go of her face.

'It's time to eat.'

'We've had lunch.'

'Would you like to eat with me tomorrow, Nathalie?'

'Yes, Papa.'

She stood still, her hands hanging limply by her sides, looking up at him, waiting to be dismissed. He knew she did not want to eat with him. She never spoke to him except to answer his questions. She just watched and waited like an intelligent gun dog. When she was with her mother she was quite different, he knew. She was bold and graceful and on some mornings, when he was still in bed, her laughter filled the house.

Coco pointed to the top of the stairs and clicked his fingers.

'There's too much wind for a walk.'

As she turned he had to stop himself from catching hold of her. She was sixteen; the thought appalled him. She ran up the wide stairs and he watched her dark plait bouncing on her back and, just below her skirt, the creases behind her knees.

He walked through into the kitchen, unbuttoning his shirt as he went. It was a lilac colour, chosen by Evelyne and made of silk. He only ever wore silk now that he could afford it, because his skin was softer than a woman's and any other cloth caused him discomfort.

In the kitchen he took off his shirt and handed it to his wife.

'It needs washing.'

She folded the shirt over her arm and watched him sit down at the table. He unclasped the heavy gold bracelet of his watch, which he took off and laid on the table beside him. Liliane put the shirt in the sink to wash and set about feeding him.

'Where's Nathalie going?' he asked.

'For a walk.'

'What's this walking business? She shouldn't be walking all over the place. It's unhealthy.'

He listened to the sound of Liliane's slippers brushing the flagstone floor. She shuffled back and forth between the larder and the kitchen table.

'You're old,' he told her, without looking up.

'Yes,' she said. 'Is everything all right? Stuart was here early this morning.'

'What did he want?'

'It was about the child.'

Liliane put a plate of *charcuterie*, some goat's cheese and a bowl of black olives in front of her husband. She fetched the bread, which she held against her stomach and cut, drawing the knife upwards. Her husband inspected the slice she handed him, turning it over, then took a bite.

'He's gone crazy,' he said as he chewed.

Liliane poured red wine into a glass, which she set on the table with the bottle.

'Get me the phone,' he said, taking a sip. 'It's on the table in the hall.'

Liliane wiped her hands on her apron and left the room. Coco sat at the table and ate. He was proud of his torso, which was as smooth and broad as when he was a young man. It was just his belly that had changed. In his forties it had swelled to make room for his intestines, which had turned against him and refused to digest what he enjoyed. His stomach ached and groaned whenever he ate, squeezing out vindictive farts that were punishment only to his entourage, for Coco liked their warmth. Sensitivity to temperature was an important component of his sensuality. What he prized in Evelyne's body was the contrast between her hot mouth and her cool cheeks, her warm stomach and her cold buttocks.

Liliane handed him the phone. He put down his knife, wiped his mouth on his napkin and punched out Georges' number. Liliane filled the sink to wash his shirt. Coco clicked his fingers at her to indicate that the noise bothered him, and she left.

'Did you find Mickey?'

'Not yet,' Georges said.

'Get Karim to look. I need you to set up a meeting for me. I want out with the FNL, Georges. They've got to empty the cache. Do you understand? I want to see Jean, by himself. I don't need this relationship when Stuart's all over me about this kid.'

When Coco hung up, Liliane was standing in the doorway.

She watched him punch out another number and left him alone.

'Evelyne,' he began.

'Coco. Hi, baby. Come to the club later.'

'No.'

'I can't talk,' Evelyne told him. 'I've got Gino asking for more money.'

'Say no. He's got nowhere else to go.'

'It's a bad atmosphere. He's stopped fucking the brunette and now she wants to leave the band. He's asking for more money because he feels like shit and he doesn't want it to show.'

'Say no.'

'He's now fucking the blonde, the one you liked. The one with the big shoulders.'

'She hasn't got big shoulders.'

'The atmosphere is really bad. The two girls don't talk. There's no musical cohesion any more. They're drowning each other out. The brunette's doing the dance moves like a traffic warden. I can understand her point of view. She's feeling underconfident. There's nothing worse.'

'I can't listen to this. I'll be over later.'

He hung up.

Liliane stood in the doorway and watched Coco lay his napkin on the table, clip his watch back on to his wrist and then rise to his feet.

'Babette called. She says could you go up and see the woman.'

'What woman?'

'The Aron woman. About her boy. Babette says she's going wild.'

He stared at her as though he was trying to remember something; then he nodded and she moved aside to let him pass. She listened to him cross the hall and climb the stairs. He would have a shower and wash his body thoroughly in his slow and ordered way, and now that he had broken what he called the summer regime, he would go back down to the villa. Something was bothering him.

She tidied up the remains of his lunch, washed his shirt and went out through the back door to hang it. The fly curtain, red and white strips of plastic, flapped violently. She hung the shirt and watched the wind chase her eight chickens round and round the paved courtyard looking for shelter. They ran in a swirl of dry eucalyptus leaves, scattering and regrouping, riddled with ticks. She held out her arms and advanced towards them, clicking her tongue and coaxing them into their pen. Since the *maestrale*, they had stopped sitting on their eggs.

Liliane kept two aluminium chairs under the lime tree in the far corner of the enclosed courtyard. Every afternoon Babette would come and sit with her. She usually brought with her a magazine or a mail-order catalogue, and they would sit together turning the pages and talking as if they really might just buy something. But because of the business with the child, Babette was stuck up at the house. She said the mother couldn't look after the younger one, in the state she was in. The bedraggled eucalyptus towering behind the stone wall creaked in the wind.

She fetched one of the aluminium chairs, placed it in the doorway, climbed on to it and unhooked the fly curtain, which she took indoors. In the kitchen she laid it out on the table to wash it. She pulled rubber gloves over her beautiful white hands and heard Coco slam the front door behind him.

In spite of everything her life was her own. She had made it against the odds, like her vegetable garden that she had created out of an arid, rocky slope. People recognised the quality of her life. They came to her to sit with her, ask her advice. It was her will and her silence that enabled her to keep her life apart from her husband's. She did what was necessary to keep him happy. She fed him, clipped his beard, washed his back and cut his toenails. Since the birth of their daughter she had not been expected to sleep with him.

Babette was puzzled by Liliane's determination to ask nothing of Coco.

'Your husband is one of the richest men on the island and you live in that black housecoat and won't even get your yard tarmacked. You could at least ask him for a new pair of slippers.'

'What would I do with a new pair of slippers?' she answered.

Nathalie's voice echoed in the hall. She could hear Raymond Battesti, too, and thanked heaven Coco had gone. One day he would have to accept that Nathalie would leave. She was a good girl, only a little stubborn. In this she was like her father. Liliane heard Nathalie's laughter and their footsteps on the stairs. They were going up to her room. Liliane glanced up at the ceiling then went back to her work.

Of course the Aron woman was going wild. Take a woman's child from her and she'll lose her mind. Liliane had lost hers long ago. What was left of her former self was a perfect imitation. Another burst of her daughter's laughter came through the ceiling. Liliane did not talk to Nathalie about her brother. She believed that her daughter should not be made aware of her pain. Her life must be kept as light and free as that laughter.

Nathalie did not even know that in two weeks her brother Rémy would be thirty. It was twelve years since Liliane had seen her son. He lived in Paris with a wife and two children whom she had never met. Other islanders back from the mainland had told her that he worked for the Central Post Office; otherwise she would never have known. She once sent Betty to see him while she was on her trip to the International Manicure Fair. Betty had telephoned him and they had met for a drink in a café near his work. Betty had always liked Rémy. When she came home, all she could talk about was how surprised she was by the photo of his wife. She had expected her to be much prettier.

'What about the children?' Liliane had asked.

'He showed me pictures,' Betty said. 'He's got two. A boy and a girl.'

'What are their names? How old are they?'

'I don't know their names. Oh, they must be about three and one. One of them was a baby. The other one was on a swing.' Then, seeing Liliane's disappointment, she said, 'They were very sweet-looking. I think they looked like Rémy.'

Liliane could hear Raymond's tennis shoes squeaking on the flagstones. They were coming into the kitchen. She took off her gloves and threw them into the sink. She hurriedly replaced the fly curtain. As they came in she was sniffing her hands, which smelled of bleach.

Nathalie smiled at her mother.

'Has he gone?'

Liliane nodded. Nathalie went straight to the fridge. Raymond hung in the doorway.

'Hello, Raymond. Come in.'

'Hello, Madame Santini.'

He was a handsome boy but he looked ill. His skin was very pale and he had purple shadows under his eyes.

'Are you hungry, Raymond?'

'No thank you, Madame Santini.'

'Liliane.'

'Liliane,' he repeated.

He smiled at her, a sweet smile. He was a gentle boy, always had been. She watched him fold his thin body into Coco's chair. She looked at Raymond's bony chest, livid against the scarlet of his tracksuit top, which he wore unzipped to the navel.

'Will you have a Coke?' she asked.

'Yes, please.'

Nathalie stood behind the open door of the fridge, gulping

[96]

from a bottle of strawberry-flavoured yogurt. When she had finished she brought Raymond the Coke. The way she set it in front of him with a glass chosen from the cupboard and inspected for cleanliness spoke to Liliane of how she felt about him.

'I'm going to see what the wind has done to my vegetables,' she told them, and left the room.

The wall had protected her garden. She walked along the narrow paths, muttering, letting the wind carry off her prayer. 'Keep her a child. She's my little girl. Please make her stay a child. A little longer.'

Outside Liliane cast her eyes across the floor of the garden. Every plant had been touched and tended by her own hands. Every leaf that sprouted, too violently green from the yellow soil, was the result of her labour. This was the domain she had been left. She was filled with rage at the sight of the garden, growing obscenely intact behind its high walls. She felt the urge to spit upon it, but turned away and walked back into the house.

Chapter Twelve

Though she was expecting him, Alice started when Babette opened the door of the sitting room and showed him in. Coco Santini did not look at her but strode across the flagstones in his silent shoes to the three French windows that gave on to the terrace and threw open their shutters, one by one, letting the afternoon heat and the sound of the cicadas into the room.

'It stinks of spinsters in here.'

Alice stood near the fireplace and watched. When he had finished he went and sat down on one of the frail pieces of upholstered furniture that were arranged around the fireplace. It was a sofa that offered room for no more than two people of average build. He spread his arms out along the back.

'Why don't you sit down?' His voice was very deep. It sounded as if he had not been wound up properly.

For the first time Alice felt her own tiredness washing over her pleasantly and leaving her a little worse off. She went and sat opposite him on a small, uncomfortable chair with thin, bowed legs. A circular rug with a pattern of garlands in pink, yellow and red lay between them. The upholstery too was predominantly pink. Santini looked incongruous in the room. But Constance Colonna had never had to share her home with a man.

He sat with his legs crossed and his arms draped over the back of the sofa. He wore no socks and she saw his pale feet, streaked with blue veins. His beard was dark blue. Bluebeard was Sam's favourite villain.

They both spoke at once.

'I'm sorry,' she said. 'Go ahead.'

He smiled, brought one leg on to the opposite knee and gripped his ankle.

[98]

'I was one of the last to hear about your son. I was in Massaccio at the time. I wish I had been here.'

'Why? Could you . . . Do you know anything?'

He glanced at her and then continued. She was not expected to interrupt.

'I gather the police now think it's a kidnapping.'

'They wasted time,' she said.

He put both feet on the floor and leaned forward, his palms pressed together as though praying for silence.

'I can't tell you what has happened to your boy. All I can say is that it's the work of an outsider, someone not from the island. It's also someone who's not very careful.' His hands made a series of soundless claps while he considered. 'They took him in the square at noon, which was very stupid. It's a miracle nobody saw them.'

Alice realised that in any other circumstances she would have strongly disliked this man.

'I know who's in charge of the case and I don't need to tell you what I think of him. You probably know already.' He paused, but she now knew not to interrupt. 'I think Stuart is a bitter, incompetent little shit,' he said, 'but you'll soon find that out. Meanwhile, I'll make my own inquiries. We'll see who gets there first. How's that?' He grinned and she caught a glimpse of gold at the back of his mouth.

When he rose to his feet, she realised how rigidly she had been holding her body, for her neck ached and her upper arms were numb. She stood up and faced him. He had an inappropriate spattering of freckles across his nose and his eyes were a pale green, almost yellow.

'As soon as I have anything, I'll let you know. Through Babette.'

When he spoke to her he looked at her mouth.

'Would they hurt him?' she asked.

His expression seemed to darken. Perhaps she was expected not to speak at all.

'Of course they wouldn't. These are wannabes. No one

who's established would make a hit like this. Stuart should know this.' He suddenly smiled at her. 'No, they won't hurt your boy. He's their only hope for stardom.'

He held out his hand. His skin was soft and remarkably cold and dry. She inwardly recoiled from this man. He let go of her hand. He was standing too close to her. She stepped back.

'They'll be in touch soon. You've got to make sure the money is somewhere you can get at it. The money must be to hand. Then we can make them wait a little. Not too long. But we must be in control.'

'We're not in control,' she said. 'They are.'

His impatience returned.

'That depends on who they're dealing with.'

He was looking at her mouth again. She was aware that her personality was immaterial to him. This was why her voice so irritated him. His technique was to seek out only that in a person which was of use to him. Women, she suspected, were principally for sex. This was what Babette had called womanising.

'How much will they want?'

'How much are you worth?'

She hesitated; she wanted to be truthful.

'It doesn't matter,' he said. 'If they've done their homework, they'll know. When did you lose your husband?' he asked suddenly.

'Three years ago.'

'I'm sorry. How did he die?'

'A skiing accident.'

He said nothing, allowing the fatuousness of this fact to speak for itself. He was taking in her eyes now, first one, then the other. She held his stare until he suddenly smiled. He patted her on the arm in a gesture of unexpected simplicity, and left.

She stood in the empty room. She felt she had hardened in his presence and she knew this was a good thing, better for her purpose than the spilling over that had occurred with the policeman. It worried her that Stuart was so widely despised. To her both men seemed equally strange and equally repulsive. If Mathieu had been with her, they would have kept a respectful distance from her grief. But if Mathieu had been there, Santini would not have offered his help.

A silence had settled in the room. The metallic sound of the crickets had stopped. The pain in her head had gone. For the first time since her childhood, she closed her eyes and prayed: Please give me Sam back, Dear Lord. She began again. Heavenly Father, please don't punish me. She opened her eyes and looked round the room. There was a large bunch of gladioli standing in a vase in the fireplace, giving off a strong peppery smell.

Please. Give me Sam back.

What could she give in return?

She would give whatever was asked of her. Anything.

When she opened her eyes, one of Stuart's men was standing in the doorway.

'Do you want those open?' he asked.

She looked over at the French windows.

'Yes,' she said.

'The wind's dropped,' he said.

'Yes.'

He nodded, trying to drive his hands into the pockets of his jeans, but they were too tight and he gave up. He scratched his eyebrow with his index finger, hesitating.

'Santini was here,' he said, indicating the door behind him with his head. 'I just saw him leave.'

Alice folded her arms, facing him head on.

'Yes.'

'Babette showed him in.'

'Yes.'

'What did he want?'

'To introduce himself, I suppose.'

'Please don't receive people without telling us.'

Alice nodded, suddenly eager to get past him. She looked

at the closed door. She would not be reprimanded.

'I'll be by the phone,' she said, skirting round him. She opened the door and left the room.

Chapter Thirteen

Stuart took the coast road to Evelyne's night-club. Gérard sat beside him, making his ritual search for a radio station. He would soon give up. Stuart looked out of his window at the sea, slick and impenetrable as celluloid, and at the lights at the mouth of the bay.

'I want you to go and pick up Raymond Battesti,' Stuart said.

Gérard sat back in his seat.

'You think we'll get anything out of him we can use? Junkies have a sixth sense. It's called knowing what people want to hear.'

'Coco's overfed him,' Stuart said. 'He's dying. You look into his eyes and you can see it.'

'When did you last look into Raymond Battesti's eyes?' Gérard asked, trying the radio again. 'Raymond's no use to Santini any more.'

'Raymond will do anything for heroin. There begins and ends his usefulness,' Stuart said. 'But Coco's going to unplug him. It's only a matter of time. He's chasing his daughter.'

'How do you know?'

'Beatrice told me.'

'Beautiful Beatrice,' Gérard said.

'You stay away from my sister,' Stuart said.

Gérard smiled and looked out of the window. Stuart drove fast through the salt marshes, pushing the tired engine.

Gérard never drew attention to the familiarity between them. He was the only person who had seen Stuart outside the island and the only one who had ever seen him with a woman. They had met as inspectors in Paris. Gérard had watched Maya pick Stuart and marry him in the first two months. He had seen their cramped, circular flat in the experimental tower block with lilac clouds painted on it and tear-shaped windows. He had teased them about being on the thirteenth floor, the last frontier for whites, because the upper floors were for the Arab families who threw their rubbish out of the windows. And he had probably seen Maya's desertion long before it happened. Stuart remembered coming home and finding his letter box in the entrance dripping with piss. He remembered retching at the smell of his burned doormat that was a smouldering, sticky mass; stepping over it and nudging open the door; contemplating the ransacked interior through a snow of feathers (the cheap furniture had buckled under one firm kick); and knowing all this was a signal that his brief marriage was over. In fact, there turned out to be no link between her departure and the destruction of his flat. Some kids in the building had simply discovered his profession.

That night he had slept on Gérard's sofa and never moved back. When Stuart turned commissaire and got his posting on the island, Gérard had asked him if he could find something for him, too.

Gérard was watching him.

'What's so funny?' he asked.

'Nothing,' Stuart said.

They were on the dual carriageway a few kilometres short of Evelyne's club. The needles were quivering in their dials and the dashboard was rattling.

'There's been a real change,' Stuart said. 'For the first time it was the FNL who got Russo in.'

Gérard tried the radio again. It was a nervous thing.

'You know what I think?' The radio hissed and flailed under his fingers. 'Coco's looking for respectability. Russo's in and his interests are safe. He's not going to sabotage that now.'

'Who fixed the deal with the FNL?' Stuart asked.

Gérard left the radio alone but didn't answer.

'What do they need most? What do they always need?'

'Ammunition.'

'And?' Stuart urged.

'Funds,' Gérard said.

Stuart lifted a hand from the steering wheel.

Up ahead was the sign bearing the name of Evelyne's club. At the top of a ten-metre pole, 'La Bomba' was scrawled in blue neon over an orange sun. The sign rose up out of the flat marshland and concrete plains of Massaccio's airport and industrial zone. Stuart pulled into the car park. It was empty but for Evelyne's red Mazda convertible. Monday nights the club was closed. Stuart parked and turned off the engine.

'He doesn't need to get involved in something like this,' Gérard said.

'He's getting old,' Stuart said. 'He's tightening his grip.'

Gérard stared ahead of him and shook his head. Stuart pulled the keys from the ignition.

Evelyne had decided not to open up. Gérard went to get the megaphone from the car and Stuart began gathering pieces of driftwood, cardboard and pampas from the surrounding wasteland and making a brittle pile on the doorstep of the club. Gérard raised the megaphone to his mouth.

'Okay, Evelyne, sweetie,' he called, his voice blasting into the night. 'Open up or we'll take in all your girls and you'll have to get pinball machines instead.'

Stuart was already sitting on his haunches, lighting the small bonfire. Smoke curled up into the brown sky. On the ground beside him was one of Evelyne's large metal dustbin lids.

'Evelyne!' Gérard called again. 'We've started a fire on your doorstep.' Above the entrance, which was of Moorish design, was a horizontal window of coloured glass. A light came on and Evelyne's legs, deformed by the convex panes, passed before them. Gérard lowered the megaphone. 'Okay,' he said to Stuart.

The fire flared and spat impressively. As the door opened,

Stuart lowered the dustbin lid over the flames. He rose to his feet and stood face to face with Evelyne.

'It's after nine. I'm not letting you in,' she said, staring calmly at Stuart.

'I don't want to come in. Thank you.'

Evelyne looked at Gérard and then back at Stuart. Stuart noticed how rare and slow Evelyne's gestures were. She held herself still as if to mark her own delicacy. When she spoke she hardly moved her lips and she did not blink but lowered her lids over her eyes like a reptile. Her mouth was wide and thin and painted red. Her dark hair, scraped brutally from her forehead, lay flat and sleek on her skull. What looked to Stuart like cherries hung from each ear. Slowly, she folded her arms.

'What are you doing anyway? I heard about the kid. Shouldn't you be out looking for it instead of pissing around with your gorilla here?' She did not bother to designate Gérard but kept her lazy eyes on Stuart. Her heels enabled her to look down on him.

'Where were you Sunday afternoon?'

'At the villa.'

'Who with?'

She stared at him, full of weariness.

'Who with?' he said again.

'You come and see me when you're going in circles. You never get anything but you keep coming, don't you? You've got to keep sending him that message: I'm on your tail. But you're not. There's never been so much ground between you.'

'Who were you with?'

Evelyne sighed. 'Coco.'

'He broke the summer rule then?'

She blinked.

'Why was that?' Stuart said.

'He had a stiff neck. He needed a massage.'

'Excellent,' Gérard said. At last Evelyne looked at him. 'That's excellent.'

She blinked at Gérard and then turned back to Stuart.

'The boy disappeared on Sunday afternoon,' Stuart said. 'It's July. For the first time in at least ten years Coco wasn't in the village.'

Stuart saw Evelyne select and reject a number of responses. She was not one to waste her breath.

'Coco's retired. Why don't you?'

'Come on, Evelyne. You know Coco can't retire. The minute he retires he's a dead man. He's surrounded himself with half-wits, so he hasn't got an heir. The teenagers from the Pescador are snapping at his heels and he owes one to the FNL. No wonder he's got a stiff neck.'

Slowly Evelyne raised her hand and scratched her eye-brow with the point of her red nail.

'If he was involved, he wouldn't tell you. But what inter-ests me is how much you can accept.' Stuart paused, but Evelyne's mask of boredom was unchanged. 'He's done some repulsive things, but a child.' He looked at her hard mouth. 'You don't have children . . .'

'And you do,' Evelyne said, folding her arms.

'If you can't think of the mother,' Stuart said, 'think of the child. You were a child, weren't you?'

Stuart held her stare. Her hatred was as palpable as desire. Her earrings swung back and forth, the only signal of the dis-array inside her. Stuart waited for her last word. But she stepped back, two sure, steady paces on her narrow heels, and closed the door.

Before Gérard could speak, Stuart turned away and walked back to the car. He felt no gratification, but a great tiredness that overcame him suddenly.

Inside the car, the green letters 'call received' glowed on the telephone. Stuart called the house. The two men sat side by side in the car, listening to the pleasant breathiness of the ring tone.

'Yes?' Paul Fizzi's voice sounded from a great way off.

Stuart picked up the receiver.

'The call came ten minutes ago,' Paul said. 'They played a recording of the kid.'

'Did you get it?'

'It's a call box in Massaccio.'

'Where?'

'The one near the Fritz Bar.'

'Did they let her talk?'

'No.'

'I'll go and collect the tape, then I'll come up to the house.'

'Stuart?'

'Yes?'

'The prosecutor wants you to call him and Zanetecci. Lasserre has been waiting for your call all day.'

'There's no point calling her when I've got nothing to tell her. I'm coming up.'

'Mesguish has arrived. He's brought twelve people and four cars.'

'Good. That's fine. They can watch call boxes.'

'And Stuart,' Paul said. 'Coco was here.'

'What did he want?'

'He wanted to talk to the woman.'

'And did he?'

'He did.'

Stuart did not answer. He replaced the receiver and then turned on the ignition. He reversed, spinning the wheel, numb with anger. The car swerved out of the car park, leaving a twisted tyre track on the road.

They did not speak on the way to the office. Stuart drove fast along the coast while Gérard watched the road in respectful concentration. The compound gates opened haltingly. Stuart swore, driving the heel of his hand into the remote control.

Fifteen minutes later he ran down the steps of the office clutching the cassette in a brown Ministry of the Interior envelope. He climbed back into his car and paused a moment before turning the ignition. Santini had been to the house. He had met the woman. He had rested his eyes on her, considered her, carried her away with him in his mind. Stuart started the car and drove out of the compound. When he was on the road into the mountains he loaded the cassette.

The recording was poor and there was a hissing noise. The speaker had a handkerchief over his mouth. Stuart took his foot off the accelerator to hear better. He could detect an accent. He rewound. They only wanted nine million. Even though he was expecting it, when it came the child's scream made him start. He played it back, once, twice. He stopped the car on a sharp bend in the road and played the scream a third time. It was not pain, he believed, but fear in anticipation of pain. He started forward again and listened to the end. They gave no deadline, just a bouquet of threats.

As he drove past the petrol station at the entrance to the village, Stuart thought of the woman and Coco's visit. He accelerated so sharply his tyres shrieked, filling the silent village, waking Beatrice, who rose in time to see her brother's car race beneath her window.

Chapter Fourteen

Alice stood in the narrow corridor that led to the kitchen, her back against the wall and her hands resting on Dan's head. His face was pressed against her stomach and she stroked his hair, trailing her fingers through it and letting it fall. She was thinking of an English prayer she had tried to teach Sam. He had got the words wrong and she had never corrected him. She was careful not to smile when he said it:

> Gentle Jesus,
> Make 'em wild.
> Look upon
> A little child.
> Supper my simplicity.
> Supper me to come to tea.
> Amen.

Dan now spoke into her stomach. She held him away from her and he looked up, his eyes bleary.

'I want milk.'

She stared at him, as if anything outside Sam had suddenly become indecipherable to her.

The back door opened, letting in a gust of wind that sent an eddy of dry leaves scattering across the flagstones. Alice and Dan turned and looked at Stuart. He nodded at her and closed the door carefully behind him. She realised she had been waiting for him and turned away in disappointment.

'You're going to bed,' she told Dan.

'Milk,' he moaned.

'All right. Then bed.'

She steered him before her to the kitchen.

The policeman in tight jeans was sitting at the table, studying a crossword magazine. He flicked his lock of hair from his face and stood to attention as she and Stuart walked in.

She sat Dan on a chair and went to the fridge. She poured milk into a glass and set it on the table in front of him.

The policeman zipped up his jacket and patted himself, delaying his departure.

'I'll call you later,' Stuart said.

A metal chain hung from the policeman's belt and disappeared into the back pocket of his trousers. Alice wondered what was on the end of the chain; there was not room enough for keys.

Dan gulped down his milk.

'Any message for Mesguish?'

'No,' Stuart said. 'Just give him the list of call boxes. Gérard's got it. Thanks, Paul.'

The policeman patted his pockets again, nodded sheepishly at Alice and bounced out of the door on his elaborate tennis shoes.

Stuart was standing with his hands in his pockets, looking down at his feet.

'They called,' she said.

'I know.'

She turned to Dan.

'You're going back to bed.'

She picked him up, went into the corridor and called Babette. She became impatient waiting for her to appear. Babette wiped her hands on her apron and held them out for Dan.

'Come on, little man. You're coming with me.'

Alice turned away from his cries, which faded as she closed the kitchen door behind her.

'What did Santini want?' Stuart asked. Something in his voice made her turn and look at him. His face had changed; his eyes were threatening and he seemed charged.

'He offered his help,' she said. She stared him out, challenging his anger.

'Two things,' he said without meeting her eye. 'One, they're amateurs.'

'That's what Santini said.'

He did not react.

'They only asked for nine million. You can afford more. That's a good thing.'

'I can't get it fast enough. It's in shares that are impossible to sell. It's not an industrial empire any more. They're functioning at a loss. It's basically finished but my brother-in-law won't let go.'

'What about him, your brother-in-law?'

'He hasn't got it. He put everything into the company.' She sat down at the head of the table.

'They haven't given a deadline,' Stuart said. 'That's good too.'

She slammed her hand down on the table, making Dan's empty glass jump.

'They hurt him!'

'No,' he said. 'They threatened to hurt him. They scared him.'

'They said they'd cut his finger off.'

He did not answer. She nursed her hand, sore from the blow.

'They could do that, couldn't they? Oh God.'

'They're in town,' he told her. 'They used a call box in town. Tomorrow morning we'll be watching fifty call boxes in the area.'

'What if they go somewhere else?'

'They won't move. It's an additional risk. You shouldn't –' He stopped himself.

'What?'

'You shouldn't trust Coco Santini.'

'I'm not trusting him. He came and offered his help. I said nothing. Then he left.'

'Those people don't let you near them without getting you to pay.'

[112] ✺

'I know,' she said.

'How on earth would you know?'

'I just do.' She held his stare. 'Listen. I don't care who he is and I don't care about your petty rivalry. I care about getting Sam back. If this man is in touch with the terrorists . . .'

Stuart shook his head.

'They're not terrorists.'

'Who are they, then?' she shouted. 'Who is it, for God's sake?'

But he was looking past her at the door. She turned on her chair and saw the little girl from the Hôtel Napoléon. Standing behind her was a beautiful woman, who spoke directly to Stuart, her voice hardly audible: 'I've been trying to reach you all afternoon. Ophélie saw something.'

Stuart pulled out a chair and looked kindly at the woman, as though he were coaxing her forward. Alice did not recognise him.

'This is Madame Aron,' he said. 'My sister, Beatrice Molina. And Ophélie, her daughter.'

The woman nodded shyly at Alice and went and sat down on the chair Stuart had offered. She sat very straight, her hands folded in her lap, her shining face turned on Stuart. The child stood beside its mother and watched Alice with her weary eyes.

Stuart squatted down before the child but did not touch her. The child looked down on him.

'What did you see?' he asked her.

Ophélie turned and looked at Alice as if she were an intruder. Then she returned her gaze to Stuart.

'I saw a big black car and a man pick the little boy up and put him in the car and slam the door.'

Alice covered her mouth with her hand. The child looked at her.

'You saw the man put the boy in the car,' Stuart said. 'What was the boy like?'

Ophélie turned back to him.

'He had blond hair. I saw him at the hotel. He had green glasses on.'

'What about the man?' Stuart asked. 'Did you see the man?'

'Yes.'

'Did you know him?' he asked cautiously.

She shook her head. Stuart paused.

'What did he look like?'

'He was fat and he had sunglasses on.'

'Fat like who? Like Daddy?'

'No.'

'Tall? Was he a big man?'

Ophélie nodded slowly. She was beginning to lose interest.

'He was tall,' Stuart repeated. 'What about his hair?'

'Don't know.' She looked at her mother, whose grace seemed to set her apart from everything that was occurring around her, as though she was not concerned by any of this, only waiting for the child to finish her business.

'You saw the blond boy get in the car. What was the car like?' Stuart asked.

'It was all black.'

'And big?' Stuart said.

Alice could not bear to watch. She stood up, walked round the table and squatted beside Stuart. She took hold of one of Ophélie's hands. The child looked at her sleepily.

'Tell us about the car,' Alice said. She smiled at the child while her eyes filled with tears. 'Tell us about the car that took the little boy away. Did the boy want to get in the car?' Ophélie shook her head. 'Did he make a noise?'

'He wriggled.'

Alice let out a little cry.

'Was the car like Daddy's?' Stuart asked suddenly.

Ophélie shook her head without bothering to look at him.

'It made a screeching noise.'

'What did?' Alice asked.

'The car. It had a round thing sticking up on the front.'

'Did the man hurt him?' Alice asked, squeezing her hand.

The child grew uncomfortable; she was starting to close down. She pulled her hand free.

Stuart was drawing in a notebook. His hand shook as he held the drawing out for the child. Ophélie stared at Stuart's shaking hand.

'Like that? The thing on the front,' he said. 'Like that?'

It was the Mercedes symbol. She nodded.

'Did the man put the boy in the back or the front?'

'The back.'

'Did he get in the back or the front?'

'The back.'

'Was there anyone else in the car?'

'I couldn't see. The windows were black. It was all black.' The child looked up at its mother. 'Can we go now?'

Stuart's sister looked at her child, then at Stuart.

'Nothing when the gendarmes were here,' she said. 'Then out of the blue, she starts talking about the boy with the green glasses.'

Alice was still kneeling, looking into the child's unyielding face.

'Can we go now?' Ophélie asked again.

Stuart's sister glanced at her daughter.

'I tried to call,' she told Stuart. Her voice was just above a whisper. 'I kept getting the secretaries. I didn't know what to do. I wanted to tell you. Then I heard you drive past, so I woke the child up, got her dressed and came straight over.'

'Thank you. It's helpful,' Stuart said, standing up. She nodded and rose to her feet. She looked down at Alice and seemed to be attempting a smile. Alice could see something of Stuart in her, the same curves in the mouth and the same straight line of the nose, but this woman's face was perfectly smooth, as though life had attacked his and left hers alone. Alice thought of a nun.

Suddenly she did not want to let the child go. It seemed to her that Stuart was letting something slip away.

'Wait,' she said, holding the child's arm. 'What else did you see?'

The child looked at its mother for help. Stuart touched Alice on the shoulder and she felt overcome, as though she and the child had had a long fight and the child had won. She sat down in the chair at the head of the table. She did not notice the mother and child leave the room.

'I'm going to call them about the car,' Stuart said. 'I won't be a minute.'

Alice did not answer. She gripped the edge of her chair until her fists ached. 'It's good what the child said,' he went on. 'We're looking for a black four-door Mercedes with tinted windows. And we have a description. There were two of them or more. I'll talk to her again. In the morning.' He smiled at her. 'We have something,' he told her, and left the room.

She could feel the chill settling in her upper body again and gripped her chair to stave it off. She could see Sam wriggling in the fat man's arms. If only Dan had not stopped on the stairs to stare at Ophélie. If only she had gone to fetch Sam herself a few moments earlier. Where had she been when he was being snatched, when he was calling for her, and why didn't he scream? He couldn't: the fat man had his hand over his mouth. She saw Ophélie poking her head round the door in the dining room. Then Dan beside her, telling her he could not find Sam. Ophélie had seen him taken even before that, before they came downstairs. When she had met them on the stairs, those sullen eyes had just seen Sam struggling in the man's arms.

The telephone was ringing. She jumped up, snatched the phone from the wall.

'Yes?'

'You have three days.'

'No!' she shouted. Stuart was standing in the door. 'It's not enough time,' she said. 'Listen. Wait.'

'You've got till seven o' clock Thursday evening to get the

[116]

money. In used notes. Buy one soft sports bag to put it in. You'll receive instructions on where to make the delivery.'

'Wait. Listen to me. Please.'

'If you don't get the money, we'll kill the child.' There was a pause. 'Without hesitation.'

'Wait. Sam. Sam.'

She held the phone tight against her ear and listened to the beeps. She held tight because she was hanging over a precipice. The beeps stopped, giving way to a long tone. The tone began to waver. She saw a tunnel, the light fading at the edges. The tunnel grew narrower as she fell.

Chapter Fifteen

Liliane sat in the Colonnas' laundry room watching Babette holding the little boy in her lap. She longed to have a turn but dared not ask. She had always been a little afraid of her friend, who had the unbridled temper of a childless woman.

'What's his name?' Liliane asked, looking at the boy. His eyes were heavy with sleep. 'How old is he?'

Babette smiled down at the boy.

'Why don't you ask him, dear?'

Liliane hesitated.

'What's your name, darling?' But it must have been the wrong tone, for the boy seemed afraid and turned his face towards Babette.

'He's called Daniel. Aren't you? And you're five.'

Babette began to rock him gently and his eyes closed. The room was warm and smelled pleasantly of ironing. Liliane stared miserably at them.

'Shall I get him a drink?' she asked.

'It's all right. He's asleep,' Babette said.

'Does he speak French?'

'He speaks both. French and English,' Babette said proudly.

The door opened. Stuart stood in the doorway. He looked at Liliane – she was not allowed to be here – but he was addressing Babette.

'Madame Aron isn't well. She fainted.'

'Where is she?' Babette stood, taking control.

'She's lying down in the sitting room. What should I give her?'

'I'll be down in a minute. I'll just put the boy to bed.'

Stuart left them, without looking at Liliane again.

Babette adjusted the child, settling him more comfortably on her hip.

'Shall I take him?' Liliane asked. 'Just while you look in on the mother?'

Babette seemed to take pity on her. She laid the boy in her lap.

Liliane did not notice her friend leave the room. She was looking at the sleeping face of this unknown child, experiencing a rush of warmth, greater than anything she had felt, even towards her own children. The boy's head rested in the crook of her arm. She watched his mouth, slightly open. Sometimes his lips moved as though he were half-forming words. One of his little hands lay on his chest. She wanted to touch his fingers.

Her heart jumped as Babette opened the door.

'She's fine. She wants me to put him to bed. Poor woman.'

Babette's compassion for the woman downstairs was suddenly too much to bear. Liliane's eyes filled with tears. As Babette took the child from her, she saw her friend's distress. For an instant Liliane believed she was angry. Babette held the sleeping child on her hip and studied her.

'I'm sorry. I can't help it,' Liliane said.

But Babette held out her hand. When Liliane took it, the tears fell.

'Of course you can't. It's all right. You can cry.' She began to make soothing noises like the most tender of mothers and Liliane cried silently, clasping her friend's hand as tightly as she could. And as Babette soothed her, she let her mind run on and on, gathering all the severed threads of her memory.

She had lost her son. She let her mind say this. I have lost Rémy. She would have liked to tell dear Babette what she remembered but she must not wake the child. She would have liked to tell Babette how happy she had been when Rémy came home that Christmas Eve on leave from National Service. How he had helped her shake the olives from the trees and gather them up in plastic sheets. She had hardly spoken to him, she was so happy to have him with her, and there would be plenty of time, she thought. They would spend a whole week together. He would catch up on his sleep in the mornings and watch TV in the afternoons. They would have a bite together in front of *Guess the Price* before he went out.

Liliane looked up. Babette was looking down on her, her face full of compassion.

'Tell me,' she said. 'Tell me what happened.'

Liliane wanted to tell Babette about Coco: how she now understood that her husband was the animal that would kill its offspring rather than be challenged by it. But she was afraid.

Babette rested her hand on Liliane's head. Liliane spoke to the floor.

'You remember when Rémy came home that time? Every evening Coco took him into Massaccio. To show him off, his handsome son.'

Liliane looked up. Babette smiled at her.

'I remember.'

'Coco was at the top then. In one year he had taken over all the best clubs. Remember?'

Babette nodded.

'He had Russo on his side,' Liliane went on. 'The north of the island was his. He was so full of himself, he even offered Rémy his new mistress. Evelyne. He wanted his boy to share everything he had. But Rémy wasn't like that.'

Liliane looked at the sleeping child in Babette's arms.

'New Year's Eve is the anniversary of Titi's death. Well, that night some drunk told Rémy it was Coco who had had him killed. Rémy admired Titi. Like everyone.'

Liliane paused. She was tired.

'Go on, Liliane.'

'It was Titi I couldn't forgive. For having let himself be killed. It had been a year and people had accepted it. They accept everything in the end, don't they? Everything here, however wicked, becomes part of the natural order of things. Doesn't it?'

'I'm afraid it does. It's our strength too, though.'

'Rémy stayed out all night and all the next day. I'd just got into bed when I heard him come in. I could tell from his voice that he'd been drinking. I heard him shout at his father and then there was a crash and what turned out to be all the *bibelots* smashing to pieces. He'd tried to kick his father and Coco had grabbed his leg and tipped him back into the display cabinet. I just sat there in bed trying not to scream.'

Still clasping the child to her, Babette sat down on the chair opposite her friend. Liliane was aware that nothing would be the same between them after this, that Babette might not thank her for breaking the silence.

Liliane told her friend about how she had listened to the front door slam, how she had run downstairs in her bare feet and seen her son lying on the sitting-room floor. He had hit the coffee table as he fell and there was some of his blood on the tiles beside his head. All night, she sat by him and held his head in her lap, dozing and waking. The alcohol kept Rémy unconscious. When at last he opened his eyes, he smiled at her and then closed them again at the pain because his lip was split.

Later she washed him as she had when he was a boy, and scrubbed his back and helped him dress, easing his shirt over his rib cage, which was badly bruised. Before he left he picked one of her broken figures from the floor. It was a little statue of Our Lady that she had brought back from her trip to Lourdes. The Virgin's head had come clean off. He looked at the statue.

'Can I keep this?'

'I could get you another one if you like it.'

'No. I want this one.'

She looked at him standing on the other side of the room, broken china around his feet.

'In case I ever forget,' he said.

'Then he left,' Liliane told her friend. 'And I never saw him again.'

Babette looked long at her and Liliane felt fear in her stomach as though she had sinned. Then Babette pressed her lips to the boy's head and Liliane saw her forgiveness.

'And Coco?' Babette's voice was free of spite.

'He came home the next evening, packed his things and left. For a whole year he lived at the villa. When he came back to Santarosa the summer after, I knew we'd never speak of Rémy.'

Babette stood up. She rested her hand on Liliane's head and began to stroke her hair. She stood there for a long time smoothing the soft, grey hair.

'There,' she said. 'It's all out. It wasn't hard, was it? It's only when you accept you've lost something, Liliane, that you can ever hope to find it again. Now come and help me put this boy to bed.'

Chapter Sixteen

Sam was dreaming of his mother. He was not asleep but still he was dreaming. He lay curled up in the dark with his cheek on his praying hands, his eyes closed.

She was lying in her bed. She often slept in the morning and he knew not to wake her because it made her bad-tempered. He stood over her and watched her face against the pillow. He wanted to kiss her cheek, but he knew if he did she would disappear. He looked at her closed eyes. Her eyelashes were very black and tangled. She had a freckle darker than the rest under her eye and one on her lip. He tried to smell her, but his dream didn't stretch that far and he was back in the dark again, too thick to breathe, and he could hear the clicking noise coming from somewhere above his head.

Since his fall he had not climbed up to the holes again. It hurt when he stood up, so he lay on his back with his knees bent and his feet flat against the wall. His breaths were quick, like they were when he was tired out from treading water in the deep end.

He had stopped crying because he did not like to hear his own voice. It reminded him of where he was. Now he slept and woke and slept and woke. He knew when he was awake because of the clicking sound. Sometimes he counted the clicks, but he never got far because his thoughts chased the numbers away.

His shorts were wet with pee. He had dreamed that he was walking down the stairs at home. There was a blue darkness that he could see through. Dan's door was open and he could hear his breathing as he passed. He reached the door to the bathroom and opened it. The tiles were cold under his feet.

He sat down on the loo because he was too sleepy to stand and watched a silverfish play dead, then disappear into a crack in the wall. He watched the crack and waited for the pee to come. It flowed out warm on to his stomach and woke him up. Later they had put the glasses back on and taken him out, sat him on a blue plastic bucket; but he couldn't do anything, so they shut him in again.

He didn't know how long he had been there because there were no days to count, but the darkness did not scare him. It was the light when the door opened and the smell of the place where the men were.

He closed his eyes and tried to get the dream of his mother back, but all he could see was his fish opening and shutting its mouth and dying in his dark, dry rucksack.

His mother would be crying now, like she did every time he got lost. The other times he had lost her, in the shops or in the woods or on the beach, he saw had just been for practice. He loved the way his mother's face looked when she cried. When she found him she would kneel down and he would put his arms around her neck and press his face into her bosom and let her hold him until she calmed down. This time it was real.

He sat up, held his legs folded against his chest and bit his knees, one after the other. He did not bite hard but gently. He liked the taste of his skin and the spit rolling down his thighs.

They had put his finger in the trap again. They had opened the door and the one who talked all the time had told him they were going to make a tape for his mother. He had not been able to open his eyes because of the light.

'Say hello to your mother.'

But he could not speak. He held his eyes tight shut. Then they had put his finger in the trap and closed it a little. That was when he had screamed. He wished he hadn't. For his mother's sake.

Ever since then he had kept silent. He had not tried yet, but he thought that even if he wanted to speak, the words would not come out. Instead there was a lot of talking in his head: sometimes his mother's voice, and sometimes Dan's.

'You're so shellfish,' Dan said. Sam laughed. 'It's not shellfish, silly. It's selfish.' In fact Dan was the selfish one. He never let him play with his toys. Even the pirate ship, which he never used. It stayed on the shelf all the time. 'You'll lose the bits,' Dan said.

'Yes, Sam,' his mother said. 'You'll lose the bits.'

But he didn't care. He still liked the ship without the bits.

This was prison. He had always been scared of prison. Now he was here. His worst dream was about prison. He had not dared tell his mother about it because just talking about it frightened him too much. Now he was in it.

He was hungry. He hadn't eaten since the ravioli. They put things in his prison, but the smell made him feel sick and he sat with his eyes buried in his knees, waiting for them to take the plate away. He did not want to eat but he was afraid they would get angry.

He let go of his knees, lay down in the dark and rested his feet against the wall. His back still hurt him if he took a deep breath, so he breathed very gently. He closed his eyes and saw the different darkness of his mind. He watched the shapes moving behind his eyes and began to count the clicks.

He could see that things were easier for other kids but he didn't know why. His head was always so full of questions that he sometimes didn't bother asking them because the answers he got just provoked more questions. He could feel them shuffling in a queue in his head, some, often the most stupid, forcing themselves to the front. When he had asked his mother on the way from the airport whose idea it was to build all the shops and houses, he knew as he was asking that this was not the question he meant to ask but another, nonstupid question that hid itself from him.

Sometimes she got angry with him because of the questions, but sometimes she asked for them and was pleased with them. He had not learned which ones made her angry and which ones made her pleased. But this he could not learn because his mother was soft and hard. Like her name. 'Alice,' he said aloud. 'A-lice. Hard, soft.'

Mickey stood in the middle of the room and mimed his favourite number: Jorge Ferreira singing 'Ai Ai, Meu Amor, Ai Ai'. He wished there was a mirror in the room. Maybe he would ask the Scattis to get him one. He knew all the words but not what they meant. This didn't matter because the song spoke to his soul. He could move just like Ferreira and make the same facial expressions, but he mouthed the words. If he tried to sing, a dead sound came out, nothing like what he had in his head.

He clicked his fingers as if to snap himself out of a trance and did a little rotating jump. He faced the kid's cupboard and listened. He had stopped whining. In fact he hadn't made a sound for a while now. He'd have to start eating soon or else they'd have problems. Paolo had told the mother they would send her his finger if she didn't get the money in time.

'And they would, too,' he said aloud. He didn't want to take the kid's finger off. 'I'm not into that kind of thing.' He saw the child's head tilted back in agony and felt a rush of adrenaline. 'Look at me,' he said. 'I've gone all weak at the thought.' He had sent her the video first. That was subtle.

He walked over to his chair and sat down for a smoke. Three million francs all to himself. They should have asked for more. He tilted back his head. 'Ai ai, meu amor,' he sang in his head. 'Ai ai.'

Mickey drew a chair up to the wall of the kid's cupboard and sat down. He tilted the chair so that the back of his head rested against the wall. The kid was quiet. There had been a lot of tears in the night, a lot of noise, causing the numbness in Mickey's fingers that occurred when he wanted to hit someone. The kid whined, which was unforgivable. He had never whined as a kid. Of that he was sure.

'Can you hear me in there?'

Silence. Mickey banged on the wall behind him three times with his fist.

'Hey! I'm talking to you.'

Silence.

'Don't make me open the door.'

Three weak knocks sounded.

'Okay.' Mickey lit a cigarette. 'Smoke?' He grinned, allowing the smoke to roll out over his grey teeth. Mickey smoked all day and most of the night. Smoke was his element, had become as much a part of him as his blood. It was in his voice, in the pores of his skin, behind his nails, his ears, between his teeth and his fingers. If they cut him open, his insides would be charred, like a rotten pomegranate turned to dust.

'I was smoking at your age. Can't remember when I started. All I can say is I can't remember not smoking. What do I remember? I don't remember the islands. I don't remember my old man. I remember my mum before she screwed herself up. Because there was a time when she was all right. She was all-right-looking. Better-looking than your mum. Not so skinny. She was half-Portuguese, half-African and she had the best of both. Portuguese hair, silky black, and beautiful dark skin and a beautiful arse like a watermelon. My dad was pure Portuguese. That's why he fucked off in the end. He thought she was too black for him. Then José came along and frankly, he was beneath her, but she followed him here and we moved into Les Mimosas and I went to school and it was downhill from there on. But I never whined. I can't imagine ever whining with José.' Mickey banged on the wall once. 'Did you hear me?'

A knock sounded.

'You shouldn't whine. I can teach you things and this is one of them. Whining annoys people and it's the fastest way of getting hit. I'm not going to hurt you. I would say I'm favourably disposed to you. Can you understand that? Favourably disposed, which means I don't hate you. You're my ticket out of this shithole. If you don't whine we'll get through this, both of us, and I'll be leaving on a jet plane, don't know when I'll be back again,' he sang, in his high, trapped voice. 'Cacilda, her name was. Cacilda. Isn't that a beautiful name? Isn't it?' Mickey sat forward. He dropped his cigarette and trod it out. He stood up and plucked at his groin. He picked up the chair and swung it against the wall of the cupboard. One of the back legs clattered to the floor. He let go of the chair and kicked it. 'Isn't it?' he shouted.

Mickey stood still in a pair of cowboy boots two sizes too big for him, which curled upwards at the tip. He stared with his good eye at the door of the kid's prison.

'Hey! Answer me.'

Two faint knocks came from within.

Tuesday

Chapter Seventeen

Coco drove his car into the car park of the Géant Casino supermarket. He saw a space in the far corner. Keeping his eye on the white Peugeot in his rear-view mirror, he crawled slowly towards it. He couldn't see who was at the wheel and he didn't recognise the car. Stuart must have been sent back-up.

He turned off the engine, threw the keys under the seat and climbed out. Just as Stuart's boys were beginning to wonder, Georges would come and pick up the car. The white Peugeot pulled up next to the trolleys fifty metres away. Coco walked towards it, took a trolley and greeted the men in the car, inclining his head ceremoniously as he walked past. He did not recognise either of them and he noticed with disgust that the driver was wearing a ring in his left ear.

As he weaved through the parked cars, he began to sweat. The midday sun was not joking. He stepped into the shade thrown by the awning of the supermarket and turned round. The white Peugeot hadn't moved. He walked through the automatic doors into the air-conditioned cafeteria.

It was a nice concession; plenty of people for a weekday. You would have thought they'd be on the beach in mid-July but no, they preferred gliding along the cool, clean floors of the hypermarket, their kids hushed with sweets picked straight from the shelf, safely imprisoned in the trolley. Afterwards, a snack here in the cafeteria and before they knew it they'd killed three hours.

Coco passed the row of people queuing doggedly, sliding their trays along the food counter. Karim was standing behind an icy slope of cheese platters, grinning stupidly at him. He had shaven his head down to a stubble. A pearly gash on his cranium shone like the Muslim new moon.

Coco pushed the door to the toilets and went straight to the disabled cubicle. He took the heavy metal cover off the toilet-roll dispenser. Hanging on the rod instead of the roll were the keys to Karim's car, which he put in his pocket before replacing the metal cover. On the way out he glanced at his reflection in the mirror above the sink. He wet his hands and ran them through his hair, checked his teeth for stray foodstuffs and left.

He pushed open the fire door that led out on to a patch of yellow lawn at the back of the hypermarket. He crossed the lawn, climbed a steep bank planted with laurel bushes heavy with diesel dust and, brushing himself off, stepped out on to the tarmac. The sun had melted the road and as he walked towards Karim's black BMW, he felt the tar sticking to the soles of his shoes.

The inside of the car was so hot, it hurt when he breathed in. He cursed Karim for having parked in the full sun. He wound down both windows and drove carefully over the uneven slip road and on to the motorway that ran north out of Massaccio.

Surrender nothing. He must surrender absolutely nothing. He could feel Jean Filippi's hand in his gut and he was squeezing. Those small, waxy hands, unfit for honest work, had got hold of him after twenty years. Coco saw Jean's hands as he sat in meetings of the executive committee. They lay pasty and inert, one upon the other, while their owner, with his soft, thinking-man's voice, talked of the long march towards the edifice of peace.

Jean Filippi's job was killing. He was the boss of a service industry; his business was the fulfilment of the island's irrepressible appetite for violence. With the push of the young beneath him, Jean was expanding: hence the Sam-7s. Jean was not a man of violence, he was a man of power; but he knew what people wanted. More kids were flocking to the FNL every day, looking for a free handgun and a uniform and something to do with the spare time that was all they had. Jean would like to have kept his cottage industry, but he knew he'd get pushed out if he didn't give them what they wanted.

Coco looked at himself in the wing mirror. This new pain in his gut was beginning to show in his face. At least he didn't look as bad as Stuart, who was ten years younger than him.

Where was the capital going to come from for this expansion? Jean needed considerable funds for a modern army. Coco could help but not in kind. He'd have to get the stuff out of his swimming pool. I'm not comfortable with things as they are, Jean. We're going to have to renegotiate.

He came off the motorway and followed the sparkling river winding through the wide valley that was always green, even in summer. A forest of eucalyptus sprawled up from the sea, stopping in a line where the pastures began. This valley was his favourite place. It rose very gently at its narrow end to meet the foot of the mountains. Some promoters from the mainland had tried to get hold of this valley for a theme park, but Russo had put a European preservation order on it and blocked the sale.

Coco opened the window and breathed in the smells that were coming off the hills to his left. After the eucalyptus from the coast the *maquis* was delicate and he thought of the Englishwoman and wondered what she would smell like. He was glad she was dark because he did not like the smell of blondes so much. He knew who had her child. A black Mercedes 500 had been abandoned in the main square. The police had been crawling round it all morning. The plates were from another Mercedes of the same model, same colour. Stealing cars was the one thing Mickey da Cruz did well. She had nothing to worry about. You having nothing to worry about, madame. I'll find your son for you.

No villages had been built along this road. A witch had cursed this mineral land so long ago, no one could remember why, and it was unfit even for goats. As the road climbed, the *maquis* thinned, giving way to a plateau of granite. He drove along a ridge on either side of which was nothing but scree for fifty metres. Three vultures hung about like delinquents, drawing circles round each other in the sky.

Soon the graffiti began. Every decent expanse of rock beside the road was daubed with red letters. He was surprised to see that even the MPC came up into this wasteland to mark their territory. The kids had shot out every road sign, leaving the triangular panels full of holes dripping with rust.

Coco parked in a lay-by, in the shadow of a wall of smooth, pink rock that rose straight upwards and out of sight. He turned off the engine and prepared for the wait. He was ten minutes early. In the shade the air was cool. A pleasant breeze came through the window. Coco pushed back the seat and closed his eyes, trying, as Evelyne suggested, to visualise the hand stirring his entrails: if you can see it, she said, you can make it disappear. But Coco could see only three vultures circling above a pool of blood.

Coco woke as Jean opened the passenger door and climbed in. Sleep seeped away, leaving him bereft. He did not appreciate being caught unawares. He wiped saliva from his beard.

Jean held out his hand. Coco shook it briefly, then turned on the engine. He closed the electric window, drove out on to the hot road and made his way further up the mountain.

'How are things in town?'

This irritated Coco. Jean always spoke as if he were some kind of hermit, the island's John the Baptist. But he got around. Georges had seen him last week at Las Palmas. Soulas had given him a job at the source over the hill. The island's only mineral-water company was surviving on subsidies – fifty people had been laid off since the beginning of the year – while Jean was getting a salary and expense account big enough to entertain at Las Palmas.

'I'm up at the village,' Coco said. 'There's no room for me in Massaccio at this time of year. It's full of people wearing thongs. I feel overdressed.'

Coco had not looked at Jean yet, but he knew he would not smile at this. Jean only smiled where it was inappropriate, blinking patiently at all manifestations of humour. Coco glanced at Jean's hands, one resting on each thigh. The nails were horribly bitten, making nubs of his finger-ends. Coco should have looked at his fingers before having suggested him as head of the Executive. Jean sat at his side quietly surveying the wilderness as if he owned it. Thankfully this was about all he owned.

Coco realised that Jean was not going to speak first. He had hoped that he would refer to the cache. Coco now wished he had brought Georges. He had miscalculated: it was not a good thing for him to be at the wheel. In this position he could not face Jean and look straight at his ruined mouth, imperfectly hidden by the thick moustache. Coco turned and looked now. From the side, the hare-lip did not show.

'So,' he began. 'We had a bit of a surprise the other night.'

'Oh?'

'The Sam-7s.' Jean gave no sign. 'You're building quite an armoury.'

Jean turned and looked at Coco, who kept his eyes on the winding road.

'This is a war, Santini, not a hobby.'

'I know, I know. And I notice they've sent in two new CRS units. They're talking peace to give themselves time to arm their troops.'

'Exactly.'

Coco was looking for a place to pull in. He was sick of this arrangement. He was not the man's chauffeur.

'Of course, they do generally send in more CRS for the summer.'

'It's a provocation.'

'Of course.'

'I assume you didn't come all the way up here to be sarcastic,' Jean said.

Coco pulled into a lay-by. A single acacia tree sprang from a cleft in a sheet of rock. Coco stopped beneath its frail canopy. Patches of sunlight quivered on the bonnet. He turned off the engine.

'I'm not in a position to keep Sam-7 missiles under my swimming pool. You talked about a "stop-gap" last April. I have considerable heat on me at present. A child has been kidnapped and Stuart is hoping that I'm involved. At the moment I have a minimum of three cars trailing me at all times. I think it's time you made alternative arrangements.'

Jean was looking nervous. Coco opened the window to breathe in the sweet smell of the acacia.

'If you're being followed . . .'

'Don't worry. I lost them in town.'

'If you're being followed, I said, you're not going to want to move anything now. Do you mind closing that window?'

'Are you cold?'

Jean simply nodded at the window.

'Do you mind?'

Coco closed the window. Jean's tone disgusted him. He was worse than a priest.

'We're very grateful for the space. We shouldn't be needing it for much longer. I'm glad, though, to have this chance to talk to you, because we were meaning to ask you. It may be a little premature, but things have been shifting lately. The MPC has retreated, leaving a lot of open ground. We're interested in acquiring Las Palmas.'

'What?'

'We've approached Edouard Getti, but he seems reticent.'

'You must be joking.'

Jean blinked at him.

'Edouard is an old friend of yours, we know. We wanted you to talk to him.'

'Ed's not going to sell Las Palmas. He'd sell his mother first.'

Jean just stared. His hair had turned greyer and lent a cartoon quality to his thick moustache, which was still jet black.

His eyes shone as any charismatic leader's should.

'We have plans for it that go far beyond anything Edouard could achieve. He's sentimentally attached to the place and it's stagnating.'

'You want to put machines in,' Coco said. 'You want to take over the best club on the front, the only place you can eat a decent meal without having a pair of tits in your face, and you want to turn it into a twenty-four-hour pay-and-puke joint.'

'Coco, I'm going to have to reason with you on this. You're not being objective.'

'No way.'

'You don't want what happened to Monti to happen to Edouard.'

'Get out.'

Jean did not move.

'I said get out.'

'You're making a mistake, Santini.'

'Get out of the car. Don't threaten me. Get out of the car.'

'I think . . .'

'Get out or I'll throw you out.' Jean opened the door. 'Hurry up.'

He climbed out and slammed the door. Coco reversed and turned round. In his rear-view mirror he saw Jean standing beneath the acacia tree. Coco paused a moment, feeling the tug in his gut. His foot hovered above the accelerator, poised to slam the man against the rock. Jean stood there waiting, his fat arms that would not lie straight floating out to each side of him. Jean had no gun. That, Coco thought, was the secret of his success.

He put Karim's car in first gear and pulled out into the road. He forced himself to drive slowly, calming himself, counting his breaths and letting them go.

In just two months the FNL had slipped out of control. I made you, Jean. I even allowed you the luxury of thinking you were a free agent. Coco slammed his foot on the brake.

He sat there in the middle of the road, his hands sweating on the wheel, the *maquis* coming at him, hammering at him this time, through the open window.

They wanted Las Palmas. Now it was Ed but tomorrow it would be The Pescador and The Palace of Glass. Last year two men on a motorbike had shot Monti as he was coming up the steps that led from his club to the main road that ran along the seafront. Monti's body had fallen back into the bamboo below the steps and it had taken Stuart three days to find his body, for the bamboo had grown over him. Coco had not worried too much about the killing because he knew Monti was Stuart's grass and Electric Blue was never a good venue anyway, too small and isolated. Now he saw that it had been Jean's first move. Something was twitching in his cheek. Coco wiped his hands over his face in an attempt to smooth out his nerves which were twisted like cables. Jean had threatened him. How had things degenerated so fast?

His nervous system partially untangled, he moved on. The scrub on either side of him went on banging under the hot sun. Coco accelerated, hurrying towards the valley. The idea came to him as he passed a lay-by that was marked by a large 'P'. Some grey-faced moron from the tourist office had put out a couple of tables with benches. As though anyone would choose to have a picnic up here.

The idea may have come to Coco as he drove by that certain things were not put to their proper use. Perhaps it was the P-sign, but out of the image of the inhospitable lay-by, snatched as he drove past, came that of Philippe Garetta, sitting out his days at the darkest table in The Pescador, violent and idle. Coco thought of the Englishwoman. He saw her pulling back her hair to reveal her shoulders and her neck, curved in offering. In his plan, he saw a way of winning her too. Garetta was dangerous; he was the only one who still talked about revolution. The question was, if he wound him up, could he stop him? As he passed the first eucalyptus trees fringing the road, Coco felt a slackening inside. The banging of the *maquis* was just blood pumping in his ears. Still, he kept the idea that had come to him when he was not entirely himself. He would start a new movement, make a war.

Less than an hour later Coco was lying on the back seat of Evelyne's new black-and-gold Cherokee. Her scent filled the car and though it was still a pleasure to him, he would not miss it.

'Okay,' she said. 'I'm going in now. There's nothing behind us.' Her voice was bad, always had been.

'Don't talk,' he answered. 'Just park and let me out.'

'What time do you want me to pick you up?' she asked.

'I'll make my own way back.'

He climbed out, slammed the door and began to walk towards the lifts. The stench of piss rose up in front of him like an invisible wall, sending him off course. There was no ventilation he could see and he could feel petrol fumes filling his lungs and lead seeping into his pores. He was quite angry now, to be hiding in an underground car park like a rat. There had long ceased to be any pleasure for him in the business of losing cops.

The lift doors opened with a three-chord chime and he stepped into the eternal dusk of the shopping mall. Mauve-tinted neon brought the meat out in people's complexions. In this place no one was desirable. He could put the Aron woman in here, on the second floor next to Champion Sportswear, and she would lose all her charm. She would look like a laboratory animal. There was some music that came and went like bad breath.

Outside he breathed in the balm of daylight. He crossed the street to Éve Beauté. Evelyne's sister Marie-Laure was sitting behind the till painting her nails. There was a pleasant smell of lacquer and leg wax in the shop. Two middle-aged Italian women were leaning over the coral jewellery in the display counter, deliberating in their belligerent language. Marie-Laure did not greet Coco. Instead she screwed the lid on the polish, raised her wide bottom from the narrow stool she was sitting on and gave him four routine kisses over the counter. She had accumulated all Evelyne's physical defects. Her lips were thinner and wider, her eyes more globular, and while with Evelyne there could be some hesitation, with Marie-Laure there was no doubt she resembled a frog. Coco waited while she served the Italian women. There was always a kind of grave sexual assurance in Italian women, however ugly. When they had gone Marie-Laure led the way through the bead curtains, past the 'treatment room' where she flayed, daubed and scalded her customers, to her flat. The TV was on and her five-year-old son was sitting on an untidy floor zapping with an advanced boredom inherited from his mother. Marie-Laure stepped forward and snatched the remote control. The boy looked up and Coco saw an instant of fear turn to resentment.

'Go out and play,' she said.

Coco watched him drive his hands into the pockets of his tracksuit and pick his way through the toys with a grace and precision that gave him hope for the child. How boys survived their mothers was always a mystery to him.

When he had gone Marie-Laure flashed him a smile. 'I won't be a minute. Do you want anything? Pastis?'

Coco shook his head. He felt superstitious about exchanging words with her on any subject now that he had made his decision about Evelyne.

When she had gone he sat down at the table where she and her son ate their meals. There was a plastic tablecloth with a cherry motif, sticky to the touch. He pulled the chair away from the table. The carpet stopped abruptly and became lino where the kitchen area began. He recalled Evelyne and Marie-Laure discussing the idea of building a bar to separate the two areas. The two women talked incessantly and about nothing.

When Marie-Laure pulled back the bead curtain and ushered in Philippe Garetta, Coco did not stand up. The man was too tall for the room and he took possession of it. At the sight of his black leather biker's garb, his long dark hair hanging in ringlets about his face, Coco thought he had made a mistake. Then Garetta leaned forward and Coco was reassured by the handshake. The leather creaked as he moved. He sat down on a chair beside Coco and rested his clasped hands neatly on the table. A whiff of tobacco came off him.

'You wanted to see me.' His voice was inappropriately gentle.

'Are you from Marseilles?'

'My dad was.'

'You have his accent.'

Garetta eyed him.

'I was brought up there till I was thirteen. When he died we came back to the island.'

'You and your mother?'

'And my brother.'

'Do I know your brother?'

'He works for Soulas.'

Coco nodded, unwilling to waste more time.

'You're interested in politics.' He leaned back in his chair for emphasis.

'It depends what you mean by politics. I'm not interested in the kind that gets men like Russo elected.'

Coco smiled.

'Well well.'

Garetta glanced down and then took a fresh look, this time holding his hair away from his face in an unnervingly effeminate gesture.

'I can't be bought, Santini.'

'I didn't think you could. I have a proposition for you, though. I'm interested in your zeal. It's your zeal I need.' Coco paused. 'I wonder how far you'd go for your ideals.'

Garetta blinked attentively at him. He had a gaunt face with an unhealthy, grey complexion and deep-set eyes. Coco could see a disquieting passivity in them that made him doubt the man's reputation for a moment.

'How far would you go, Garetta?'

Garetta folded his arms.

'What are you offering?'

'I want some idea of how far you would go for your ideals.'

Garetta looked away and smiled at some unseen object.

'We don't speak the same language, Santini,' he said, facing Coco again.

Coco looked at the pale face, neither young nor old but haggard.

'Do you take heroin?'

Garetta turned his head away again to hide his smile as if it were some shameful tick.

'No, I don't take heroin. There's not enough time to be a junkie and a revolutionary.'

'Why aren't you in the FNL, Garetta?'

'They're not radical enough.'

'They believe in the armed struggle.'

Garetta puffed out a laugh.

'The armed struggle. The armed struggle's become the island's family business. Joining the FNL is an economic not an ideological decision. They're not interested in change; they just want to hold on to their piece of the cake.'

'And you want a revolution. Do you have a following?'

'Small.'

'Do you know Mickey da Cruz?'

'I do.'

Coco hesitated.

'Would you kidnap the child of a rich industrialist for the cause?'

Garetta folded his arms and stared at him. It was not passivity Coco had seen in his eyes but an unblinking, animal detachment.

'Certainly.'

'And would you kill the child? Would you carry out the threat?'

'Absolutely,' he said in his soft voice.

'It's against the island's deepest values.'

'I believe in progress.'

Coco detected no irony in the remark. He stood up and stepped over the child's debris to the glass cabinet behind the TV set.

'I'm going to have a drink. Do you want one?' He took two glasses from the cabinet, holding them in one hand. 'Pastis?'

'No thanks.'

Coco found a bottle of Ricard in the lower half of the cabinet and poured himself a drink. He went to the sink for water, letting the tap run on his finger until it grew cold.

'I think it's time for a new independence movement,' he said, keeping his back to Garetta.

'I'm not stupid, Santini. Nothing you could create could lead to revolution.'

Santini turned and faced him across the room.

'You're not going to get a revolution without a movement, and you can't start a movement without funds.' He walked back to the table and sat down. 'I love this island as much as you do, Garetta. I can feel the place is sick. Deeply sick. If I've contributed to that . . .' He drained his glass.

'If a revolution is what it takes,' Coco said, putting down his empty glass. Garetta continued to watch him with the intelligence of a wild animal. 'The kids need something new. They need new ideas, a new agenda; they'll come flocking. Use tough words, the harder the better.' Coco opened his hands. 'Let me help you,' he said, watching with satisfaction as Garetta prepared to light a roll-up. 'For the world your group will begin with a bombing. Modest, unpretentious. Like yourself, Garetta.'

Chapter Eighteen

Alice knelt on the floor in the dark, looking up at the viscous blank of the TV screen while the kidnappers' videotape rewound. It had arrived with the post early that morning.

When Stuart handed her the package, he had warned her, 'It's their aim to make you suffer.'

The machine stopped with a click and she pressed PLAY on the remote control. She reached out and touched the screen. She was quiet now and exhausted from crying. She hoped by watching the film over and over again to inure herself. She now used the FREEZE-FRAME button, setting herself against the pain.

There they were again, the three of them walking across the tarmac towards the camera. The image was distorted for a moment and then cleared, revealing the boys at her side, Sam skipping around her, weaving close to her and moving away again, impeding her progress. She pressed PAUSE as Sam trod in her path, his arms raised at quarter to nine. There: she could see her irritation. She pressed PLAY and watched herself step aside to avoid him. Stay close to me, Sam, she had said. Here, take hold of my dress. And you, Dan. She pressed PAUSE and stared at this tableau of the three of them, her two boys holding on to a piece of her dress. She stared at the three of them blurred by the PAUSE function. She pressed PLAY and then PAUSE. His knee was raised in mid-skip, his feet turned in. Please don't be cross, Mummy. Every frame showed her how it was. She had not loved him enough and so he had been taken from her.

Stuart had sat through the film with her. Then he had watched it again, as she was doing now, pausing, rewinding. He wrote down time codes in a little notebook. Then he went to the airport to see if they had been picked up on the closed-circuit system. Outside the shutters she sensed the heat of the afternoon. She had been sitting there for hours. She picked up the mobile and called David's number again. As soon as the secretary heard her voice she put her straight on hold. Alice listened to *Carmen*, speeded up a little.

'Alice.' His voice was the same as Mathieu's. 'Nothing yet. I'm waiting for Gerbier to call me back.'

'David . . .'

'I know, Alice.'

'We've only got two days.'

'It'll be all right. Gerbier's going to work something out. His family's been looking after our money for a hundred years. I'm confident, Alice. Trust me.'

In his voice Alice heard Mathieu's love of a crisis.

'Why won't they take the house as collateral?' she said. 'It's worth more than nine million. I can't mortgage it, David. It'll take a month. We've got two days.' Her throat was dry.

'It's all right.' He spoke softly. 'Gerbier knows, Alice. He knows. He's just got to convince the others to take an affidavit. He can't get the cash out alone.'

'They said yes, then they called back . . .'

'Alice? I'm getting another call. If it's him I'll call you straight back.'

'Call me back, David. Please.'

She hung up and stared at the phone. She longed to call her mother. She suddenly wanted her here. She was ready to be gathered up, not tenderly but ineluctably, in her mother's way. 'There there,' she would say. 'Old thing,' she would say; her mother's mark of camaraderie in the face of their fate – that all they'd ever have was each other. This was how her mother had arranged things, at least. She had organised her life to fit her low expectations. She would have no man and Alice would have no father. Mathieu had called her the Immaculate Conception. His joke had been sweet to Alice then and the memory of it made her smile again. No, Sam had always been the buffer against her mother. She would not call her in.

She pressed PLAY again. They were in the terminal building, filmed from behind. How had she not noticed someone with a camera so close to them? She watched herself taking Dan into her arms and then held the frame. The camera remained on Sam, at his reaction to this moment of exclusion. She saw his shape in profile. His resignation was discernible in his bowed head and in his shoulders that hung forward a little as though to protect his chest from the slight. She pressed PLAY again. She felt that all this was very precise and very careful; that Stuart was wrong: this was no amateur. She watched the three of them waiting for the luggage. She saw how Sam was never still. At this moment he was imprisoned somewhere, perhaps in the dark. As her greatest fear was drowning, Sam's was being confined. He had once told her that what frightened him about being dead was that you couldn't move. She sat in the dark, her head resting against the back of the sofa, and watched the three of them disappear, rubbed out by the bright sunlight.

She sat there, TV light splashing over her face, adhering in her eyes.

When the phone rang, she leapt to her feet. She picked up Stuart's phone from the table by the sofa.

'Hello?' There was silence. 'Hello?' They had gone.

The policeman, Paul, was now standing in the doorway, looking inquiringly at her. 'Hello?' She hung up but still clutched the phone. She looked at Paul. He was about to say something so she turned her back on him. She picked it up before the end of the first ring. She heard a man's voice.

'Who is it?'

'This phone isn't working properly.'

It was Stuart. Her shoulders dropped in relief.

'Where are you?'

'Someone's planted a bomb in town. A new group. It could be linked.'

'A bomb? Stuart, wait.'

'I'm going to the site. I'll call you afterwards.'

'What about the video at the airport?' she asked.

'Nothing. They've been through the footage of the day you arrived. He knew where the cameras were.'

'You see, they're not stupid.'

He did not answer.

'What's the bomb? Is it them?'

'I don't know. I don't think so. I'll be up by six,' he said.

'Stuart?'

He had gone. She turned round. Paul was standing just behind her, his hands a little out to his sides as though he was trying to corral her. There was a smell of alcohol on his breath.

'Get out of here!' she shouted. 'Leave me alone.'

He hesitated a moment, weighing up his options, then turned and left the room, quietly closing the door behind him. Alice strode after him towards the door, suddenly eager to see Dan and hold him. She found him in the laundry room on the first floor, sitting on Babette's knee. He was crying.

Alice went to him and gathered him in her arms. She clasped his little body to her, welcoming him back. She kissed his hair and rocked him back and forth.

'Don't cry, darling; Mummy's here.' She held him tight and closed her eyes, feeling how great the gap between them had become. 'Mummy's here.' It did her good to say this. Over and over again she murmured, 'You're Mummy's little boy.' Babette sat on the chair, her hands covered in gold, resting on her knees, watching them.

Alice carried Dan downstairs into the study and sat down with him in front of the flashing TV set. His tears had died down but she still held him tight. She understood that whatever happened, she must go on being a mother to both of them. For the first time she considered Sam's death. She knew that even if she were to lose him, her future lay in her love of both boys. With this thought, she made a decision. She would never again cut herself off from Dan. She stared at the TV screen, holding Dan until she could hear the breathing of sleep. Then she carried him next door and laid him down on Stuart's camp bed in the corner of the sitting room. She went back to the study, turned off the TV and picked up the mobile phone. She punched out Santini's number.

Her heart beat faster as the phone rang. His deep voice, in isolation from his person, calmed her a little.

'They sent a video,' she said, afraid to speak too loud. 'They want the money on Thursday, by midday. I can't get it in time. I have to ask you. Can you lend me the money? I'll pay you back within the month. I can get . . .'

'It won't be necessary. I think we might have them.' There was a moment's silence. 'Where are you calling from?'

'A mobile.'

'Yours?'

She hesitated.

'Stuart's.'

He hung up.

Alice stared at the phone. She tried to recall his exact words. She felt she had lost the capacity to decipher language, but with the words something in her had come unsprung. They had found him.

Chapter Nineteen

The *maestrale* had left the sky surgically clean. The light was now so sharp Stuart could barely open his eyes. He squatted behind the ribbon of orange plastic a hundred metres from the car, buried his face in the crook of his arm and waited for the explosion. For some reason, Mesguish was there, and Van Ruytens, who always came for a bomb and who now settled beside him with his pipe in his mouth and his hands over his ears. It was more the pipe smoke than the imminent explosion that made Stuart bury his face.

'Twenty-eight minutes,' someone said.

Stuart looked up to see who had spoken. It was Mesguish's deputy, who was staring back at him, chewing on a piece of gum. They were waiting for the long hand to reach six. It was impossible to get anyone from Bomb Disposal to go in any more. They had to wait the full half-hour, and make do with the detritus when it did explode, policy now being zero risk. Mesguish's man grinned sarcastically at him. When he turned away, Stuart saw he was wearing an earring and flushed with anger.

In the thirtieth minute the bomb exploded. Stuart felt the blast on his face. It was too late to cover his ears. The sound vibrated in his chest and throat. Glass and debris began to fall like rain. Something flew through the air towards him; he thought of a body. People were scattering all around him. It was the bonnet of the car that now rocked to and fro a few paces from him in the deserted square.

Stuart stood up. The man with the earring was grinning and chewing at the same time, busily looking about him for an echo of his excitement.

'Fuck,' he was saying. 'Fuck me.'

Stuart saw Van Ruytens brushing dust from his trousers. He was saying something to Mesguish and smiling. Stuart could see the back of Mesguish's cropped head and two rolls of bristle-covered fat resting on his collar. The prosecutor patted Mesguish on the arm, put his pipe in his mouth and began to climb over the plastic ribbon. Stuart leapt on him, grabbing him by the sleeve.

'No. No one's going on to the site.'

Van Ruytens had managed to take the pipe from his mouth with his free hand. He now stared at Stuart, his mouth open.

'It's all right. I'm not going to touch anything.'

'It's not all right, Prosecutor. No one's going in there. Not anyone. Not Mesguish and not you. The only people going in there are me and the forensic experts. Do you understand?'

Van Ruytens blinked at him.

'I'm amazed at your rudeness.' He was smiling.

'I don't care,' Stuart said. He let go of the prosecutor, noted the aghast faces around him and stepped over the ribbon. Stuart walked across the deserted square towards the car's scattered remains, his ears still ringing from the blast.

Gérard and Paul, wearing plastic gloves, were already picking their way through the debris. Fabrice was moving about on his own, taking photos. There was a neat crater about thirty centimetres in diameter where the bomb had been. The area was still hot and Stuart could see the tar oozing beneath the crust like toffee. He shielded his eyes with his hand and watched Paul peel off his surgeon's gloves. In spite of the heat, Gérard was wearing his mac. He took a piece of folded paper from his pocket and handed it to Stuart. Stuart held it at arm's length from his failing eyes. It was a copy of the communiqué that had been read over the phone to a news trainee at the *Islander* that morning:

> Our island has become a capitalist backwater, the Continent's sick cell, infested with all her evils – unemployment, greed, corruption and moral decline.

The independence movements are polluted, sinking in the quicksand of crime and social disintegration.

A total and unnegotiable breach with the Continent is the prerequisite for a New Society.

Let the masses of this Eden rise up and throw off centuries of exploitation, pillage and humiliation. It is time to act.

The Revolutionary Committee of the FAR (Front for Anarchist Revolution)

Stuart looked up. Gérard was a few paces away, pointing with his foot at a piece of blue metal like a plate.

'Gas cylinder,' he said. 'And they used sugar.'

'Who was it for?' Stuart asked, looking about him as though the target might reveal itself. He could feel the crowds gathering behind the barricades. The heat in the white square seemed to isolate them further. 'There's a Crédit Lyonnais,' he said stupidly.

Paul blinked at Stuart, waiting for him to ask something sensible. The alcohol was beginning to show in his boyish face; he had pouches beneath his eyes.

'It's cheap,' he said.

'What was the target?' Stuart asked again.

'Maybe it's just an inauguration.'

Fabrice moved efficiently through the scattered remains of the car. He had seen enough not to need guidance. Gérard was gliding gracefully behind him, holding a roll of plastic freezer bags for samples. Stuart watched Paul slipping his bare brown foot in and out of his shoe. In winter he wore brightly coloured socks and Stuart had noticed that one pair had 'Snow Time' printed on them. He could see why women loved Paul; he was touching.

'They're novices,' Paul said. Gérard came and stood beside Paul and squinted at Stuart. 'It looks like novices,' Paul told him.

Stuart folded the paper and put it into his pocket. He looked at his two friends. They were his friends, that was suddenly clear to him, as the three of them stood there in silence, enjoying this moment of respite, aware of the hundred-metre perimeter behind which a tidal wave of shit was being held back by a plastic ribbon.

'I manhandled the prosecutor,' Stuart said.

'Did he like it?' Gérard asked.

Stuart smiled.

'The prosecutor, Zanetecci, Mesguish and his pirates, even Lasserre. They're all waiting for me to make a mistake. And that woman . . .' He noticed their intent expressions and paused. 'She's sitting up in that house. Just waiting.' He stood in the hot, white square and looked at the charred spring of the car's seat, lying on the ground. He looked up. 'And why in God's name is Mesguish here?'

'The fire brigade got the call,' Paul said. 'They used the radio to call the commissariat and Mesguish picked it up.'

Stuart stared at him.

'There's something odd about this bombing,' he said. 'Look at the name. FAR. Anarchy's not a word people use any more, is it?'

'Too radical,' said Paul.

Stuart didn't answer.

'The communiqué's from another planet,' Gérard said.

Stuart was following his own thoughts.

'Raymond's not talking,' he said. 'Do you think we should let him go?'

'How long have you got left?' Paul asked.

'A few more hours,' Stuart said.

Paul had taken up his bouncer's posture, feet apart, arms clasped across his chest.

'You might as well use up the time,' he said.

Stuart could feel Gérard's disapproval. He stood between them, delaying his departure. They waited politely. He found nothing else to say. They nodded goodbye at him, Paul jerking his chin upwards, and watched him cross the no-man's land towards what was coming to him.

Mesguish was waiting for him. Stuart climbed over the ribbon and stood facing his large skull glowing with a halo of white bristles. He had a face like a gargoyle, full of exaggeration: fiery eyes, a bitter mouth and a belligerent chin. Stuart felt weary looking at him.

'So?' Mesguish said. 'What's the Front for Anarchist Revolution?'

Stuart spoke quietly to expose the man's unnecessary loudness.

'They're new. They're nothing serious. They used sugar. And there doesn't seem to be a target.' Mesguish stared angrily at him, lost. 'It's not a splinter group because there's no expertise. It could be outsiders.'

'You're saying it's not connected in any way to the business at hand?'

Stuart woke up.

'The business at hand? The business at hand seems to be the surveillance, the scrupulous surveillance of the three or four streets around the Fritz Bar. The call box is the only lead we've got. I'm still trying to work out what you're doing here.'

Mesguish's mouth drooped more steeply at the corners. With his scowl, a marble of fat appeared on the bridge of his nose.

'Zanetecci told me to check it out.'

Stuart was aware of someone standing behind him, too close. He turned and saw Lopez looking up at him, a pencil between his teeth. He grinned, then removed the pencil.

'Who let you in?'

'The prosecutor did.'

'Wait for me over there. I'll be one minute.'

Lopez held up his hands and stepped back, then he turned and walked over to a group of Mesguish's men. He reminded Stuart of that dog in Santarosa, foraging in the rubbish.

'Talking to the press now,' Mesguish said, nodding slowly.

'Listen. You were called in as back-up. You have one task,' Stuart said, striking the air with his index finger. 'Surveillance. That's all. Do you understand?'

Mesguish's hands were in his pockets, so it was his nose he thrust at Stuart.

'Listen, you little shit. If you knew just how long you had left on the top of this dung heap of an island, you might show me more respect. Central Office is sick of telexes spewing out complaints about your incompetence. You're on the way out.'

Stuart stared at the ball of fat between his eyes.

'You shouldn't let your men wear earrings, Mesguish,' he said. 'It reflects badly on the police.'

As he walked away, the back of his head tingled where he expected the blow. He even hoped it would come. But he cleared the car park unscathed. Lopez was standing beside the prosecutor, taking notes. So far he had kept his part of the bargain. There had been a short side-bar on the search and the following day an interview with the gendarme, Morin, saying that it looked like a runaway. This theory would be well received. It would just confirm what everyone knew: that continentals had no idea how to treat children. Stuart was too angry after his conversation with Mesguish. He would call Lopez later and he ducked into the crowd that had gathered on the other side of the CRS barriers.

As he drove away from the scene he smiled at the thought of the prosecutor's indignation. In one day he had undone years of grudging obedience and caught a glimpse of his own potential. It occurred to him that it was this sense that had driven Titi and he asked himself, for the first time, if Titi had ever loved anyone.

Two men with black visors passed him on a bike. In a reflex motion he swerved away from them, though if they had wanted to shoot him they would have had time. As the adrenaline subsided he thought of the woman alone in the house, waiting for news, and he felt useless again and overcome. He accelerated along the seafront. Through the open window a siren, heralding some other disaster, sounded further and further away.

There was a hot, dry wind blowing in his office. Someone had opened the window and left the fan running at high speed, and the room was slatting. A paper folder was opening and closing on his desk. The smell of his office, hitherto his element, now made him feel nauseous. Stuart sat down at his desk and opened the folder.

Inside were several large black-and-white surveillance photos from the day's shift. They were poor, slightly overexposed and the grain was swollen. They must have been taken from about 500 metres away. The first was of a car in a lay-by with the driver's head tipped back and in profile. On the back of the photograph Stuart read: SANTINI, Claude Augustin: 12H47, 17/7/99.

They had noted the registration number beneath. He didn't know the car, but Santini's profile was unmistakable. He leafed through the other photos. The last one was of Jean Filippi standing alone in the lay-by with his dick poking from his flies. Stuart judged from his expression – eyes raised to heaven in an expression of contrition – that they had caught him in that split instant before the flow begins. Stuart pulled out a shot of Jean climbing into the car, in which Coco's face was recognisable, and laid it on top of the folder for inclusion in the file.

He pulled out Raymond's file and began to read through Gérard's interrogation. He read the first three sentences without taking them in, then reached out and put his hand on the telephone. He held it there for a few minutes as though he were taking its pulse, thought better of calling her before he had some good news and went back to Gérard's assertively juvenile script. He could tell from the PV that Gérard thought Raymond's custody a waste of time. He had let him ramble and the narrative was full of unexplored threads fluttering like kite tails. He stopped reading and looked at his watch. He would see her in a little over an hour. He unlocked the drawer to his desk, looked at the tiny plastic bag of brown he had kept from the last bust and closed the drawer again. What was Coco risking a meeting with Jean Filippi for? He took his notepad and wrote down Filippi's name with an arrow beside it. Then he opened the drawer and began to make up a dose for Raymond.

In the basement Raymond sat in the cell, tugging at the side of his hair that had not been cut. His mother always did first one side, then the other and they had snatched him from the chair in the alley before she had finished. He had had his eyes closed and was enjoying the sun on his face when they appeared from nowhere, bursting into his dream, brutalising him but still not managing to reach him, he felt so good. They had dragged him off to the sound of his mother's cries. That had been yesterday morning. Now he was sweating all over and hair cuttings were sticking to his chest and neck. His legs were heavy but weak, as though they had been stretched thin like two long pieces of plasticine hanging over the edge of the bed and running along the floor. There was a dragging sensation in his hips and thighs and he wanted to kick out but couldn't. He retched twice, but there was nothing inside him and he closed his eyes and retched again and then again until his eyes were filled with spaniel's tears, thick and gluey. They had left the light on and the bulb hung above him, white and blinding; they had done it on purpose. He shouted into the empty corridor, 'My head! My fucking head.' He hugged himself. It was so cold in here and damp, he could feel the moisture on his skin, like a poisonous film. His nose ran and ran and the skin on his face hurt, felt as if it were hanging off in strips like dirty hotel wallpaper. He was so dirty he could smell himself like old onions in a pan and his clothes clung to him and offered no warmth against the cold. He pulled the hood of his tracksuit over his head. 'Turn the light off!' he screamed. But his voice stuck in his throat and no one could hear him down here anyway. 'I want coffee. Get me some coffee, for Christ's sake.' He tried to lift his legs in order to lie down, but his dick, standing between his legs like some stupid sentinel faithful to his post when the city had been destroyed, barred his way so that he could not move and he could not get his dick to lie down. His arousal was like a sick torture he was inflicting on himself and his dick strained upwards, taking with it all his energy. 'Get me a cigarette.' He retched again. 'Please.' His eyes were still weeping glue. 'I need a cigarette. Somebody. Please.' And he rocked to and fro, gripping the hard, cold edge of his camp bed. 'Mum,' he moaned. 'I want my mum. You bastards!' It hurt his head to speak and he rocked and whimpered, 'Mum.'

Stuart descended the concrete steps to the basement. The place was cool and smelled pleasantly of damp. He went to Raymond's cell, which was at the end of the L-shaped corridor next to the rest room.

Raymond was clutching his head. Stuart could see he was far gone. He opened the cell door and stepped inside. Raymond was shaking. He grabbed him by the collar.

'No. Fuck off. You're hurting me. I want a lawyer. Don't touch me.' His voice was hoarse.

Stuart took him into his office and sat him down, cuffing one hand to a metal ring in the wall beside his desk.

'Give me something, you fucking bastard,' Raymond said. His nose and eyes were streaming. Stuart just stared at him. 'Please.'

'What can you tell me?'

Raymond sat in the chair, clutching himself with his free arm. He wore a shiny red tracksuit top with the hood pulled up. His handsome face looked as though it was rotting from the inside. His dark skin was liver-grey; he had purple bruises beneath his eyes and he was sweating.

Stuart put his hand in his pocket and held out the heroin on his palm. Raymond looked down at the tiny white envelope. He reached out for it. Stuart closed his hand. Raymond cried out and passed his hand over his face. He had scabs on his knuckles.

'This is better than what Coco can give you. What's he up to?'

Raymond thrust his hands further into his pockets.

'Please. Give me something. I can't think.' He leaned forward, gripped his thighs with his free arm and buried his face in his lap. 'Please. My head.'

Stuart turned his back on Raymond and went and closed the shutters; then he took his chair from behind his desk and carried it over to Raymond. He sat down two metres away from him in the dark and asked again, 'What can you tell me?'

Raymond sat up. His voice trembled.

'Please. Can't you give me something? I'm dying.'

'What is there of interest in the market streets behind the Fritz Bar? Who hangs out there?'

'No one. It's dead.' Raymond clutched his stomach and moaned.

'We've got a black Mercedes 500 with doubled plates. Who took it? Come on. I've got it here,' Stuart said. 'It's good. What do you know about the Mercedes?'

Raymond watched Stuart's closed fist resting on the desk.

'Come on,' Stuart said.

'I don't know anything,' Raymond whined.

'What would Coco have to discuss with Jean Filippi?'

Raymond retched.

'He doesn't trust me any more. Please.'

There was a discreet knock and Annie entered the room. Raymond began to shout. 'Let me out! You can't keep me any longer.'

'I can,' Stuart said. 'Possession,' he said, opening his hand. He glanced up at Annie. 'What is it?'

She came forward, undisturbed by Raymond's screams

and the darkness and put a Ministry envelope on the desk.

'They picked it up on the scanner,' she said.

'Anything interesting?'

'They didn't say. Zanetecci called. He asked why your direct line wasn't answering.' Stuart did not answer. 'He wants you to call him,' she said.

Stuart picked up the envelope and looked inside.

'Prosecutor Van Ruytens wants you to call him as well,' she said gently. 'Soon as possible. And Lopez.'

'Thank you,' Stuart said.

'He's like a dog with a rag,' she said.

'Yes. I'll call him. Thanks.' He could feel her hesitating but he did not look up. When she had left the room he went and fetched the envelope from his desk. 'Think, Raymond. I'm leaving this on the desk. To jog your memory. Jean Filippi. Think.'

Raymond began to sob. Stuart left him, closing the door gently behind him.

Annie looked up and smiled at him as he walked past. He attempted a smile in return, reneged, then felt ashamed. He made for the recording room but the thought of having to talk to the technician made him change his mind. He took the stairs to the first floor and went and shut himself into Gérard and Paul's office. The room was cramped and hot. Paul's side was covered in posters of sites of great natural beauty, all places he claimed to have been. Gérard's side was bare. The shelf behind his desk was empty but for one large book: an encyclopaedia of mushrooms. On his desk was a tape recorder.

As he listened Stuart looked out of the window on to the flower beds neatly planted by Gérard with red, white and blue flowers, in three neat rows.

Coco's voice made him turn and look at the machine. He stopped the tape and rewound.

There was something in her tone: 'I can't get it in time. I have to ask you. Can you lend me the money?'

It was intimacy.

Then Coco gave his answer and Stuart held his breath. The inevitable pause came and he hung up.

'Too late,' Stuart said, snatching the tape from the machine. He ran down the narrow stairs. 'We might have them' – it was incriminating enough. Annie looked up as he passed her and said, 'Lopez.'

'I'll call him from the car.'

Raymond was sitting in the dark, panting like a dog.

'You're free,' he told him. 'You can make a call. One call. So you'll have to choose between Nathalie Santini and your dealer.' He took his keys from his desk drawer and unlocked Raymond's handcuffs. He helped Raymond to his desk. 'Here, sign this. It's the end of your custody.' The youth leaned on him and Stuart got a whiff of his acid smell. When he had signed, Stuart closed the file and took it with him.

As they left the room Raymond said, 'You're a sick fuck, Stuart.'

But Stuart did not stop to answer because his anger was driving him again, pushing him forward, and he was glad to give in to it.

Chapter Twenty

Liliane sat quietly beside Babette as she drove into Massaccio for the demonstration. It was due to begin at six. Babette always marched: for the fun of it more than from any deep conviction. When Liliane had told her she would come, Babette could hardly contain her excitement. She now kept glancing sideways at her as though she were afraid Liliane might change her mind and jump out of the car.

Liliane knew that what she was about to do would make her life lastingly difficult. But she was deeply affected by the disappearance of the woman's child. She believed it might be what was making her sick and she felt the need to do something, make some gesture that would take her, if only for a moment, out of her marriage. Walking through Massaccio with the Women's Peace Movement would be seen by everyone as an act of rebellion against Coco. He referred to them, even in public, as 'the harpies'.

They were behind a tractor that was moving, high-haunched and imperious, down the steep stretch of road that led to the main drag into town. Babette sounded her horn twice. When he passed the lay-by she gave him a long blast.

'Bastard,' she said under her breath.

At last the road straightened out and she overtook him in the wrong gear, making the engine scream, but she sat facing straight ahead of her, her enormous breasts resting on the steering wheel. Liliane glanced up as they passed. A young man with black curly hair and an imbecile's grin bounced behind the wheel.

Liliane looked at Babette's hands on the steering wheel. The fingers were swollen and chapped from washing-up.

As she pulled out on to the main road Babette smiled at

Liliane, her big tattered smile. She was wearing the lovely headscarf with sunflowers on it and she had put on some lipstick.

'You all right?'

'I'm sick. It won't let up.'

'It's the violence. Women have a sixth sense. When things get this bad we feel it physically. I can't sleep; you feel sick.'

In Massaccio they drove straight into a traffic jam at the port. The sound of horns mingled with the sound of sirens. Babette crossed herself.

'Can you smell burning?'

Liliane nodded, too nauseous to speak. Babette leaned out of her window and hailed a policewoman in a short-sleeved shirt and white gloves who was standing on the pavement surveying the chaos with expert detachment.

'What's happening?' Babette's voice was shrill above the noise. The policewoman stepped towards her, cupping her ear with her hand. 'What's going on? Why all the traffic?'

'There's a demonstration.'

'I know. We're trying to get there. Why the sirens?'

The policewoman turned her head away and squinted into the sun for a moment. She was wearing a pair of inappropriately large gold hoops in her ears.

'There's been another bomb.'

She stepped back as Babette prepared to ask her next question and began gesticulating aggressively at the stationary cars in a sudden galvanic fit. Babette edged forward.

'What is all the fuss about?' she complained. 'I mean, it's not as if it's rare, is it? You would have thought they'd be used to it by now. If they're not going to arrest the bombers they could at least direct the traffic properly so we can get on with our lives. Wouldn't you think?'

'This island is like a prison with no warders.'

Babettte looked at Liliane.

'Who said that?'

'No one. Me.'

Perhaps it was Rémy. It was the kind of thing he would say. Liliane often prayed that he would come back before Coco died. She also prayed that Coco would die before she did, which she knew was tantamount to praying for his death.

'I'm going to park,' Babette said. 'We can walk to the Palais.'

Babette made for the pavement, craning above the wheel, her eyes carefully avoiding the indignation of the other drivers. At last she drove on to the pavement and parked between two palm trees. It was a relief to Liliane to get out of the car. She squinted at the light in town, which always seemed more blinding than in Santarosa.

'Ready?' Babette was smiling at her over the roof of the car. 'Off we go then.'

Babette took her arm. There were only three years between them, but she allowed Babette the illusion that she was much younger. They turned into the long avenue that led up to the Palais. The street was empty of traffic and people were walking in the road, all in one direction. Perhaps it was the white light, or the absence of cars, but there was a strange atmosphere in town, like an absence of purpose.

Liliane enjoyed Babette's supporting arm, the sound of her quick step and her narrow heels on the stone pavement. She could hear a woman's voice shouting into a loud hailer and she recognised what it was that was so different. It was the presence of so many women on these streets usually filled with men: idle or purposeful but always lordly; for the street was their domain and women and girls were tolerated as passers-by, not as occupants. She squeezed Babette's arm and returned her smile. Up ahead was the Palais with its seven arched doors. Liliane looked out for television cameras. Her secret hope was that Rémy might see her on the news. It was unlikely but she still hoped.

Babette took her by the hand and led her through the crowd to the steps of the Palais, where most of the committee had gathered. The leader was a lawyer called Suzanne Vico, a woman in her thirties who had returned to the island after studying in France and America. She was clever and tough and shrill as a vixen. The men hated her.

She was calling on them to break the immemorial silence, handmaiden of violence. Only the women, she believed, could do this.

Someone was taking photographs beside her. It was the journalist, Angel Lopez. Liliane tried to move away, but he lowered his camera and smiled at her.

'She has nice imagery and the ideas are beautiful but she has a flaw: the big unspoken enemy.' He paused, nodding encouragingly at them. 'If you break the silence, who do you talk to? The police, of course. But she can't call on islanders to do that, can she?' He waited good-naturedly for them to agree. 'The police. Come on,' he said, with exaggerated incredulity. 'So what can she suggest? Taking the law into your own hands? A posse of vengeful women? That would be perpetuating the old codes. Am I right? Babette. You look very glamorous today,' he said, nodding at her headscarf. 'Am I right?'

'I'm afraid I wasn't listening.' Babette gave him a coy smile and turned back to Suzanne Vico.

'I am surprised to see you here, Madame Santini. Glad, but surprised.'

Liliane did not believe he was glad. As far as she knew, he had never once said anything in his paper to indicate that the violence wasn't nourishment to him. But she kept silent.

'This movement, whatever its weaknesses, might just be the thing that saves this place,' he said, raising his camera to his eye. He took several photographs of Suzanne Vico and then turned back to her. 'Will you march then?'

Liliane nodded.

'Why now?'

'Don't answer,' Babette said, taking Liliane by the arm. 'Come on, they're moving. Do you want to be a few rows back?'

'No, no. It's all right,' she said. 'We'll walk in front.'

'You're brave, madame,' Lopez said.

'She's just had enough,' Babette said.

Lopez followed them as they moved towards the foot of the steps where Suzanne Vico and the other committee members had gathered. Liliane felt his hand on her arm, gently but firmly restraining her. She turned and looked into his face.

'Please,' she said.

'I just want to give you my card. In case you ever want to break the silence.'

She looked down at the card in his hand, then took it and put it in the pocket of her skirt.

'They've gone too far this time. No?' He looked sincere for a moment, then grinned with disconcerting suddenness. 'Good luck, Madame Santini.' And he turned and disappeared into the crowd.

Babette took her left arm. A young woman with a pink T-shirt, a black bra showing through and a swinging ponytail smiled at her and took her other arm. Through the eerie hollowness of the microphone, one woman's voice called out a slogan and the crowd echoed with a deep, rich sound that rained down on them. Liliane was filled with an unfamiliar happiness as she stepped forward into the street.

Chapter Twenty-One

Alice and Dan were playing a game of Pelmanism on the floor. While Alice gave in to waves of sleep, Dan concentrated hard on the game. One pair of shutters was open, just enough to let in a slab of light that heated the rug and revived locked-in smells. Dan had marvelled at the golden dust motes, disturbing them with his splayed hand. He was now frowning at the game, resting his truculent chin on his hand. He glanced up at her occasionally as if he mistrusted this new mood of hers. She smiled at him.

'Have you had enough?'

He didn't bother to answer but went back to the game. He was on a roll, turning the matching pairs over, one by one – banana, cherries, bus, canary, grapes – putting them calmly and efficiently in a pile between his knees. Dan always finished. He did not have Sam's rampaging boredom. He could put his mind to anything provided winning was involved. He cleared the floor and looked up at her triumphantly.

'Well done,' she said.

'Is Sam coming back?'

Behind his laughing eyes, his hard little chin, she could see his fragility. She reached out and took hold of his hand.

'Your brother's coming back.'

He swallowed, keeping his eyes on her, waiting for more.

'Mummy loves you very much, Dan. We're going to get Sam back. But we have to be brave and patient. We'll help each other. All right?'

'Why did they steal Sam?'

She wondered what he had overheard.

'They want money,' she said. 'They took Sam and said

they'll give him back when we give them the money.'

'Blackmail,' said Dan. He knew the subject well.

'Yes.'

'Will they hurt him?'

'No.'

'Mummy?'

'Yes, darling.'

'I want Sam.' His chin began to tremble.

'I know you do.' She pulled him towards her and clutched him. 'Listen. Can you hear? They've put the sprinklers on. Let's go outside.'

She picked him up and they went out into the garden. The air was still hot but the afternoon had slipped; there was a sense that things had come unsewn in the heat, that Nature had let herself go. They stood on the stone step and watched three standing sprinklers, scattering rainbows. Alice put Dan down. He was barefoot and he jumped off the hot stone on to the damp lawn.

'Come, Mummy.'

'I'll watch you.'

Dan never insisted. He ran off into the mist and began to play, as he and Sam had played only three days before, opening his mouth to the water and holding up his arms in a gesture of worship.

Stuart was standing beside her.

'You were smiling,' he said, keeping his eyes on the child. She went back to watching Dan. 'Any news?' he asked.

She looked at him. His smile was strained.

'Has something happened?' she asked.

'You tell me,' he said.

'What do you mean?'

He shook his head and smiled again briefly. She turned away from him to watch Dan. The man beside her was all over the place. She had been right to go to Santini.

'Dan!' she called. Dan stopped and looked at her. 'I'm going in now, Dan! Come on, please!'

Dan dropped his arms and trotted across the engorged lawn and she wished she hadn't stopped his game. She and Stuart watched him approach.

'What was the bomb?'

Stuart shrugged, his hands in his pockets.

'It's as unlikely a bomb attack for this island as a kidnapping is.'

She looked at him, expecting more, but his face was hard. Inwardly she turned against him, shifting the last of her faith over to Santini.

'I have to go and change him.' She cupped the back of Dan's head with her hand. 'His clothes are wet.'

Stuart just drove his hands deeper into his pockets. She picked Dan up and put his wet body on her hip, but Stuart did not stand aside.

'I don't know yet how Santini's involved . . .' He looked beyond her at the sprinklers. 'But these lunatics couldn't make a move without him knowing about it.'

She saw the shadows under his eyes, his ravaged face. Now that Sam was found, Stuart was in her past. She felt a remote affection for the face, as though it were some piece of archeology.

A phone was ringing in his pocket. She put Dan down.

'Go and ask Babette for some tea,' she said. 'I'm coming.'

Dan ran round the side of the house to the back door. She followed Stuart into the sitting room. He was talking on the phone, his back to her.

'Maybe,' he said. 'But you screwed up badly today. You put Mesguish's man on to him.' His voice was quiet and calm. 'The report's incomplete. There's a big hole between two and four. After the meeting with Jean Filippi he returns to his villa. They pick him up again in Santarosa two hours later. Two hours.' There was a pause. 'So where is he? Is anyone with him?'

Alice sat down on the sofa. He stood with his back to her, hunched over the phone, his left hand hanging from his sleeve, his feet apart on the elaborate rug. He looked ungainly and yet strongly rooted.

'Can you hear anything with the laser?' he went on. 'What about Georges?'

He hung up and paused for a moment, looking at the phone. Then he turned and faced her. His anger seemed to have drained away.

'You spoke to Santini,' he said, staring down at her. His eyes did not seem to be focusing on her properly.

'I rang him to ask him for money. I can't get it fast enough.' Her voice failed; she tried again. 'They've given so little time. He said he'd help me.'

'He told you he had located your son.'

She looked up at him, feeling disadvantaged suddenly.

'Yes.'

'You trust him,' he said gently.

'I don't trust anybody.'

His eyes seemed to come into focus.

'More than you trust me.'

She shouted at him. 'He said he'd found Sam!' She clenched her teeth, determined not to cry. 'I sit here in this house, waiting. Imagining my son.' She looked down at the rug. She found herself invoking Mathieu again, felt the rush of anger towards him. 'Santini is the only person who has given me any sense that he has any control. You don't seem to have any.'

'I don't pretend to.'

She looked up.

'Santini knows who took him,' she said.

'Of course he does. He's involved.'

'I don't care. If he was, he can get Sam back.' Stuart was silent. 'Can't he?' But he was staring beyond her. 'Santini can get him back, can't he? Stuart.'

He looked at her. She considered pressing him, but his remoteness alarmed her and she held back. He stepped towards her and sat down beside her on the sofa, leaning

[169]

forward, resting his arms on his knees. Quietly he addressed his hands.

'If he wants to, he can.'

She watched him rub his hands softly together, turning them over, inspecting them.

'Who is he?' she asked. 'How did he make his money?'

Stuart sat back and locked his hands behind his head.

'First drugs. In Marseilles. He spent ten years in prison in the sixties and seventies and came out a rich man. Then amusement arcades. Since he came back his trail's got cleaner and cleaner. Now he has the best real estate on the island.'

He turned and looked at her, taking his hands from behind his head. His face had lost its savagery. She noticed his mouth, sharp and curved like a boy's, and a tiny scar like a cleft on his chin.

'He's a dangerous person,' he told her. 'I really believe the only limits he ever had were the island's. And they seem to have gone.' He raised a hand and let it drop wearily into his lap.

'Why?'

'Don't know.'

He smiled fleetingly at her.

'Even the FNL is his. They always act in accordance with his wishes. They never touch any of his real estate. They blow up beach complexes but never his. But now they've got their own financial interests. Maybe he showed them there was money to be made. Maybe that's why things have changed.'

He leaned forward again. She looked at the back of his neck where the dark hair was cropped and grew to a point. She thought of Sam's blond spiral.

Again he spoke to his hands. 'Say he isn't involved. It's a new group with no connection. He finds out who it is and he decides to tell you. He wants to help a woman in distress. If Santini isn't a kidnapper, he is a criminal. It's not in his nature to do something for nothing. You know that.' He sat up and looked at her. 'You sensed you'd have to pay somehow. He made you understand that, didn't he?' She stared back at him. 'The temptation to take risks will be enormous for him.'

His reasoning was following some autistic pattern.

'What do you mean?' she asked.

'What's he going to do? Rush in there and shoot them all? Mount a rescue operation in the middle of town? If he wasn't involved he'd try and negotiate, try and take a cut.' He leaned back against the sofa. 'You have to protect yourself. Go with Santini. But have us follow, a little way behind. It won't cost you anything.'

His eyes were shining. In the yellow light of the room, in the old maid's decor, he looked gentle suddenly and, in spite of the vertical lines in the hollows of his cheeks, almost youthful.

'All right.' She kept her voice cold.

He smiled at her.

She had the feeling that something was slipping away from her, that she had relinquished something important. She felt exhausted and confused.

'Just don't use this to get at Santini.'

He shook his head. He had become passive and remote, as though he had made some decision satisfactory to himself.

'You don't have any children,' she said.

'No.'

'You're not married.'

He hesitated.

'Separated.'

'You have no idea what it's like, have you?'

'No,' he said. Then he took her hands and held them. 'I won't let you down,' he said.

She pulled her hands away.

'Don't leave me in the dark any more. You've got to tell me everything. All the decisions you make, I want to know about,' she said. He looked charged again.

'Santini's assuming that I overheard the conversation, so he's not moving. He's at home, in the village. Call him back and say you're on your own mobile. He thinks I bugged mine but I didn't. I can't. I scanned the call. I can pick up a call if it's on the right frequency. It was pure chance but he doesn't know that, so call him. Say you want to meet him.'

'Why?'

He nodded at the phone on the table.

'He knows who has him.'

She reached forward and picked up the phone. She punched out Santini's number.

'Hello? It's me.' There was a long pause. She could hear him breathing. 'It's Alice Aron.'

'Yes, what is it?'

'Is everything all right?' she asked.

'I can't talk at the moment.'

'It's okay, it's my phone,' she told him.

'I can't talk to you now. I'll call you in the morning.'

'But you said –'

'I said I can't talk now.'

He hung up and she was left there, her heart beating too fast.

'What did he say?' Stuart asked.

'He was tense and he sounded angry. He kept saying, "I can't talk now".'

'He's already made one mistake today,' Stuart said. 'Talking to you. He's going to make another one. We just have to wait.'

Alice was feeling faint. She wanted to leave the room, to go and find Dan and Babette, but she could not move.

'You should lie down for a while,' he said. She shook her head. 'Lie down, just for a moment.'

He touched her elbow briefly as if to test her. Then he held her arm and she let him help her to her feet and guide her to his bed in the corner of the room. She lay down on her side, drawing her knees up. For the first time in three days she was hungry. He covered her with an imitation fur rug that smelled of dust, lifting the cover over her shoulder. Then he went and stood on the other side of the room, near the fireplace.

Chapter Twenty-Two

Stuart was on the road down to the plain. Wisps of mist were hanging in the trees. The sun was low and merciful and the birds were now singing cockily. Alice had slept; Stuart had watched her, holding his position by the fireplace, aware of the fragility of her sleep, until Gérard had come for the evening shift. The sound of the door opening woke her and Stuart left quickly, suddenly afraid to see her awake.

The image of Alice, asleep in the corner of the room, came to him with an unpleasant rush of adrenaline. He looked at his eyes in the rear-view mirror. They looked angry. He tried to change the expression in them but could only manage surprise. He turned on the radio for noise, then turned it off. He had not changed his shirt for three days. He decided to go home and take a shower before going back for the night.

Stuart took the hairpin bend where Titi's dog had been killed. She was a mongrel – half-poodle, half-coyote with pointed translucent ears and bowed legs. She followed Titi everywhere. A bearded Englishman on his way to the coast to fish had run her over. He ran straight over her bloated middle. The Englishman picked her up from the middle of the road and stood there, looking helplessly about him. Titi watched from behind a fig tree. His dog lay in the Englishman's arms, whining softly and staring at the sky. The dog saw the crumpled bars of a bird cage and at the same time felt something swimming about inside her, something that had broken loose. She felt the boy watching her from behind the tree. The man was turning round and round. Then the loose thing escaped. Titi and the Englishman heard the dog make a sound like a long sigh. The Englishman stopped turning. His face was bright red and he looked as though he might cry.

Then he made a decision – perhaps he decided that this was, after all, an island of savages – and he walked to the side of the road. As he was laying the dog in the ditch, Titi came out from behind the fig tree and sneaked round to the far side of the man's car. Through the open window on the driver's side he saw a jack-knife with a carved ivory handle. He reached in and took the knife. That afternoon, before he put his dog in the ground, he cut off one of her ears with the knife. He wore it round his neck until it curled and dried like a waxy leaf.

Stuart had not thought of the incident for years. Now it seemed to him to have been curled there at the back of his mind waiting to be discovered like some clue to Titi's life and so to his own.

He drove through town, past the dark sea, flat as a lake. The barricades from the afternoon's march were stacked neatly along the side of the road. Otherwise the women had left no trace. They never did. They could weep and scream but the violence would go on. Stuart wondered why they were thus condemned to spectate. Perhaps it was that thing in them he envied, that his sister had and his mother and even Alice Aron, with her grief – an elusive quality, as though they were inoculated against life itself.

Gérard had told him that Liliane Santini had marched. She had been seen at the front with Vico. Stuart smiled. Poor Liliane: Coco would make her pay.

By the time he reached home, the last of the sun was gone. Driving over the humps in his street, he told himself he would get a new car when this was over. When this was over. He drove up the ramp to his garage and his heart sank.

In his flat Stuart moved quickly and efficiently. The place was filled with his own loneliness like a strong smell and he was anxious to get out.

After his shower, which was a thin ribbon at this time of day, he put on a clean shirt and then drank a mini-carton of chocolate milk. He threw away the jar of gherkins in the fridge and washed up the spaghetti saucepan. Then he made his bed. At the door he stopped. He would give her something. He went to his bed and pulled the box from beneath it. He took the brown-paper bag with his mother's gun in it and slipped it into his jacket pocket. Then he left the flat hurriedly, as if it were contaminated.

It was dark when Stuart pulled up in front of the Colonna house. He recognised Lopez's car, a maroon Honda Civic, parked so that the two back tyres bit into the lawn. Stuart walked round the car. He looked at the Basque flag stuck on the rear window. Alone in the dark, Stuart grunted with contempt. Lopez could not claim ethnic persecution. He came from San Sebastian but he was no more Basque than Stuart was. At this thought, Stuart turned and bolted up the steps to the terrace, holding on to his mother's gun in his pocket.

They were in the kitchen. She had her hair tied up in a ponytail. The change felt like a kind of betrayal. She and Lopez looked up at him as though his entrance were overblown.

'Hello, Stuart,' Lopez said.

Stuart flushed and went to the sink to pour himself a glass of water. He faced them and drank.

'What are you doing here, Lopez?'

'I'm meeting Madame Aron. Properly. I've just given her my card. That's all. Don't worry. I'm not importuning her. Actually, I expected to see you here. I'm doing a story on the march. The changing tide.'

'What changing tide?'

'Liliane was there.'

'What march?' Alice asked.

Stuart looked angrily at Lopez.

'It was a march for women,' Stuart told her. 'A peace march.'

'Who's Liliane?'

'Liliane Santini,' Lopez said. 'It's the first time she has participated in a women's march. Her husband won't like it.' Lopez smiled at Stuart, who stood leaning against the sink.

'You can read my piece, Stuart. There's nothing in it to compromise our agreement. It's very general.'

'I'll read it.'

Lopez laid his hands on the table.

'I'm done.'

'You can leave then.'

'I can.' Lopez did not move but looked up at Alice. 'Thank you, madame.'

Stuart felt the blood rush to his head. He watched Lopez stand and hold out his hand. Alice took it without rising. 'You have my card.'

Alice nodded. Stuart watched Lopez until he had closed the door behind him.

'What did he want?'

'He wanted me to talk to him first.'

'He's a journalist.'

'Quite.'

Stuart put his hand in his pocket and touched his mother's gun in its paper bag.

'Did Santini call?'

'No.'

'Did Lopez mention Santini?'

'No.'

He held the gun. What a ridiculous idea to give her a gun. Alice looked at her watch.

'I spoke to Santini four hours ago. Why hasn't he called back?'

'He won't call tonight. He'll call tomorrow.'

'Oh God,' she said, rubbing her face with her hands. 'Another night.'

Stuart took the gun from his pocket and laid it on the table in front of her. She looked up at him, her long hands on her cheeks.

'It's for you.' He nodded at the brown-paper bag. 'It's a woman's gun. My father gave it to my mother.'

Alice looked at him. He was staring hard at the paper bag.

'A gun,' she said, her hands still on her face.

He shrugged without looking at her.

The bag was thin to transparency in places. She pulled out the object. It was small, the size of a manicure kit, but heavy. The brown suede case was unmistakably gun-shaped. She unzipped the case and pulled out the gun. She looked up at Stuart, but he kept watching her hands.

'It's all right. It's not loaded,' he said. 'The bullets are in the bag.'

She held the gun on her palm, the barrel resting on her index finger. She gripped the textured butt. The words *Manufacture française d'armes et cycles de Saint Etienne* were engraved along the barrel and the initials 'MF' inside a garland. On the other side the words 'Type Policeman'. She pulled the tiny catch and the barrel sprang open. She looked at the brownish purple of the metal, the colour of bruises.

She returned the object to its little case, zipped it up and put it back into the paper bag. When at last he looked at her, she saw the same expression of hopefulness Sam wore when he gave her a drawing. There was nothing to understand from this gift except that it was a gift.

'Thank you,' she said.

Chapter Twenty-Three

The room stank. Through his tobacco-charred nostrils Mickey could smell burned spaghetti sauce. He sat on the floor with his back against the boy's cupboard and smoked the first beautiful cigarette of the day.

They should have thought of getting a TV. The Scatti brothers were now seriously annoying him. Paolo was petty and Sylvano was stupid. He had asked them for some music. A Walkman was all he wanted, to pass the time, but Paolo had said no, it was too risky to buy anything, and Sylvano had stood there staring at him smugly.

Mickey considered his job much harder than theirs: confined day and night with the boy, who had turned into an animal. It was hard on his nerves. The boy lay curled up on the floor, wouldn't eat, wouldn't speak, just whimpered when he opened the door to empty his pisspot. The kid could die from dehydration, the Scatti brothers wouldn't care. They had killed people, working for the Camora, on an informal basis. Mickey had only hurt people, sometimes badly, always for Coco Santini, and he had never got the recognition he deserved because Coco was a racist. Yes, his job was harder.

Mickey stubbed out his cigarette on the cement floor. He would get the kid to drink something. He would be gentle and coaxing. He could stay calm when he had to. He did not want to have the kid's death on his conscience. He stood up and his joints cracked. He walked like Jorge Ferreira over to the sink. He smiled to himself, unsure whether his pleasure came from the applause in his head or from the new idea that was lying there, only half-formed, by which he would secure for himself the largest share.

He filled a mustard glass with Coke. Lucky Luke, his favourite character, was printed on the glass. As he approached the door of the cupboard, he felt overcome with love towards the child he had been. How could his mum have resisted him? He had been adorable, more beautiful than this kid. But he hadn't grown properly. Only his torso had grown and this, he knew, was because he hadn't had his share of mother-love.

'The day after tomorrow you'll be free,' he told the boy. He crouched in front of the door of the cupboard. 'I'm going to open up so shield your eyes. I got you some Coke. You've got to drink if you want to see your mum.'

Mickey could hear the heavy metal door of the garage opening and the bang it made as the weights came down. The brothers were back. They had no style. They could only buy tinned food and spirits, never wine or cheese or fruit. Sylvano only ate sweet things. They had no idea how to live. He'd wait until they had gone before getting the boy to drink, because they'd only scare him. This place, too, was his find. The whole hit had been planned by him. He prepared to adopt a different attitude towards Paolo. Still crouching, Mickey turned round at the sound of Paolo, who always came first, pushing open the entrance to the hideout.

He saw the face and heard the shot and reached into his boot for his weapon in the time it took to recall Garetta's name. On the impact, his arm was flung from his side, the glass bounced once on the cement floor and then smashed into hundreds of geometric pieces. Mickey fell back and hit the boy's wall. He could feel cold air rushing into him, chilling his stomach, which he tried to clutch but his arm wouldn't come. He knew he would survive this wound to his abdomen and he had time to congratulate himself on his muscular armour before realising that Garetta was going to shoot him again. He was coming towards him and Mickey knew not to meet his eye, that this would be a mistake, so he looked to his right. His vision was sharper than normal. He took in the thick, white paint that covered the brick wall, the inexplicable dog's footprints, three of them, in the cement floor, the shiny, tubular metal table legs and the rubber stoppers on the legs of the chairs like the ones in the canteen at school. Garetta was up close and aiming at him. His weapon had a silencer. Mickey had always loved the pristine sound of a silenced shot. He had never possessed a silencer himself. He reached into his boot again, knowing he had no chance. But the shot still didn't come. He could feel the textured wood of his gun with his fingertips but did not have the strength to grip. The blood seeping out of him felt like the strange but pleasant sensation of a bath emptying around his naked body. 'Please, Garetta,' he said, closing both his eyes, good and bad. Garetta read his words as a signal and Mickey saw the scene fold in even before the bullet entered his brain.

Sam floated high up near the breathing holes and watched the big hands pull him out into the light. He saw his own body curled up in a ball in the man's arms. He saw his own eyes and mouth shut tight, his whole body closed and empty, because he was up here, watching the man with the long black hair, and even though the man was a giant he looked small from here. Then he saw the other man dressed in black lying on the floor. He saw his skinny legs, bent the wrong way like his Pinocchio puppet. And then he saw his head and he began to fall through the air, and as he fell he closed his eyes and said 'I must not land in the blood. I must not fall there.'

As Garetta pushed the child through into the garage, Paolo knew something was wrong. He had an urge to run, but his brother was stuck in the back of Garetta's car between two armed men. Paolo tried to help the kid up. But it lay on the ground curled up in a ball, fists closed. It had silver tape over its mouth, and around its hands and feet. Something had scared the kid so badly it had shat itself. Paolo pulled back as

Garetta came through. Garetta picked the child off the ground like a small package and walked towards the car. Paolo considered asking him about Mickey then decided against it. Garetta had appeared on the boat at dawn. He had stood at the end of his bed with one hundred thousand francs in a plastic bag: 'From the FNL,' Garetta had said. 'To cover costs. We're taking this over.' Looking at Garetta now as he put the child into the boot of the car, Paolo did not believe he was FNL; there was something wild about him, too wild for obedience.

Paolo looked at the Arab in the back. On the boat that morning he had taken his Baretta from the bedside table. He now prepared his words: 'I'd like my weapon back; it belonged to my father.' But Garetta was coming towards him and he had always been intimidated by very tall men.

'I need you to clean up in there.'

'Clean up,' Paolo repeated, his mouth dry.

Garetta turned and signalled to the Arab kid. Paolo's heart faltered and he took a step back. The Arab got out of the car and Sylvano climbed out after him.

'You and your brother,' Garetta said, smiling.

Paolo saw then that the man was a wolf. He had seen such a man once before and he knew he must hold perfectly still. As Sylvano came towards him, Paolo said a Hail Mary in his head. He did not close his eyes but he did not look at the wolf-man either. He followed his orders with slow, careful movements. As he crawled through after Sylvano into the hideout he knew what it was to be the prey and he heard himself whimper.

Paolo stood in the room and looked at Mickey's body. Sylvano was shaking out his legs to make his trousers fall straight.

Tears of rage burned Paolo's throat.

'*Figlio di cane!*' he screamed.

Sylvano glanced incuriously at Mickey's body, then back at his brother. He plucked at the cuffs of his suit.

Paolo spun round and kicked the small square door in the cement wall, but he already knew without looking that they were trapped there with the dead man, whose blood all around him appeared to be forming a skin.

Philippe Garetta drove through the Cortizzio valley, past the sawmill where he had once worked. He had liked the place, the smell of the pine and the men who worked there, but not the boss, and he had left one winter morning when there was frost on the ground. He had asked for a pair of gloves and the shithead had told him the company didn't provide gloves.

The child was lying tied up and gagged in the boot, with the provisions for the hideout. Garetta turned on the radio. Denis had tuned into some terrible teenage radio station. A girl was shrieking and swearing at the DJ, who had just told her she had won ten thousand francs. 'Thank you. Thank you all. Thank you, Radio Heaven. I love you all! Oh my God!' Garetta looked for the local news channel. Frigari was shooting off about quotas. Garetta shook his head.

'You're all finished, you hippie fuckers,' he said.

Karim and Denis were following on the bike. They would occasionally appear in the rear-view mirror, a black tick on the road, then fall back.

Garetta sat through the sports results. There was nothing about the bombing. He must have missed it.

Coco had given him Karim for his expertise but no equipment. Santini had said there was no one more deft than Karim. The explosion had been considerable, considering. Karim had said that with the junk he had to hand it was the best he could do. It was a pity he wasn't an islander. Denis came with Karim and he was not an islander either, but from Arles, and he had gypsy in him. Still, Garetta thought, it was early days. And as Santini had pointed out, it was because they were not islanders that he could ask him to get involved in a kidnapping.

'You can get your group started with this,' Santini had said.

'Get a good sum, buy some decent hardware; I might throw in some bazookas.'

Garetta had never liked Santini. He talked about revolution as if he was talking about a real-estate opportunity.

In the end Garetta had accepted Santini's offer of Karim. When it came to it, he didn't have much choice. There were few people he could trust with something like this. He'd bring in the others once he'd laid the groundwork. It was a real organisation he wanted, with perfect discipline, like the Red Army Faction or ETA. He'd create links with other groups fighting for the same goals. He'd win back some respect for the island.

He had written the speech for the paper by himself. He had been pleased by its density, by the economic expression of so many ideas and by the images of sickness and decay. He thought with disgust of the Scatti brothers, of their big white vedette moored in the marina, their flash suits. He should have rid the island of them, too. They were a lot worse than Mickey da Cruz.

He searched for some decent music on the radio. He had a weakness for heavy metal, but it was harder and harder to come by and he gave up. He drove down into the valley, over the single-lane bridge that crossed the dry river bed and on to the road towards Castri, home territory. As he drove, he tried to consider the sum of thirty million that Santini had told him to request for the child. He was thrilled, not so much by the sum, which was a little abstract, but by the power his demand would represent. He felt immensely powerful. In fact he had always felt immensely powerful. Now, he thought, it was time to show it.

Wednesday

Chapter Twenty-Four

Stuart walked quickly along the wide market street that led from the Old Port to the Fritz Bar. Stunted palms giving no shade sprang from the hot granite pavements. There was an unpleasant smell in the air of burned rubber and rotting vegetables. He had thought the street deserted; now he noticed a silent audience of old women standing, alone or in pairs, on the rectangular pedestal of shade offered by their doorsteps. He stepped into the road to avoid passing too close to them and trod on a slice of pineapple fermenting in the gutter. He scraped his shoe clean, aware of the women's scrutiny. They were looking at his fluorescent orange arm band with 'Police' printed in black, hovering between their desire for a little entertainment and their lifelong habit of obstruction. On the island there were different codes for men and women. The women never talked and never signed their statements, while for the men there was nothing that couldn't be discussed at the right price. It was this combination of the women's silence and the men's loquacity that made his work so hard.

Paul's call had come when Alice was still asleep. Stuart had taken it in the kitchen in front of Babette. The hideout had been found and an as yet unidentified body, but the child had gone. In the background Stuart listened to Babette noisily preparing a tray for Alice. Perhaps it had been the sight of Babette pushing through the swing doors with the tray for her – he did not know – but he had left without telling her.

He now turned into the narrow street that ran behind the Fritz Bar. A jagged line divided the street between sun and shade. People leaned out of the windows high up in the decrepit façades on either side of him and he knew he was nearing the site. Someone shouted out something he didn't hear and there was female laughter. He looked up and saw a middle-aged man in a vest, leaning from the third floor of the Hôtel Majestic. The shutters of the ochre building opened upwards, casting rhomboid shadows on the wall. The man in the Majestic was smoking a cheroot. He waved it in the air as he shouted.

'You're too late! You're always too late. How can you ever expect any order on this island? They're a bunch of kids but they run rings round you.' The man had an Italian accent. 'How old are you, anyway? You should have retired!' he yelled.

As he turned the corner, Stuart smiled.

The street was barricaded. A CRS nodded at his ID and stepped aside to let him pass. Romano's Pizza was at the end. The *sapeurs'* red van shielded the entrance from view. He had told Paul to wait for him; he wanted to look at the body. He could now see Romano, a fat man with a grey ponytail, red shirt and black trousers, standing with his back to him, smoking with a raised elbow. Stuart walked past the proprietor without greeting him: the man was a big-mouth. A couple of teenagers in aprons stood beside him, their hands bleached with flour, looking impressed.

Two uniformed policemen were standing beside their vehicle not far from the entrance to the garage. Stuart recognised one of them, a blond youth with a crew-cut and a red face, whose uniform always looked too small for him. His face lit up when he saw Stuart.

'How are you, Commissaire?' he said, holding out his hand.

Stuart took it, patting him on the shoulder.

'Good to see you.' He held out his hand to the other cop who saluted with great austerity. Stuart nodded and smiled and turned back to the blond youth. 'Not fed up yet?' he asked him, moving away towards the garage door.

'No, no, I love it here,' he said, breathing in the freshness that was a figment of his imagination.

The boy came from La Rochelle. He was always enthusiastic when he saw Stuart, who was ashamed that he could not remember his name. The boy followed him to the entrance of the garage.

'Is it a reprisal killing?' he asked.

Stuart looked down the slope into the cool, dark interior. The garage was deep and narrow, wide enough for one car. There was a smell of diesel.

'No,' he said. 'I don't think so. I don't know what it is.' He moved down the ramp towards Paul, who was standing at the far end with a small man in a suit.

'Fausto Ribeira,' Paul told him as he approached. 'He owns the garage.'

Fausto had an exaggeratedly worried expression on his face and he stood there fingering the brim of the cane trilby in his hands. His moustache was the two pencil-thin strokes favoured by the Portuguese of his generation.

He pleaded with Stuart. 'I have told everything to your colleague. I didn't want to let the garage. It was for sale. I put an ad in "Person to Person". He called because he saw by my name I was Portuguese. I said okay. He seemed a nice boy on the phone; he was respectful. He said he was from Lisbon. I'm from Braga but, as I said, he sounded nice.'

'What name did he give?'

'Santos.' Fausto looked consolingly at them. 'It's a very common name. He said he was only staying on the island for the summer. He had a sweetheart. He said he wanted somewhere to keep his bike, just for the summer. He had plenty of money.'

'He offered cash?' Stuart asked.

Fausto hesitated. He looked down at his hat, then at Paul, then at Stuart.

'Things are difficult for me. I done two bathrooms and a patio last month without getting paid. I had to lay off my

[189]

nephew. There's no work and when there's work they don't pay you.'

'You'd never seen him before?'

The man shook his head.

'He was young. I thought he was a bit young to have so much cash. But this island is full of kids loaded with cash. I don't have to tell you that.'

'You said you didn't think he was an islander. Why?'

Fausto looked hurt.

'He said he was on holiday. When I met him he was . . .' He stroked his cheek with the back of his fingers.

'What?' Paul said.

'He was coloured.'

'Black.'

'No, not quite black. Tanned. Very tanned. He spoke very bad Portuguese.'

Stuart turned to the boy from La Rochelle.

'Take him back to the office, will you? Someone will take your statement, Monsieur Ribeira.'

Fausto followed the youth up the ramp into the sunlight, keeping a respectful two paces behind.

'Let's have a look,' Stuart said.

Stuart listened to Paul Fizzi's explanations. There was a workbench two and a half metres long and fifty centimetres wide, running the full length of what looked like the wall of the garage but was in fact a breeze-block screen built by the kidnappers. The workbench had been pulled back to reveal a heavy wooden panel low down in the screen wall. The panel, about seventy centimetres square, had served as a door. It now hung open on its hinges. On the inside, there was a plaster wall, thirteen millimetres thick. They had shot away an area of plaster and uncovered the metal case containing the electric locking mechanism. There were four .38 bullets, two lodged in the cement wall and two, found on the floor of the hideout, that had been compressed by the impact on the metal case. One of the compressed bullets must have triggered the locking device, enabling their escape. Paul had counted five impacts. If the shots were fired with a Smith and Wesson .38, as he suspected, then the kidnappers had been extremely lucky: only one bullet had remained in the chamber when the door had clicked open.

When Paul had finished he stood there awkwardly, scratching his eyebrow. It was sad that the more conscientious Paul tried to be, the more Stuart was aware that he would never make a good policeman. He turned away and crouched down in front of the entrance to the hideout.

There was a strong smell in the room, like unwashed feet. As he stood up, Stuart realised it was the corpse. The hideout, which was about two metres by three, was already overcrowded; there was Fabrice with his cameras, Gérard, the dead Portuguese and now himself and Paul.

Fabrice made for the exit.

'I've finished,' he said. 'I shot a roll. I think there's plenty.'

The others did not acknowledge his departure. Everything about Fabrice – the red spectacles, the grey, curly hair, the biro on a string round his neck – was in keeping with the dogged, disapproving behaviour of the militant unionist, and yet Stuart had come to like him.

Stuart stepped towards the body. Broken glass crunched beneath his feet. He bent down and touched the spilled liquid, still sticky. It looked like Coca-Cola.

Gérard and Paul stood and watched him as he peered at the body, keeping his shoes outside the limits of the congealed blood. From the look of the man's clothes and his small, smooth hands, he was young. He had been shot twice. The bullet in his lower abdomen had caused abundant bleeding, which suggested a hollow bullet. The one in the back of the head had caused instant death. He had not been shot with the same weapon that had been used to open the door. He must have fallen forward on to what was left of his face and then been turned over.

'To get the keys to the cupboard,' Stuart said out loud.

'He's got a holster in his boot,' Paul said. 'They took his weapon.'

'After they shot him,' Stuart said. 'They shot him first, in the stomach, from there.' He pointed to the entrance. 'He was holding a glass so he was taken by surprise. He must have trusted them.'

'They had a key,' Gérard said.

Stuart looked up at the sound of his voice, slightly effeminate, theatrical.

'We think it was an accomplice,' Paul said.

Stuart nodded.

'Who had to shoot their way out,' he said.

'They open the door, shoot the person guarding the kid, take the kid and leave the other member of their gang shut in with the dead man.' Paul paused, looking perplexed. 'And they leave him a gun.'

'They took the weapon from the dead man,' Stuart said. 'From the holster. It's the right size for an S and W.'

Stuart stepped carefully around the body. He peered into the cupboard and was struck by the smell of urine. He thought of Alice waking up to discover that he had left without her. As he had driven through the gates he had imagined her watching him from the window. Now he was relieved that she had not had to see this place. There was no light for the child and no ventilation except for a few holes high up in the partition wall. There was a desiccated piece of ravioli on the thin foam mattress. If the boy had had a blanket, they had taken it with them.

'Maybe somebody lost it,' Paul said.

'It's either a sudden, very stupid fight, or it's a second group who came in and took over,' Stuart said.

'How many people are there on this island ready to do a kidnapping?' Gérard asked.

Stuart nodded at the corpse.

'What did the doctor say? How long had he been dead for?'

'Six to eight hours,' Gérard said.

'When is the autopsy?'

'Three,' Gérard said. 'I'll go.'

Stuart looked at Gérard and then at Paul.

'You know who it is, don't you?' he said.

'Who?' Gérard said.

'Mickey da Cruz,' Stuart said. The three of them looked at the dead youth. 'Look at the boots,' Stuart said. 'And the legs. Look.'

Gérard and Paul looked down at the corpse with its bowed legs and its gory head, their faces full of respect now that it had a name.

'What got into him?' Paul said.

'Funny,' Gérard said. 'I always thought Mickey was an Arab.'

'He always dressed like Lucky Luke,' Paul said.

The words sounded like a kind of homage. They stood still for a moment, the three of them bound together by the ugliness of all the things they had seen. For a moment none of them was in a hurry to leave the stinking room and the dead Portuguese boy and go back to the surface where they were despised, in part for what they saw. Stuart welcomed back the familiar sensation of detachment. He was free, for a moment, from the terrible longing that had been growing inside him over the past few days. It was a pain that he recognised, not as something he had experienced before but as something that had been lying there all along, waiting to declare itself. Stuart realised that he missed Alice all the time, even when he was with her.

Now Paul and Gérard were watching him and he scanned the room for something with which to cover the boy's ruined head. He fetched a checked tea towel from by the sink and laid it over the head, but it only lent a more cartoon appearance to the legs.

Chapter Twenty-Five

Alice walked down the narrow alley to the main square. She was light-headed with lack of food and sleep. It had been three days since she had dragged Dan behind her up this street. She now looked at her surroundings: at the golden light of evening cutting long shadows on the walls, at the cobbles and the weeds growing between them, at the telephone wires, running back and forth in slack lines and at the swallows far above. Like a convalescent who has long had to do without it, she felt the beauty of the object world and its irrelevance. The alley steepened and she slowed her pace. Santini was waiting for her. He had the money: nine million in the correct notes. Her heart beat faster at the thought of it.

She had been woken that morning by her heartbeat, chill with panic. She had run downstairs in her nightdress and met Babette in the hall. She was carrying a tray. The inappropriateness of the tray, the guilt at having slept, if only for a few hours, and the knowledge, even as she asked, that Stuart had gone, made her burst into tears. A policeman she had not seen before, crossing the hall, had looked up and seen her sitting on the stairs, weeping. Babette had made her some coffee, which she had drunk in silence in the kitchen, Dan on her knee. Stuart's empty cup was still unwashed on the table. She had stared at it as if it were a fetish, willing him to call her. She had waited all morning, playing Pelmanism with Dan on the kitchen table, then noughts and crosses in spilled salt. This he enjoyed and he had wanted to play again and again. The policeman had sat hunched over Paul's crossword magazine, raising his head occasionally to give Dan a wink and a smile. Babette stood at the sink, scrubbing mussels in a deep pot: God only knew who they were for. When the policeman had left the room to go and piss, Alice had jumped up, pushing Dan too brutally from her lap and knocking over her chair. Babette and Dan had watched while she called Santini. His wife's voice was full of kindness and Alice had felt herself weaken. She had delivered her message quickly and hung up.

At six, Babette had taken Dan for a walk and she had shut herself in the study to watch the kidnappers' video and wait. While she sat there watching, the images of her son had begun to take on the colour of archive. Santini and Stuart had both disappeared. Sam may have been found but something had gone wrong. When the call came at last and it was Santini, she took it as a sign: she would cut herself off from Stuart. As the eight o'clock news began, she had turned the TV on loud and climbed out of the study window.

She emerged from the narrow alley into the main square. Three old women were sitting on folding chairs, their backs against the wall of the *mairie*, facing the orange sun. She felt them watching her as she walked towards the chestnut trees. She passed quickly beneath the trees, steeling herself against the sound of the breeze in their leaves.

She had taken Sam's rucksack instead of her handbag, which her mother had bought for her in Rome on their last trip. The bag suddenly seemed like an ugly object from someone else's past. Inside the rucksack she had put Stuart's gun. She could feel it hitting the small of her back as she walked.

He had let her down. The kidnappers had made their request. All that mattered was that they got their money in time.

'It won't help you to give them the money,' Stuart had told her. His remark now struck her as morbid, cruel even.

She found the entrance to the four flights of stone steps, a narrow gap in a wall covered with ivy, angry with starlings. She could not see the birds but she could hear their screeching. She made her way down the steps, weaving through ten or fifteen cats, some warming themselves on the stone, others gliding back and forth, taking no account of her. At the bottom of the steps there was a low wall on the other side of which was a steep drop to the brown sluggish stream below. Santini's house was to the left, at the end of an alley. There was a smell of open drains and the sound of a radio coming from somewhere above her head: the news jingle as it ended. She passed under a bridge linking two houses and stopped in front of the wrought-iron gate. The bell rang inside the house and she heard a door open and soft shoes slapping the ground. An old woman stood before her, holding the gate open. Behind her was a courtyard full of chickens. The woman said good morning and stood aside to let her pass, betraying no curiosity. Alice followed her across the courtyard and up three steps to the front door. They stepped into a dark hall.

'He's in the kitchen,' the woman said. She sounded out of breath. 'Through here.'

They passed along a narrow, very brightly lit corridor. The woman halted in front of a door and looked at her.

'I'm sorry about your son,' she said. Alice recognised the gentleness from the phone call. The woman's dark eyes shone. 'I'd do anything to help you.' She found Alice's hand and gripped it hard. 'Anything,' she said. Then she let go and threw open the door to the kitchen, standing aside to let her pass.

Santini was sitting at the head of the table. He was wearing a short-sleeved shirt with a tropical motif. He ran his fingertips up and down his forearm, folded across his chest, as though he were nursing himself. He did not stand up but let his wife pull out the chair to his right. She lifted it carefully so that it did not scrape the floor. Alice took off Sam's rucksack, clutching it on her knee, and sat down. Santini put his hands, palms down, on the table, looking at them while he spoke.

'I was right. Your son was in town . . .'

'What do you mean was?' He was not looking at her. He

would not be interrupted. 'Where is he?' She shouted: 'Where is he now? Tell me!'

Santini looked calmly at her.

'He was being held in a hideout in Massaccio by a group of three.' He spoke without altering his tone, slowly and quietly, his deep voice reverberating in the small room. 'The boy who organised it was shot this morning. They shot him and took your son.'

'Who did? Where did they take him?' Alice felt the room was listing. She reached out and gripped Santini's arm. 'Do you know who it was?'

He looked at her coldly. His eyes were like two yellow fishes.

'No,' he said, placing a hand over hers. 'But we'll find out.'

'Take me there,' she said, standing up. She was weak and dizzy and she could feel herself swaying. She fixed on his blue beard that floated above the dense jungle of his shirt. 'Take me there.'

'I can't.'

'Why not?'

'Stuart's there.'

'So what? Take me there.' Alice felt the floor was rising up to meet her. Someone was beside her, holding her elbow. 'Please,' she said.

'Will you drink something? *Sirop de menthe*?' His wife was helping her back into the chair. Alice heard her slippers on the floor as she moved about the kitchen and her voice, continual and soothing. 'You have to take something, you're very weak; you can see in your face, you haven't had enough to eat, you need sugar. Then we can help you. You've got to get your strength up, hasn't she, Claude?'

Alice looked into the glass of green liquid that was placed before her on the table. There were clouds on the surface. She picked up the glass and took a sip. The drink was ice-cold and sweet. She put the glass down.

'Please take me there.'

[197]

'Where do you want to go, dear?'

Santini's wife sat down beside her. Alice faced Coco.

'Please,' she said.

'Where does she want to go?' his wife asked again.

Coco glanced at her, then back at Alice.

'How do you know they took Sam? I want to see where they had him. I want to see.'

'No. Stuart's still there.'

'What does it matter?'

'You could drop her off, Claude,' the woman said. 'My husband wants to help you. It's just that Stuart's always hounding him, isn't he, Claude? He'd hold Claude responsible for your son if he could. That's why he has to be careful; but he will help you, won't you, Claude?' Santini looked at Alice, ignoring his wife. 'You could drop her off a little way away.'

Santini rose to his feet. He walked past his wife and stopped at the entrance to the kitchen.

'I'll take you to the Old Port. It's a ten-minute walk from there. You meet me an hour later in the post office on the main square. If you're late you make your own way back. But you should prepare yourself. They won't let you through.'

Alice stood up and let Santini's wife feed her arms into the rucksack.

'Please eat something before you go.' But Santini was out of the room and Alice followed him.

In Santini's car on the road down to the coast, Alice looked out of the window at the hills, slipping into the distance in varying degrees of purple. The sky above the sea was red. She closed her eyes against the breeze.

She saw Sam's skinny frame running towards her, up a sandy slope, the sea shining behind him. He was standing over her, grinning, with sand on his face.

'Stay out of the water, will you? There are big boys in there with harpoons.'

'Why?'

'They could be dangerous.'

'The boys?'

'The harpoons.'

'Okay.'

He could fight her long and hard and then suddenly relent like that, as though he were showing her that he could yield and was her superior because of it. Something inside her that she did not care to look at made her want to dominate him. So often she thought she could feel his spirit fighting hers, resisting her, and she admired him for it. She saw his little legs kicking up the sand as he ran towards the sea and his pointed head on his frail neck.

Santini was driving fast along the waterfront. He turned and smiled at her.

'All right?' he asked. She stared back at him. 'Don't go putting your trust in the wrong people any more. It wastes time.'

He pulled up in front of three cement blocks that barred the entrance to the market streets.

'You walk down that street. Take the second on the left and then first right. It's a garage at the end. One hour,' he said, reaching over her and opening her door, brushing her breast as he did so. She climbed out of the car and did not look back.

Alice began to run, following Santini's directions. When she reached the garage she was out of breath. A young policeman in uniform was standing in front of the closed door. He stared impassively at her as she stood before him panting.

'Where's Stuart?'

'Madame?'

He was burly and red-faced with a crew-cut.

'I'm the child's mother. Where's Stuart? It's urgent.'

'The commissaire left a couple of hours ago.'

'Is this where they kept him?' she asked, looking at the garage door. 'Let me in. I want to see.'

'I'm afraid I can't do that, madame.' He stared at her, his

thumbs hooked in his belt. 'Did you say you were the mother of the victim?'

'No. Oh, for God's sake, where's Stuart?' She looked round for help. The street was empty. The muffled sound of accordion music came from a restaurant a few doors down. 'You're going to be in trouble when he finds out how slow you were.' She could feel the weight of her gun and she wanted to use it. 'Listen to me. I have to see him. It's important.' She could feel his doubt. 'Hurry up!' She spoke to him like a mother.

She followed him towards the squad car parked at the entrance to the street and watched him reach in through the driver's door to use the radio. She heard a woman's voice, then random noise. The sky was now dark blue and a chill breeze was blowing. She shivered.

'Someone's coming to fetch you.'

She nodded and turned her back on him, folding her arms against the cold. She could feel him hovering behind her. She crossed over to the other side of the road to wait for Stuart. The youth walked back to his position in front of the garage door.

When the brown Datsun pulled up it was not Stuart at the wheel. The driver leaned over the passenger seat and opened the door for her. It was Paul.

'Where's Stuart? What's happened?'

'Nothing. It's all right. Get in.'

He drove fast along the narrow backstreets of the old town, using his horn to make people scatter, sometimes driving along the pavement, working the gears. Alice sat in silence, pressing her foot on to an imaginary brake. They pulled up in front of the gates to the compound. Paul opened them with the remote control.

'Tell me what happened,' she ordered.

He was chewing gum. He looked at her, interrupting his chewing for a moment; the expression in his eyes was bovine.

'You'll have to ask Stuart,' he said. He drove into the compound and came to such an abrupt halt, slamming his foot on the brake and releasing it again, that her head was thrown against the seat back.

Without waiting for him, she climbed out of the car. Lamps like searchlights flooded the compound with artificial daytime. She ran up the steps to the building. The door clicked open before she had time to press the intercom.

She stopped in the doorway of Stuart's office. He was standing behind his desk. A man sitting opposite him turned in his chair and smiled at her: it was Lopez. Stuart was looking in her direction but not at her.

Paul's voice came from just behind her: 'We found the video recorder. It was the size of a lipstick. Fabrice doesn't think you can buy them on the island. He's checking.'

Stuart nodded at Paul. Lopez rose to his feet and held his hand out across the desk.

'No TV, no radio,' Lopez was saying. 'Nothing that could make a noise and alert the neighbours. Why jeopardise everything and look for another place? It was carefully chosen.' Stuart was walking him to the door. 'Why risk moving?'

Alice stood and watched. She could hear them talking but the meaning floated somewhere in another realm, inaccessible to her. She felt suddenly overcome with the kind of desolation she had not experienced since childhood.

'There were three or four of them,' Stuart said.

Alice watched, dazed. In her head she could hear the sound of wind in pine trees. She could not move. Then someone said her name and she reeled away from·them into the room, making for the open window. Behind her the door closed. The sound of men's voices faded in the hall. She pulled the rucksack from her shoulders and laid it on the window sill. She leaned out and looked down at the floodlit compound, feeling the breeze on her face.

'Sam,' she whispered.

The sound of the weakness in her voice appalled her. She tilted back her head and banged her forehead as hard as she could against the edge of the shutters. For a moment she was numb. Then she felt hands gripping her shoulders and she heard a moan that was not hers, and she fell back and the room turned.

The pain in her head was considerable. She smiled in deference to it and closed her eyes.

'You made a promise,' she said.

Stuart did not answer. He sat cupping her head in his lap, hunched low over her.

Her voice was strangled: 'You should have woken me up.'

Stuart nodded, laying a hand on her cheek.

'Santini knew who had Sam,' she said. 'You didn't. Now someone else has got him. You don't know who it is. You don't know. Do you?'

He was searching her face.

'You don't know where he is,' she said again.

'Are you in pain?' he asked.

Alice touched her forehead, running her fingers back and forth over the lump.

'Tell me,' she said.

He took her hand and held it, keeping his eyes on her.

'Someone went in and shot the person who was holding Sam. His name was Mickey da Cruz. He worked for Santini.'

Alice listened. Hot tears ran down her temples into her hair.

'Mickey had two or three accomplices. They weren't killed. They were shut in but they got out. It looks like they were Italians. Their boat was seen in the marina. Whoever took Sam left these men alive. They took the risk that they might be caught and interrogated.'

She swallowed, closing her eyes against the pain in her head. 'Sam was here. In the middle of Massaccio.' She smiled. 'I had the money. I was going to give them what they wanted and get him back. Now he's gone. No one knows where.' She paused again, her mouth trembling. 'Whoever took him is a killer.'

[202]

Stuart squeezed her hand harder.

'Santini knows who took him.'

She closed her eyes again.

'What was it like?' she asked. 'The place where they kept him?'

'He had a mattress and a duvet,' he said.

'What was it like?'

'It was like a little flat with a kitchen unit.'

'What, was he on a mattress in the corner or something? Was he tied up?'

'No. They made a separate place for him, a small space, just big enough for his mattress. He wasn't tied up.'

'Was he in the dark?'

Stuart hesitated.

'Did they have him in the dark?' she asked.

'Yes.'

She stared at him, her mouth open.

He reached under her shoulders and lifted her towards him.

'I'll find him,' he said, talking into her neck.

He was holding her against his chest. She could feel a bone pressing into her left breast, otherwise nothing. She rested her chin on his shoulder and stared at a brown smear on the white wall.

'I'll find him,' he said again.

Alice wondered if the stain was blood.

He was telling her that he would drive her back to the village. She could feel his voice reverberating in her chest. She had no wish to move: all movement seemed futile.

The lights in the car park hurt her head and she closed her eyes. He led her to his car. She rested her head against the seat and closed her eyes. She listened to the car door slamming, the ignition, the gates opening. As they moved further away from the compound, the darkness deepened. The pain in her head was now a tight crown. She opened her eyes and looked out of her window at the same road they had taken the day Sam had disappeared: the waterfront with the containers like floating skyscrapers, the strip of shabby urban coastline, the road up into the hills. The recurring scene filled her with despair.

As if he could feel it, he pulled over. They were in a lay-by. He turned off the engine and sat staring ahead of him at a whitewashed tree trunk in his headlights.

'I can't help you.' He reached for the key in the ignition and held it a moment. Then he let go and leaned back against his door. 'I can't pretend I can help you.' He gave her a sad smile.

She found it hard to breathe. She held her mouth open, waiting to breathe like Sam's fish. She looked at his hand gripping the handbrake. She was afraid to speak. That he might take his hand from the handbrake filled her with an inexplicable anxiety. She held still, breathing shallowly now; very careful.

He let go of the handbrake and reached for the key.

'Please.' He looked at her. She watched his hand on the key. 'Please help me, Stuart.'

He took his hand from the key and looked out at the tree.

'Your husband hated this place?'

She nodded.

'I do too,' he said. The quick smile came again. 'I've spent my whole life trying to be at home here or trying to turn it into a place where I can be at home.' He let go of the key. 'I wanted to leave but I couldn't. I found out there was nowhere else to go. Even though I hate it here, I can't survive anywhere else.'

She watched his hands moving as he spoke. There were three gestures that recurred like a code.

'There was someone I admired as a child,' he said. 'He was a kind of hero for people here. They still talk about him. His name was Titi Ciccioni and he was from Santarosa. He was the one who started the movement for independence. Santini had him killed and took over. He brought in his people and it became his mafia. The whole place became corrupted by his

system.' He rubbed his eyes with his thumb and forefinger
and put his hand back on the key.

'Tell me,' she said.

He looked at her.

'You're kind,' he said.

'I'm not.'

He smiled.

'No.'

He took his hand from the key and folded his arms, clasping his chest closely for protection, trapping his hands.

'Go on,' she said. She could feel his mind selecting the
words and rejecting them. She had practice at mind-reading.
But he shook his head. She rested her head against the seat
back, staring at the blanched tree trunk in his headlights.

'I've forgotten what he looks like,' she said. 'After three
years I can't picture him any more. I think that's why I kept
coming back here. I could feel him here. It's strange that this
was what he left me.'

'He left you the boys. Dan looks like him.'

He was still trapping his hands as though they might
betray him if he let go of them.

'How do you know he looks like him?'

'I remember him.'

'Who?'

'Your husband.' He paused, but did not face her. 'His aunt
used to give tea parties for the village children. I went a few
times.' At last he looked at her. 'I was older than him by about
five years.'

He looked happy, suddenly, and Alice smiled in marvel.

'You can help me, Stuart.'

His hand flew to the key again. The ease had vanished.
Again she could feel the inner shuffling as he searched for the
words.

'What is it?'

He folded his arms.

'When I was about Sam's age something happened. I did

[205]

something I can't forgive myself for.' There was an urgency in his tone, as though he feared she might stop him. 'My mother had died. About two years before. Me and my sister were very close. She followed me everywhere. There was this place we used to go after school, this man's place in the hills behind the village.' He passed his palm over his mouth.

Alice was suddenly afraid to hear what he had to say. The windows were up and it was too hot, but she held still.

'We'd go up to this man's place. Lucien, his name was. He made knives, good ones in layered steel. People came up from Massaccio to buy them. We'd go and watch him in his workshop, slicing the steel thin as paper, folding it.' He freed his hands, resuming his code. 'He had wood, different essences for the handles, and he let us make things. Beatrice was only small but she could carve. So he let us use his tools. Anyway, it was one Sunday, after Mass.' He paused again, pressing his thumb and forefinger into his eye sockets. Alice watched, hardly daring to move. 'Me and Beatrice were round the back of the workshop. Lucien was inside and I remember the sound of the machinery. He asked me to chop some cherry logs. I did it all the time. I don't know how it happened. All I remember is raising the axe and letting it fall and suddenly Beatrice's hand was there. I remember looking at her and then looking at her bloody fingers lying on the block. I remember thinking they looked like giblets from a bird. I didn't understand at first because she wasn't making a sound. Her mouth was open for a scream but she was silent. I was screaming.'

Alice watched him swallow, his Adam's apple rising and falling. She held still. He rubbed his eyes then began using his hands again.

'After that she fainted. Lucien carried her down to the village and I ran behind. He had her two fingers in a hand-kerchief. I heard him tell my dad not to be too hard on me. He said it was punishment enough what I'd done to her. But my dad shut me in the dark until the first day of school.

It was the beginning of summer, so it was almost three months alone in the dark.' He nodded his head as if he were congratulating his father for his rigour. 'Anyway, when I saw Beatrice again, everything was different. It's never been the same between us since. Not so much because of the accident but because she wasn't allowed to be attached to me after that.'

He looked out at the tree in his headlights. Alice studied his profile, traced it in her mind, learned it, like an object of value, worthy of respect.

'It was these two,' he said, moving his hand back and forth like a gentle knife over his index and middle fingers. 'I've never mentioned it to anyone before.' He shrugged. 'Don't know why.'

Alice looked at his hands, now quiet in his lap.

'You're telling me because of Sam. You know what it's like for him.'

He shook his head.

'I can't say that. It's not the same. I'm telling you because . . . I don't know why I'm telling you.'

Without raising her head she held out her hand, palm upwards. He put his hand on hers and she closed her fingers. She sat still, looking down at his hand in hers.

'It's not the same,' he said. 'Sam's done nothing wrong.'

'Nor had you.'

She was not prepared for the look of gratitude he gave her and she let go of his hand. He seemed to return to himself in an instant. He turned on the ignition and drove. She looked at his hand on the gear lever, at the smooth dark skin, the swollen veins. She looked at his face, slashed with lines, and recognised what she felt as pity.

Chapter Twenty-Six

When Coco hit her, Liliane believed it was proof that the edifice was crumbling. His ring struck her molar through her cheek and made the inside of her mouth bleed. The taste of blood had always made her sick and she went into the bathroom to throw up. She knew that if she had stayed in bed, he would not have struck her. But she had stepped in his way as he paced up and down in the bedroom and he had seen her smallness and her ugliness, and it had just made him angrier. When she still denied knowing where Nathalie was, he gave up. He had always overestimated his effect on her, in every matter, even sexual.

Liliane spat the last of her vomit into the toilet and flushed. The process that she had set in motion when she had joined the marching women was even darker and more threatening than she had imagined. She looked at her face in the bathroom mirror and give herself a ghastly smile, then went back into the bedroom and climbed into bed.

Coco was dialling Georges Rocca again. On the dressing table, which had belonged to her mother, were a lace doily under a pane of glass and several framed photographs of Nathalie, none of their son. Coco had destroyed them all. He used to like saying, 'I'm not a violent man.' He had said it so often in the beginning that he and everyone else came to believe it. Liliane had always known how violent he could be. He only delegated the violence as a way of not falling prey to it.

From the look on his face, she saw that Georges was telling him what everyone else knew. It was a look of disgust. Coco looked at her while he listened to the details of his daughter's liaison. Liliane held his stare. His instructions were calm and addressed to her.

'Get him, Georges,' he said. 'Deal with him as soon as you can. Give him what he wants. Use the strong stuff. You know where it is.' Then he looked at the telephone and hung up. 'You', he said jabbing his finger at her, 'are an unfit mother. You knew about this.'

Liliane touched the ragged edge of her sliced cheek with her tongue. She knew not to answer him. She could see the weakness in him, flickering there. All her being told her to stay quiet, to protect her daughter.

'Liliane.'

'Yes, Claude.'

He gestured vaguely towards his face.

'Your mouth . . .' He jerked his head up. 'There's some blood.' Liliane wiped her mouth with the back of her hand. 'You know where they are,' he said.

'I don't.'

She faced him. She knew how he saw her: her face, round and pale and flaccid, with black pebbles for eyes, too ugly for dishonesty.

'I'm going to punish her,' he said. 'She has to be punished, otherwise we'll lose her. You understand that, don't you?'

Liliane looked down at her neat hands, smeared with blood, resting on the bedclothes.

'You understand that, Liliane!' he shouted.

'Yes,' she said. 'I understand.'

But there was still a little tremor inside her, left over from the march, and she lay back and cupped her bosom beneath the covers, as if she were cupping a flame in the wind.

Chapter Twenty-Seven

In a small, bare room that smelled of paint on the fifteenth floor of Les Mimosas, Nathalie Santini lay beneath Raymond, listening to the sound of his breathing. She stroked his back with the tips of her fingers. He was her man, she told herself. Whatever happened. He was heavier now that he was fast asleep, and he was breathing into her hair. She wanted to laugh. This was the feeling she had been waiting for all her life. She closed her eyes and asked God to let her die now.

He had called her from the police station. He was crying. 'I'm sick,' he told her. She knew how sick he was and she understood his wish to destroy himself. It was a part of him and she respected it. He had told her he had no money to score with. 'I lie to everyone,' he said. 'I can't lie to you.'

'Raymond needs me,' she had told her mother. She had taken the bus into town. He was waiting for her outside the gates of the police station. She had thought he was dying. His skin was grey and he was sweating. He could hardly walk, he was so out of breath, but he had smiled at her. 'My angel,' he had said. She had given him her communion necklace, which was gold with pearls and more than enough, and they had walked to his dealer's house. She had waited for him outside. 'I'll be five minutes,' he had said and he had taken an hour at least, but even the waiting was a kind of bliss.

She turned her head and looked towards the window. A beautiful blue light was coming through the net curtains. She had given her body; that had been easy. He had not even needed to ask. There had been such a silence between them – in the hall of Les Mimosas and in the lift – there had been no room for words. The feeling was so strong, she had found it hard to breathe.

He had undressed her carefully, as though he needed to concentrate. When she was naked he had knelt down, as if he worshipped her, and she had knelt down too. She had not made a sound, even when it hurt. He had wiped the tears away and kissed her without consoling her. There was no need. Her lips and face still hurt from his kisses. Before he fell asleep, he told her again that she was his angel and that she could save him. He had spoken with great seriousness and she believed she could.

She wanted to leave Raymond while he slept. She didn't want to say goodbye. She slid carefully from under him. He sighed and turned on to his side. She sat on the edge of the mattress and looked at the smooth curve of his back and the dark gully that ran down the middle. She wanted to touch him but she stopped herself, believing that love required great discipline. She thought of her mother, who had only ever wanted her happiness. She would be waiting up for her, would pretend that she had slept and ask no questions. This thought made Nathalie rise, gather her clothes and quietly leave the room.

Downstairs in the utility room, Georges Rocca held his sleeve to his nostrils to block out the sickly smell that was emanating from two community dustbins. He had a good view of the entrance to the building and could not be seen. He had just told Coco that he had found them. 'Call me,' he had said. 'Day or night.' When Nathalie Santini came through the glass door, Georges was scrutinising his tie, just back from the cleaners, noting with irritation that the pale mark was indeed a stain and not part of the bright, diagonal brush-stroke motif as the Vietnamese woman had insisted. When he looked up the girl was halfway across the courtyard. In her walk she was still a child. For Georges, eliminating Raymond posed no problem whatsoever. He didn't have a daughter himself but his sympathies were right behind Coco.

When she had gone, Georges picked up the leather attaché

case from between his feet and emerged from the utility room. The case contained three hypodermic needles, a very large dose of uncut heroin, a pair of miniature brass scales, a copy of *Penthouse*, twenty-three parking tickets in an envelope addressed to 'the care and attention of Lieutenant Capelli', a packet of four fluorescent markers, a gold fountain pen, a description sheet with interior and exterior photographs of a property for sale in The Hesperides beach complex, a packet of Lexomil and a box of fifty .38 'special' bullets.

He made his way towards the building, his metal heels striking the concrete and echoing all around him. One leg was slightly shorter than the other and so his gait was distinctive, a little unsettling, he felt. The two skinheads were on either side of him before he reached the door. They were a whole head taller than him but this in no way diminished his authority. He'd told them Raymond was an Arab, to incite enthusiasm. They wouldn't know the difference.

'This is easy,' he said, as they stepped into the lift. 'Too easy for you two,' he said, winking at them. The boys grinned eagerly at him. He could see them both trying to avoid looking at the growth on his nose. One of the boys had a left ear that looked as if it had been gnawed by a dog. Otherwise you could hardly tell them apart. They were wearing exactly the same clothes: black bomber jackets, white T-shirts, jackboots, pale jeans, even the belts with the New Order symbol for a buckle.

'He'll still be stoned,' Georges told them. 'So let's try to do it without waking him up, shall we?' The boys nodded earnestly. 'I want neatness and precision. I want no adrenaline in the blood. Right? You hold him down while I shoot him up. Couldn't be easier. If you're disciplined I'll use you again. Is that clear?'

The skinheads nodded.

With the nonchalance of a TV cable sales team, the three of them stepped out of the lift and walked down the freshly painted corridor.

Thursday

Chapter Twenty-Eight

Since Raymond had come into her life, Nathalie had let her hair out of its plait. It now hung down in an undulating mass, stray pieces clinging to her tear-stained face. Her mother, sitting beside her on her bed, tried to tidy it a little. The news had come to the village in the early afternoon and they could still hear Raymond's mother, Incarna Battesti, and the terrible monotony of her crying, echoing in the courtyard next door. Habit told people not to believe in the overdose. Then, when they discovered Nathalie had slept out, no one doubted Coco was behind the boy's death.

Liliane contemplated her daughter's misery. The horror of it had worn off. Now that she was bent on action it didn't hurt so much so see her child's suffering. Soon they would both be rid of him.

As if he'd heard her thoughts Coco banged once on the door, hard. She imagined the gesture, a clenched fist and a lateral punch outwards from the chest.

Liliane stood up and walked towards the door. Nathalie sat on her bed clutching her knees to her chest.

Coco stepped into the room and jabbed his finger at Nathalie, who hid her face.

'I forbid you to shed a single tear over him. He was a junkie. He'd give you up for one dose of his drug. Don't you understand that, you stupid child!' He turned on Liliane. 'You knew that!' He flung an arm out, pointing to his daughter. 'Why did you let her see him?' Suddenly his face softened. 'Did you have him here? he asked. 'Did you receive him?'

Liliane faced him. She called to mind what she was about to do, how he would soon fall anyway. She closed her eyes.

Then he struck her for the second time that day. The force of the blow knocked her against Nathalie's little desk. Her child's clutter, carefully arranged, fell to the floor. While Liliane gasped for breath she saw Nathalie run at her father.

'I hate you!' she sobbed. 'I hate you. I've always hated you and I always will.'

Coco watched her sink to the floor. She knelt on the carpet, her legs splayed on either side of her, shaking with tears. Coco towered over her, a new expression of detachment on his face. Without looking at Liliane, he left the room.

Liliane went to her daughter and put her arms around her. Downstairs the front door slammed.

'He's gone,' Liliane said. 'He'll stay at the villa now. Nathalie?'

She looked up at her mother.

'Why didn't you call me? I could have told you he was coming home,' Liliane said.

'Why didn't he stay with his whore?'

'He's in trouble.'

'Good. I hope they kill him.'

Liliane was shocked. Nathalie had never indicated that she was aware of what her father was. Now it came as a relief to her. For the first time in her life, she felt she had an ally.

'Mum.'

'Yes, my angel.'

'I loved him. I could have saved him.'

Liliane looked into her daughter's face. The childishness was still there, in the swollen mouth, the full cheeks.

'I know you loved him.'

'I don't want to go on living, Mum. I don't. Do you understand?'

Liliane nodded, unable to speak.

'They were the best moments of my life. They were the only moments.'

Liliane knew she had not acted quickly enough. But there was nothing to stop her now. She could avenge her daughter and her son. She breathed in the smell of Nathalie's hair and moved back and forth to the lullaby in her head. She would sit by her tonight and tomorrow night, and every morning she would be there when her child woke up.

Chapter Twenty-Nine

Karim watched Philippe Garetta moving further away in the moonlight. A canvas army sack filled with their bedding hung across his back. He was walking too fast along the narrow path, loosening the splintered rock with his tread. They were on a narrow shelf overhanging a drop to their right so deep he could not see the bottom. There was something that spooked Karim about Garetta. His movements, his whole bearing, made him nervous. And he had noted the Browning that Garetta kept in his right boot.

Karim hugged close to the cliff wall, his eyes averted from the gorge. He was carrying the child on his shoulder. He could feel its body was stiff with fear. As soon as the path widened a little, he stopped. Denis halted behind him.

'Garetta!' Karim called, but Garetta carried on. Karim watched him, then turned to Denis. He was carrying a cardboard box and two holdalls, one on each shoulder, full of provisions.

'Here. We'll swap. You can carry him. He's so stiff, he weighs a ton.'

'I'm not taking him here,' Denis said.

Karim studied him. His dark eyes shone like an innocent's no matter what he put into his body and no matter what evil he did. But there was a leak in the left eye, a little of the black had spilled into the white like a tiny worm. Karim patted him on the cheek.

'I need a smoke,' Karim said.

'Let's move,' Denis said. 'Or we'll lose him.'

Garetta had disappeared.

They walked on. The child on Karim's shoulder was in some kind of spasm. It occurred to him that he might die.

'Inshallah,' he said aloud.

The path curved sharply to the left and stopped in front of a steep rock. Karim looked up to find Garetta leaning over him, his long curls hanging down.

'Pass me the kid,' Garetta said.

An unpleasant hierarchy seemed to have settled between them: Garetta at the top, then himself, then Denis. Karim was not used to taking orders from anyone except Santini, who had led him to believe that Garetta would be his equal in this. But Garetta had forced him into a two-hour ride on the back of a trial bike when there was room in the car. Denis rode Garetta's Cagiva hunched over and with such concentration, it was tiring to be a part of it. Karim had so far not found the opportunity of talking about his feelings. Relieved to get the child off his back, he held him up to Garetta, who grabbed him under the arms and hauled him out of sight. Karim stepped away from the rock face to avoid the shower of dust and stones that fell in his wake.

'This is no good for me,' Karim said to Denis. 'We're going to have to have a conversation.' He reached out to find a hold on the rock and pulled himself up.

Before him stretched a plateau of long grass flooded with moonlight that sloped gradually upwards to a wood in the distance. Garetta was already halfway towards the trees, the child and the sack on his back. Karim stood there looking at the silver plain until Garetta had disappeared into the wood.

'Hey, Karim!'

Karim turned and looked down at Denis.

'Take the fucking box.'

He knelt down and took the box. There seemed to be a lot of tinned cassoulet.

'Shit. He knows I don't eat this shit.'

'Karim! For fuck's sake.'

Denis handed up the bags to him, one after the other, then climbed up.

'You can take the bags,' Denis said and he picked up the box. 'Where's he gone?'

Karim nodded towards the wood and Denis walked off.

Garetta had flattened the grass, leaving a trail that caught the moonlight and shone brighter. Karim opened his eyes wide. It felt as if he was experiencing night for the first time and he did not like it. Night in the city was nothing like this. This sky with all its stars was too close. It felt as if the night were pressing up against him like some whore licking his face and the moon coating everything with its sleazy light.

Denis was far ahead of him. Karim hung the bags from each shoulder and followed. The long grass brushing against his legs as he walked sickened him. Nothing had prepared him for a place like this. Not his life in Massaccio where he was a prince with a black BMW 328i which yelped and flashed its headlights when he pressed the remote-control locking device; not his origin, which he draped over his person like a mantle but of which he knew nothing, for all he had from Algeria was a photo of the Djijelli football team taken in 1965, his father in the front row, second from the left. His dad had died the year he was born in a stupid accident at the port and so he told people he had been killed by the French during the war of independence. Karim had managed to live his whole life on the island without ever coming near a place like this. As if he had known all along that if Allah was anywhere, He was up here.

When he reached the trees, Denis had disappeared. The wood was so dark, for a moment he could not see and he held his arms out in front of him, moving forward step by step, afraid to breathe. He wished he knew one prayer, just one of the many his mother had sung to him at bedtime when he was little, before she had lost him. She had never learned French and he had never learned Arabic, and so they had been separated and all her weeping and kissing had just set them further apart.

When he emerged from the wood into the clearing, Garetta and Denis were waiting for him. Garetta had a smug look on his face.

'You got a problem?' Karim said, dropping the bags.

Garetta shook his head slowly.

'You,' he said, adjusting the position of the child's body on his shoulder. 'I think you have a problem. I think you're out of your depth.'

Denis was staring at him too and Karim realised he was perspiring heavily.

'Let's just move, okay?' he said. 'How far is it?'

'We're here,' Garetta said.

On the far side of the clearing was a low stone hut with no windows. The roof had caved in at one end and a tree had sprung up inside the hut, its branches growing out through the hole.

'That?' Karim said. A toothpick had materialised in Denis's fingers and he began picking his perfect teeth. 'If they find us here, there's no way out,' Karim told Garetta. 'We're trapped.'

But Garetta was carrying the child towards the hut.

'They won't find us,' he said, ducking to pass through the door.

Karim looked at Denis but he was still picking his teeth. It was impossible for him to think straight in this place, so he sat down on one of the bags and began to roll a spliff.

Sam could feel the hard ground against his back but it still felt as if he was falling through the air. His whole body was tense, waiting for the landing. His legs and arms were tied up so tightly he couldn't feel them any more. There was a small hole in the roof and he could see the big round moon. He knew that if he turned over and faced the ground, the falling might stop, but he could not take his eyes off the moon, which was trying to tell him something.

Sam wished they had left him in the cupboard. When they had pulled him out he had felt like one of his stick insects being ripped off its branch. He wished they had left him in the dark with the man talking to him through the wall. The new men didn't talk. The tall one looked like his wolf puppet. Sam kept his eyes on the moon. As long as he looked at the shining moon he would not see the skinny man's head again, all bloody on the floor.

As he fell backwards Sam felt that he was un-growing. He was seven years old – the age of reason, his mother called it – but now he was going back through his life to before he was born. He could remember what it had been like inside his mother. It was warm, as though he had an invisible blanket on him that weighed nothing. Sometimes tiny bubbles ran along his skin and burst, which felt like the lightest rain in the world. He had heard his father's voice and felt him pressing down on his mother and he had smiled and said, Hello, Dad, but his dad couldn't hear. He remembered being a little kid, too. His nose ran all the time and he could hardly walk and hardly talk. His life was like a dream. Then he had woken up; when Dan arrived, he had woken up. Now he was back in that dream again. He was un-growing.

When he had come out of the dream he had wanted to know what other people saw when they looked at him. He had held his mother's face in his hands and looked into the dark mirror of her eyes.

'Mummy. What do you see when you look at me?'

'A handsome boy.'

'No, I mean what do you see?'

His mother never completely understood.

The moon was her face smiling down at him in his cot.

Karim woke up with a headache and a dry mouth. He was lying on the long, brittle grass, his head resting on his bedroll, which he had not bothered to undo. It was the moon-light that had woken him and there was a noise, like a distant motorway, which had reached him in his sleep. He stood up and looked around. The moon was still covering the clearing with its obscene light. Denis was asleep a few paces away from him, tucked up in his sleeping bag like a dead knight, his hands folded on his belly. He was forcing air out through his closed lips with little puffing noises. Garetta was in the hut with the child.

Karim walked round to the back of the hut. He walked through the long grass to a track that disappeared into a gorse thicket. He followed the track towards the noise. The gorse pricked his legs through his jeans. The track began to descend steeply and the gorse was replaced by thin, twisted trees that rose on either side of him. Karim began to jog, keeping his knees bent, down the track that had become a staircase of stones. A breeze had come up and there was a smell of mildew. The track levelled out and stopped suddenly on the edge of a precipice. He was standing on a ledge, looking into another gorge. Down below him the waterfall sprang from the dark forest into a deeper darkness. He could see its white foam shining in the moonlight and feel the cold air it generated on his face. The sound of the water was terrible.

He stood there swaying on the edge of the precipice, the noise emptying his mind. Then he pulled back and ran up the path as fast as he could.

When he reached the hut he stood beside the entrance breathless, his back against the wall, and listened to Garetta talking on the phone.

'He's asleep,' he said. There was a pause. 'If you don't, he'll sleep for ever,' he said. 'No. Thirty million or nothing. You've got a week to get the rest.'

Karim waited, listening to the sound of Garetta moving about inside the hut. Then he stepped through the door. Inside it was cold and it smelled of goat-shit.

'You called her,' he said.

Garetta was standing in the middle of the hut with his back to him. His head almost touched the rafters. He turned round. His expression was calm.

'You said we'd call in the morning,' Karim said.

'It is the morning,' Garetta said.

'We should have made the call together.'

[223]

'I heard you get up and I went out to get you. But you'd disappeared.'

Karim stared. He recalled his terror before the waterfall and felt ashamed. He drove his hands into his pockets.

'So what did she say?'

Garetta glanced at the boy, who was lying on his back in the corner, his knees up. Karim could not see if his eyes were closed or open. Garetta stooped as he passed through the door. Karim followed him outside.

'So?' Karim said.

'No more weed,' Garetta said. 'I don't want you stoned up here.'

Karim smiled.

'Let's talk about the phone call.'

Garetta pointed at him.

'No weed up here or you're out.'

Karim looked at him. He was not taking orders from Garetta. Still he grinned and swiped the air with his palm.

'I need all my faculties, right?' he said. Garetta studied him. 'So what did you say to the woman?'

'I told her we wanted thirty million and I gave her a week.'

'And? What did she say?'

'She said she wouldn't even talk about ransom until she'd heard her child's voice. I told her he was asleep, so she said she wouldn't pay a penny until she heard him. I said if you don't pay he'll sleep for ever.'

Garetta reached into the pocket of his leather jacket and pulled out some tobacco and papers. Karim watched him roll a very thin cigarette.

'And?' he said.

Garetta lit the paper.

'She asked me to take the nine million she already had.'

'What did you say?'

'I said I wasn't interested.'

'What?'

'I said I wasn't interested.'

'What's all this "I" shit?'

Garetta was concentrating on smoking his roll-up.

'This is Santini's deal, not yours. I'm here because Santini hired me. I'm not working for you.'

Garetta exhaled the smoke noisily, studying the roll-up in his hand.

'Listen, Garetta. I'm not staying up here in this shithole for another week.'

Garetta looked up.

'Do you know how long ETA holds people?'

'I don't fucking care.'

'They can hold a man for two years. Do you understand? They cut themselves off from the world and they sacrifice their petty appetites for a higher cause. They're strong and they're focused. You've been up here five minutes and you're already shitting yourself.'

'All I'm saying is you're going to have to be a bit cooler, man. I mean share,' he said, making a give-and-take motion with his hands. 'We're in this together.'

Garetta appeared not to be listening. Karim shifted slightly and Garetta turned on him.

'And this place is not a shithole!' he shouted, stepping towards Karim. 'This is the most beautiful place in the world.' The man was too close. Karim could see his jaw muscles working. 'You're not up here to get rich,' Garetta went on. 'You're up here so that we can take back this paradise for the oppressed.' He flicked his roll-up into the long grass. 'I'm not interested in her nine million. I'm not going out for nine million. We won't even get started on nine million.'

Karim looked up into Garetta's dark face. The moon was behind him.

'You're not joking, right? You never did have a sense of humour, so this isn't a joke. Right? Am I right, or what?' Garetta folded his arms and waited. He was much too close but Karim did not move. 'Listen, man, I don't give a shit about politics,' he said. 'If I needed politics I'd have joined the FNL, but I didn't. I chose to work for Santini because the man has an independent mind. If I'm up here' – he paused, looking around him – 'in this shithole, it's because Santini asked me to come. And if you're here it's because Santini wants you here. So if the woman offered nine million, I think you should have talked to Santini before you turned it down.'

Garetta grabbed hold of his sweatshirt at the neck. Karim could feel how the weed had taken the edge off his reflexes. He looked back into Garetta's eyes while all his nerves hummed uselessly.

Suddenly Garetta let go of him. Karim turned round and saw Denis sitting up in his sleeping bag, watching them.

'Denis,' Karim said. 'Okay. Now we can all have a talk.'

'You can talk,' Garetta told them, walking off into the hut. 'I'm going to sleep.'

Karim watched him go, aware that he had lost.

'It's this place,' he said, turning to Denis. 'What the fuck are we doing here, anyway? What was Coco thinking of when he hired this lunatic?' He smoothed out his sweatshirt. It was white, with the word 'Thermocooler' printed in black sci-fi letters across the front. He had not seen the point of it when Nadia had given it to him and he had been angry. Now he stroked it lovingly. 'I mean what is this shit about the oppressed?' He looked at Denis's patient face and made a decision. 'I'm calling Santini.' He clicked his fingers at Denis for the phone that was in Denis's jacket.

'You can't.'

Denis was still sitting up, his legs trapped in his sleeping bag. Karim strode towards him and punched him hard on the upper arm, right on the nerve. It took a few seconds for the pain to show on Denis's face.

'Give me the phone.'

Denis clutched his shoulder and with his free hand found the phone. Karim leaned down and snatched it from him.

'I'm a professional,' he said. 'I haven't kept clear of those nutcases in the FNL all this time just to end up in some headbanger's fantasy.' He punched out the number of Evelyne's mobile. 'The mother offered to give him nine million straight up,' he told Denis. 'He should have taken it then seen about the rest. We'd still have the kid, but at least we'd have some cash.'

'It'd be a risk collecting the money,' Denis said.

Karim ignored him.

'Pick it up, pick it up, Evelyne.'

'It's the middle of the night,' Denis said.

'Shut up, Denis.'

Karim called the main number for the villa and waited. It rang seven times, then Evelyne answered.

'Yes?'

'It's me.'

There was a pause, then Santini's voice.

'Yes?'

'It's me.'

'Don't call here.'

'Wait!' Karim shouted. He was still there. 'Call me from a clean phone. It's important.'

Karim heard Santini's breath in the mouthpiece. Then a kind of grunt, which Karim knew was acquiescence. He hung up and began to pace while he waited. Santini was being watched but he'd think of something. Karim smiled at Denis triumphantly then went over to his own bedroll to make up his bed. How could Garetta sleep in that stinking hut? Karim climbed into his sleeping bag and lay back clutching the phone. It was good to know that Santini's voice could reach him up here in this shithole.

Friday

Chapter Thirty

The bathwater had begun to cool and tiny air bubbles had settled on Alice's skin. Here in the water she could get through the night. Her sternum was red from trying to rub away the pain in her chest. In the water, she could feel her heart, the poor beating thing, for the hanging sac of blood that it was. The tap, dripping slowly on to her left foot, was a more soothing pulse on which she could focus.

She sank beneath the water, tilting back her head. When she was beneath the surface she believed Sam was alive. Underwater she found a preternatural logic. Their bond was inviolable. She was his mother. So long as she was here, so was he.

She came up and gasped for air. The bubbles on her skin had gone. She added more hot water. She recalled the kidnapper's voice, the calm brutality in it. He had not let her speak to Sam and she had not been afraid then, only very angry. Now she was afraid and she began to sob. She reached forward, turned off the tap and sat clutching her knees, weeping. She sobbed deeply, begging it not to happen. 'Mummy,' she said. 'Please help me.'

She lay back and let her tears subside underwater. She was the mother. No one could rescue her. She was the one.

When she came up again she was calm. She looked down at her body in the water. She had always felt towards it a detached appreciation, as though it did not belong to her but was on loan. Mathieu had made love to her as though he too believed that her body was beside the point. She closed her eyes and ran her fingers up the middle of her abdomen and between her breasts. She opened her eyes and looked at her hands on her breasts, the long fingers not quite able to contain them. She thought of Stuart, downstairs in the kitchen. His love for her filled the house. She saw his head resting on her breasts, kissing away her fingers. She saw his hair, wet from the bath.

Downstairs Stuart opened his eyes and reached for the alarm clock on the floor beside the bed. It was 5 a.m. He had been asleep for less than two hours. Accustomed as he was to a hollow, dreamless sleep, the sensation of the dream now slipping through his mind was a little unpleasant. He got up, put on his underpants and opened the shutters, then the French windows, and stepped on to the wet grass. There seemed to be no light in the sky and yet the garden was so sharply defined, the pine trees on the lawn looked like cut-outs. All was too still and too luminous and Stuart felt as though he had burst in on the natural world while it was undergoing some secret mutation. He went back in to dress, leaving footprints of dew on Constance Colonna's parquet floor.

He made his bed, his throat burning from the packet of cigarettes he had smoked in the night to keep himself awake. It was good to be smoking again. He picked up his watch from the side-table. He was aware that he was running out of time: Mesguish was filing a report to Central Office about his treatment of the case. The idea of losing his job did not alarm him. Only Gérard's distress, carefully dissimulated over the phone, had bothered him. He recalled his deputy's plaintive tenor: 'Be careful, Stuart. He can do you a lot of damage.'

'It's much too late for that.'

He went into the kitchen. The room was quiet and filled with the bizarre grey glow of dawn. He did not turn on the light. He poured a mountain of coffee into the filter and turned on the machine. That night he had sat here, at the table with Alice, waiting for the call. She had drunk whisky and he had smoked. She had talked to him – about her son mostly, about his problems at school and with other children. She had been so careful not to talk about herself and he had still heard the anguish in her. He had been careful himself – careful not to look at her, because he knew if he did, his eyes would make some impossible request. At 2 a.m. the call had come and she had stood up and walked calmly over to the phone on the wall. When he nodded, she had picked it up. She was composed and determined and he had wondered if it was the whisky. He had feared that the strange energy would subside in the night and leave her with the knowledge that her son was further, much further, from reach.

'Stuart.' He spun round. She was standing in the doorway. 'The water. You forgot the water.'

The coffee machine was spitting and smelled of roasting metal. Alice sat down at the table. Her hair was wet.

'It's early,' he said, filling the machine with water. She was wearing jeans and a white T-shirt. Her face looked different in the morning; he thought he could see the child in her. She sat with her bare arms folded on the table.

'Do you want some coffee?' he asked.

'Please.'

He could see that the energy was still there. He felt a sudden urge to smile and he turned his back on her to watch the coffee machine.

'Did you sleep?' she asked.

'A little.' Stuart's dream came and went. He turned round. 'You?'

She nodded.

He touched his forehead: 'Your head okay?'

She ran her fingers over the bruise.

'It's fine.' She scratched her arm. 'Do you think they'll take the money?'

Perhaps this was her making conversation.

'Yes,' he said. 'I do.'

She stared at him, but this time he did not look away. Her face flushed and he saw her swallow. She looked down and he thought she might cry.

He took what coffee there was, found two cups and set them

on the table. She watched him pour, still scratching her arm.

'Mosquitoes,' she said.

He sat down beside her. She took a sip of coffee.

'When the next call comes you tell them you're finding the rest,' he said. 'Keep the tone you had last night. It was good.'

She put the cup down and listened. There again was the child in her. She must have always done everything right in her life; hence the question he sometimes caught in her eyes: What have I done?

'They'll only consider negotiating with someone who's in control,' he went on. She considered this a moment, then drained her cup. 'You take your car to Santini's,' he said. 'Like we said. I'll be waiting outside. You won't see me, but I'll be there.'

She nodded.

'Make him feel you're depending on him. Maintain whatever thrill he's getting out of helping you.'

Stuart regretted the tenor of the remark, but her expression did not change. He could see the faint stripe running down the middle of her smooth forehead, a shadow of the vein that marked her distress.

'You think he's killed two people in one week. First the kidnapper and then the junkie.'

'I do.' He finished his coffee, now cold. He was aware of her watching him.

'Your colleague, Paul,' she said. 'He doesn't like women very much, does he?'

Stuart looked at the freckle on her lip and then turned away.

'I've never thought about it. You may be right. Yes. You're right.'

'They admire you,' she said.

Stuart realised that she pitied him. He smiled, stood up and took the cups to the sink.

'I'll go and get dressed,' she said.

He nodded, keeping his back to her as she left the room.

*

At six Gérard came for his shift. As Stuart climbed into his car, Alice appeared just behind him. She was barefoot on the gravel path. She rested her hands on the open window. She was wearing the same blue dress she had worn when they met.

'Will you call me straight after Santini's?' she asked.

'Of course.'

He turned the ignition key and she stepped back. In his wing mirror he watched her turn and walk towards the house. As he drove out through the iron gates he felt a sense of purpose entirely unfamiliar to him.

On the way down the hill he called Christine Lasserre. He had begun to feel uncomfortable every time he thought of her and was about to hang up when he heard her voice.

'Madame.'

'Where have you been?' Her voice was low and calm. Stuart wound up the window. He still did not know how much he would tell her.

'Did you get the report from ballistics?' he asked.

'Yes. What are you doing, Stuart?'

'Going into the office.'

'What's going on?'

'The new kidnappers called last night at two a.m. They asked for thirty million.'

Lasserre was silent.

'This is quite a different case,' she said at last.

'Why? Why is it different? It's the same case.'

'What's the matter with you, Stuart?'

'Nothing.'

There was another pause.

'Do you have anything on the first group?'

'The boat was dumped in Rimini. The Italians are looking for two members of the Camora. Brothers.'

'Do we know them?'

'No.'

'Do you trust the Italians?'

'Yes. We have a good relationship. It's one of the things

that's been held against me, my relationship with the Italians.'

'Stuart, could you talk to me as if I weren't your enemy for a moment? It's very tiring. I'd like to know what you think.'

'You know what I think.'

'Tell me again,' she said.

'Where's Mesguish?'

'At the commissariat. Awaiting your instructions. Like the rest of us.'

'Did you see his report?'

'I did.' She paused but Stuart kept quiet. 'He wants Central Office to transfer the case to Paris. Zanetecci is seriously considering it.'

'So what's stopping them?'

'I am.'

'Why?'

'Stop being childish. Your job is to keep me informed.'

Stuart hesitated. He was too isolated without Lasserre.

He took the short-cut through the industrial zone in the eastern suburbs of Massaccio. Ahead of him was a huge grain silo like a great pink cathedral in the dawn sun.

'We picked up a conversation between Madame Aron and Santini,' he told her.

'What do you mean "picked up"?'

'On the scanner.'

'So it can't be used,' she said wearily.

'No.'

'And?' she said.

'He told her not to worry. That he thought he knew who had Sam.'

'When?' she asked.

'Just before we discovered Mickey.'

'What were his exact words?'

'He said, "I think we might have them."'

'Too ambiguous. You can't use it anyway,' she said.

'Santini's lent the woman nine million francs.'

'What did he do that for?'

'He . . . He likes her.'

Lasserre let him wait.

'You think Santini had da Cruz killed, then took over the kidnapping using some of his people.' Stuart saw her sitting there fingering that pendant of hers. 'Why?'

'He's in trouble. The FNL are all over the place. They're taking over some of the best clubs.'

Stuart knew how unconvincing he sounded. He looked at the palm trees along the seafront and wound down the window. The air was close and there was no wind.

'You think he's behind the new group, don't you?'

Stuart did not answer.

'Are you still there?'

'Yes,' he said. He hoped she would go on.

'You opened a new file for the bombing. Why was that? Did you think it was linked?'

'No.'

'Do you now?' she asked.

'I don't know, but I don't think it's a good idea to link them anyway. It just reduces our options.'

'What are you hiding, Stuart? I'm bored of guessing.'

It was good to talk to somebody.

'I had Raymond in custody in connection with the bombing. As soon as I let him out someone went in and administered a rhinoceros's fix of pure heroin. He was sleeping with Santini's daughter.'

Lasserre whistled.

'He's careful. You'll never get him for something like that.'

'We can squeeze him, though.'

'Probably not. Listen, Stuart. Use Lopez. Get him to do a story on Raymond.'

'Lopez is scared,' he said.

'Send him to me.'

'All right.' He opened the compound gates and drove through. 'I'm here.'

'Good. Keep me informed, Stuart. I'm on your side.'

He hung up. As he opened the door of his car he heard the phone ringing in his office. He ran across the compound and up the steps. He punched out the door code. The ringing stopped.

The Cesari boy was in the hall, standing beside the coffee machine waiting for it to deliver. He had been on night shift, monitoring calls. The boy plucked the plastic cup from the machine and held it out to Stuart.

'No. You have it.' The boy hesitated. 'How was your night?' Stuart asked him. 'Did you manage to get anywhere with that call?'

The boy's face brightened.

'It's a mobile. I got the area. But it's quite large.'

'Where is it?'

'In the hills behind the Palomba Rossa. The relay covers about fifty square kilometres. It's mountainous, though, so Telecom can eliminate the areas that are unreachable.'

'Call Fabrice,' Stuart said. 'He knows someone straight at Telecom. I've forgotten his name.'

'Commissaire Mesguish called just before you arrived. He's coming at eight-thirty.'

'Anything else?'

'Someone called Santini at two-twenty a.m.'

Stuart stared at Cesari.

'Where?'

'At the villa.'

'Why didn't you tell me?'

Cesari raised his arms and dropped them hopelessly at his sides.

'Sorry, Commissaire. I didn't know . . .'

'Did you recognise them?'

'No, I didn't.'

'No one you've ever heard before?'

'No.' The Cesari boy looked worried.

'Can I hear it?'

'Yes, of course.' The boy led the way, but the phone began

to ring again. 'Commissaire,' he said as Stuart turned away. 'I'm sorry about the other day. I don't know how we lost him.'

'Forget it,' Stuart said, heading towards his office. 'He's easy to lose.'

But it was not his number that was ringing: it was not Alice. He picked up the switchboard phone on Annie's desk and pressed line one. The woman's voice was familiar.

'Who is it?'

Cesari was pointing at the ceiling to indicate that he was going back to the recording suite. Stuart nodded at him and watched him disappear through the swing doors. 'Who is this?'

'Search his villa,' the woman was saying. 'Le Losange.'

'Is that you, Babette?'

'There's a cache there.'

'A cache? Wait.'

'You want to put him away. Search Le Losange. There's a big arms cache.'

It was Liliane.

'What about the child? Liliane? Wait.'

She had hung up. The light on the switchboard blinked and then went out. He had not even recorded the call.

Stuart went into his office and closed the door. The room was dark. He went to his desk, turned on the anglepoise and began to look for his old notebook in the drawer. Liliane's voice persisted in his head. He found a small black notebook with the red spine that contained Monti's brother's number. He dialled the number and waited. He could not stop smiling.

'Yes. Who is it?'

Dominique Monti was abrasive but he was straight. When his little brother had been killed he had turned up in Stuart's office and told him that if ever he needed any help dropping a black flag on Coco Santini, he just had to call.

'It's Stuart.'

[239]

'What is it?'

'You said I could call you.'

'Yes. What is it?' His voice was identical to his brother's.

'Could you meet me at Santini's villa in town?' He looked at his watch. 'In an hour. Nine-fifteen. Do you know Le Losange?'

'I do.'

'Monti, I need a drill. Two of them. For floor and wall drilling.'

'No problem.'

Stuart put the phone gently into its cradle and let his heart settle. He sat down behind his desk and leaned back in his chair. He had never had an opportunity like this and it would never come again. He sat staring into the light of the anglepoise, telling himself to think. At last he picked up the phone and called Paul. As he gave his instructions, he heard his own voice floating in the room. It struck him as remarkably calm and he listened to the words flowing out of him and his tone, more solemn than he felt because he wanted to laugh, and when Paul said, 'Okay, I'll see you in an hour,' Stuart heard the reverence in his voice.

He called back Lasserre.

'I need to search Coco's house.'

'Why?'

'Raymond's murder. It could turn something up.'

'What's happened? What have you got, Stuart?'

He paused.

'Monti's brother, Dominique,' he said. 'He overheard something two nights ago at Enrico's. I've just spoken to him.'

'You're putting Raymond back in the file.'

'Yes.'

'What are you looking for?'

'It's to put pressure on him.' He hesitated. 'I'm taking Dominique Monti with me.'

'What for?'

'For his drill.'

'Stuart. What are you looking for?' He didn't answer. 'I said what are you looking for?'

'Nothing. I haven't got anything. I need to scare him. You can understand that.'

He heard Lasserre sigh.

'Thank you,' he said. 'Thank you. I should go before he has time to shit and shave.'

'I'll fax you the order now.'

'Thank you,' he said again.

'Call me,' she said. 'I'll be at the tribunal from nine.'

Stuart turned off the anglepoise and left his office. He found Cesari with his head on the desk, fast asleep. He reached over the boy and turned on the tape recorder. At the sound of the reel rewinding the boy sat bolt upright. Stuart held up his palm.

'Where is it? The call to Santini.'

Cesari looked in the exercise book on the desk in front of him. He pointed to the time code.

'Here.'

Evelyne's voice was pristine for 2 a.m. Coco had clearly been asleep. Stuart listened to the short conversation three times but could not recognise the caller.

'Let's see where the relay is.'

Cesari carefully unfolded the map.

'Here,' he said, pointing to the circle he had drawn in red crayon.

'Good. Thank you.' Stuart noted down the reference. 'Make a copy and give it to Paul as soon as he comes in. We're searching his villa this morning.'

'What do I tell Commissaire Mesguish?'

'Tell him I'm searching Le Losange. We have no secrets.' He winked and the boy relaxed. 'Tell him to call me in my car.'

He picked up Lasserre's fax and ran out to his car to call Alice.

'Go to Santini's villa now,' he said. 'Tell him you couldn't wait. Keep him talking; let him console you.'

'He doesn't console.'

'Just try and keep him there. I'll be there in less than an hour.'

'What's happening?'

'We're going to search his villa.'

'Why?'

'I'll tell you later.'

'Is Sam there?'

'No, no. But he knows where he is and we're going to get him to tell us. Alice?'

'Yes.'

It was the first time he had said her name.

'I'll tell you about it when I get there.'

As he replaced the receiver and raised his hand to the ignition, last night's dream rose to the surface. They were in the canteen at school; he recognised the white-tiled walls and he could hear the cries of the children as they ran down the stairs on their way into the refectory. She was clutching him, but he could not see her hands on his back nor could he see her face; he could only feel her breath on his neck and her hips pressing against his as she moved with him, and in his dream he closed his eyes and knew this was all the shelter he would ever find. As the children's cries came closer he suddenly needed to see her face and he tried to shift so that he could see more than his own back working like an animal, but as he did so he felt her slip away and he was alone, naked, his forlorn penis waving at the blank wall and the children rushing in.

He held the ignition key and closed his eyes. Then he sighed, turned on the engine and drove out of the compound, past the parasol pines where Santini's men had once stood watch. It seemed a long time ago. He considered how little his life had changed in the interim. It did not matter. It may be a good thing, he thought. Perhaps a man could make his life mean something in the actions of a single day.

A lime-green street cleaner was crawling along in the middle of the road ahead of him, spraying the pavements. He wound down the window to let in the smell of damp street dust. He watched the young man in overalls that matched the machine, hanging off the side of the dustcart, spraying the streets with a vague wave of the arm. He had a Walkman on and he was singing with his eyes closed. Stuart smiled. 'Thank you, Liliane,' he said aloud. His mother had always said she was a good woman.

Chapter Thirty-One

Stuart coasted past the entrance to Santini's villa, past Dominique Monti's van parked on the opposite pavement. He followed the road, which curved sharply towards the sea. Beyond the turn was a lay-by with three municipal dustbins, spilling waste. He parked in the shade of a scrub oak and turned off the engine. Alice was already inside Coco's house.

He reached over to unlock the glove compartment, the door of which came off in his hands. He looked at his gun lying on top of the radio, picked it up and turned it over on his palm; then he put it back, replaced the door and locked it again. He climbed out and walked back along the road towards Dominique Monti's van.

Along the side of the white van were printed the words 'Ets. Dominique Monti, BTP, SARL' in neat black letters like a surgeon's credentials. Stuart could see a dusty foot in a beach thong holding open the door. He caught Dominique's face in the wing mirror a second before he looked up from whatever he was reading. When he saw him, Dominique slid open the door with his foot and climbed out. He nodded and gripped Stuart's hand hard. He was wearing a pair of faded blue satin football shorts and a yellow vest with the number nine on the back. His chest was as broad as a cement-mixer – he could carry two standard sacks of cement on each arm – and his legs were grey to the knees with cement dust. He had the same boxer's nose as his dead brother. Stuart recalled his informer's face, full of excitement, while he told him of his plan to have plastic surgery in Belgium.

Dominique was looking up at him. His face, too, wore the colours of pastis, all yellow and indigo.

'Can we sit in the van a moment?' Stuart asked.

Dominique held out his arm. When they were inside Stuart said, 'We're going to search his place.'

Dominique raised his eyebrows.

'Whatever you say.' He leaned forward, peering through the windscreen at the sky as if for rain, and then nodded in the direction of the villa. 'Whenever you're ready,' he said.

'I'm waiting for back-up,' Stuart told him.

'You look in better shape than you did last year,' Dominique said. Stuart looked at him. 'You do,' Dominique insisted. He leaned forward and looked up at the sky again. 'I'm waiting for the Devil Divers. You know, the fighter pilots.' He craned his neck. 'They're supposed to be flying over the bay this morning. Amazing.'

Stuart nodded. The other Monti had been better company.

'I'm going back to wait for them,' he said. 'Join us at the entrance. Have you got everything?'

'Course I have.'

Stuart climbed out and walked back to the lay-by. A white haze covered the sun and he could smell a storm. He turned and looked at the hills. Behind them the sky was filling up with churning cloud like volcano smoke. Up ahead, over the sea the sky was still blue, but he could feel the storm in his joints and smell it in the tarmac. He looked down at the hand she had held in the car, turning it over, and he smiled to see how it shook.

The squad car he had asked for was parked beside his. The fat boy from La Rochelle was sitting behind the wheel. Beside him was a young woman and in the back was a youth, neither of whom he knew. The fat boy beamed at Stuart and got out.

They shook hands over the bonnet.

'This is Mireille, Commissaire.'

Stuart shook the woman's hand but could not compete with the enthusiasm of her smile. Central Office had published a pamphlet at the beginning of the year that announced a new public relations offensive for the police. Paul had said it was a euphemism for an end to ugly women on traffic duty. Mireille, he would say, was new policy. Alice was right; Paul did not like women.

The youth now climbed out of the back of the car. He was small and wiry with a juvenile face and bad acne. He introduced himself with three syllables that Stuart did not catch.

Stuart turned to the boy from La Rochelle.

'Your name, I'm sorry,' he said.

'It's tricky sir,' he answered. 'It's Joachim.'

Stuart told them it was a routine search in a homicide case and they were to cover the front gate.

The villa, as Coco liked to call it, had been built by Jug Nordstrom, the Swedish architect who had designed first Russo's place, then Coco's, then Rimini's, the Milanese real-estate man. The last of Nordstrom's creations had been blown up a year after completion. Apparently, Rimini had gone to see Coco with tears in his eyes.

'Why? I don't understand. You said it would be okay.'

Coco said he'd make enquiries and get back to him. A week later Coco met him at The Pescador and told him, 'There's been a mistake. You can rebuild.'

Some kids from the FNL had taken the initiative without checking first. They had had to use 300 kilos of explosives to get rid of it.

Coco's villa was made up of four tent-like structures in wood and glass, linked to each other by narrow footbridges of steel and wire mesh. The tents were arranged in a diamond around a central courtyard, and so Evelyne had named the house 'Le Losange'. People said Evelyne sometimes went naked along the footbridges.

Paul arrived in his own car with Gérard. Behind them came Fabrice in his van. Stuart took them aside and briefed them while the three cops waited in the squad car. He noted the same calm in his voice and felt the same detachment he had experienced earlier. Before he had finished Fabrice began to unpack his equipment. Stuart could feel his disapproval.

He held out his hand for one of the camera cases.

'Does the magistrate know?' Fabrice asked, pushing his red glasses further up his nose.

'Christine Lasserre's right behind me.'

Fabrice handed him a camera case.

'She's right behind the man with the drill, is she?'

'She knows.'

Fabrice nodded and carried on unloading.

As all seven of them walked towards the gates to the villa, Stuart wondered why he had chosen to leave his gun behind.

Chapter Thirty-Two

Coco liked having the Aron woman sitting beside him at the table while Evelyne waited on them. He liked watching the expressive arch of Evelyne's back as she stalked out of the room. Twice she had attempted to stay and each time he had sent her to fetch something unnecessary: some sugar for his coffee and then his telephone. Either the Aron woman did not notice Evelyne's fury or she was an impeccable actress.

Evelyne called this place the sun room. To Coco it looked like an air-traffic control tower. The young woman was sitting on the high-backed cane armchair Evelyne had brought back from a furniture fair in Milan. Behind her was a bullet-proof plate-glass window with a view over the bay that had always disappointed him. The greenish glass made the pool in the foreground murky.

'What happened to your forehead?'

'I banged it.'

'I can see that. You look tired,' he said, looking at her mouth. She had a beauty spot on her lower lip. When she blew on her coffee it disappeared. 'Are you eating?' he asked her. 'I'll ask Evelyne to get us some croissants.'

'I'm not hungry. Thank you.'

'You should eat.'

She put down her coffee cup and looked at him. There was a candour in her stare that he appreciated. It was a rare thing, especially in a woman. He leaned back in his chair and let her look.

'Why did you lend me the money?' she asked. The large red sports bag full of cash lay at her feet, under the table.

'You asked me to.'

'The last time we met you suggested that it would be easy

[248]

for you to find out who had him. And you did, very quickly.'
She hesitated, looking for the right words. Unlike Evelyne,
she didn't chatter.

'Yes?' he said.

'Can you find out who has him now?'

Coco stroked his beard and studied her. She had a few lines
on the bridge of her nose. Her skin was otherwise smooth, but
it would wrinkle early. If he got her son back she would fall
into his arms.

'Yes,' he answered. 'Yes, I can.'

'How come?'

'That's my secret,' he said, smiling.

She was not as vulnerable as she looked. There was something tough about her that he liked. She was wearing a blue
dress with small white buttons all the way down the front. It
was open at the neck and he could see a dark freckle on her
milky skin beneath her left collarbone and another one lower
down. He imagined undressing her and smiled again: he
could play join the dots.

At the sound of the doorbell she turned and looked towards
the door.

'Are you expecting somebody?' he asked.

She smiled, a polite rictus. 'I'll have some more coffee, if
there is any.'

'I'll get it for you.'

As he walked round her chair to the door he glanced down at
the shadow beneath her breastbone but could divine nothing.

Standing in the doorway blocking their path stood Evelyne,
a Dobermann disguised as a poodle. She was dressed in a
white-and-gold cowgirl outfit fringed with tassels. Gérard
swore at the sight of her, out of admiration or disgust, Stuart
did not know which. He was relieved when Santini
appeared. At the sound of his voice Evelyne pulled back,
making the satin fringes quiver. She let Coco take her place
but she never took her dead eyes off Stuart.

'What do you want?' Santini asked. He was carrying a coffee cup. He glanced at Dominique Monti, who was standing beside Stuart with his drill. 'What's going on? Are you all bored?'

'We'd like to search your house, Santini,' Stuart said.

'You've already searched it. Come back another time. I'm in a meeting.'

'We'd like to search it now.'

'In connection with what?'

'In connection with the death of Raymond Battesti.'

'Oh come on, Stuart. He was a junkie and he died of junk.'

'Just let me in, Coco.'

'Where's your warrant?' Evelyne asked.

'You watch too much American TV,' Stuart told her. 'Tell her, Coco. You're a better jurist than I am.'

'Who's the magistrate?' Coco asked.

'Christine Lasserre,' Stuart said.

Coco stood for a moment facing them, then he turned his back on the open door and walked away across the hall towards a broad arch in the far wall.

'You deal with it, Evelyne,' he said. 'If they damage anything, we'll sue them.'

Stuart stepped into the hall. The walls and the floor were covered with a blinding white marble. It was the same marble Santini had chosen for the mausoleum he had built for himself on the promontory overlooking the bay. The hall was cool and smelled of Evelyne's perfume.

'I suggest you stay, Santini,' he said. 'We're going to use the drill.'

Coco turned round. The others had followed Stuart into the hall and were standing behind him. Coco glanced again at Dominique with his drill. Stuart could see his anger in the tension in his mouth.

'You can do what you like,' Coco said at last. 'But you'll have to pay for it and you always end up paying for your mistakes, don't you, Stuart?'

He turned and passed through the arch and up a flight of steps. Stuart was not going to run after him. When Coco had gone he wrote down the time of his refusal to attend the search, then turned to Evelyne.

'I'd like the plans of the house, please.' Evelyne folded her arms and stared at him with her dead eyes.

'Give us the plans, Evelyne,' Gérard said. 'Or we'll drill through every wall in the house.'

She did not move.

'You should go and get Coco,' Stuart said. 'He has to be present at the search.'

Evelyn blinked slowly at him. There were mean brackets around her mouth that he had not noticed before.

'If you don't get him, we will,' Stuart told her. 'Check the whole house,' he said to Gérard and Paul. 'We're going outside to have a look around. Dominique?'

Dominique Monti nodded.

'And Fabrice.'

The three of them climbed the steps that led through a pampas thicket to the front drive where Dominique had left his compressor. Stuart glanced at Alice's Mercedes, then led them along a narrow path that passed through a bed of spider cactus to an unnaturally green lawn. The house was to their left. Ahead and out of sight was the pool set in a paved terrace overlooking the sea. Stuart walked across the damp grass towards the house. There were no sprinklers. Dominique walked beside him, tugging on the giant flex that attached the drill to the compressor and swearing at the opulence. Fabrice followed behind, looking about him with feigned boredom, taking in every detail.

Stuart knew he would find the cache quicker in Coco's presence. He stopped beneath one of the bridges made of wood and steel cable. Two glass pyramids overhung the high cement-rendered walls. The entrance hall was below the ground and lit by glass tiles that paved the internal courtyard. There was no visual access to the house except from the air. Stuart and Fabrice walked round to the back. Dominique followed with his drill. Stuart stood with his back to the blind façade, facing the sea. Coco would have taken her to a room with a view.

'Dominique.'

Dominique stopped beside Stuart on the path.

'Can you drill over there?' Stuart asked, nodding at the terrace ahead of them.

'I can drill where you like,' he said.

They crossed the strip of lawn to where the terrace began. The rubber flex dragging behind Dominique left brown welts in the tender grass. The terrace was made of the same white marble as the hall. Stuart watched Dominique set up his machine. He thought of Alice being breathed on by Santini.

'Where?' Dominique asked. He was standing, legs apart, gripping the machine.

Stuart pointed randomly at a slab of marble at his feet. He was conscious of Fabrice watching him in disbelief.

'Block your ears, Fabrice.'

Monti's brother began drilling. The machine was so loud and so powerful, holding it transformed him into a maniac. The drill sank into the marble as if it were icing, and churned up the earth and sand beneath. White dust spiralled into the sky. Dominique cut out a jagged square metre and stopped. When he looked up, his black hair and eyebrows were coated white.

Fabrice stepped forward.

'Just wait,' Stuart said, holding up his hand. He had never questioned Fabrice's special status. Conferred by his quasi-scientific role, it was confirmed by his quiet authority and his integrity. Fabrice stayed clean and Stuart had never held this against him: somebody had to. But today there was no place for him. He would just have to write his report when it was all over.

Stuart was still holding his hand in the air like some crazed prophet. Fabrice and Dominique were watching him in silence. There was the sound of a door sliding on rails and then a shout. Gérard and Paul were weaving across the lawn towards them, carrying Coco. Each one had hold of an arm and a leg. Coco did not appear to be struggling, but Evelyn ran along beside them, lashing out at each of them in turn, forcing them to defend themselves as best they could without their arms. Above and behind them five jets dived in formation towards the sea. As the sound ripped through the sky Stuart saw Dominique Monti mouthing his awe-struck obscenities.

'I was not present when you did that,' Coco said, nodding at the mess in the immaculate terrace.

'Yes you were,' Stuart said. 'You can put him down.'

'He did the Gandhi routine,' Gérard said, setting Coco down on the terrace. 'He sat down on the floor.'

Paul looked down at Coco: 'It's an insult to true revolutionaries the world over.'

Coco stood up. He brushed the marble dust from the back of his trousers. The sky was dark with cloud.

'Anyone else in the house?' Stuart asked.

'Madame Aron. In the room overlooking the pool.' Paul turned and pointed to the glass pyramid. 'There.'

Stuart looked but could not see her.

'You're out of control, Stuart,' Coco said. 'These people know it and you're scaring them.'

'I'm scaring you, Santini,' Stuart said. 'What's Madame Aron doing here?'

'You brought a pneumatic drill to look for Madame Aron?'

'No. I brought the pneumatic drill to look for an arms cache.'

Coco's amusement vanished and returned in an instant. Stuart looked at Evelyn, who fixed her eyes on him. Too late. He had seen them flick towards the pool. He turned and looked at the pool. It was what they called an 'eternity pool', with an overflow system. He could see that it was not quite full. Coco had built the cache underneath, then filled it up.

[253]

There would be an access from the outside. Stuart looked hard at Coco and Coco stared back, his watery green eyes entirely free of expression. Emotion showed in his mouth, which was why he wore a beard, Stuart thought.

'Come with me, Coco. I have an idea.'

Evelyne stepped forward.

'Wait here,' Coco told her.

The two men walked side by side towards the house.

'We're going to find Madame Aron,' Stuart said. 'She's your only hope.'

'What are you talking about?'

'You'll see.'

They stepped through the front door into the hall. Stuart could see the sweat beginning to soak through Santini's silk shirt.

'You've got an arms cache under your pool, Coco,' Stuart said.

'You've always had shit informers.'

'You've got a cache under the pool. There's nothing between you and twenty years inside but a pneumatic drill.'

Stuart looked at Coco. His eyes still carried no expression, but there were tiny pearls of sweat all around them. Stuart knew from this silence that he was right about the pool. His heart sang.

'Which way is Madame Aron?' Stuart asked. 'Let's go and see her. Maybe she can help you find a way out.' Stuart walked towards the arch. 'Up here?'

Coco overtook him and led the way up a flight of marble stairs to a landing. Straight ahead was a narrow arch through which Stuart could see part of the enclosed courtyard: steel, glass and foliage. There was a sound of water trickling.

'A fountain,' Stuart said. 'Nice.'

Coco turned left and opened a door in another arch. Stuart followed him up more stairs that were covered in a thick, green carpet that matched Coco's shirt. At the top they stepped into a sparsely furnished room with white walls and a white ceramic floor. They were in one of the glass pyramids overlooking the sea. Alice was standing on the other side of the room before a plate-glass window. She walked round a smoked-glass table with two empty coffee cups on it. Beneath, Stuart could see a red holdall. Inside was Santini's money. Alice shook his hand and he noted how cold hers was; then she turned to Santini.

'What's going on?'

'Ask him,' Coco told her, walking away from them both. He stood with his back to them, looking through the greenish glass at the pool, his hands in his trouser pockets.

Stuart looked for something in her face for him, but she carried on.

'What's going on?' she asked again.

'Mr Santini is in trouble. Who does the gear belong to, Coco?'

Coco did not move. The back of his shirt was drenched with sweat. Stuart could see that he and Alice were reflected in the plate glass, that Coco was watching them. Stuart spoke to Coco's back. 'Is it for the new group. For the FAR?'

Coco turned round.

'Don't be ridiculous.'

'Just the FNL, then?'

'What do you want, Stuart? Either drill the fucking hole or get to the point.'

'I want you to tell this woman who has her child,' he said.

'I've got no idea who has her child.'

'You said you did,' Alice said quietly. 'You said you could easily find out.'

'I said I could find out.'

'Well, find out, Santini,' Stuart said. 'Very quickly or I'll drill.'

'Come on, Stuart. You know I wouldn't go anywhere near something like this.'

'You've got five minutes to decide.' He looked at his watch. 'I'm not leaving them out there. It's going to rain.' He felt weightless but not, for once, with anger. He could feel how close he was to Coco, how carefully he had to tread. 'Five minutes,' Stuart said, 'and I give them the signal to start drilling.'

Coco grew more unsettled as the silence gathered. He began rubbing the back of his neck with a repeated movement. All the time he kept his eyes on Alice. Suddenly he dropped his arm and walked over to Stuart. He stood so close, Stuart could feel his breath on his face.

'You know I don't know who has her child.'

'You're going to find out,' Stuart said.

Santini stared into Stuart's eyes and Stuart stared back. He saw tiny brown spots floating in the pale green; like shit in the sea, he thought, and he wanted to laugh suddenly at this moment, at the solemnity of two enemies locked together like this and at the smell of Coco's aftershave, overwhelmed by the odour of his sweat.

'Okay,' Stuart said, pulling away. 'That's five minutes.'

'I don't trust you, Stuart.'

'Course you don't. But you have no choice.'

'First call the magistrate,' Coco said as Stuart moved away. 'Call Lasserre now, in front of me, and tell her you didn't find anything.' Stuart shook his head. 'Then I'll look for the kid.'

'No!' Stuart shouted. His voice reverberated in the bare room. 'I'll call Lasserre when you've told me who has the child and where.'

'What about the others?' Coco said. He walked towards the window and looked out, rubbing his neck again. 'Call the magistrate and cancel the search, then we'll go. All of us.'

'Go where? Out of here so you can lead me on a wild-goose chase while Evelyne empties the cache?'

'He knows where he is.' Alice's voice broke in. She was now looking at Santini, her black eyes full of anger.

Santini glanced at her, then addressed Stuart again.

'We leave together,' he told Stuart. 'Everyone. You cancel the search in front of me, then we leave.'

'Leave and go where, Santini?' Stuart asked. 'To pick up

the child? Are you telling me you're able to do that? Is that what you're saying?'

'No. That's not what I'm saying.'

'Where are they?' Stuart asked.

'I've no idea.'

'They're in the *maquis*,' Stuart said. 'Aren't they?'

'Probably.'

'How many of them are there? More than three?'

'I've told you,' Coco said. 'We all leave and I'll find out what I can when we're up there.'

'Forget it. You're not in a position to make conditions.'

'You can forget it, Stuart. You can forget it!'

Stuart had never seen him so angry.

'We all go,' Stuart said calmly. He nodded towards the window to indicate the group by the pool. 'I'll call Lasserre when you tell me where we're heading, otherwise we drill.'

There was a pause.

'Drill then,' Coco said.

There was a flash of lightning.

'No!' Alice said.

Stuart glanced at her. He shouted against the thunder: 'We're drilling.'

'Stuart!' Alice cried, but he walked out of the room.

As he walked quickly down the stairs he could hear her running behind him.

'Please, Stuart!'

He stopped in the hall and looked at her. Coco was right behind her.

'I'm starting the search,' he told her.

'Karim's with them,' Coco said suddenly. He was looking at Alice again, delivering the news to her.

'Karim,' Stuart said. 'You sent Karim in.'

'That's what he'll tell you. But it was his own crazy initiative. Like Mickey. I don't know what's going on in the minds of these kids.' He flipped his hand over beside his head. 'There's no . . .'

[257]

'Who else?'

'No idea.'

Stuart turned to Alice.

'I need to talk to him alone.'

'No.' She shook her head. 'No, Stuart. You're not making any deals without me.'

Stuart watched her, waiting for her distress to subside.

'Alice. Please.'

'I have to come.'

'It's all right.' He wanted to touch her. 'I promise.'

Santini was picking up every nuance of this little exchange.

'Please. Ask the others to come in. Trust me.'

She hesitated, then she looked once at Santini and left them. When she had gone Stuart took a chair and sat down at the glass table. He kicked the soft bag with the toe of his shoe.

'I can send you down for this,' he said.

'Not for long,' Coco said, walking to the window.

'Ten years,' Stuart said.

Coco clicked his tongue twice. He had his back to Stuart, who now lit a cigarette.

'Who told you?' Coco asked suddenly, turning round. Stuart ignored him, drawing on his cigarette. Coco hesitated between standing or sitting down. He took the chair.

'Just tell me this: was it Evelyne?' he asked.

Stuart waited. When the silence started to hum, he leaned across the table, close enough to see the grain of Coco's skin.

'You got a call last night at two-twenty a.m. From Karim,' he said softly. Coco settled back into his chair and crossed his legs. 'You're going to call Karim back like he asked you to,' Stuart went on. 'You're going to get them to take this money.' He kicked the bag at his feet again. 'Tell them it's not in their interests not to. And you're going to set up a meeting to hand it over.' He paused. 'Now who are the others?'

But Coco was looking past him towards the door. Evelyne was leading Alice and the men into the room.

Coco uncrossed his legs.

'I want to talk to you,' Coco told Evelyne. 'Go to the study.'

'We'll all go to the study,' Stuart said. 'There's nowhere to sit here.' He put out his cigarette in one of the empty coffee cups and stood up. 'Perhaps you could make some coffee, Evelyne.'

Evelyne had moved into the new situation like an amphibian crawling on to the shore. She glanced at Coco sitting in the chair. As if he were a thing of the past, she counted the people in the room with a long red fingernail.

'Six coffees then,' she said and left the room.

Alice was standing between Gérard and Paul.

'We're postponing the search,' he said. He paused while Paul shifted, folding his arms and placing his yawning tennis shoes further apart from each other. 'Dominique, you can go home, but I'd like you to be ready in case I need you.'

Dominique nodded solemnly. When Stuart did not continue he said, 'So I go then?'

'I'll call you if I need you.'

'No problem,' Dominique said. 'Any time you need help putting him away, I'm your man.' He looked down at the person he took for his brother's killer, but when Santini met his eye, Stuart saw how afraid he was.

'Show him out, Evelyne,' Coco said. 'Then wait for me in the study.' He was sitting in the large cane chair, stroking his beard. At the sight of him Stuart felt a rush of doubt. Evelyne raised her eyes to heaven and led Dominique out of the room. Coco was watching Stuart, and as he held Santini's stare the room seemed to tighten around him. Pressure was building up in his head and his ears were burning. Santini dropped his eyes for only a moment, then raised them again.

Go on, Stuart thought. Go and talk to her. You won't get another chance.

Santini stood up. He looked at each of Stuart's men. He had no control and yet he could command. He stepped out of the room and Stuart closed the door.

'We've got a lead for the child,' he told them. 'A good one. I haven't got any choice. I have to pursue it now.' He glanced at Fabrice but Fabrice said nothing. He just stood there, his eyes blocked out by the reflection of the window in his glasses. 'We'll take the three cars we've got; that includes Madame Aron's...'

His voice came clearly and reliably again and he created an illusion of certainty with what little he had. He unfolded a plan to them, all the transgressions of procedure and the unspoken dangers dissembled behind the fluency. At every moment as he spoke, he was aware of Alice watching and judging him. When he had finished no one spoke. The questions were too many. He looked at Fabrice, standing there with his hands in the pockets of his anorak.

'We'll need someone to go with the tracking equipment. Fabrice?'

'There's a technician for that. Presumably you're going to ask Central Office.'

'Everything is going to be regularised. Lasserre is behind me. We just don't have time . . .' He stopped himself. 'This only works if we move quickly. Otherwise we'll lose him.'

Stuart looked at Fabrice and decided to let him go; he would have to do what his conscience told him to do.

'Paul? Can you do it?'

Paul shrugged. He was not familiar with the equipment. 'Sure.'

'Any questions?' Stuart asked.

'The technician can come with me in the van,' Fabrice said.

Stuart nodded at him, careful not to embarrass him with his gratitude. He turned to Alice.

'Madame Aron?'

The others turned and looked at her. She was standing by the door, cordoned off as always by her sex and her class and her grief.

'Can you drive your car?'

She looked at Stuart and nodded and for a moment Stuart believed it would be possible for him to love her.

Chapter Thirty-Three

Lopez stood at the bar staring grimly at his reflection between the shelves of liquor. No one came to this bar because the owner's wife had a germ phobia and the place stank of bleach. He liked the smell because it reminded him of the prison hospital that had been a sanctuary for him. There, hope had trickled back like the smell of bleach in the throat: it was a nice line – he would try and use it some time.

He took a sip of his Kir. He liked the syrupy sweetness of this bourgeois, woman's drink. He had been introduced to Kir by a sausage heiress in Barcelona. Her name was Maria Teresa and he had loved the self-love with which she purred her own name. He looked at his watch. Stuart had not called as he had promised and it was already ten-fifteen. He took his mobile from his pocket to make sure it was on and laid it carefully on the bar. He would give him another fifteen minutes, then he would ring the *Islander* and start his series. He took another sip of his drink, then swallowed it all. No, he would not wait. Stuart had not treated him well.

He called the paper. Thierry, the news trainee, picked up. The editor was in a meeting.

'Tell him it's me, Thierry. Tell him it's about the kidnapping.'

'What kidnapping?'

'Just get him.'

'Sure. Lopez?'

'Yes.'

'You told me to monitor the police radio.'

'Yes.'

'I wrote it all down. I've put it on your desk.'

'You don't have to write it down; just tell me if there's anything interesting.'

There was a pause.

'Like what?'

'Oh, come on, Thierry. Like names even you've heard of.'

'There was a call for a squad car to Coco Santini's.'

'When?'

'Wait a minute. Just one minute. I've got it here. It came at eight-thirty-three.'

'Santini's place where? In Santarosa or in town?'

'In town. His villa on the bay. I've got the address. Just a minute.'

'That's okay. I know where it is. Thank you.'

Lopez knew as soon as he arrived at Santini's place that he was too late. He could feel it as he looked through the wide-open gates at the empty drive. As he climbed down the bank on to the road, the first drops of rain began to fall. When he reached his car, his hair was wet.

He sat in his car and lit a cigarette. He still smoked Ducados and he liked the smell of brown tobacco and rain, mixed. Maybe it was time to go home to San Sebastian. He took his mobile from his jacket pocket and dialled Stuart's number. The secretary answered. She had a whining voice.

'I know it's not your fault, madame. Just be kind enough to let him know that the story will be in the *Islander* tomorrow morning, in full.'

He hung up and while he finished his cigarette he looked for his opening line. A beautiful young woman, still grieving for the tragic loss of her husband, has been struck . . . Young woman or young widow. Which? It needed a link with the island. The young widow of a member of one of the island's oldest families . . .

Lopez saw the moving shape in the wing mirror before he turned his head to look. He held perfectly still until the car had driven in through the gates. It was Georges Rocca's car.

He stubbed out his cigarette in the ashtray and climbed out.

He stood in the rain and looked for a way in. Santini's villa was notoriously impenetrable. It was a bunker. That was why he didn't need security guards. Security guards just took bribes. Lopez smiled, letting the rain drip into his mouth. He felt young again and excited. It was too soon to go home.

He followed the steep path that led from the lay-by down to the flat rocks and the sea. He could see the gulls standing down there, all facing in the same direction, standing stupidly in the rain, waiting for some gull messiah to scud in across the sea. He slipped in the mud and tore his suit vent on a root that was sticking out of the path. A ribbon of catholic oaths rolled from his mouth.

When he reached the shore he ran at the gulls, rain and sea stinging his eyes, and the moment of doubt came as the birds held their ground – they were preparing an attack. But they stepped lazily forward in response to some invisible command and lifted into the air, curling off to the next cove where Santini had built a little harbour and beach, all of cement. Lopez followed the narrow path over the rocks, his heart still beating from his moment of doubt with the gulls.

Only Santini's mausoleum was visible from the cove. It was built on a piece of rock that jutted out beyond the cliff face. The mausoleum was the work of two brothers from a village in the north-east of the island that had produced stonemasons for generations. The marble was from Italy and the work was said to be very fine. Lopez had written a piece while it was being built questioning Santini's right to burial on his own property. He had checked: Article L2223-9. Any person may be buried on a private property provided that the said property is situated at the prescribed distance from the confines of a town or village. Le Losange was not beyond the prescribed distance. It was a feeble assault, but Lopez knew that Coco's mausoleum was a matter of the deepest significance to him and while it was not possible to make the authorities put a stop to it, they had been forced to think up a way round the illegality. In the meantime they had halted the building work, which had been a source of considerable irritation to Coco. Still, Lopez thought, Coco had him on a short leash. He knew if he ever sought to do him any real damage, he could forget his peaceful retirement in San Sebastian; no port would be far enough. It was a sad thing to discover that after all he had been through he was so afraid.

Lopez heard a clap of thunder in the distance. Coco no longer used the cove now that he had his pool, and his cement installations were daubed with gloomy obscenities. The old access up to his property was barred by a tall wire fence that had collapsed in places and lay curling in the undergrowth. Lopez climbed over and looked up through the rain at the cliff. The first part of the climb was easy. He followed the old path, hoisting himself up where a step had subsided, making his suit muddy at the knees. He talked to himself under his breath as he climbed, clasping on to the ice-plants when the path disappeared. He was grateful for being close to the ground. His size had never been a disadvantage. He could sneak and crawl still, past police barricades, into rival rallies, past ticket booths at *corridas* and football matches and also into women's beds, into their mothering arms, where they would press their lips to the top of his head and in no time their wistfulness would turn and their mouths would slide from the O of surprise to the Ah of concupiscence and it was too late: he had insinuated his way past the turnstile of their desire. For he was in fact none other than a real-life, flesh-and-blood sex dwarf. Lopez smiled as he climbed up through the rain. It was the sausage heiress's phrase and he liked it, for that was exactly what he was: a sex dwarf. No woman was safe.

He had reached a dead end. The rock on which the mausoleum was built rose up before him, impregnable as Colonel Moscardo's *alcázar*. The thunder was still a long way off. Lopez looked for a hold. The best face was where the rock overhung. If he fell from there he would hit the lower part of the slope about a hundred metres below. He would have to climb the smooth part where the rock met the cliff and a muddy stream now trickled. He took off his socks and shoes. His feet had been broken with cables by the Guardia Civil when he was in his twenties. When he had been released he had gone to see a physiotherapist, who had restored them with exercises that Lopez had joked were at least as bad as the torture. But he was a dour man from Huesca and he had not laughed. Lopez used his little feet to claw at the mud and he climbed slowly and steadily, trusting them with all his weight, using his fingers only lightly to correct his balance. The cliff was perfectly vertical and as he climbed he marvelled at his own agility.

He heard them before he reached the top. He recognised the sound immediately as metal striking stone. He gripped the long waxy grass that fringed the cliff edge and gazed at the white mausoleum, glistening in the rain. The banging was coming from inside. If they found him, they would shoot him, but if he tried to go back the way he had come he would break his neck, so whatever happened, he was going out through the front gate, be it dick or feet first.

He pulled himself up and lay on his stomach on the wet grass, his legs still hanging over the cliff. Santini's house was further up the hill and out of sight. Lopez crawled on to the lawn and crept round the side of the mausoleum. He heard a woman's voice. It was Evelyne.

'Lay them like that. Like bottles. Yes.'

'Careful!' Lopez started. 'What do you think we're dealing with here?' It was Georges Rocca.

'Hurry up,' Evelyne said. 'I'm getting wet.' She was outside the vault. Lopez took a step back. He realised that if they found him, he'd simply go over the cliff.

'Okay,' Georges said. 'Now the ammunition.'

It was an arms cache.

'Okay, now seal her up.'

Lopez listened to them slide the stone drawer back into place.

'Smoother than that,' came Evelyne's baby-doll voice. 'It's got to be smooth. Look, there. It shows.'

They were applying the cement.

'Dog's work,' Georges said. 'Let me do it.'

'Hurry up, for Christ's sake,' Evelyne said. It was a voice job she needed, Lopez thought. 'Hurry up!'

Go on, Georges, hit her. You know you want to.

'I'm going back to the house,' Evelyne said. 'Leave the gate open when you go. Clean up all that. I don't want to see a speck of dust here in the morning.'

When she had gone he could hear them set about clearing up. There was a sound of splintering wood.

'Okay. Let's go,' Georges said.

Lopez waited a few seconds, then advanced to the corner of the mausoleum and looked out. Georges was walking up the path that led to the house. Behind him were his two new skinheads. They were carrying the tools and a bucket of cement and Georges was carrying the broken pieces of crate. Lopez could see red Cyrillic lettering on one of the pieces and he whispered a long, liturgical oath.

Chapter Thirty-Four

Stuart drove Santini's Saab up the hill to Santarosa. The rain was hanging in swathes on the road. The wipers could not move fast enough and it clung to the windscreen like a caul. Alice sat beside him, the only one in the car wearing a seat belt.

'How's she handling?' Coco asked him.

Stuart glanced at him in the mirror. He was sitting behind Alice with his hands cuffed behind his back. Next to him was Joachim, the youth from La Rochelle.

'Good,' Stuart said, for he could not deny it; there was some pleasure in driving a good car.

Santini's Saab was from another world, a long way north from here, in another Europe where people wore seat belts and drank decaffeinated coffee and only rarely killed each other. The idea that he should have chosen a car from such a place amused Stuart. He guessed it was Evelyne's idea. Evelyne, Santini's longest-standing mistress, whom he treated like dirt and who gave unswerving loyalty. She was the kind of woman the island produced: a cold heart capable of blind devotion.

They drove past the entrance to the cemetery.

'Madame Aron?' Coco said. 'Can I ask you to move forward a little? The lever is under your seat.'

Alice obeyed in silence. Stuart could feel her hatred of Santini coming off her like heat.

Santini had relaxed a little since they had left the villa. Stuart had made the call to Lasserre from the car while they were still parked in the lay-by. When he told her the search had produced nothing there had been a prolonged silence. For a moment he had thought that he had lost her support.

'Are you with Santini now?' she had asked.

'I am,' he had answered. 'I'm going back up to the Colonna house. I'll call you from there,' and he had hung up quickly.

The rain thinned as they drove past the petrol station into the village. Paul was behind them in his own car. Sitting beside him was the blonde cop, Muriel or Mireille. Gérard, who was driving Alice's Mercedes, was with the spotty youth. With Fabrice there were seven of them and four cars; it was not enough. No matter how invincible he felt, it was not enough.

When he drove up the narrow alley to the Colonna property the rain had stopped. Beneath the asphalt sky the lawn and the cedar glowed with their own light. He turned off the engine and watched Alice open her door. He hoped that she would turn and look at him before climbing out, but she did not.

Alice stood in the kitchen with Dan in her arms and hugged him hard while Babette waited patiently for her to return him to her. Babette carried Dan everywhere. Alice realised she was not in a position to object.

'Little Dan. My man,' she said. But he was not hers; he could be taken from her at any time. 'Mummy loves you,' she said, correcting herself.

He clung to her when she tried to hand him to Babette.

'Dan, Mummy has to go into the room with the policemen. They're going to get Sam back for us.'

'I want to come.'

She hugged him again and kissed the top of his head.

'I want you to wait here, Dan the Man. I want you to be here when I come back. I want to know that you're safe here, with Babette, waiting for me. I'll have something to look forward to then. Do you understand?'

Dan relaxed his hold on her and she delivered him to Babette's arms. Then she brushed his cheek with her hand and left.

Alice stopped in the doorway of the Colonna sitting room. In the golden light that was now coming through the windows, they looked like characters overacting the drama of waiting. Paul and Gérard were sitting side by side on the undersized sofa. Paul was leaning forward, inspecting his hands, and Gérard sat bolt upright, his arms crossed over his military raincoat. Santini was sitting on the edge of Stuart's bed between two policemen, one of whom was the fat one who had barred her way the other night. They had both changed out of their uniforms into tracksuits. Santini's hands were still cuffed behind his back. Stuart, who was standing by the fireplace talking into a mobile phone, seemed to be the only one not trapped by the languor.

She stayed by the door, repeating in her head fragments of what she had been told: they knew what area Sam was in; there would be a transmitting device in the bag of money; there would be four cars, all in radio contact. But the old anxiety had filled her, leaving no room for thought. Her body was cold with panic again and her mind slid off the facts.

She watched Stuart put his hand into the pocket of his trousers and take the weight off his right foot. He was wearing a clean shirt. Alice noted the shift in her perception of him and how her mind had covered its tracks, masking the way back. She was aware that she had placed all her hope in him, that this man who had been worthy of pity had somehow become heroic to her.

Stuart was punching out another number.

Santini shouted from the bed.

'Hang up. I said hang up. We said no calls, otherwise there's no deal. Hang up, Stuart!'

Stuart looked at Santini while he yelled, but did not hang up.

'Mesguish, please,' Stuart said into the phone. He kept his eye on Santini, who did not move. 'It's me. I'm at the Colonna house. I need back-up. We have a lead to pick up the child. Lasserre knows. Call her.' There was a pause. Stuart kept looking at Santini. 'I can't go into details . . . I have four cars here. There's a technician on his way with the tracking equipment. It's beyond that, Mesguish. We're moving to pick up the child. I need you to get everyone on standby. When I give the signal, you go in and get the child.' There was another pause. Santini tried to stand up and the police- man with the crew-cut gripped his arm and held him down. The policewoman stepped closer in case she was needed. She had taken off her jacket and tie and rolled up the sleeves of her shirt. 'I don't know that yet,' Stuart was saying. 'I hope I'll be covering the drop-off. Do you have Cesari's map? He eliminated the valleys. Yes, they're on high ground. It's about an hour and a half from you. Get two opaque vans. Take your men if you have to but take Cesari with you. He knows the terrain.' There was a pause. 'No. We need men, not cars. They're in the middle of nowhere. Just take one car with a decent radio. Call Morin and ask him for his dogs. Not trackers, Alsatians. Mesguish. This is your rescue operation, all right? It's yours. Do you understand?'

He hung up and put the phone in his jacket pocket.

'I'm not joking, Stuart.'

Stuart glanced over at Santini.

'Can we have some light?' he said.

The policewoman turned on a standing lamp beside her.

'If you want my help, Stuart, you're going to have to play straight.'

'What are you talking about?' Stuart said. 'You got what you wanted. I'm here with you. I'm not digging up your villa, am I? Let's see you play straight.' He looked at Alice for the first time. 'This woman trusted you. You boasted you could get her son back for her.'

Coco did not answer. He looked at Alice as though sud- denly acknowledging that she was the real audience. She looked down and he turned back to Stuart.

'What makes people sick about you is that you pretend to be a good man when what you are is a coward. There aren't any good men on this island. They don't survive,' said Coco.

'They don't survive because you kill them,' Stuart said.

'They don't survive,' Coco said. 'Full stop.'

'There's the difference between us. You think people here are born corrupt. I think they just follow a leader. But you agree with me,' Stuart added. 'Otherwise you wouldn't have killed Titi.'

'It sticks in your throat that, doesn't it?'

'It sticks in everyone's throat.'

Santini glanced again at Alice. This time she faced him. The effect of the handcuffs behind his back thickened his neck, forcing his head forward.

Stuart looked at his watch.

'It's two-fifteen. We're going to call Karim.' He looked over at Santini. 'Ready?'

'First let me out of these,' he said to Stuart.

Stuart nodded at Joachim. The youth unlocked the handcuffs and delivered them over to Stuart, who then turned to Gérard and Paul.

'Wait in the kitchen, will you? When the technician comes, make him wait with you.'

Alice sensed that Stuart and Santini were preparing to act out their own private drama, that she would have to fight for a place in it. Santini was sitting with his ankle resting on the opposite thigh. The memory of their first meeting returned, filling her with disgust.

She stepped aside while the others left the room. She was afraid for a moment that Stuart would ask her to leave with them, but he did not. She stood by the door and watched him cross the room to Coco.

'You can use my phone,' he said, holding it out. Santini looked at it but did not move. 'Come on, Santini. For God's sake.'

Coco reached out and knocked the phone from Stuart's hand, sending it sliding across the parquet and spilling its battery.

'I'm not making any calls until I get some guarantees.'

Alice watched Stuart retrieve the phone and replace the battery.

'It's not broken,' Stuart said. 'You're lucky.' He walked over to Santini. With his left hand he reached down and gripped his wrist. Santini went rigid. He seemed mostly to be struggling against the indignity of resisting. With his right hand Stuart took the handcuffs from his jacket pocket. Alice heard the clicking as the handcuff bit several notches deeper and the chime of metal as Stuart hooked Santini's right hand to the bar at the end of the bed.

'This is illegal,' Santini said.

'No,' Stuart said. 'As soon as I began that search, you were in my hands. If I want to put the cuffs on I can. No justification needed. Do you understand?'

'There are no grounds, Stuart. The search is over. You pulled too hard and the rope's bust.'

'I don't give a shit about your arms cache, Santini. I've got plenty to put you away. Just think of the word betrayal, Santini. That should put you straight. I don't need a cache. I've got a little bird now.'

Santini glared at Stuart. 'No deal,' he said. Chained up he became more threatening. Alice stepped forward, forcing herself to overcome her fear of him. 'And get that woman out of here, for Christ's sake!' Alice jumped at the bark of his voice. 'What in God's name is she doing here anyway?'

'You didn't mind having her around before, Santini. You didn't mind her being there so you could play Godfather. You lent her the ransom, remember. How much did she tell you she could afford? Thirty million at the most? Then, *bam!* they ask for thirty million. You're trapped, Santini. You trapped yourself.'

'I offered her my help because she came asking for it. Ask her.' He flung out his free arm. 'She came to me because she saw straight away how fucking useless you were.'

Stuart's face did not change.

'You're trapped, Santini. You can't pull out of the deal because I'm sending you down anyway for kidnapping. I've got plenty. Trust me.'

'Bullshit.' Stuart turned his back on him and went to the fireplace. 'Who was it?'

Santini's face looked shockingly pale against the blue-black beard. Alice now stood in the middle of the room, afraid to move.

'Who grassed?' Santini asked again. 'Tell me who it was.'

'Why would I do that?' Stuart said.

'Without me, you don't get the kid.'

'Is that your opinion? Then you must be right.'

They stood there facing each other in silence, each waiting for the other to speak. At last Santini said, 'Take these off.' He nodded at his right hand.

Stuart looked at Santini. Then he crossed the room and freed him. As Stuart straightened up, Santini rubbed his wrist.

'Who was it?' he asked again. 'Tell me.'

Alice could see the mechanisms working between them like a fine machine.

'Forget it,' Stuart said. 'Just forget it. It won't make you feel any better.'

'I'll be the judge of that. Who is it?'

Stuart fetched one of the chairs from the fireside and set it down two paces away from Santini. Alice was tired of standing, but she did not want to draw attention to her presence again.

'Now we call Karim and you get him to take the nine million. We give them time to dream up the meeting. You're going to take the money . . .'

'No way,' Santini said. The two men were leaning towards each other. 'You're not getting me to walk in there so you can book me with the others.'

'I'm taking the money,' Alice said. 'No one else.' Her ears were ringing and her voice was louder than she had intended. 'I'm not letting anyone take any risks with my child.' She

[273]

looked at Stuart, lowering her voice. 'They'll feel less threatened if I go. Santini can set up a meeting with them and I'll take the money.' Her heart was beating fast and her face was flushed. 'Stuart?'

'I'm sorry,' he said, shaking his head.

She felt dizzy.

'I'm taking the money.' She was using her own voice to steady herself. 'No one else.'

'Of course she's got to take the money,' Santini said. 'If I go, they'll know something's wrong. I'd never do it and they'll know I've been set up. All she has to do is dump the bag and leave, right? She'll be fine.'

Stuart was staring at Alice as though he was not seeing her. She saw his fear and she saw how little in control he really was.

'Please,' she said, gently. 'It must be me.'

He seemed now to be taking her in. His face was full of sadness.

'You can't go.'

'Stuart.'

'It's too dangerous. I can't let you. I'm sorry.' He held out the mobile to Santini. 'Call Karim,' he said.

Alice closed her eyes. She felt all the strength drain from her. She heard Stuart strike a match to light his cigarette and the rain falling. She thought of Sam and saw his body. He was lying on his side with his knees brought up to his chest, fists and eyes closed. She felt Stuart taking hold of her hand. She knew the feel of his hand in hers, the size of it, the texture of the skin.

'Please, Stuart,' she whispered. 'Let me go.'

He held her hand tighter, so tightly it hurt her. The pain helped to tether her to what she perceived. Santini was dialling the number. 'Please,' she whispered for the last time. But he did not let go.

Chapter Thirty-Five

The rain battered the tent, which had begun to leak through the zip.

'Fucking Go Sport,' Karim said, touching the drip with his fingers. 'Cheap shite.'

He had chosen the tent because it was silver and shaped like an igloo; it had not occurred to him that it might rain. Denis was lying beside him in his dead knight position. Karim could feel the damp coming up through the ground-sheet and his bedroll. The end of his sleeping bag was wet through.

'How can you just lie there?'

'What do you expect me to do?' Denis mumbled, keeping his eyes closed.

'This is fucked. I'm cold.' He was wearing all the clothes he had brought. He patted the pockets of his tracksuit for his hash. From somewhere within the bedding came the trill of the phone.

'Quick, where is it?' He kicked Denis to enliven him and then found the phone nestling between his legs. He composed himself. 'Hello? The line's shit.'

'Are you alone?'

'Denis is here.'

'Just Denis?'

'Yes. Why?'

'I'm going to give you some instructions and I want you to listen. Don't answer. Just listen. When I've finished you'll tell me you've understood, that's all. Is that clear?'

'What is it? What's going on?'

'Karim, I said listen.'

'Sure. I'm listening.'

'No questions,' Santini said.

'Right.'

'How many of you are there?' Karim hesitated. He had a bad feeling. 'I said –'

'Three.'

'Okay. I want you out of this,' Santini said.

'Fucking right,' he said.

'What did I say?'

'Sorry.'

'The mother has nine million francs ready and waiting. You're going to take the nine million. I want this over.' Karim moaned with relief. 'I want to talk to whoever's behind this. You're going to pass me to the third man and I'm going to get him to accept the ransom.'

Santini paused and Karim listened to the rain beating against the tent; he looked at the dead joint in his fingers. What was he talking about, the third man?

'Yeah right,' Karim said.

'I'm going to get him to take the money. As soon as he leaves to collect it, you call me. Do you understand?'

Karim looked down at Denis, who was lying with his arms behind his head, watching him, relaxed as anything.

'I'm going to give you a number . . .' Santini was saying.

'Santini, you behind me?'

'Have I ever let you down, Karim?'

'Fuck,' Karim said.

'The number is –'

'Wait, wait. I'm going to write it down. Shit.' Karim was trembling. 'Denis, you fuckhead. Give us a pen.'

But Denis had no use for pens.

'Just remember it, Karim.'

'Yeah, right. What is it? What's the number?'

'0609363635.' Santini's voice was eerily patient.

The first four digits were the same as his own. He just had to remember 36 twice, then 35.

'Karim, have you got that?'

'Yes.'

'Now where are you?'

'We're in a shithole.'

'Directions, Karim. Come on. I'm going to get you out of this.'

'Okay. Right.' Karim looked pleadingly at Denis, just lying there with his hands behind his head. But Denis always followed, so he never had to know where he was going. 'Drive through Cortizzio and take – what is it? – the left fork. It leads to a rubbish dump, okay? There's an electricity plant just before it. On the right. Just there you'll see this track that leads into the woods. It goes down into a kind of valley and then you lose the track and you have to follow the valley upwards.'

'Wait,' Santini said. 'What valley?'

'Not a valley. It's like a big ditch in the woods. Shit, Santini. I don't know the *maquis*; I'm trying to think. When you follow the path down it leads to a ditch. You follow this ditch up – I mean to the right – follow it for a long way; it's about half an hour's walk uphill, then it disappears, I think, and you're on a hillside. Fuck, I can't explain.'

'Just go on.'

Karim kept talking but he did not believe he was making sense.

'You see a track – it's a goat track that runs uphill – and you follow that until it runs into a ridge with a steep drop on your right. It's like a gorge, deep as hell.'

He went on talking into the phone and when Santini didn't interrupt him he knew he was being recorded. 'It's a stone hut with a tree growing through the roof.'

'How long from Cortizzio?'

'About forty-five minutes.'

There was a pause.

'How's the child?' Santini asked.

What did Santini care about how the child was? There it was, spelled out for him: police.

'He's okay. I suppose.'

Karim saw a room full of cops in leather jackets with big bunches of keys hanging from their belts, the head man holding his finger to his lips, the mother standing there, crying silently, and the tape recorder turning round and round. Karim wondered if Santini had dreamed the whole thing up like this from the start. He was not the kind who got nailed. He must have planned it this way.

'Call that number as soon as he leaves.'

'Yeah. Just get me out of this.'

'I'll speak to him now. Put him on.'

Santini's was the only voice Karim had ever heard that carried any authority for him. He climbed out of his sleeping bag and squatted in front of the entrance to the tent.

'We're bailing out,' he said to Denis.

Karim knew the trouble they were in but he did not care at this point. All he cared about was getting out of the *maquis* and back to his car, his flat and his girlfriend, Nadia; seeing her in the bath, painting her toenails, her plump, golden body and all her black hair piled on top of her head.

He brushed the water from his hair and stepped into the hut. Garetta was sitting on the tarpaulin with the radio quacking in his lap. The room smelled of paraffin from the lamp beside him on the floor. The boy was also on the tarpaulin, curled up in a ball in the corner, as far away from Garetta as he could be. Karim took the phone from inside his jacket and handed it to Garetta.

'Santini.'

Garetta turned off the radio.

'Why didn't he call me on my phone?'

Karim shrugged and thrust the mobile at him.

'He's waiting.'

Garetta took the phone and held it to his ear, listening suspiciously. He was a caveman.

'Go on,' Karim said. 'Talk to him.'

The boy in the corner was very still.

'Yes?' Garetta said.

Karim watched Garetta listening to Santini. His face was gaunt and the skin was grey with stubble. He had thick sacs beneath his eyes. With his long black ringlets he looked like a pirate and this thought cheered Karim up. The rain, dripping through the hole in the roof, collected in a puddle at the base of the tree and flowed in a little stream along the floor, between his legs and out through the door. The smell of paraffin and rain and Garetta and the terrified child made the air thick as a hammam.

Garetta was listening to Santini and keeping quiet. Karim realised it was not necessarily a sign that he was giving in. It looked like mute resistance.

At last Garetta said, 'Okay, I'll call you back,' and then hung up. He contemplated Karim's phone, then looked up at Karim and then back at his phone.

'So?' Karim said.

Garetta put the phone in his pocket.

'Hey!' Karim clicked his fingers at him. 'My phone.'

'I'm going to call him back,' Garetta said. 'I'm going to sleep on it, then call him back.'

'Use your own phone,' Karim said.

Garetta folded his arms, making the leather of his filthy Perfecto creak.

'Give me my phone back, man.'

But Garetta ignored him.

'My phone, man. Use yours.' But Karim could hear the defeat in his own voice.

Garetta ignored him. He leaned forward and turned down the paraffin lamp. The room was filled with a dim, hissing light.

'Shit, man. It's only six o'clock and it's already night. What a shithole.' He could make out Garetta leaning back against the wall, his legs stretched out in front of him, his huge feet resting one on top of the other. Garetta had been in the Legion in the north where a man learned to sleep hanging upside down from a tree. Karim was in good shape. He exercised enough to be proud of his body, to parade his perfect torso for the women, but he knew that it was cosmetic compared to Garetta. He'd told Santini where he was. Santini was behind him. And Santini equals the whole island, he told himself. He glanced at the bundle in the corner, then turned and went back into the rain.

Chapter Thirty-Six

The rain had ended, leaving no memory behind in the sky, which was a deep, Order of Merit blue. The sun had gone down behind the hills without colour or ceremony. Stuart and Alice sat in the hired Mercedes. They were parked in front of the closed gates to Santarosa's cemetery, set back from the road and shielded from view by a row of cypress trees on either side of them. They had been waiting there for nearly an hour for Karim to call back with the meeting place.

Further up the road, in the lay-by opposite the petrol station, Gérard was sitting at the wheel of Santini's Saab. In the back were Joachim and Santini. Paul waited in his car with the other two cops, Mireille and the spotty youth. Fabrice waited in his van in the main square. Stuart told himself that even if he did call Central Office, it was too late to send reinforcements. The last plane from the mainland had already left.

Sitting beside Alice, he could feel her anxiety come and go in waves. She was resting her elbows on the steering wheel of her car. Her lips were pale and she looked weak.

'Do you want me to drive?' he asked. 'I can drive first, then you can take over.'

'No, no.'

'Do you want something to drink? Paul always has some whisky in a flask. I'll get him to bring it.'

'I'm okay.'

'Are you sure?'

She nodded and smoothed her face with her hands.

'Mesguish is good,' Stuart said. She looked at him. 'Not as a human being but as a policeman. He is.'

'Are you convincing yourself?'

'No. I promise you.'

'Don't promise.'

The radio spat and Gérard's high-pitched tenor cut in and cut out again.

'You should have let me go,' she said.

He looked at her. Her remoteness was alarming.

'I can't let you go.'

The radio hissed again.

'Stuart,' came Gérard's voice. 'Channel seven's no good up here . . .'

Stuart told him to switch to five and put the scrambler on. He gave the same instructions to the two other cars. Paul's voice cut in. 'Pass me Santini,' Stuart said, cutting him short. He didn't want any radio banter in front of her.

There was a pause, then came Santini's baritone.

'What is it now, Stuart?'

'Tell me about Denis.'

'What about him?'

'Where's he from?'

'No idea.'

'Come on, Santini. What can he do?'

'Pick locks.'

'What else?'

'Nothing. He's simple. He obeys Karim. That's it. Now it's my turn. Are we on air?'

'No.'

'Who turned me in?' Santini asked.

Stuart looked at Alice. He waited.

'It was Georges Rocca,' he said at last.

There was a long silence.

'Bullshit.'

'Who do you think it is, Santini?'

'You're finished, Stuart.'

'So are you.'

Alice looked away.

'I bet you my Sig Sauer you'll be on an early retirement by the end of the year.'

Santini's solid-silver weapon, the only remnant of his former days. Stuart smiled. He could not help it. There was
something satisfying in this talk.

'What does that mean? If you're wrong I get your Sig
Sauer? What happens if you're right?'

'There's nothing of yours I want,' Santini said.

'There's a big rush to get me buried,' Stuart said. 'You
could put me in your mausoleum and we could be together
till the end of time.'

Alice was watching him. He hung up.

'You think you've got him, don't you?'

'It's not so much that.' He hesitated. 'It suddenly seems' –
he looked at her as though she might be able to tell him what
it was – 'childish.'

But she said nothing.

'Are you all right?'

She nodded slowly. She was very far away. He saw that
what he was doing, the operation he was orchestrating, did
not concern her. She seemed to be involved in another, far
greater matter. He guessed she was praying.

Alice opened her eyes. Stuart was looking at the map on his
lap, his face lit by the orange glow of the dashboard. It was
now dark outside and there was no moon that she could see.
She closed her eyes again. Sam was there, huddled with fear.
She had not slept. Her panicking heart had lashed her awake
each time she dozed off. She had heard the growing discon-
tent over the radio. It had been a long wait. She opened her
eyes again. Stuart had put away the map and was looking at
her.

'What are they doing?' she asked. 'Why are they taking so
long to call back?'

'Sleeping maybe.'

'How can they sleep?' She rubbed her face. 'There's no
moon,' she said, looking out through the windscreen.

'No. But we've got infra red. A good pair made by the

[283]

Israelis. We found them in a search. They belonged to the FNL. I never declared them.' She looked at the hard cut of his profile. 'Mesguish has them,' Stuart was saying. 'He'll need them tonight.'

She remembered sitting with Mathieu in his car, watching his face like this while he drove. It was early on and they were in Paris and he was taking her to lunch. It was winter and the sky was white and she could feel the cobbles under the wheels. She sat leaning into her door, holding herself away from him, preventing herself from reaching out and touching him. Then suddenly he had turned and smiled at her, a smile full of kindness, and he had pulled over, turned off the engine and kissed her. She had felt overcome with shame because she knew the kiss was a reward.

She looked at Stuart and saw herself leaning towards him. She would make sure he did not feel ashamed. She would kiss his face, his mouth, his neck.

He was looking at her.

'Without you, none of this works any more,' he said. 'I won't be able to do this.'

She held out her hand. He took it again and held it hard and she closed her eyes. Sam was still lying there waiting. She did not move for fear of losing Stuart's hand. She felt as though she were being held unequivocally. This was what it was to feel safe.

The radio broke in and she let go.

'Come in, Stuart. It's the call. Do you copy? Over.' She could hear the tremor in Gérard's voice.

'We copy. Over.'

They could hear the high-pitched ringing of the mobile phone, the third ring and Santini answering.

Stuart found her hand and held it hard.

'I understand,' Santini was saying. 'The call box in Cortizzio. Fine, but she needs time to get there. Give her an hour. Of course she'll be alone. I'm not coming. It's a dark blue Mercedes.'

They could hear someone exhaling, then silence. Stuart let go of her hand.

'Stuart? Did you get that? Over.' It was Gérard.

Stuart slammed his hand down on the dashboard.

'Pass me Santini.'

There was a pause. Stuart took the map from the side pocket.

'He wants Madame Aron to go . . .'

'Fuck you, Santini.'

The radio went dead.

Stuart began to hit the dashboard over and over again. Alice reached out and touched his face. He stopped still and looked at her. Placing his hand over hers on his cheek, he closed his eyes.

'You're not going.'

She spoke gently to him. 'I have to go. It'll be all right. I promise.'

Gérard came on the line: 'Stuart. He said he won't pick up if it's anyone else. What do we do?'

She put her hand gently over his mouth.

'You must let me go, Stuart,' she whispered. She wanted to tell him that she loved him.

Gérard's voice came again: 'Stuart?'

Alice took her hand from his mouth. It would not be fair to tell him now. Stuart picked up the radio.

'Okay, Gérard. Put Santini on.'

'Fuck you, Stuart.'

'Yes, all right.'

'I'm not making the rules.'

'Of course you are, you liar.'

'If you're going to insult me you're on your own.'

'Shake your handcuffs, will you, Santini? I want to hear them.'

There was a pause. Alice could hear Santini's bass growling in the background.

'Stuart, it's Gérard. She has to go to the call box in Cortizzio.

There's only one. At the entrance to the village. When you're coming from Massaccio it's after the signpost on the right. She has to wait in the call box and pick up when it rings. He'll give her instructions.'

Stuart shouted into the radio. 'Who is it, Santini? I'll give you one more chance.'

Santini came back: 'Screw you, Stuart.'

Alice watched Stuart regain control. It occurred to her that this was the kind of person Mathieu had sought to be.

'Cortizzio's forty minutes away,' Stuart was saying. 'I'm going to send Fabrice and the technician ahead with the van. They can park in the village and wait. I'll give them a ten-minute start, then we'll leave. I'm going to get Paul to follow without his headlights. He can take Mireille and her colleague with him. You follow on when I give the signal. When Karim calls, you signal Mesguish straight away. Do you understand? Over.'

There was a hiss, then Gérard said he copied.

Stuart turned and faced her.

'Ready?'

She nodded, unwilling to look at him for too long and risk weakening. She turned the key in the ignition. Her hands were sweating and her fingers slipped on the key. She tried again and drove slowly over the gravel, stopping at the entrance to the road. Stuart was leaning forward in his seat, talking into the radio. She was aware of his voice, calm and authoritative, the meaning coming to her only sporadically. She tried to breathe slowly and deeply to settle her heart.

'. . . Come in, Mesguish. Do you read me? Over. You're going in with the dogs as soon as I give the signal . . . All right, everyone, we're moving.'

The image of Sam was still there in her mind, like a curled fossil.

'You're going to drive to Cortizzio,' Stuart told her. 'I'm going to duck down. We'll go slowly. It's a forty-minute drive from here. You're going to go to the call box in Cortizzio. You'll see it on the right as you come into the village. He'll be watching the call box to make sure you're alone.'

'You can't be in the car. What if he sees?'

'He won't. You're going to drop me off on the way. I'll tell you when. You'll pick me up after the call. I'm not letting you go alone.' His tone was gentle and inexorable.

She looked at his face with all its poignant lines; then he turned and reached into the back. He was checking the bag, which was lying on the back seat. The transmitter was taped to the bottom. He reached up and flicked a switch above the rear-view mirror. 'So the light doesn't come on when I open the door.' He sat back. 'You'll be with him soon,' he said. 'You'll get your boy back tonight. Turn right out of here.'

Chapter Thirty-Seven

When he reached the wall of the hut, Karim turned again and walked back along the muddy floor towards the child. He was trying to think, but his mind seemed to be confined by the six paces it took to cross the room. He stood still and looked down at his orange cheesecloth trousers, spattered with mud at the hem. The rain had stopped but he was still cold and damp.

Denis was sitting in Garetta's place on the tarpaulin, picking his teeth. He must have run out of toothpicks because he was using the point of his knife.

'Think of something, for fuck's sake, Denis.'

Denis took the knife blade from between his teeth, to show that he was trying.

'He doesn't trust us, right?' Karim said. 'So he could do anything.'

'He doesn't trust you,' Denis said.

Karim looked at him.

'What are you talking about?'

'He took your phone. He didn't take mine.'

'You don't have a phone.'

'No, but he doesn't know that.'

'I'm getting out,' Karim said suddenly. 'You can do what you like, but I'm out.'

Denis scrambled to his feet.

'I'm coming,' he said, folding the knife.

Karim looked at Denis, then at the child.

'How long's he been gone? Five, ten minutes?'

'More like ten,' Denis said.

'Why did he take my phone? What's he planning?'

'He doesn't trust us,' Denis said.

Karim moved him out of the way with his arm.

'Okay, now listen. We're going to take the kid. Santini wants the kid back to its mother.' He approached the child and leaned over it.

'Look at it. If it dies, we go down for sure,' he said, looking at Denis. 'We go down just about for ever.'

Denis scratched his eyebrow.

'So what do we do?'

'We take the kid and get out of here. I told Santini where we were. I don't want to be around when Garetta gets back.' Denis nodded like he always did when he didn't understand. 'We're going to give the kid back.'

'Good idea,' Denis said.

'Help me, you dickhead.'

Denis crouched down beside Karim and looked at the unmoving child.

'Shit,' Karim whispered. 'All that money.'

'What happens if –' Denis began.

'Shut it and help me. We've got no choice.'

Karim reached his arms under the child's back.

'Get his legs.'

'He's all stiff,' Denis said.

They picked up the child, who stayed curled up in a ball. Karim looked at his face for the first time and wished he hadn't. He did not know what he had been expecting, but the sight of the child's eyes, wide open and knowing, scared him.

'Fuck, man. You carry him.'

Denis turned and rounded his back obediently. Karim tried to lift the child on to Denis's back, but the child seemed to stiffen even more and would not uncurl.

'Fuck, Denis. Just take him.'

Denis turned and held out his arms.

'It's okay,' Denis said to the child, speaking with a gentleness that surprised Karim. 'We're going to take you back to your mum now.' The child did not move but went on staring at God knows what. 'Okay. Give him to me,' Denis said. Karim passed him the child and Denis went on talking in his new voice. 'That's okay, now off we go.'

Karim backed out of the hut into the black night. He had never thought he would ever be grateful for Denis.

Sam knew someone was talking to him but he could not understand the words. It was as if there was a wall between him and the words and he was only getting the voice. He could not feel his body any more, but he knew he was moving. He was looking into the sky, which was far above him, and he saw that the sky was like the surface of the water for his fish and above was another world that he did not understand. He could hear feet brushing the grass and the trees moving in the wind.

He looked for the moon but it had gone. He knew that this was sad, but he did not feel anything.

He had flown before, in the bathroom in his flat in Paris, when everyone was asleep. He had held on to the shower rail and kicked his legs outwards like they did in swimming lesson. He remembered the feeling of sinking in the air and kicking harder to stay up. He would soon open and fly up to the surface. He didn't want to be in a world where his mother wasn't.

Chapter Thirty-Eight

They were nearing Cortizzio and Karim's call had still not come. When Mesguish's voice, shrill with doubt, asked him for a decision over the radio Stuart simply told him to stand by. He did not want Alice to detect his apprehension.

He was crouching on the floor in front of the passenger seat. He knew the road so well, he could visualise it, identify every turn and every straight line, without having to ask her. She had her window open a little and he could hear the route: the emptiness of the valley and the sound intervals between the pine saplings as they passed the Cortizzio plantation. In the changing quality of her silence Stuart could feel her fear rising and falling.

'Remember,' he said. 'When you've taken the call you get back into the car and drive into the village. In the square, park and call me. You're okay about the radio?'

She nodded.

'Here,' he said. 'You're going to slow down to twenty. Good. Now stay at twenty. On the next bend I'm going to jump out. You'll have to reach over and shut the door behind me.'

He looked up at her face leaning close to the steering wheel, at her chin thrust forward. He opened the door with one hand and with the other gripped the radio to his chest.

'Now,' he said, and he rolled out.

Alice pulled the door closed behind him, veering only slightly as she did so. She breathed slowly and deeply, concentrating her mind on the road ahead of her. The road curved and revealed the lights of the village. When she saw the neon light of the call box, she caught her breath. She read

the signpost carefully, trying to pin her mind to its percep-
tive function only and calm herself. She pulled over, feeling
her hands on the steering wheel and listening to the road
beneath the wheels. She looked at her hand as she turned the
ignition key. 'No,' she murmured. 'Keep it running.' She
restarted the engine then climbed out. She slammed the door
for the noise it made, but the night seemed to absorb the
sound. 'Here I am,' she whispered to whoever was watching
her. She pulled open the door to the call box. It did not come
easily but ground on its hinges. She heard her step on the
metal floor. She put her hand on the receiver and waited.

Stuart walked along the side of the road. He rubbed his
shoulder, which had been bruised in the fall. Around the
next bend he would be in sight of the village. To his right the
forest climbed steeply; to his left was a drop to the valley. He
looked for access into the forest, but the rock face was a wall
covered in wire mesh to protect the road. He crossed over to
the other side and looked down. The trees straggled thinly
out of the dark. It was too steep; he would have to stay on the
road. He gave thanks that there was no moon.

The village was up ahead. He could see the call box and
Alice's shape inside it. He thought he could see from the tilt
of her head that she was holding the phone. The sight of her
so far from reach made him anxious. If Karim had not called,
it meant either that he was unable to or that he had decided
not to co-operate. Perhaps Santini had given him some signal
during the conversation. The reassuring constancy of his
hatred of Santini settled him.

He spoke into the radio: 'Come in, Gérard. Still nothing?
Over.'

'Nothing, Stuart. Over.'

'Okay. I'm calling Mesguish. We're moving. Tell Santini
he screwed up. Remind him. If anything happens to the
child, he dives. Over.'

He looked at Alice, perfectly vulnerable in the glass box.

[292]

She had picked up the phone. They had to move now; they would not get a second chance.

'Come in, Mesguish,' he said. 'Move now. Do you copy? Move now. Put the dogs in front. Over.'

While Mesguish was making the appropriate response, his voice charged with excitement, Stuart saw Alice turn and step out of the call box. He gripped his radio until his fist hurt. He watched her walk over to the car and climb in. She moved off immediately. It was at least ten minutes' walk to the village from here. Mesguish was still talking.

'Call,' Stuart whispered. 'Call, Alice.' The car disappeared. He stood in the dark and closed his eyes. 'Alice,' he said again.

The radio went quiet. Stuart heard an engine not far off.

'Come in, Paul. I'm standing by the road five hundred metres before the village. Is that you I can hear? Where are you? Over.'

'We're coming very slowly. It's hard to see. It's dark as hell.'

'I can see you. Slow right down. I'm fifty metres ahead of you. Pick me up. Over.'

Paul's car stopped. Joachim climbed smartly out of the passenger seat and greeted him with a pat on the arm. Stuart ushered him into the back, closed the door quietly behind him, then climbed into the front. Paul's car smelled of women's perfume and stale fags. The pump-action shotgun, the weapon Paul always chose, lay across his knee.

'Just stop here a moment until we get her call,' Stuart told him.

Paul leaned forward, resting his elbows on the steering wheel, and rubbed his eyes. Driving with no lights on a mountain road was tiring.

'Stuart?' The radio cut out.

'Hold the button down,' Stuart urged.

'Can you hear me, Stuart?'

'I can hear. Go ahead. Over.'

'He wouldn't let me talk to him.' Her voice was high pitched. 'I thought they'd let me hear him.'

He waited. But there was silence.

'Alice, come in. Tell me what he told you to do. Try and remember his words. Over.'

'He said to go up to the Col du Palomba Rossa. He said drive through the village and take the only road out. He said it's twenty minutes away. It's marked with a blue sign. Just next to the sign there's a lay-by. He told me to put the bag down in the centre of the lay-by; he said dead centre, then drive back down the way I came.'

Paul was unfolding a map.

'Wait there, Alice. Paul's driving me into the village.'

The radio hissed.

'No! Stuart. They'll see you. You can't. They were watching me.'

Stuart counted three seconds.

'How do you know they could see you? Over.'

'He told me. He said, "I'm watching you."'

'Alice, listen to me. They've gone to get Sam. We must give them time. Now sit there and start counting. No one's going to see me. You just count and I'll be there before you get to two hundred. Do you understand? Over.'

'Yes.'

He could hear the tears in her voice.

'I'm coming. Just count.'

Chapter Thirty-Nine

Karim walked along the ridge. Without Garetta ahead of him and without the moon, he moved more slowly than the night before. He advanced, feeling the cliff wall with his fingers, listening to Denis, who was a few paces behind, talking continually to the child. Karim felt like he was in a dream; the unfamiliarity of Denis's tone made it worse.

He thought of home, of his hanging wardrobe with all his clothes, arranged according to colour, starting with black from the left, moving through the greys, then white, then red, then orange. He would not wear any other colours. Nadia wanted to move in; maybe he would let her, on a trial basis. He had only been up here for one night but it seemed like months since he had seen home, his car, Nadia. He would surprise her – crawl into her bed and fuck her, gently, from behind – and she wouldn't know whether she was awake or dreaming. If she tried to turn and talk to him he would cover her mouth with his hand and hold her still and whisper in her ear. He imagined her back arching and her arse moving; then he remembered he didn't have his key.

'Hey, Denis. You'll have to let me into Nadia's flat.'

He turned and saw that Denis had disappeared.

'Hey, Denis!'

'I'm here.'

In the grey darkness, Karim could just make him out – Denis and the bundle in his arms.

'Get a fucking move on.'

When Denis had caught up Karim said, 'You've got to let me into Nadia's flat. I want to surprise her.'

Denis was panting and Karim could smell cough lozenges on his breath.

'All right?' Karim said.

Denis nodded. Karim looked down at the kid, still curled in a ball in Denis's arms. Its face was buried in Denis's filthy jacket.

'Poor kid,' Karim said. 'You must stink. Let's go.'

'Where are we going?' Denis asked, his voice normal again.

'To meet Santini. We go to Cortizzio and we call him from there. Now listen: when we get off this ridge we head for the woods and hide until Garetta has passed. Then we head down to the village as quick as we can. Right?'

Denis nodded and Karim had the sudden impression that Denis dragged him down. It was not a good thing to spend too much time with an idiot. When this was over he'd cut Denis loose.

When they reached the end of the ridge Karim stopped to take a gorse needle from his socks. His trainers were damp and ruined. The thought of having to buy more trainers brought a flash of anxiety: he was giving up three million francs. He had three million francs within reach. He could buy a villa with a crescent-shaped pool in The Hesperides compound and he would be set up for life. But then he would lose Santini and without Santini he would get nowhere. He stood up and walked on, bringing to mind Nadia's swaying arse to banish the thought of the money.

When they came in sight of the woods below them, Denis asked for a rest.

'You can rest in the woods,' Karim told him. He looked at the woods, a black cloud stretching out below him, the last band before real life, he thought. He kept on walking down the narrow track. He could hear Denis was tired. 'Pick your feet up, you'll fall.'

Suddenly Denis stopped.

'Listen.'

Karim had already heard, but the nature of the sound only revealed itself to his consciousness now, as he watched the two shadows emerge from the forest, moving towards them up the hill, not fast but smooth and unrelenting.

'Dogs,' Denis said. Karim saw the fear in Denis's face and adrenaline rushed into his body. 'No, no,' he heard. 'Don't run!'

But Karim did run. He ran back up the path, moving so quickly it felt as if he was being pulled up the hill. He had seen a tree, a tall tree, on a bend in the path. It was not far. If he could reach it he would be safe. But he could not see the tree and the path steepened, his trainers began to slip in the mud and he was using his hands too, clawing at the path, looking for the tree. He was still scrambling up the path but he had stopped breathing, for everything had suddenly gone quiet. Then up ahead he saw the tree and he breathed again, and at that moment he heard men's voices and now behind him, instead of barking, was the sound of dogs panting closer, but the tree was closer still and he reached up for its branches that stretched out over the path and he heard a sound, not like an animal sound but human, like a man with water in his throat, drowning, and he knew where they'd get him and he put his hand there and thought, I can lose a hand for stealing, but it was too late and he felt the fur against his fingers and a hot pain between his legs and everything flooded with red darkness.

Chapter Forty

They were on the road up to the ridge called Palomba Rossa. Stuart sat crouched again in the front of Alice's car. She was driving with her head forward, too close to the steering wheel. Stuart did not like it up here. He never had. Here, the sky and the wind took over. The crude wind moved the dark pines and the bracken. It was like the end of the world. Compared to this place the *maquis* was a scented garden.

In winter the road they were on was often closed because of heavy snowfall and the few villages beyond were cut off. It was a dead end, running out in an abandoned farm in the village of Castri. The map showed a forest track as the only way out. Stuart guessed that his man had either a four-wheel drive or a trial bike.

'What can you see?' he asked her.

'There's an open drop to my left and on the right there's forest. Pine trees. We're coming to another hairpin bend.'

It was the last one before the ridge.

'Good. You can drop me off there. On the turn.' She nodded, keeping her eyes on the road. 'Take the bag and put it on the seat beside you.' She had slowed right down. She reached into the back and tried to lift the bag. 'That's all right,' he said. 'Stop the car a moment. Stop and put it in the front.' His heart was beating too fast. She stopped and put the bag on the passenger seat. 'I'll be right behind you,' he said. 'Watching over you. You just leave the bag and drive away.'

'Stuart?'

'Yes?'

But she just stared at him. There was the pity again. He smiled at her.

'I'll be watching you,' he said.

As he climbed out of the car he thought he heard her say something, but she had slammed the door and when he straightened up and turned she was already round the corner and out of sight.

He followed the steep road after her, but she had gone, and he ducked into the forest, which was now to his left. He moved quickly through the thin pines, keeping close to the road where the slope was gentler. For once there was not a breath of wind and he could hear the water dripping from the trees. He was trying to think what Alice had said to him, to decipher the words in retrospect, but he was left with nothing but the sound of her voice. Up ahead there was a fire-break like a grand avenue, leading straight down the hill to the lay-by. His man could park in the trees and get a clear view, unseen. When he came in sight of her tail lights through the trees, he spoke into his radio: 'Fabrice. Come in. Where are you?'

'I'm coming up behind you, Stuart. I've just passed a sign to the Palomba Rossa. Over.'

'You're a kilometre and a half away. Stop there. Park so you can cut off the road if necessary. In case he goes out that way. I'm going to wait at the lay-by. When I see him I'll signal you. Then I'm switching off.'

'Okay, Stuart. We're here. Over.'

He could see most of the lay-by now. Alice had parked. He called Paul, who was making his way on foot with the two young cops.

'I'll signal when he shows, then I'm cutting out,' he said.

'We're down below. I just caught sight of her lights. It's not far but it's steep,' Paul said.

Stuart took his gun from its holster and watched Alice walk into the middle of the lay-by. She stopped a moment, holding the bag, and looked about her.

'Not there,' Stuart whispered. 'Nearer me.' But she obeyed the instructions she had been given and set it down, dead centre, in front of the fire-break.

As he watched her walk back to the car he began to feel very cold. He watched her car back and turn gracefully out of the lay-by and he felt as though all the heat were leaving his body. As he listened to her change gear he knew he had made some great mistake.

He stood with his hand on his gun, watching the bag. He gripped his gun and held his eyes wide open in the dark. He could hear owls calling each other in the forest behind him. The lay-by was like a silver lake. He felt the shock of recognition, as though the lay-by ahead of him, the thick darkness around him, this loneliness and sense of readiness were all he was. Everything he felt now was everything he had ever been.

He heard the sound of a bike sawing through the night and received it calmly like some signal he'd been waiting for. He called Fabrice, then Paul, and told them that an individual on a powerful trials bike was approaching along the fire-break, that they were to stand by, he was cutting out. He switched off his radio and took his gun from its holster.

The bike moved down the gentle slope. When he hit the lay-by the rider stood up a moment on the foot-rests and Stuart saw he was tall. He was wearing black leathers and a black helmet with a visor. He stood astride his bike and looked about him. The bag was a few metres away. He drove slowly up to it and stopped on the other side of the bag, facing Stuart. He put his left foot on the ground and Stuart saw he was in neutral. He kicked the bag with the toe of his boot. It would feel too soft. Get off the bike, Stuart thought. But the rider kicked the bag again. You want to check. You know you do. Get off the bike. Stuart counted four to five paces between them. But he was not going to get off. Stuart saw him let go with his left hand and pause for an instant. When he reached down Stuart was already out of the forest. By the time he had straightened up Stuart had thrown all his weight at him, hitting him in the chest with his shoulder, heard the grunt as the wind was knocked out of him and heard him swear, clearly enough in spite of the visor to know that he was an islander. The bike was on top of him with the motor still making its ugly hacking sound. The man was on his side, flailing like a big black insect. Stuart stood over him and, using both hands, each shaking in perfect synchronicity, pointed his gun at him.

'Take off your helmet,' he said.

Stuart could hear an engine and he recognised the sound of Fabrice's van. The thought of Fabrice with his red glasses, the one man he did not need at this point, reminded him that his man would try for his gun and then there it was, conjured from beneath him, from his right boot, of course. And as he looked down at the man's weapon pointed steadily at his chest, Stuart thought: he's taking my pulse and even though I have the positional advantage, he can feel my hesitation and he knows now that I've never shot anyone in my life and never will. Then there was the strange muted ping of the silenced bullet and the impact high up in his thigh, and to his astonishment he fell back and he heard Paul's shout and, as his head hit the ground, he wanted to laugh, because he knew that one way or another Santini had probably won his bet.

Epilogue

A gentle wind was blowing in Massaccio, warm and dry and unhealthy. It came across the sea from the desert and left an invisible coating of sand that clung to the back of the throat, dried out the nasal passages and caused a barely perceptible frosting of the windscreen of Santini's Saab. He ran his finger along the glass, then raised it to his tongue and tasted the salt.

The trial was in its third day and Santini was enjoying himself. There were police barricades forming a solid chain around the Palais de Justice. He walked towards them, kicking out his feet slightly with each step, like the actor Lino Ventura, whom he believed he resembled. A bus stopped just in front of him as he prepared to cross the street and a large group of teenagers began to pour forth, noisy and oblivious and overladen. Coco scanned the girls' faces, each one uglier than the next. He thought of his beautiful Nathalie, then, stepping into the road, pushed her out of his mind.

A gendarme checking IDs looked mechanically at the twenty-five-year-old photo in his driving licence that bore no resemblance to him and opened the barricade to let him through. As he walked up the steps of the Palais he could feel a dusting of Sahara sand beneath his feet. His shoes were of the softest Italian leather and he wore them without socks, even in winter, because he disliked the feeling of elastic against his skin.

Things had been going his way. The case had taken a year and a half to come to court because Christine Lasserre had decided to put Mickey and Garetta in the same file. It meant they could not close the case until an exhaustive search had been made for the Scatti brothers who, to their credit, had still not been found. This had given Coco plenty of time to convey his position to Karim and Denis in prison.

He pushed the door to the Palais and stepped into the cool marble interior. Lawyers in their robes were sitting on the stone benches all along the corridor, talking in hushed voices to their harrowed clients. There seemed to be more and more women in the profession. Coco decided that next time he would find an attractive woman to represent him. He was walking behind one now as he made his way to the main courtroom, admiring the coil she had made with her hair and the wisps of it on the nape of her neck.

Another gift had been Christine Lasserre's transfer to Strasbourg three months after his arrest. She had carefully briefed the new investigating magistrate, a young Protestant from Uzès, and managed to offend him. He had let Coco out of prison, announcing in a press conference that there were insufficient grounds for his incarceration and that he was against remand anyway, except for rapists. Coco found the blond-haired free-thinker repulsive, both physically and morally. Three months later the charges against him were dropped and he became a witness. That it should be luck and not Russo that had provoked his release made Coco happier than anything.

The foyer outside the courtroom was filled with people, all of whom he knew. He stood on the edge, in the grey light coming through the dirty atrium, avoiding their greetings. The journalist Lopez was talking to the female gendarme at the entrance to the chamber. When the Spaniard looked up and saw him he turned away. He could not see Alice Aron anywhere. She was due to appear today, but the trial had got off to a slow start because Karim's lawyer had tried to push his mutilation charge through. Perhaps she would not come until the afternoon. Coco was more disappointed than he would have expected. He made his way towards the witnesses' entrance, cursing himself for being so early.

*

Alice walked across the tarmac away from the plane. This time she had only a bag over her shoulder and nothing in her hands. As she walked towards the terminal it was not the former experience she remembered but the kidnappers' video of it. She remembered his shot of Dan holding her dress, of Sam with his goggles on, jumping around, and of herself, her former self.

She walked through the same smells that now worked on her like an insinuation: kerosene, asphalt and the scent of the *maquis*, warm and cold like patches in a lake. Only the light was different and the people around her moving with her towards the terminal, looking trussed up for winter and peevish. This time she had no luggage to collect and as she walked towards the exit, she took in the scene – the conveyor belt, the trolleys and the waiting crowd – and she found herself looking in the empty spaces between these things, straining to see into the gaps in memory and perception and discover what she had never seen: the man with the camera.

The palm trees planted in two rows in front of the terminal had been encased against frost in huge bamboo crates. The sight was disappointing and she hailed a taxi and climbed in, eager to get away. But she did not know what to tell the driver. It was too early to go to the Palais de Justice and she did not feel like sitting in a hotel room. She could not remember the name of the main square in Massaccio, so she asked for the only place she could remember.

'The Fritz Bar.'

She looked out of the window at the freight depots and the car-dealers and the vacant lots, reading every sign, listening to the driver's background humming against a barely audible radio, trying to keep her mind from wandering in search of Stuart.

She had not been back to the island since. When Madame Lasserre had called her a week later for the reconstruction of the shooting she had said that she could not leave Sam and they had managed without her. As they drove past an orange grove laden with fruit, she wound down the window to capture the scent, but she caught only the smell of wood smoke. She looked at the plane trees lining the road, their trunks blanched by winter and their mutilated branches pruned to nubs, and she thought she remembered Stuart saying he preferred winter, but she was not sure when he had said this. Most of her memories of him were truncated, like those trees. They drove past the tall ferries in the docks. This island, she realised, was where she had left herself behind.

The driver dropped her off at the same entrance to the pedestrian zone where Santini had dropped her. She walked to the main square and was relieved to see that here the palm trees were loose and moving in the warm wind. She sat down on an empty bench beneath a statue of an heroic islander on a very high pedestal, closed her eyes and lifted her face to the sun.

She remembered sitting in the back of a police van in Cortizzio holding Sam. The sight of his pale face and his huge hollow eyes were a shock to her, but it was his silence that told her of the depth of the damage that had been done to him. She had sat there rocking him in her arms, believing in the illusion of her own calm until she screamed at the first-aid personnel, refusing to let them take him from her.

She remembered the consultant in intensive care, with his sleeves rolled up and thick dark hair on his arms, gently prising Sam from her. He shone a torch in his eyes, tested his reflexes and took his blood pressure with an abstracted air, as though he were trying to hear something a long way off. He had told her in an inappropriate sing-song voice that her son was out of danger, that the speech would return. In no time, he had said. It had taken Sam six months to speak. One month for every day in captivity. He would play with Dan, even fight with him, in perfect silence. Then one morning at breakfast he had told her that he wanted more sugar on his cereal and she had burst into tears.

She smiled at this thought and opened her eyes. She could

smell something delicious on the breeze, like warm caramel. Across the square was a dark green kiosk that sold crêpes. She rose and went to buy one with chocolate sauce. She returned to her bench and ate it, a little self-consciously and too fast, wiping the chocolate from her mouth with the back of her hand.

She saw herself on the morning after Sam was retrieved, walking out of the hospital with him in her arms. The same consultant was standing in the sun with a cigarette in his mouth, rolling down the sleeves of his white coat. With him, their backs to her, were Paul and Gérard. Something had made her walk over to them and, as they turned and she saw their faces, she had guessed, exactly as she had guessed when Mathieu's best friend had telephoned her, seconds before he told her. It was Gérard who said it: 'Stuart was shot last night. He died this morning.' He had looked down on her, his face hard only for a moment, and then he had looked away, over her head, and squinted into the sunlight to hide his grief. She had stood there unable to speak, with Sam too big in her arms, and nodded slowly as the familiar coldness of loss crept over her.

Back in Paris she had looked at herself in the bathroom mirror and seen, with curiosity more than regret, how changed she was. Stuart's death worked on her slowly, over months. She could not stop thinking about him dying that night while she was in the hospital with Sam, perhaps in the next room. She would wake up in the middle of the night and her heart would feel like a heavy stone she had swallowed. She sometimes felt as though she had dreamed of him and she punished herself for not remembering the dream. Anger settled in her. She hid it from the boys, but when she was alone it gripped her hard. Once she had picked up a plate and hurled it against the kitchen wall, then another and another until all twelve plates were broken and she had swept them up, terrified by her capacity for dissimulation, even to herself. What made her angry was the understanding

[306]

that she would survive whatever happened to her.

When her mother came from England she had tried to talk to her about him. But she had found herself unable. There was so little to say. She could not tell her mother that she suspected he had loved her in a way that no one had or ever would. She did not even know his first name. Instead she began to talk, using his hand gestures. She remembered his codes perfectly.

She kept his present to her in a locked drawer. Sometimes she would take out his mother's gun and look at it. She would smell the metal, rub it over her hands and smell her palms. She could taste it. She would pull out the cartridge and the barrel would spring open. She would practise loading the tiny bullets, sliding them one by one, the last in the chamber. He had given her a box of twenty-five. On the box was written in yellow and grey fifties lettering: 'FIOCCHI cartucce pistola automatica. Smokeless 6,35 mm bullets'.

She stood up, moved by a sudden urge to speak to Stuart's men again. She wanted to talk about him. She went to the call box and dialled the number, which she still knew by heart. She recognised Annie's voice.

'Hello. It's Madame Aron. Is Gérard there, please?'

'No. He's not here any more.'

Alice thought she could hear her resentment.

'Is Paul there?'

'Hold on, please. I'll see.'

The call box stank of cigarettes. While she waited, she pulled the neck of her sweater up over her nose.

'Hello?'

'Paul?'

'Yes.'

She could not help smiling.

'It's Alice Aron.'

'Yes. What can I do for you?'

'I wonder, I'm in Massaccio, for the trial. Could we meet for a coffee?'

'I can't. Sorry. I'm on desk duty; I can't leave the office.'

She felt herself flush with shame.

'I see. Well maybe at the trial, then.'

'Not today. I was up yesterday.'

'Paul?'

'Yes.'

'Can I talk to you? Please.'

'Of course you can talk to me. What's the problem?'

'I just wanted . . . Oh, nothing.' She felt his silence as an act of cruelty. 'Forget it.' She looked out through the glass door of the call box at a group of middle-aged women in fur coats. 'Where's Gérard?' she asked, wanting to punish him.

'He went back to Paris. Aubervilliers, to be precise.'

'Who's commissaire now?'

'Mesguish.'

'And what about you? What are you doing?'

There was a moment's hesitation.

'I've been sidelined.'

'What does that mean?'

'I work with the airport police. Professionally speaking, it's a luxury grave.'

'What happened, Paul?'

'I don't want to talk about it, Madame Aron. If you don't mind.'

Alice did not answer. She was wondering what she had done to deserve this.

'Okay, Paul. I'll see you, then.'

'Yes. All right. 'Bye.'

She hung up, slamming the phone into its cradle.

She stepped out of the call box and began to walk towards her hotel. She walked fast, trying to shake off her anger and shame. When she reached the Hôtel Majestic she was out of breath. She was about to climb the steps to the lobby when she felt a tap on her shoulder. She spun round and was surprised to see that it was not Paul. It was Lopez.

He was panting, holding a hand to his heart.

'I'm sorry,' he said. 'I smoke too much.' He held out his hand and she shook it. 'Lopez. We've met once.' His smile looked more like a grimace in response to the pain in his chest. 'You walk very fast.'

Alice smiled.

'Your hair,' he said, pointing at her. 'You cut it all off.'

She touched her head.

'Yes.'

'It looks nice. Can I talk with you for a moment? Do you mind?' He glanced once up and down the street. 'Maybe in the bar. Can I buy you a coffee?'

The bar was poorly lit by a candelabrum covered in opal spheres that hung from the middle of the ceiling. The room was large and empty except for a few low tables and chairs clustered around an ornate wooden bar in the corner. The carpet and the chairs and the curtains were all plum-coloured and so was the teenage barman's uniform. There was a smell of dust and fried food.

'Here is good. No?' Lopez said, holding his hand out to the triangle of chairs furthest away from the bar. 'We can talk here.' He waited for her to sit, then sat down himself. 'I saw you in the call box in the square. I have been wanting to talk to you for a long time and when I saw you I thought it's now or never.' He smiled again, his brief, pained smile. 'How can I begin?' He rested his small hands on his knees and slapped himself smartly. 'All right. I am a journalist. This you know.'

'I do.'

'Right.' He smiled. 'I'm not a famous journalist or even a good one. I have worked for the daily newspaper here, the *Islander*, for many years. I'm not brave' – he raised his eyebrows at her, inviting her to share the joke – 'not at all. I like my job but I don't think of it as useful in any way. Do you understand me?'

Alice nodded.

'When your son was kidnapped I was sent to cover it. You remember the commissaire? Monsieur Stuart? Well, he asked me to keep the story out of the paper. I did not like Stuart. I thought he was just a narrow-minded policeman. But I said I would do what he asked because he said he would give me exclusive access and I believed him. I did not like him, but I knew he was honest.'

The barman appeared. She ordered a Coke and Lopez ordered a Kir.

'Stuart was not a liar. He made me angry because he did not call me often enough, but he kept his word. He would have kept his word if he hadn't been killed.'

'How was he killed? How exactly?'

'I am surprised you don't know.'

She did not answer; her throat was dry.

'I think that it was Paul Fizzi's fault. He was a cowboy, but Stuart never saw this. And he was a drunk. He shot Garetta with a pump-action shotgun.'

Lopez paused as if for him this information was enough in itself.

'But he shot him because he was aiming at Stuart,' Alice said.

'Maybe. Maybe not. What is certain is that he aimed at Garetta's head. The bullet went right through the helmet and out the other side.' Lopez sliced his hand through the air. 'When they took his helmet off the skull fell open like the lid of a teapot. Fizzi got away with self-defence because Garetta did take a shot at him. Lucky for him they found the bullet.'

'Are you saying that if Paul hadn't been there, Stuart would not have been killed?'

Lopez considered this.

'I don't know. Philippe Garetta was a dangerous man. He may not have needed Fizzi there to kill Stuart but maybe Fizzi scared him. Maybe something could have gone on between the two men. Maybe Stuart could have talked him out of it. He was subtle. But with Fizzi rearing up with his weapon . . .' Lopez threw up his hands. 'What is certain is that Stuart could not have survived Garetta's second shot. He fired a high-velocity bullet into Stuart's chest and at close range. It would have fragmented inside his body. So . . .' He opened his hands.

Alice covered her mouth.

'Are you all right, Madame Aron? I'm sorry. It's nasty.'

She shook her head. She needed air. She stood up and walked away towards some double doors leading on to a dark courtyard covered in ivy. She would not cry. Lopez was behind her.

'Madame Aron. I'm so sorry.'

She pushed open the doors and went outside. The smell of frying was being propelled into the yard by a ventilator in the wall. She turned her back on Lopez and threw up on to the ivy. When she had finished, Lopez handed her a clean white handkerchief.

'I'm sorry,' he said again, shaking his head. 'I didn't come here to make you sick.'

Alice wiped her mouth and stood up. She felt tired out and relieved.

'I think I fell in love with Stuart,' she said. 'I didn't realise at the time, but I only knew him for five days and I loved him. I can't seem to get over his death.' She smiled at Lopez. He held out his arm.

'Come. Come inside. It smells bad here.'

She took his arm and followed him back inside. They sat down again.

'Coke is good for nausea,' he said, nodding at her glass. She took a sip. 'I wanted to talk to you. Now I am very glad that I came. Are you feeling better?'

'Yes.'

'Today you are going to court. This afternoon you will testify. Do you know what you will say?'

Alice looked away. She had not been able to think clearly about the trial and she now felt ashamed.

'I don't know. I'm very angry that Santini's been let off. When I heard about it I lost heart. I don't think the trial's of much importance without him, really. I suppose I'll just answer the questions.'

Lopez held up his finger. His eyes were shining with excitement.

'Listen, Madame Aron. I told you I wasn't brave. But there's someone who is.' He looked at her, full of eagerness. 'Liliane Santini.'

Alice nodded.

'I'm sure.'

'She is.'

'I believe you. I met her once.'

'After the new magistrate let Santini out of prison she called me.' He paused.

'What did she say?'

'She wanted your address.'

'Why?'

'I don't know.'

'She never wrote.'

'Yesterday,' Lopez said, 'she called me back.' He held up his hand in case she should decide to speak. 'I have some details that will help you answer the questions today.' Lopez took a sip of his Kir. 'Now. Santini is getting off. They've got nothing on him. He has sent a clear message to his accomplices in prison, Karim and Denis. The only ones on trial for the kidnapping. He has sent them some threats and some promises. Now both of them are denying Santini had anything to do with it. You know that?'

'Yes. I know.'

'So. Karim will get away with twelve to fifteen years for bringing your boy back and for having his balls eaten off. Denis the same, probably, and they'll be let out in six to pick up their reward.'

'From Santini.'

'From Santini. Do you want another Coke?'

'No.'

'Sure?'

She nodded. Lopez waved at the waiter and ordered another Kir.

'Okay. So Santini is walking free even though we know he organised, maybe not the first but certainly the second kidnapping. Stuart knew this but he never got any proof together because he was alone; he had no support from his hierarchy, not really, and he was in a hurry. For you, perhaps.' The waiter brought his Kir and he took a few sips and put down the glass. 'So.' He leaned forward. 'When the President asks you today why you think Santini was involved, you can say that you are speculating on the basis of what Commissaire Stuart told you. "And what was that," he will ask. And you will answer: "He has an arms cache on his property." And whatever they throw at you just say that Commissaire Stuart told you that there was an arms cache at Santini's villa and that's all you know.' Lopez grinned and leaned back in his chair.

'Evelyne emptied that cache.'

Lopez raised his eyebrows.

'You knew about it?'

'I was there when Stuart searched his property.'

'Where were the weapons?'

'Under his swimming pool.'

'Why didn't Stuart take him in?'

'He made a deal. If he led us to Sam he'd let him off.'

'I thought this and I tried to put it to Paul Fizzi, but he told me to fuck off. He thought I was just digging up the dirt on Stuart. I wanted Fizzi to talk about the cache, but I couldn't be sure he wouldn't reveal me as his source.'

Alice watched Lopez take another sip of his Kir.

'Evelyne moved the weapons,' she said. 'As soon as we left, she moved them.'

'But' – Lopez raised his index finger again – 'Evelyne, who is quite a clever woman, thought it would be too risky and too obvious to move the weapons off the property, so she moved them from the pool to his mausoleum. I know this, because I was there. I saw it.'

Alice looked at his beaming face.

'Why didn't you testify, then?'

'I told you. I am not brave. Someone would kill me sooner or later.'

She smiled.

'So who's going to kill me?'

'No one. You'll leave the island. You'll leave it all behind. Nothing ever spills beyond the island. All the shit stays here.'

Alice took a sip of her Coke. A pleasant feeling of excitement was growing in her.

'How do you know the weapons are still there?'

'I don't know for sure, but Santini's been under house arrest ever since his release from prison. So I'm assuming he wouldn't take the risk.'

Alice sat back in her chair and looked at Lopez, who was staring hard at her. They were like two children with a plan.

'It was Liliane Santini who told me to come to you,' he said. 'She is the one with the courage. Will you do it?'

'Yes. I think I will.'

'You just answer the questions. Like I said.'

'Will Santini be there?'

'Yes.'

'Will you?'

Lopez shook his head in mock terror. She smiled.

'We'd better go,' Lopez said, looking at his watch. 'You only have an hour.'

Alice hurried up the steps of the Palais after Santini. He must have heard her footsteps and he turned round. As he waited for her to catch up, she felt his yellow eyes on her. He held open the door for her and she smiled graciously at him.

'You look good,' he said, pointing at his head. 'The hair.'

'I'm happy to be back here.'

Santini tilted his head.

'Really?'

'Yes. Shall we walk together? We mustn't be late. Do you know where it is?'

'Follow me,' he said.

As they walked along the corridor, he had his hands in the pockets of his blazer and he kept glancing sideways at her as if he could not believe his luck.

'You sold the place in Santarosa, then? It's a shame.'

'Yes.'

'It must be painful for you to return here.'

'Not at all,' she said. 'I'm so happy.'

They were in sight of the main courtroom. She let him go first into the space, barely large enough for them both, between the inside and outside doors.

'I wonder,' she whispered, 'do you know, by any chance, what Commissaire Stuart's first name was?'

'Antoine. Why do you ask?'

'Antoine,' she repeated. Santini looked at her mouth. She smiled at him. 'Thank you.'

She noted the strong smell of wood polish and knew that it would always remind her of this moment. As he pushed the second heavy wooden door into the chamber, she spoke to the back of his neck: 'I'm going to testify against you, Santini.'

He stopped dead. Alice felt her heart fluttering in her throat. She thought of Stuart's hand in hers. 'You'll go to prison.'

There was an infinitesimal shift in the tilt of his head and she felt a rush of fear as she waited for him to turn and face her. But he held still and she was suspended a moment in this strange air-lock, between her past and her future. Then he pushed the door and stepped into the chamber.